"An engaging paranormal roma   *ly*

"A really good, really enticing, really passionate romance . . . Patricia Coughlin has gone the distance and made my toes curl in anticipation of her next venture into romance . . . one of the most delightful romances I have read in a while. The passion is electrifying! The story is captivating! The characters are incredible! My hat is off to Ms. Coughlin for making my heart sing and bringing a smile to my face with every page! Incredibly wicked! A lesson in seduction you will never forget . . . one of the greatest mixes of character and plot you'll ever find! Patricia Coughlin fills every chapter with passion . . . every page with desire!"   *—Booklist*

"An enjoyable romantic fantasy . . . an exciting tale."
     —Genre Go Round Reviews

"[Patricia Coughlin] . . . draws you into the story with each and every word she writes; her characters are full of wit and vitality."
     —Night Owl Reviews

"There is great wit and delightful repartee within the pages of another sparkling gem from a real talent of the genre. A nonstop read with a cast of wonderful characters. One of the ideal . . . romances of the season. To be savored. SENSUAL."
     —Romantic Times

Berkley Sensation Titles by Patricia Coughlin

THE LOST ENCHANTRESS

WEDDING MAGIC

Wedding Magic

Patricia Coughlin

BERKLEY SENSATION, NEW YORK

THE BERKLEY PUBLISHING GROUP
Published by the Penguin Group
Penguin Group (USA) Inc.
375 Hudson Street, New York, New York 10014, USA

Penguin Group (Canada), 90 Eglinton Avenue East, Suite 700, Toronto, Ontario M4P 2Y3, Canada
(a division of Pearson Penguin Canada Inc.)
Penguin Books Ltd., 80 Strand, London WC2R 0RL, England
Penguin Group Ireland, 25 St. Stephen's Green, Dublin 2, Ireland (a division of Penguin Books Ltd.)
Penguin Group (Australia), 250 Camberwell Road, Camberwell, Victoria 3124, Australia
(a division of Pearson Australia Group Pty. Ltd.)
Penguin Books India Pvt. Ltd., 11 Community Centre, Panchsheel Park, New Delhi—110 017, India
Penguin Group (NZ), 67 Apollo Drive, Rosedale, Auckland 0632, New Zealand
(a division of Pearson New Zealand Ltd.)
Penguin Books (South Africa) (Pty.) Ltd., 24 Sturdee Avenue, Rosebank, Johannesburg 2196,
South Africa

Penguin Books Ltd., Registered Offices: 80 Strand, London WC2R 0RL, England

This book is an original publication of The Berkley Publishing Group.

PRINTING HISTORY
Berkley Sensation trade paperback edition / August 2011

Library of Congress Cataloging-in-Publication Data

Coughlin, Patricia
  Wedding magic / Patricia Coughlin. — Berkley trade pbk. ed.
    p. cm.
  ISBN 978-0-425-24123-3 (trade pbk.)
  1. Women dressmakers—Fiction. 2. Weddings—Planning—Fiction. 3. Female friendship—Fiction.
4. Domestic fiction. I. Title.
  PS3553.O7698W43 2011
  813'.54—dc22

                                                                                    2011005545

PRINTED IN THE UNITED STATES OF AMERICA

10 9 8 7 6 5 4 3 2 1

For Eileen Fallon, BAE
Best. Agent. Ever.

One

Sophie rose early and dressed for battle in a sleeveless black linen dress with white piping and a matching cropped jacket. It was more tailored and less comfortable than what she usually wore to work; she just hoped it was worth the effort.

For luck, she added the single string of pearls that had been her mother's.

One corner of her mouth lifted in a rueful smile as she fastened the clasp, thinking it a particularly fitting gesture, reminiscent of the knights of old who carried a lady's favor onto the field with them. If anything could bring her luck today, it would be conjuring her mother's spirit, and she had a feeling she was going to need all the luck she could get.

Fashion tips would also be useful, she thought as she turned her attention to the age-old dilemma of what shoes to wear. Arms crossed, lips pursed, she reviewed the options lined up like good little soldiers on her closet shelf. Life would be so much simpler if her style sense were as well honed as her organizational skills. Her gaze moved quickly over her favorite sandals and the ridiculously high—and expensive—designer creations she'd allowed herself to be talked into on a rare shopping trip with her sisters. The never-worn stilettos were Exhibit A for why she did her best to avoid those outings. Tucked away at the very end of the shelf was a glossy black shoe box tied with pink ribbon. She never looked inside the box at the sparkly party shoes she'd worn exactly once, on the night of her thirtieth birthday. Part memento, part cautionary tale, they were a reminder that the past consists not only of what happened, but of what might have happened and didn't.

She finally settled on a pair of black, open-toed pumps with a moderate heel. It was the safe choice, and Sophie was a big fan of playing it safe.

As battle garb went, the finished outfit lacked the intimidation factor of, say, a Kevlar vest or chain-mail trench coat, but it was infinitely more practical given the forecast for sunny skies and temperatures climbing into the nineties, well above the norm for June in Rhode Island. If her upper arms were more toned or tanned, she might have thrown caution to the wind and ditched the jacket. But they weren't and she didn't.

Her outfit also wasn't terribly au courant . . . at least she didn't think it was. She was never quite sure since, try as she might, when it came to fashion she always seemed to be a season—or two—out of step with whatever was currently in vogue. Okay, so maybe saying "try as she might" was a bit misleading. It would be a lie to claim she *tried*, as in putting any actual effort into keeping abreast of style trends, but in her own defense, when stuck in the dentist's waiting room, she did choose *Elle* magazine over *Consumer Reports*. Most of the time.

To be honest, from her vantage point—which was now officially closer to forty than thirty—wearing what looked fabulous on Sarah Jessica Parker was less important than wearing something that looked good on her. SJP's wardrobe options and hers were a twain that would never, ever meet. Sarah's style was slinky and sexy and adventurous, and her own was mainly focused on drawing attention away from her flaws. This morning she was satisfied she'd done the best she could with what she had.

Her sisters, unfortunately, didn't share that assessment. And the unwritten bylaws of sisterly love—even stepsisterly love—decreed they had every right to say so. It was for her own good, of course, though Sophie had never quite figured out why most things family did for your own good just ended up making you feel bad about yourself. They wasted no time exercising their critiquing rights when she walked into the offices of Seasons, the wedding and event-planning business founded by her stepmother. Or rather, when *they* walked in, since by the time they showed up, Sophie had been in her office long enough to grab a cup of coffee, go over her notes for the day ahead, and check both e-mail and voice messages with an eye toward squelching any pending disasters that had reared their demanding little heads overnight. Among the many things identical twins share, Jill and Jenna had the same rule about setting foot in public before they were ready to be seen. They didn't do it, period. Never had, never would.

Having shared a bathroom with them for a big chunk of her formative years, Sophie could attest to their tireless dedication to the wonderful world of grooming. And hey, it worked. They were several years closer to the big four-O than she was, with husbands and kids and homes to care for, and still they appeared each day looking like they'd been peeled off a glossy magazine cover, and Sophie, well, didn't. It explained why they held court in highly visible showroom offices out front, meeting and greeting clients and projecting a properly glamorous and upscale image, while her office was next door to the supply room in the employees-only section.

Sophie had no complaints. It was a practical arrangement, especially now that her father was retired and he and her stepmother spent much of the year in Florida, leaving the day-to-day running of the business to the three of them. She was at her best working behind the scenes, averting crises, slaying dragons, and generally doing whatever was necessary to keep the train on the tracks and moving forward. She wasn't good at showmanship, and although she was too nice to say so, the Js weren't much good at anything else.

"Is that what you're wearing?" Jenna asked her. She was standing just inside Sophie's office, her head tilted slightly to the side.

It wasn't the first time she or Jill had asked Sophie that same question using that same vaguely perplexed tone and expression. Actually the first time had been twenty years earlier, on the night of Sophie's very first real date. The Js—two years and many, many dates ahead of her socially—had been on hand when she emerged from her room feeling, maybe not beautiful, but pretty damn close, in a miniskirt and knit top under a baggy blazer with the sleeves rolled up. It was the eighties and she was feeling very Madonna meets *Pretty in Pink* . . . until Jenna's offhand question zapped all the air from her little fantasy world. With no time to change, she'd answered the door with sweaty palms and her stomach in knots and spent the rest of the night yearning to be invisible.

Now older and supposedly wiser, and seated safely behind her desk, she wiped her damp palms on her skirt and fought the urge to blurt *Why? What's wrong with what I'm wearing?*

Instead she responded with what was intended to be an intimidating show of nonchalance. "That's the plan."

"Hmm," said Jenna.

Jill nodded thoughtfully. "Maybe you should stand up so we can get the full effect."

"There is no effect," Sophie retorted, wanting to stand for inspection only slightly less than she wanted to stab herself in the eye with a letter opener. "It's a dress, period, no big deal."

"I beg to differ," said Jill. "Everything about your meeting with Owen Winters is a huge deal for Seasons. Helen Archer has social clout out the ying-yang and handling her only daughter's wedding will bring us lots of new contacts, not to mention the kind of local buzz we'll get if by some miracle you convince Winters to cooperate. Think about it, Sophie, there's never before been a wedding held at Ange de la Mer. This would be monumental."

"Historical," Jenna added.

"Mind-boggling," said Jill.

"If you pull it off."

Jill nodded. "Yes. *If*. Helen Archer was very clear: if we can't deliver Ange de la Mer, she'll keep looking for a wedding planner who can. So yeah, I'd say this is a very big deal."

"A colossal deal," agreed Jenna. "And it's all up to you, Sophie."

God help us.

No one said it aloud, but it's what they were all thinking. Even Sophie. Especially Sophie. It's not that she was afraid of taking on a difficult task. When it came to her job, she'd been known to tackle the impossible and pull it off. Sweet-talking, arm-twisting, begging and bribing, it was all in a day's work. She couldn't count the number of times one of the *J*s had promised a client something outlandish that they knew nothing about and she'd had to step in to save the day—and Seasons' reputation—by finding a way to deliver on it.

This was different.

For this meeting she would be taking the lead, and along with that went taking center stage. Hardly her natural habitat. She was more like the Wizard of Oz, content to work her magic from behind the curtain. What if she messed up? It was entirely possible. Owen Winters was an unknown quantity, and when she tackled a problem she preferred to know the facts and have them sliced, diced, and lined up in neat rows ahead of time. The problem was there just weren't that many facts to be had about Winters . . . at least not on such short notice. She'd Googled, of course. And she'd shelled out $24.95 for a copy of his latest book only to find the inside cover had the same long-distance photo and paltry handful of details she'd found online: *Owen Winters has vast military experience and has traveled the known world in preparation for writing about worlds unknown.* Big help.

If only she had more time, she thought.

"If only Shelby Archer hadn't gotten lost coming back from the damn ladies' room," Jill said.

She was referring, of course, to the other night, when socialite Helen Archer and her daughter, Shelby, the bride-to-be, had come in to put forth their unorthodox request and a bit of serendipity led to Sophie being thrust front and center.

"If only you didn't have that damn picture hanging on the wall right where she could see it," grumbled Jenna, glaring at the damn picture in question.

It was a framed watercolor of a castle, the original artwork from the cover of a children's storybook that had been Sophie's favorite when she was a little girl. As luck would have it, the artist's inspiration had been the Newport estate known as Ange de la Mer, the very place where Shelby Archer had her heart set on being married. The book itself was old and not very well known, but Sophie remembered her mother reading it to her over and over; the framed cover was a way of keeping those memories close to her heart. Shelby recognized the artwork because she too loved the book and they were happily chatting away about their favorite parts of the story when Helen Archer came looking for her daughter and Shelby surprised everyone by announcing that losing her way and winding up in Sophie's office had been an omen, and that

Sophie and only Sophie was the one who should plead her case with Owen Winters.

Jill sighed. "Oh well, what's done is done. We just have to make the best of it. You know, play the lemons we've been dealt and all that."

"Jill's right," said Jenna. "What matters now is that we work together to put our best foot forward."

"Our best-*dressed* foot," Jill added.

Sophie immediately thought about her sensible black pumps hidden beneath the desk. She knew just enough about fashion to know they weren't even close to what Jill had in mind when she said "best dressed."

"So come on," Jenna urged with the kind of encouraging smile Sophie knew better than to trust, but was too polite to ignore. "Stand up and let us have a look so we can see what needs tweaking."

Reluctantly Sophie dragged herself to her feet and stepped a few inches away from the desk.

"Hmm," said Jenna, bringing them right back to square one. "Well. I like the pearls."

"Thanks," said Sophie.

Jenna folded her arms and a second later, without looking at her twin, Jill did the same. They were freaky that way. Tall and willowy, toned and tanned, they weren't identical to the point where Sophie couldn't tell them apart, but it had definitely made life easier when Jill had her pale blond hair cut in layers and Jenna left hers all one length.

"Tell me, Sophie, what do you see when you look at yourself in that outfit?"

Sophie shrugged. "I hadn't really thought about it. I guess I see someone who's sensible and who you can trust to be honest in do-ing business with you."

"That's interesting," Jenna countered. "Because what I see is someone dressed for a funeral."

"Or tea with the queen," added Jill.

"Or tea with the queen," Jenna quickly agreed.

Tugging on the hem of her jacket, Sophie shrugged again. "What's wrong with having tea with the queen?"

"Nothing. Nothing at all. It's just not exactly the image we're trying to project, is it? I mean Seasons is about glitz and glamour and big, splashy celebrations. Not about tuffets and crumpets . . . and those." She pointed at the black pumps.

Sophie managed not to shuffle her feet.

"But not to worry," exclaimed Jill, moving closer to give Sophie a reassuring pat on the shoulder. "We'll have you fixed up in no time. I keep extra clothes in my office for emergencies."

"I am not an emer—"

"So do I," said Jenna. "I'm sure that between us—"

Sophie held her hand up. "Whoa. Aren't you forgetting something? Like the fact that you're both about three inches taller and twenty pounds lighter than I am? Even if I wanted to change into something else, something . . . splashier—which, for the record, I don't—nothing that fits you would fit me. And no, we don't have time to go shopping."

That quieted them for a few seconds. Jill brightened first.

"Shoes," she exclaimed.

"Of course," agreed Jenna, already kicking off the strappy black stilettos she was wearing. "Here . . . these will work with that dress."

"I really—"

"Put them on," she ordered. And then, as an afterthought, "Please."

Knowing it would be futile to argue, Sophie sighed and put the shoes on, adjusting the narrow straps until they felt as comfortable as heels that high could feel.

"Much better," pronounced Jill.

"They pinch my toes," Sophie protested.

"They pinch mine too. You get used to it. Now, lose the pearls."

Sophie frowned, her fingers moving instinctively to the neck-lace. "But Jenna said—"

"I lied," said Jenna. "I do like the pearls. They're beautiful against your skin . . . they make it look even more creamy."

"Peaches and creamy," Jill added, tossing her a bone.

"And with the right jeans and a slinky little lace tee, they'd be fun and fabulous. But at the moment they're just screaming Grandma. Here . . . take my necklace." She reached for the clasp.

"No," said Sophie. "The pearls stay." She took a deep breath and added, "They belonged to my mother."

Jenna sighed. "Fine. But let's at least try to jazz things up with a little extra bling."

A few minutes later Sophie was wearing platinum earrings, a matching cuff bracelet, and Jill's diamond-studded Movada watch.

Jenna gave a nod of lukewarm approval. "I guess I can live with that. So what time is your appointment with Winters?"

"I don't have one," Sophie answered.

"What? How can you not—"

"I tried," she interrupted to head off the dozen questions she could see forming behind their matching expressions of confusion. "He didn't return any of my calls, and when I took a chance and stopped by after work last night, he wasn't home."

"Maybe you should try again. Like right now. There's a lot riding on this and—in case you've forgotten—not a heck of a lot of time."

"I haven't forgotten." She waved her arm—which thanks to the platinum cuff felt five pounds heavier—toward her desk with its neatly arranged piles of paper. "But I have too much work here to be making forty-minute runs to Newport for nothing. And in case you've forgotten who you're dealing with, let me remind you that contingency plans are my specialty. I don't even schlep to the post office without having an alternate route in mind in case I need it. And I figured out an alternate route for this situation. You might say it's a way to be in two places at once. So you can both relax." She pulled her cell phone from her jacket pocket and held it up. "Everything is under control."

The call she was waiting for came while she was checking on an order for sixteen dozen out-of-season white tulips being flown in from South America. She immediately put the wholesaler on hold and grabbed her cell.

"Hello."

"This is Ghostship calling Valene," replied a voice that sounded lower and huskier than the teenage male voice Sophie was expecting to hear.

Frowning, she checked the caller ID a second time and sighed. "Cut it out, Josh."

"I know not this Josh of whom you speak," said the voice. "This is Ghostship, calling to report that Osprey has landed."

"I have no idea what you're talking about; just tell me what's going on there."

There being a car parked on Bellevue Avenue, a discreet distance from the Ange de la Mer estate. At least that's where Josh Spencer, stock boy and all-around errand runner, was supposed to be. Josh was her contingency plan, sent to keep watch so she didn't make any more wasted trips.

"I just told you what's going on," Josh countered. "I said Osprey has landed."

"Who's Osprey? You were supposed to be watching for Owen

Winters. I showed you his picture on the book jacket, remember? I swear, Josh, if you're screwing around—"

"I'm not. Jeez, lighten up. I've been sitting here watching all morning, which, for the record, is boring to the max. Even my butt is numb. Sue me for trying to break the monotony. I called you as soon as Winters drove in, just like you said to do. He probably wasn't even inside yet when you picked up. I mean, I can't be sure of that because of, you know, the wall and all. But it was definitely him. The guy's got the sweetest bike ever."

"Winters rides a bike?"

His heavy sigh indicated just how lame he found her.

"Bike as in motorcycle," he explained. "His motorcycle is primo."

"Oh, right." Of course.

"And I was just being, like, metaphorical when I called him Osprey."

"Osprey? That's a metaphor? For what?"

"Osprey. You know, the birdman with the black eye patch and the silver talons and those wicked hidden wings?" When she didn't immediately say "Oh, *that* Osprey," he went on. "Heck, Sophie, didn't you even bother to read the guy's book?"

"He writes comic books, Josh. I don't read comic books. And if I did, I promise you it wouldn't be one about a birdman with an eye patch. Osprey," she muttered, rolling her eyes.

"Graphic novel. They don't call them comic books anymore, you know."

"So I've heard."

"And you shouldn't be so stuck-up; his stuff is pretty amazing. There's a spin-off video game in the works and *ParaWorld* magazine says Lucas is after the film rights."

"That would be very helpful information, Josh . . . if we were in the moviemaking business instead of the wedding-planning business. I'm leaving now. You stay where you are in case he takes off again. If he does, call me right away on my cell so I don't drive all the way there for nothing."

"What if he leaves and comes back again? Should I just stay here and keep watching?"

"Good question," she murmured.

"I could follow him," he offered, real excitement chasing all traces of boredom from his tone. "Then you could hunt him down and corner him wherever he is."

"No," Sophie told him firmly. "That's called stalking. And it's against the law." Not to mention that cornering him in public was not likely to put the man in a very receptive mood, and she definitely needed Winters in a receptive, open-minded mood to hear what she had to say. A sense of humor also wouldn't hurt.

"I could follow him without him knowing it . . . that's what Ghostship does. Covert ops."

"Still stalking," she countered, trying not to consider the possibility that in another couple of days she might have to resort to it. "Do not, under any circumstances, follow him, do you understand? Just call me if he leaves the house and . . . and we'll figure it out from there."

"Roger, Valene. Ghostship out."

She flipped her phone shut. Who the hell was Valene?

Two

The sound of the doorbell interrupted Owen Winters in the act of sitting in front of his computer and staring off into space. Staring into space was only slightly less tedious than staring at the monitor, but he'd take what he could get. The screen itself was blank, same as it had been for . . . well, a while. Blank, that is, except for the relentlessly blinking cursor, which on really bleak days seemed to be taunting him. *Loser, loser, loser.* One of these days he was going to have to get his ass in gear and prove the obnoxious little blinker wrong by actually writing a line or two. But not today.

He didn't need to get up and look to see who was ringing the doorbell to know that whoever it was, he didn't want to see them. There was no one he *did* want to see. At least no one who was going to show up on his doorstep today or any other day.

The bell rang again.

"Go away," he muttered, thinking he really ought to get an electrician out there to fix the switch for the damn gates. And maybe, while he was at it, a plumber to dig a moat. Twelve feet of piranha-infested water ought to put an end to unwanted visitors. He glanced at his watch, sighed, and reached for a cigarette in spite of the fact that he was allowing himself only one an hour and it had been not quite nineteen minutes since his last. Was it his fault the stupid doorbell had broken his concentration and punched a Marlboro Man–size hole in his willpower?

He shoved aside the blank drawing board and rummaged through the dozens of pages of scrawled notes strewn across his desk without finding the cigarettes he'd ventured out to buy just hours ago. Deciding he must have left them in the kitchen, he pushed away from the desk, gave his stiff right knee time to adjust to his weight, and went to check, trudging past room after empty room to reach the other side of the house.

There were times when he questioned his sanity for buying such an overpriced monstrosity to live in all by himself. It was exactly the kind of disgusting display of self-indulgence he despised, and at times he felt downright guilty for doing it, for having his choice of beds to sleep in when there were plenty of homeless people who'd be grateful for just one. A better man would do something to rectify the situation. Like turn the place into a homeless shelter, he mused with a flicker of perverse satisfaction. That would soothe his conscience and piss off all the snotty rich people living around him. Bonus. He hated snotty rich people almost as much as he hated himself these days. Also, any shelter worth its salt was bound to have folks coming and going at all hours, strangers setting up cots and raiding the kitchen and turning his study into a playroom for their kids. All that noise and commotion would give him a legitimate excuse for not being able to write, as opposed to the piss-poor one he had now. *Loser, loser, loser.*

When you came right down to it, he wasn't sure exactly why he'd bought the place. One day he was driving by—for the thousand-something time—and he noticed the discreet Realtor's sign on the gate and knew he had to have it. The shrink his agent set him up with had suggested he bought it because he was searching for something, and that he needed to figure out what it was and act on it before he could move on. That's when Owen had quit going to see him. He'd been poor most of his life, and just because he no longer was didn't mean he should shell out a couple of hundred bucks an hour to have someone tell him what he already knew . . . that there was something missing in his life.

There was one good thing about living there, he decided as he trudged on, limping less than he had six months ago, but still more than enough to piss off a man used to being in good shape. Make that great shape, as in finely tuned human machine shape. Not so long ago, it had been a matter of course that his own life and the lives of others depended on his physical strength and agility and the speed of his reflexes. Those days were over. Now the good news was that he could afford a house so ridiculously large he didn't have to worry about getting enough exercise. Especially not at the rate he was losing things and going around in circles trying to find them.

It was weird. He'd put a beer down somewhere, go back a few minutes later to the spot he was certain he'd left it, and it would be gone. The same thing happened with his cigarettes and with the golf clubs he liked to keep handy throughout the house. He didn't actually play golf—too passive and pointless a game for his taste—but sometimes when he got stuck for the right words, swinging a club helped him think. At least it used to. Lately that well of inspiration seemed to have dried up along with all the others.

He spotted the cigarettes as soon as he entered the kitchen, the red-and-white box floating in about four inches of water in the sink. Perplexed, he scanned the room. The window was open. Maybe he'd left them on the counter on his last beer run and the wind had blown them into the sink. Again. Ocean breezes could be erratic, calm one minute and gusting the next. Of course, the capricious wind didn't explain the disappearing beer bottles that sometimes turned up back in the kitchen, empty, or the golf clubs he found tossed by the side of the patio out back.

Weird, he thought for the umpteenth time since moving into the century-old mausoleum. Just weird. And that's as far as he was ready to take it. Just because he wrote about the supernatural didn't necessarily mean he believed in it. If there was more to what was going on around the place than his own absentmindedness, then . . . well, then he was going to need a lot better proof than an empty beer bottle or two. He was going to need something up close and personal.

"Got that?" he muttered, glancing around as if there really might be someone listening.

He fished the cigarettes from the sink and shook the water off, hoping to find one still dry enough to light. He didn't. Disgusted, he tossed the pack in the trash, thinking that if this kept up he might have to break down and start buying them by the carton instead of a pack at a time. It would be more convenient, of course, but it would also shatter the comforting delusion that having a smoke now and then was not the same as actually *being* a smoker. He wasn't ready to face the fact that ten years after going through hell to quit, he'd really been stupid enough to get hooked again.

The doorbell sounded a third time . . . or was it the fourth? Whatever, it was quickly followed by some very assertive knocking. Growing even more irritated, with himself and with the freaking wind and especially with whoever was out there banging, he headed in that direction, automatically grabbing a beer as he passed the fridge and positioning himself where he could see out the narrow window beside the door without being seen. He recognized both the black SUV parked in the drive and the woman standing on the steps from her last visit, when it had taken nearly fifteen minutes of ignoring her to get her to go away. Whatever she was after, she was persistent; he'd give her that.

He stood for a moment, watching her fidget and glance around as if pondering her next move. Out of habit, and boredom, he lingered to take a closer look. She was pretty enough, in a low-key, forgettable sort of way. Average height, average body, unremarkable brown hair pulled into some kind of twisted ball in back. She had the sort of pleasant, low-key, inoffensive look that led him to conclude she was there either to try to sell him something or to save his immortal soul. And he had no interest in either.

"Mr. Winters," she called out. "I know you're home."

Owen took a quick step back, worried she was nosy and determined enough to peer in through the window.

"Look, all I want is a few minutes of your time," she called. "Really. I'm not selling anything, if that's what you're thinking."

Okay. That left saving his soul. He backed up another step.

"In fact," she went on, "I think you may be very interested in hearing what I have to say. This could be a great opportunity for you."

Oh, yeah. Definitely after his soul. Probably had that briefcase of hers stuffed with fire-and-brimstone pamphlets. Well, she could just stand out there and bang her ass off; no way in hell was he opening the door and letting her in.

That ungracious thought had barely formed when he felt a chill, as if a giant temperature vac had sucked the warmth from the air around him, and then just as suddenly and inexplicably the front door swung open, coming at him so fast he had to lurch sideways to avoid getting whacked in the head.

What the hell . . . ?

Sophie, standing on the other side of the door, was just as startled to see the door fly open with such force it literally bounced off the inside wall. She jumped, with a little squeak of surprise, which immediately made her feel silly. After all, wasn't the whole point of standing out there, pounding on the door for all she was worth, so that someone would open it? Well, now someone had. And he didn't look happy.

On the plus side, he wasn't dripping wet, as he would be if she'd dragged him out of the shower. Of course, that still left sleeping, working, or being tied up with a matter-of-life-and-death phone call as possible reasons he hadn't come to the door sooner. She'd considered all those possibilities as she stood there pounding, just as she'd considered them on her last visit. The difference was that today she was feeling more desperate than polite.

Judging from the way he was glaring at her, *polite* wasn't at the top of Owen Winters's list at that moment either. She braced herself for an angry tirade about the evils of uninvited visitors. Instead, when he finally spoke, his deep voice was quiet and icy with control.

"Do you always go around letting yourself into other people's homes?"

"Letting myself . . . ?" Her eyes went wide as the meaning of the question became clear and she jabbed her index finger against her chest. "Me? You think I . . . ?"

"Didn't you?"

"No," she replied indignantly.

"Then who . . . ?"

"I assumed you . . ."

"I didn't," he said.

"Oh. Then, well . . ." She glanced around and shrugged. "I guess maybe the wind could have blown it open."

"Yeah. Maybe." He sounded unconvinced. And annoyed.

He stared at her with undisguised suspicion for a few seconds, not saying anything. Probably trying to think of a way to blame her for the wind, Sophie thought, using the time to regroup . . . and crossing her fingers that the man was merely rude and not bat-shit crazy. Or dangerous. Not that she had any choice but to forge ahead. Whether he was sane or certifiably batty was a secondary consideration. It was her job to win him over, and by God that's what she was going to do.

"Owen Winters?" she ventured, recovering enough to seize the opportunity the wind had blown into her path. Fortune favors the bold, after all. She waited for a response, eyeing him speculatively because, to be honest, she wasn't one hundred percent convinced he was Owen Winters. Granted the book-jacket photo had been taken at a distance and Winters had been half turned away, leaning on a tree, but the man in that photo had looked a little younger. And a lot better groomed. She tried to picture the guy in front of her without dark stubble and bloodshot eyes. Ditto the faded All-man Brothers T-shirt that had been washed so many times it was impossible to tell what color it had started out. The neck band was frayed—mauled by stubble—and it barely reached the waistband of his equally decrepit jeans with a hole in one knee that looked to be the result of wear rather than a fashion statement. Did authors use body doubles? she wondered.

He ignored her greeting. "Who are you?"

"Sophia Bennett," she replied, offering him the business card she had at the ready. "Everyone calls me Sophie."

He took it with the hand not holding the beer bottle and squinted, reading the words under his breath. "'Seasons . . . for all the occasions of a lifetime. One-of-a-kind parties, weddings, and celebrations.'" When he looked up there was no mistaking the curl of his lip. "Weddings and celebrations. What are you? Some kind of wedding planner?"

He said it with such disdain you might think she'd introduced herself as a puppy slayer or the Grinch's assistant.

Sophie nodded and proudly lifted her chin. "That's right. It's a family business, founded by my mother . . . well, stepmother actually. She's mostly retired, though she still—"

"Cut to the chase, lady. What does this have to do with me?"

Sophie couldn't blame him for cutting her off. In fact she was grateful for it. She'd been rambling and she never rambled. She hated rambling. It was so . . . disorganized.

"Good question," she told him, smile firmly in place. She refused to be intimidated by his brusque tone and unfriendly expression. Failing that, she refused to show that she felt intimidated by him. "The answer is somewhat complicated. If you don't mind, I'd like to come in and explain it to you."

"I do mind. And there's no need to explain. Whatever it is, I'm not interested."

He shoved the card back at her and reached for the door handle. This was definitely not going as well as she'd hoped.

"How can you be sure you're not interested in what I have to say if you don't give me a chance to say it? Please, Mr. Win—"

A sudden movement behind him caught her attention, but when she automatically shifted her gaze in that direction, there was no one there.

"What is it?" Winters demanded, his attention sharpening as he turned his head to look behind him and then back at her. "What did you see?"

Sophie shook her head. "Nothing. I thought I did, but it must have been a trick of the light."

He didn't respond, just stood there studying her with the same probing glare that had been in his eyes when the door first blew open. Then he startled her by stepping aside with a grudging wave of his arm. "Maybe you should come in after all. It can't hurt to hear what you have to say."

"It won't, I promise. One hundred percent pain-free, that's me."

Sophie thought he might have snorted quietly as she passed him, but she ignored it, moving inside quickly, before he had a chance to change his mind. She'd known going in that this was a long shot, but she'd told herself that if she could just get him to hear her out, she might have a chance. She clung to that hope as he closed the door behind her. For several long seconds they stood in silence, him frowning, her still working her best "Isn't this fun?" smile. He glanced around awkwardly, as if not quite sure what to do with her now that he'd allowed her in.

Something told her the man didn't do a lot of entertaining and she felt a pang of sympathy for him, quickly followed by a bigger pang for herself as it occurred to her that his recluselike habits didn't bode well for her chances of convincing him to open his home to a hundred and fifty or so strangers . . . not counting sundry support personnel and waitstaff.

"This way," he said finally, and started down a long wide hallway to the other side of the house.

Sophie followed slowly, partly because that's how he was walking, slowly and favoring one leg a little, and partly because her toes hurt and she wasn't used to walking in heels that high and she didn't want to risk twisting her ankle or falling on her face. She was probably going to fall on her face when she made her request and that would be humiliation enough for one day. The slow pace worked to her advantage because it gave her the opportunity to look around and make mental notes just in case she got lucky and Winters said yes. And on a more personal and sentimental level, it gave her time to deal with the sudden lump in her throat resulting from the simple fact that she was really there. She, Sophia Beatrice Bennett, was actually inside the Princess House. It was the ultimate dream come true for the kid who had curled up with a beloved book and wished she could crawl inside and be part of that fascinating made-up world.

The house did not disappoint. The rambling Queen Anne–style villa, which did indeed resemble a fairy-tale castle, was as spectacular inside as out, with all the style and sophistication Sophie associated with the 1920s, the era in which it was built. The foyer was spacious, with a starburst of black-and-white marble on the floor and pale gold walls that wore a faint sheen from the sunlight pouring in through dozens of curved and beveled-glass windowpanes. True, there were no talking sculptures to welcome her and no magic carpet to whisk her from room to room, but she was very pleased with what was there, from simply framed watercolors to pale silk window dressings to the timeless furnishings with clean lines and rich tones. And the humongous split staircase just like the one in the book with the banister the backward princess could slide *up*.

She only wished her mother was there to see it all with her. And she hoped she would be able to pull this off so Shelby would have a chance to see it too. If anything, the house was an even more magnificent setting for a wedding than she'd imagined. The overall mood was elegant and warm and welcoming . . . everything the lord of the manor was not, she thought ruefully.

As they passed the staircase her gaze lifted to where it divided in two and continued upward on either side of the foyer. Professionalism edging sentimentality aside, her mind automatically began compiling a list of ways a clever photographer could use the delicate, curved banister to frame a shot when again, from the corner of her eye, she saw movement. This time the impression was stronger, as if there was something sheer and white floating in the air above the staircase, like . . . like a wide ribbon of snowflakes, but once again, by the time she blinked and refocused, there was nothing there.

Nerves. It had to be nerves. *Get a grip,* she chided herself silently, taking a couple of deep breaths to try to slow the racing of her heart.

The man she had concluded must be Owen Winters led her to an immense sitting room dominated by a wall of floor-to-ceiling windows overlooking a rose-stone patio and rolling expanse of green lawn. What she assumed was a guesthouse was some distance off to the side of the patio, and in the distance, just beyond the lawn's edge, was Cliff Walk, the public pathway that ran behind the mansions on the east side of Bellevue Avenue and was a well-known Newport landmark. On the other side of that narrow walkway, silvery cliffs formed a rough, steep, dangerous drop to the ocean.

Two words popped into Sophie's head the instant she stepped into the room: *cocktail hour.* It was the perfect setting for cocktails between the ceremony and a formal, sit-down dinner. She pictured a full-service bar stretching the length of the back wall, with appetizer stations at each end, and maybe a half-dozen simple white banquettes by the windows. If the weather cooperated, the French doors could be left open and on the patio outside there would be a mix of small tables with chairs for sitting, and taller tables for guests to gather around. And maybe a few more banquettes. Also, possibly, shade umbrellas. She cast an assessing gaze at the sun high in the clear blue sky; she'd have to wait until she got the ceremony time pinned down before she could determine what the angle of the sun would be in late August.

Of course, that was just one possibility. Her mission was only to get Owen Winters on board. After that either Jill or Jenna would take the helm to actually create the wedding of Shelby Archer's dreams and she, Sophie, would slip back into the more familiar role of making sure everything went according to plan. To even think about scheduling and seating arrangements was putting the cart before the horse. If she couldn't convince Winters to play nice, none of the rest mattered.

"Wow," she murmured, drawn closer to the windows. "That view is even more spectacular than I imagined. How often do you set your alarm so you can get down here in time to sit and watch the sun rise?"

Silence.

When Sophie turned her head to look at him, he shrugged. "Never actually."

"Oh. Well. I guess living here, you must get used to seeing it. But that's what I would do, every morning, me and my coffee and the sunrise to start the day right."

"Is that what you came here to talk about?" he asked pointedly. "The view?"

"Of course not. Not exactly anyway, but the view certainly doesn't hurt." She glanced at one of the cream-and-pale-blue striped chairs. "May I?"

He nodded, though he didn't look happy about it.

She sat and opened her briefcase to remove the file containing a few carefully selected photos of past Seasons events along with the detailed formal proposal she'd put together especially for this meeting, her version of bringing out the big guns.

"Let me start by saying that your home is beyond beautiful. Whoever your decorator is did a wonderful job."

"Decorator?" he countered, giving the word the same sneer of disapproval he had *wedding planner*.

"I just assumed . . ." She trailed off with a small, chastised smile and circled her finger in the air to encompass their surroundings. "So you—"

"Bought it fully furnished," he informed her. "The old lady who owned the place died and—"

He was interrupted by a loud *thump* and they both turned abruptly to see that a book had toppled from the table behind him to the floor. Without commenting, he picked it up and returned it to the table, careful to place it close to the center this time. He turned back to Sophie.

"As I was saying, she died and left her estate to a nephew who was her only heir. He'd moved to the West Coast years earlier and had no interest in coming back east, so he let the place sit and gather dust for ten or so years before he finally decided to sell it as is."

"I see. Well, I'd say that was his loss and your good fortune. Ange de la Mer isn't only beautiful; it's unique, which brings me to my reason for being here. At Seasons, our top priority is making our clients' dreams come true. No detail is too small, no request too big. So, in keeping with one of our clients' wishes, I'm here to discuss the possibility of using your home for a wedding the last weekend of August."

He looked horrified.

"I know it sounds crazy," she went on before he had a chance to say anything. "I know because that's exactly how it sounded to me when the bride-to-be and her mother broached the idea. First, there's the time factor. Less than eight weeks to plan a formal wedding for a hundred and fifty guests? That alone is insane. Then they explained that the bride wants to be married here, at Ange de la Mer. At Seasons, we've planned hundreds of weddings, weddings at country clubs and hotel ballrooms, a few at the beach. Naturally we've also arranged weddings in private homes, but we never before worked with a couple who want to be married in a home belonging to a total stranger, someone they'd never even met, someone with no connection whatsoever to them or to their families."

"So we're in agreement," he said. "It's an insane idea."

"It would probably be more accurate to say we *were* in agreement," she countered. "I should have said my first reaction was that it was a crazy idea, but then Helen Archer— the mother of the bride—pointed out that this sort of thing is done all the time by movie producers. They send someone out to scout the perfect setting for their film and then negotiate with the owner for use of the property. That's why I'm here: to negotiate."

"Let me save you the trouble; there's nothing to negotiate."

As he spoke he crossed his arms in a way Sophie found very distracting. There was something to be said for the rumpled T-shirt look after all, she decided, something a lot more intriguing than that posed shot on his book jacket. Maybe the stubble was growing on her, or maybe it was simply that she'd moved past her first, instinctive impression of a grown man answering the door barefoot and swigging beer from a bottle, but it occurred to her that there was something about his physical presence that eluded the camera, that drew you in for a closer look.

Something about him? Who was she kidding? It was *everything* about him. Under the stubble and the rumple, the guy was dead-on fine: he was classic, all-American male eye candy, tall and lean and rough enough around the edges to be interesting. Not that she was interested. She didn't know much about the man, but she didn't need to know much to know he wasn't her type. And it was beyond a safe bet to say that she wasn't his. Omens aside, this mission might have been better left to one of her sisters. Or both. That whole twin mystique really did it for some guys.

"Lady, you got it straight the first time," he said, snapping her wayward thoughts back to the matter at hand. "It's a crazy idea. And it's out of the question. I'm sorry you wasted your time—"

She lifted her hand to stop him. "Please, won't you just sit down and hear me out before you make up your mind?"

"That would only be a waste of more time for both of us. Believe me, my mind is made up and there's nothing you can possibly say to change it."

"Five minutes. Please."

He made no effort to hide his displeasure as he ran his fingers through darkish brown hair that was not so much long as it was shaggy, the ends touched with gold. She'd bet anything those subtle streaks, like his tan, were one hundred percent natural. She could no more picture him sitting still for someone to paint highlights on his hair than she could imagine him in a tanning salon. Both were the product of long hours in the sun, the same sun responsible for the lines etched at the corners of his mouth and eyes. Laugh lines? Sophie had only known him a few minutes, but she thought not.

"I'm listening," he said finally, ignoring her invitation to sit. Instead he stood gazing down at her, his full mouth settled in a discouraging frown, his long-legged, lean-hipped slouch the most eloquent of body language: it screamed for her to hurry up and go away.

She held the proposal out to him. "I prepared some notes to make sure I covered everything. Maybe you could—"

"Tick. Tock."

She realized he wasn't even going to glance at the bullet points she'd labored over long into the night. Trying not to become flustered, she forced a smile and carefully placed the proposal on the table in front of her. "In case you haven't noticed, this isn't easy for me. Knocking on a complete stranger's door for a cold-call hard sell isn't exactly my style."

"And yet here you are."

"Yes. Here I am."

"I wonder why."

"I told you why: I have a client—correction, a *potential* client with her heart set on being married here at Ange de la Mer."

"And you have yours set on clinching the deal."

"Well . . . of course. I'm a businesswoman, Mr. Winters. This wedding will be both lucrative and high profile. And from my point of view, that's a win-win."

"In that case, my advice is to tell your potential client to check out Rosecliff just down the street. It's much more high profile and I understand weddings are a regular occurrence there. They've probably got the whole routine down to a science."

"Precisely . . . and that's the problem. Weddings aren't science. They're the exact opposite; they're . . . magic," she exclaimed, her passion creeping into her voice. "I've done weddings at Rosecliff; it's a beautiful site, but it won't do for this bride. It has to be Ange de la Mer. She claims there's something magical about this house and I have to agree. It's the way it sparkles in the sunlight as if someone sprinkled it with fairy dust, and the way the copper angels at the top of the spires spin around as if they're dancing in the wind, and those cozy little balconies where you'd swear Juliet or Rapunzel could appear any second."

Something that might have been amusement flickered briefly in his eyes. "Fairy dust?"

She smiled. "I may have gotten just a bit carried away. But the fact is that Shelby has been in love with this house since she was a little girl and sailed by here with her father."

He stiffened, that small trace of humor gone as his expression hardened into a scowl. "Then I'm afraid she's out of luck. There's a long list of reasons it's not going to happen, starting with the fact that I hate weddings."

"You hate weddings?" Her hushed tone reflected her shock. Who was the puppy-slaying Grinch's assistant now? "How can anyone hate weddings? Weddings are celebrations of love and commitment and new beginnings."

"Marked by a display of pomp and pretentiousness, signifying nothing . . . a legalized crapshoot all gussied up with champagne and white lace, and with about the same odds of success as a shady carnival game, something I happen to know more than a little about."

"Carnival games? Or marriage?"

"Both. For instance, I know both are for suckers."

"That's a pretty harsh generalization."

"Have you ever been married, Ms. Bennett?"

"Well . . . no. But I really don't see what that has to do—"

"I have. It lasted eighteen months. Six of which were happy. Most of the time."

"I see."

She did see, clearly. And somehow she had to find a way to prevent his obvious bitterness about his own failed marriage from preventing Shelby from having a shot at the wedding she'd always dreamed of.

"That must have been a very difficult time for you. And it's understandable that it had an influence on your attitude toward marriage, but perhaps you could try to think of this strictly as a business proposition. It will be as if we were shooting a movie here, but instead of taking weeks or months, we'll only need one weekend . . . obviously with some time on both ends for setup and cleanup." She thought it best not to get too specific about just how time-consuming and involved preparations for a wedding on this scale could be. That could all be explained later, in baby steps. "You could use that time to treat yourself to a wonderful vacation . . . a sky's-the-limit vacation. Helen Archer is a woman who knows what she wants and is willing to pay for it; she's made it clear she'll spare no expense to make her only child's wedding perfect."

"I'll bet," he drawled with a grim smirk. "I know the type. And for her sake I hope it happens, but they haven't minted enough money to get me to let it happen here."

Three

There was a note of finality in his tone. The realization that he wasn't going to change his mind was closing in on Sophie. She quickly reviewed the arguments at her disposal—financial gain, favorable publicity, the sheer pleasure of doing something from the goodness of one's heart—and concluded that none of those alternate routes was likely to get her where she wanted to go. That left begging and blackmail, which both her pride and her conscience prohibited. Besides, there was nothing about Winters to suggest he'd be any more susceptible to those than to anything else she'd said.

Maybe it was time to shift gears and start thinking instead of an alternate wedding site, one that would appeal to Shelby and soften the blow of losing out on her first choice. She really liked Shelby and she hated disappointing her as much as she hated losing the business. She could think of a half-dozen lovely, little-known sites that were similar to Ange de la Mer. Similar, but without the emotional connection. And there would be Helen Archer to deal with. She'd only met the woman once, but that was enough to figure out that she was someone who knew what she wanted and was accustomed to getting it. Somehow she would have to be convinced that following through on her threat to keep searching until she found a wedding planner who could deliver Ange de la Mer was a waste of time . . . time she didn't have if the wedding was to take place in a matter of weeks. At this point Sophie didn't think any other planner, including the *Js*, would fare better with Winters than she had.

She looked up to find him watching her.

"Look, this has nothing to do with you," he told her. There was a new and unexpected hint of regret buried in his gruff tone. "You gave it your best shot. But even if I wanted to go along with it, I couldn't. I'm a writer, which means I work at home, and I have a September first deadline. I wouldn't get any work done with people coming and going all the time, prancing around here bedecking things and unfurling white carpets."

She smiled slightly, a faint flicker of hope reigniting inside. It was just enough to let her see the signpost reading *Alternate Route This Way.*

"You'd be surprised how quiet my crew can be when bedecking and unfurling. And I'm glad you mentioned your writing because I was hoping for an opportunity to tell you that I'm a big fan of your work. A . . . friend recently turned me on to it. In fact we were discussing one of your books just this morning. And I can't wait to read it," she added, taking a shot that he was more susceptible to flattery than to profit. When it came to little white lies, her pride and conscience had more wiggle room.

"Really?" He looked dubious. "Which one?"

"Which one what? Oh, you mean which book . . . the, uh . . . the one with Osprey. And the Ghostship. And Valene. It sounds great."

"Yeah, that's a classic all right." He put his beer down, leaned back against the pillar between two sets of French doors, and rubbed his knuckles against his jaw. "Funny, though, I wouldn't have pegged you as a fan of sushi westerns."

Sushi westerns? Why the hell hadn't she taken a closer look at that stupid comic book? Correction: *graphic novel.*

"Really? Well. That just goes to show that appearances can be misleading. I adore a good sushi western. Which is why I would never do anything to interfere with your deadline; we would totally work around your schedule, and if at some point we did have to be here during your work hours, we would be as quiet as church mice."

"Church mice?" he countered, raising one eyebrow.

Sophie nodded, her expression solemn. "Yes, it's a little-known fact that they're the quietest and most discreet of the mice family."

Owen couldn't help smiling. It felt . . . strange. Almost painful. Which he supposed just went to show how long it had been since he'd done it. Apparently the smile muscle could atrophy just like any other. Who knew? It was worth it, though, because Sophia Bennett smiled back and he discovered that he'd been hasty in his initial assessment. There was at least one thing about this woman that wasn't even close to being ordinary or nondescript: her smile. Her smile was . . . radiant, dazzling, disarming, drag out all the overworked clichés you could think of. Her smile was amazing; it made her eyes look amazing too, like sunlight on a blue-green sea. Her smile lit up her face and there was beauty there too. Hell, her smile lit up the room. And, most amazing of all, it lit up something inside him.

Because he was an idiot. He shook his head and began talking to distract himself from things he had no business thinking about. Distance. He needed distance from those thoughts, and detachment . . . and he needed her to go. "Lady, the cold-call hard sell may not be your style, but you're damn good at it. For what it's worth, if anyone could persuade me to let the spoiled little rich girl have her way, it would be you."

"But?"

"But the answer is still no."

Accepting defeat gracefully, she got to her feet and very ungracefully knocked her notes to the floor in the process. In a quick, reflex action, Winters stepped forward and they both bent and grabbed them at the same time, straightening slowly so that they ended up standing face-to-face with just a few sheets of paper between them.

Their eyes met and Sophie felt a sudden flutter of shyness. That feeling of wanting to look away and not wanting to at the same time. Not wanting to won out. It was silly. Absurd really. And unsettling. He was just so . . . male. He was the poster child for flagrant, uncompromising maleness. Everything about him . . . his size and the way he stood, the way he was looking at her. His eyes were dark blue, blue verging on midnight, and they held a faintly speculative edge, as if he were wondering all sorts of exciting and inappropriate things about her. Sophie didn't know how she knew that, she just did. Even his scent was male. And all of it was alien to her world, alien and enticing.

The world where she spent her days—and nights—was one of . . . how did the nursery rhyme go? Sugar and spice and everything nice. It was a polite and pretty world where romance reigned supreme and the men were all spit-shined, tuxedo-clad, and on their best behavior. Winters was none of this. And that, Sophie told herself, explained why he was having such a strong effect on her. He was a novelty. A primal novelty. It was probably something to do with pheromones and musk and . . . swagger. Big surprise the guy wrote sushi westerns. Not that she knew exactly what a sushi western was, but western meant cowboy and cowboys were always big and tough and . . . well, primal. Maybe she really would read his book.

"Thanks," she said, indicating the papers, the creaking of her voice due to her suddenly dry mouth. She really hoped her cheeks didn't look as flushed as they felt.

"No problem," he replied, still without letting go. "I really am sorry I can't help you out."

"Me too. I know it probably sounds as if Shelby is a typical rich spoiled brat, but honestly she's not. She and her fiancé are great kids. They just graduated from college and signed up for the Peace Corps together. That's the reason the wedding is a rush job; they decided they want to be married before leaving for Ecuador in September."

As she glanced at the papers in her hand, one of the reminders she'd scribbled for herself jumped out at her.

"She wanted their marriage to have its start here at the Princess House because she thought it would bring them luck."

He let go as if the papers had suddenly caught fire in his hand. "What did you say?"

"That she wanted to be married here for luck?"

He shook his head impatiently. "No. The house . . . what did you call the house?"

"Oh, that." She smiled. "We call it the Princess House. Shelby told me that when she was a little girl her father used to take her sailing near here because Ange de la Mer reminded her of the castle in her favorite storybook, and it just so happens it was my favorite too. My mother read it to me so many times I knew the words by heart; she used to brag that it was the one book I could 'read' even before I'd learned to read." She tipped her head to the side, her small smile becoming sheepish. "You have no idea what a thrill it is for me just to be standing here, in the Princess House."

"Could you just stop calling it that?" he snapped.

"Sorry. I'm sure that's the last thing a guy wants to hear his house called."

He waved that off, still frowning.

"When I love something I get a little carried away: I even have a copy of the book cover hanging on the wall of my office. Until we talked about it, Shelby hadn't realized that this house actually was the inspiration for the castle in the story; she'd fallen in love with it all on her own. Her dad died when she was in high school and I think losing him made the idea of having the wedding here even more special and more important to her. It's her way of feeling closer to him and including him in her big day. *The Princess House* is actually the title . . ."

"I know what it is."

Owen also knew his tone was much too harsh and that turning his back to her while she was still speaking was rude. He didn't care. He'd heard enough.

Confused and agitated, he stared out the window, honing in on a spot at the far right of the property, just off the Cliff Walk, where a cluster of hippo-size blue hydrangea bushes provided shelter on blustery days, the perfect spot for a peanut-butter-and-jelly picnic after a couple of hours of fishing at a small cove about a fifteen-minute hike from there.

How many times had he sat in that spot staring at this house?

Once upon a time a perfectly ordinary princess lived in a perfectly extraordinary house by the side of the sea.

At the time, he couldn't afford to own as much as a square foot of lawn at a place like this. It didn't matter. On the days he got to spend just hanging out with Allie he was as happy as he'd ever been. Now he was rich enough to lay claim to every stinking blade of grass out there and happiness seemed as impossible and as far away as the make-believe worlds he created for his readers.

The Princess House. Sophia Bennett wasn't the only one who knew that book by heart. There was a time when he knew every word, and he knew where every blue bird and firefly were on every page. All that seemed far away now too. As far away as Allie herself.

But maybe he had it wrong. Maybe impossible wasn't what it was cracked up to be. Not an hour ago he was standing in the kitchen challenging the universe and anyone else who might be listening to prove to him that there was something out of the ordinary going on there. Could this be the proof he'd asked for? Was her mention of *The Princess House* meant to be a sign of some kind? A message?

He could think of only one way to find out, and it didn't involve showing her to the door and locking it behind her as he'd intended to do until about sixty seconds ago.

His mind made up, he turned to face her. "All right."

"All right?" she echoed in a tone hovering somewhere between hopeful and guarded.

"Yeah. Go ahead and tell the bride and her doting mother to start their engines. They can have their damn wedding here."

Humph. That was Ivy Halliday's thought as she stood at the front window and watched the young woman, Sophia Bennett she believed she'd said her name was, climb into her big, clunky automobile and drive away.

A wedding planner.

Humph.

Had she known that, she never would have flung open the door on her behalf. The audacity of it, to even think of arranging a wedding there, at Ange de la Mer, considering its history. *Her* history. As always, the twinge in her heart came quickly. A blink of an eye and it was 1927 again and she was standing at this very window, watching and waiting. Now she waited for the memory of those long hours and the days that followed to wash over her and recede. It was entirely possible that Miss Sophia Bennett knew nothing about all that. Young people were so focused on the future they failed to consider that places, like people, have a past, and the past cannot be undone or wished away simply to make room for the new.

Was she one of the Barrington Bennetts? Ivy wondered. Likely not. Say what you would about the Bennett women; they did not traffic in commerce. Not that Ivy wasn't a firm believer that a woman had every right to live her life as she saw fit. She had after all.

Today wasn't the first time Sophia Bennett had come calling, or the first time the ill-mannered Mr. Winters had refused to see her. Ivy had intervened in the hope that Miss Bennett was the woman he was so obviously pining over and that with a little encouragement she would keep coming back and—most importantly as far as Ivy was concerned—she would have a civilizing effect on him.

It was her dearest wish that the woman would succeed where she had thus far failed, by getting the man to use coasters beneath his odious beer bottles and close windows when it rained and to refrain from dropping wet towels on her parquet floors. She also didn't care for his habit of playing loud music at all hours of the day or night, but at least music didn't leave marks on the mahogany sideboard or make the whole place reek of cigarette smoke. In short, Mr. Winters was treating the home she'd loved and tended all her life as if it were a cheap, run-down, flea-ridden motel, and she didn't like it one bit.

And then there was all the pitiful moping about that he did. There could only be a woman to blame for that. The fact that Ivy had never married didn't mean she'd lacked for suitors, or experience. Quite the contrary. And for all that men stomped around and called themselves the stronger sex, she recalled just how easily a man's heart, and his ego, could be bruised. A woman had to tread so carefully lest she seem to offer more than she was willing, or had left, to give.

Owen Winters was a handsome enough man . . . at least he would be if he ever troubled to clean himself up. He could easily find female companionship if he only tried. Of course, he was a writer and everyone knew that in and of itself accounted for a certain degree of self-absorption . . . not that the man actually produced any writing that she could see. She checked regularly and some doodles and nonsensical phrases were all he had to show for the hours spent slouched at his desk.

Sometimes she was tempted to try to snap him out of his gloom with a good old-fashioned scare. She could do it so easily. She didn't care how nonchalant he appeared to be about her little "reminders"; she'd wager that one good ghostly *"OOOOOO"* and a bookcase crashing down on his head in the middle of the night would do the trick. The problem was she didn't want to send him running scared; she simply wanted him to pick up his wet towels. If she spooked him into moving out and selling the property, she could well find herself sharing her home with a half-dozen cats, or children, and that would mean a whole new set of problems. No, the devil you knew and all that. She would tolerate Mr. Winters for as long as necessary.

What she would not tolerate was a wedding under her roof. She was the bride of Ange de la Mer and that was that. Just because her own wedding had never taken place was no reason someone else should be the first to marry there, in the house that had been built expressly for her as a wedding present from her father. In fact, as far as she was concerned, that was reason enough why no other wedding should take place there.

What a bother. She supposed she must assume some of the blame since it was she who had seen fit to open the door to Miss Bennett in the first place, but Mr. Winters could have resolved the matter by simply being himself. He could have refused the woman's request with his usual lack of graciousness and put a quick end to the entire business on the spot. Unfortunately he had failed to do either.

That meant it was up to her.

She did it! Sophie couldn't stop grinning as she headed back to Providence, crossing the bridge over Narragansett Bay with classic Bon Jovi blasting from her car speakers and the thrill of victory a live current running through her. The only thing that would make the moment more perfect was knowing *how* she did it.

The fact was she had no idea exactly what it was she had said or done to cause Owen Winters to change his mind so abruptly. If, indeed, he had changed his mind. Not to get lost in semantics, it seemed to her that it hadn't been a change of mind so much as a change of heart, and it had come right after she mentioned the deep emotional connection Shelby felt to the house. One moment he'd been scowling and ready to show her the door, the next he was scowling and agreeing to allow Shelby to be married at Ange de la Mer.

It would be helpful to know how she'd broken through his resistance so she could file it away in her bag of tricks for future use. And because she loved delving into a good mystery and Owen Winters definitely qualified as that. A wealthy, wildly successful, and—beneath the scruff—hunky-looking beast, holed up in his luxury man-cave, seething with suspicion, cynical about love, and curiously familiar with a little girls' storybook . . . what woman raised on fairy tales and happy endings could resist wanting to know more?

As curious as she was, however, she'd understood that it was not the time to hang around asking questions. As soon as he uttered the magic words, she'd whipped out the standard bare-bones agreement she'd brought along for him to sign and beat a hasty exit before he had time to think. Or ask himself what the hell he was doing. She decided it was also not the time to mention that someone from Seasons would soon be back to take measurements and do a complete inspection of the place so they would know exactly what they had to work with, or that Shelby was sure to want a pre-wedding-day look at the house she'd fallen in love with from afar. Maybe she could schedule the two visits together to minimize the inconvenience. And, she thought, her mouth curving into a smile, she would bring along a case of assorted local micro-brews, as a "disturbing the peace" offering.

Her smile faded as it occurred to her that more than likely she would be sending the beer along with Jill or Jenna, not delivering it personally. Her assignment had been to secure the client's venue of choice; she'd done that. There had been no discussion about who would take the lead for the actual planning of the wedding—maybe because they hadn't wanted to jinx themselves, maybe be-cause no one had really expected her to pull it off. Then again, what was there to discuss?

She and the *J*s worked as a team. Translation: Her sisters worked directly with the client and Sophie coordinated and cal-culated and kept track of things behind the scenes. It was Jill or Jenna who escorted clients to sample catering menus and to audi-tion bands; they went to the cake tastings and helped the bride in her quest to find the perfect wedding dress. It was Sophie who checked and double-checked to make sure the cake tastings didn't overlap and that the band the client chose was available on the date they needed them and that the perfect dress arrived in plenty of time to allow for alterations. And when something went wrong she was more often than not the one called on to fix it. As an event took shape, all the relevant information was funneled back to Sophie and entered on the Big Board that took up a full wall in her office. At one glance she could see the up-to-the-minute status of every event Seasons had scheduled for the next twelve months.

Sometimes Sophie thought of her office as the hub of a busy airport. Each upcoming event on the board was like a huge jet circling on its assigned flight path, and she was the air traffic controller responsible for overseeing them all, for knowing who was on board and what cargo they were carrying, for knowing everything she needed to know to bring each one in for a safe landing when the time came. Her role might not be the most glamorous, but it was important just the same. No event had ever crashed and burned on her watch, and none ever would.

She really wanted to be there to see her sisters' faces when she told them she'd gotten Winters to sign the agreement, but suddenly she couldn't wait until she got back to the office to tell someone. She set her cell phone to speaker and punched in the Archers' home phone number.

"Hello, Shelby," she said, recognizing the young woman's voice as soon as she picked up. Her voice, like her overall demeanor, was smoother and more relaxed than her mother's. Helen Archer's crisp, to-the-point delivery made it clear you were but one minor blip on her busy schedule. "This is Sophie Bennett; I'm calling because I have good news . . . great news actually."

"About the Princess House?" Shelby countered, anticipation lifting her tone.

"That's right. I just left there and I have, tucked safely away in my briefcase, an agreement signed by the owner. It looks like you're going to be getting married at Ange de la Mer."

Shelby whooped with excitement. In the background Sophie heard Helen Archer's questioning tone; Shelby quickly relayed the good news to her mother.

"I don't believe it," she then said, speaking to Sophie once more. "I don't believe you actually pulled it off."

"O, ye of little faith," teased Sophie.

"Only because you said yourself it was a long shot and I shouldn't get my hopes up. I was the one who said it was an omen that you happened to have a painting of the house hanging in your office."

"And it looks like you were right. Whatever the reason, I'm really happy it worked out for you."

"Thank you. I can't believe it . . . this has been my dream for as long as I can remember, but I thought that's all it was . . . I never thought it would really happen. To be completely honest with you," she went on, her tone sheepish, "when my mother first suggested we look into it, I thought she was crazy . . . and I told her so. This is one time I'm glad she never listens to me."

Sophie was as thrilled by Shelby's joyful reaction as she was over clinching the deal in the first place. It was moments like this that reminded her why she loved her job and that made the tough days and the occasional impossible-to-please client worth the trouble.

"Well, that changes now. From here on we'll all be listening to you, to you and Matthew," she amended to include Shelby's fiancé, "and we're counting on you to tell us what we need to know to make your wedding day perfect for the two of you."

"No problem. We've talked about it a lot and we know exactly what we want."

"That's music to a wedding planner's ears; the more certain you are of what you like and what you don't, the easier our job is. It would also help to see any magazine clippings or color swatches you have, and any notes you may have jotted down."

"Oh, trust me, my mother has that covered. I think she's been secretly subscribing to bridal magazines and tearing out pictures for years."

Sophie laughed. "Well, of course she has. This will be a big day for her too, especially with you being her only daughter . . . her only *child*."

"So she tells me . . . several times a day."

"The next step is a second consultation to discuss an overall theme for the wedding—which can be very subtle or very dramatic, depending on your ideas—and we need to bang out a time schedule . . . which I don't have to tell you is going to be tight from the get-go. Once we draft a detailed proposal and get your final approval, we can start pulling it all together."

"Sounds good. When?"

"Let's see . . . can you come in tomorrow morning at eleven?"

"Eleven it is."

Four

Strictly speaking, Sophie didn't have to sit in on meetings with clients. And she suspected that most of the time neither the *J*s nor the clients even noticed that she was in the room. Blending into the background just sort of came naturally.

She went because she'd learned that being there to take her own notes—particularly during the initial planning session for an event—was preferable to depending on Jill or Jenna's listening skills. It helped stave off future misunderstandings and screwups, and since she was invariably the one called on to resolve misunderstandings and screwups, especially those of the last-minute, drop-everything-and-work-long-into-the-night variety, making time now ended up saving her time and aggravation in the end.

She especially tried to be on hand for wedding consultations. True, corporate events were at the top of Seasons' food chain in terms of profit; they also brought free publicity and resulted in the greatest number of new referrals, but in the end corporate events were . . . well, corporate. Weddings were personal and intimate; a wedding was literally a life-changing occasion for the people involved, and as far as Sophie was concerned, that mattered a hell of a lot more in the grand scheme of things than celebrating record-breaking profits or the glitzy launch of a new product line.

She felt a special affinity for the brides who entrusted Seasons with the most important day of their lives, and along with it an extra measure of dedication to making sure every detail was not merely right, but perfect. It didn't matter how many hours a day she had to work or how tired she was or how much concealer it took to hide the dark circles under her eyes, she would not permit so much as an engraved silver bubble wand or a blown-glass Cinderella's-coach cake topper to slip through the cracks and mar a happy couple's day, not if it was within her power to prevent it. First, because by the time the big day arrived, most brides were stressed to powder-keg level and even a teensy-tiny glitch could set them off and send months of careful preparations crashing like a string of dominoes. And second, because that's what she did; she made things perfect. She made dreams come true.

It was entirely possible that her soft spot for all things bridal was a genetic predisposition, or at the very least that it had rubbed off on her at an early age. Her mother had been an artist with a needle and thread and the one-of-a-kind wedding dresses she created were truly works of art. Sophie had happy childhood memories of spending time in her mother's small dressmaking shop, the sewing machine whirring away in the background as she turned the silk and lace scraps her mother set aside for her into wedding finery for her dolls. Sadly, she never developed anything close to her mother's skill . . . though she sometimes wondered whether she might have if things had turned out differently.

Instead she took satisfaction in knowing she shared her mother's passion for her work. Her mother had taken pride in making sure that every one of her brides walked down the aisle in a dress that not only made her look and feel beautiful, but that was hers and hers alone. Among the most important staples in her shop, right up there with the bolts of silk chiffon and the glass vials filled with seed pearls and crystals, had been a pretty china tea service and an always fresh assortment of fancy cookies. Madeleine Bennett believed there was no better way of getting to know someone than over a cup of tea and she insisted on getting to know a bride before she started to sew. Observing how a customer held herself and how she moved, how she laughed and even what she laughed at, had been a crucial part of her mother's creative process. As they sipped tea, she would listen to the bride-to-be talk about the man she loved and about her dreams for their future together. They also talked about The Dress, of course, as they pored over pattern books and magazine photos, debating whether it should be ivory or white, silk organza or dupioni silk, but her mother insisted it was the offhand remarks and the little things revealed between those crucial decisions that helped her to really understand the woman's vision of herself as a bride, perhaps better than the woman herself understood or could put into words.

That was another reason Sophie was always willing to rearrange her schedule to be available for a wedding consult; just as every woman had a vision of herself as a bride, every bride-to-be had a vision of her wedding day, and it was her, Sophie's, self-appointed duty to see to it that this vision became a reality. Even if it sometimes meant swimming against the mighty and well-armed tide that was the Seasons' wedding-planning machine.

Joyce Mainelli Bennett—her stepmother and the third *J*—was a sharp businesswoman and a virtuoso when it came to spotting a new trend and making it her own. One of the first local wedding planners to promote the concept of "theme weddings," over time she figured out which themes were the most popular and fine-tuned them until she had each one down to a science. When she "semiretired" she left behind what were referred to in-house as

"The White Books," a set of oversize, leather-bound albums containing dozens of professional photographs of weddings by Seasons, along with promotional photos and material from preferred vendors. Each book was dedicated to one of Seasons' *signature* themes, from Fairy-tale Princess to Romance by the Sea to Winter Wonderland. All you had to do was match the BTB—Bride-to-Be—with a theme and hand her the right book. The photographs had been strategically selected and arranged so that the client could easily see herself stepping into the prefab fantasy and living it, and before you could hum "Here Comes the Bride," she was trying to decide which of the Ice Palace floral arrangements or Sand Castle cake designs she preferred.

It was a no-brainer; weddings-by-number. Joyce understood her daughters' strengths and their shortcomings; she'd known they would be taking over the business one day and she'd planned accordingly. If the cookie-cutter approach didn't quite mesh with Sophie's philosophy, well, so be it. In theory, Jill, Jenna, and she were equals when it came to business, and to their credit neither they nor Joyce ever suggested otherwise. They didn't have to.

It had been the same when Joyce and her father married when Sophie was thirteen, the year after her mother was struck by a car and killed crossing the street in a blizzard. Joyce had known her mother slightly through business and she had been persistent and resourceful in her effort to fill the sudden hole in her father's life. Persistent, resourceful, and fast. Sophie still hadn't gotten used to her mother not being there when suddenly Joyce, Jill, and Jenna were. The *J*s moved in, bag and baggage, Calvin Klein jeans, and strawberry-scented styling mousse, and suddenly her home didn't feel like home anymore. It wasn't really their fault. Joyce was just so different from her mother, as different as Jill and Jenna were from her. They tried to make her feel like she was one of them the same way they tried to overhaul her sense of style and find her dates, and with the same lackluster results. Then, like now, the fact that they didn't go out of their way to make her feel like a square peg in their world of sleek and sexy round holes didn't mean she wasn't one.

Sophie wasn't entirely opposed to the White Books. There was no denying that they were a brilliant marketing tool and for some brides they enhanced the whole planning experience and introduced them to new ways to express themselves on their wedding day. For others, they were just plain overwhelming. A wedding was like a puzzle, with hundreds of pieces that had to fit together perfectly when the time came to assemble it, and she was a firm believer that the final piece of the puzzle should come from the hearts of the couple being wed, not from a book. *That's* what she was listening for when she sat quietly on the sidelines at meetings, that handful of words or offhand comment that would reveal the final piece of the puzzle. It was impossible to predict, but she knew it when she heard it.

One bride had casually joked about how her fiancé carried in his wallet a snapshot of her taken when she was five, playing dress-up bride in her backyard with a lace tablecloth for a veil and a bunch of wild violets for a bouquet. Sophie suggested she add violets to her white rose bouquet without telling the groom. In a church filled with people, the moment when she started down the aisle and he first saw the violets, and their eyes met, was theirs alone, and one they would carry with them forever.

Sophie was convinced that every couple in love shared something—a secret getaway, a private joke, a memory of a lost loved one—that could add personality and joy to their celebration in a way no seven-tier cake or vodka ice luge could. You just had to work harder to coax it from some of them. There were women who hadn't spent a lifetime fantasizing about their wedding day, and some who had envisioned it right down to the smallest detail but weren't good at putting their vision into words.

Shelby Archer was not one of them.

* * *

"Hemp."

Sophie immediately looked up from her notes. The *J*s said nothing and that was probably for the best. Helen Archer laughed, a high-pitched bubble of sound that had more to do with surprise than amusement.

"I'm sorry, sweetie," she said to her daughter. "I must have misheard; I could have sworn you just said 'hemp.' "

"That is what I said," replied Shelby.

"Oh. Well, then you must have misheard Jill's question; she asked what sort of wedding gown you have in mind."

"I heard her. Hemp; that's the kind of gown I want."

The five women were gathered around the conference table in the room reserved for meeting with Seasons' wedding clients. Elegant black-and-white photos of past weddings adorned the walls and a specially built glass shelf held the White Books . . . except for the Fairy-tale Princess edition. Either Jill or Jenna had— understandably perhaps—assumed that would be the theme Shelby would choose for her *Princess House* wedding and they pulled the book and had it waiting when the Archers arrived, nestled right there beside the crystal champagne flutes and the silver bowl filled with fresh strawberries.

At the moment it sat in front of Helen . . . open to the re- touched photograph of a beautiful bride wearing the quintessen- tial Cinderella ball gown. Helen leaned back in the cushy white leather swivel chair, lips pursed, and looked quizzically at her daughter.

"Hemp? Isn't that some sort of grain? Like barley? You can't make a wedding gown out of barley, sweetheart."

"It's not a grain," Shelby told her, smiling and relaxed. "It's actually a fiber . . . from the cannabis plant."

"Cannabis?" Her mother's impeccably shaped brows arched. "But that's . . ."

Her blue eyes twinkling, Shelby said, "Same genus; different plant. You could say that the kind you smoke is a distant cousin of the kind used to make wedding dresses . . . and paper and all sorts of other useful stuff. It's a legitimate crop, and fully sustainable, which is important . . . even George Washington grew hemp."

Her mother huffed. "Maybe, but I doubt he made Martha wear it. Really, Shelby, I know you have some crazy ideas, and I do try to be understanding, but this is your wedding we're planning . . . not a Greenpeace rally." She glanced imploringly at Jill and Jenna. "You're the experts: a hemp dress . . . really, have you ever heard of anything so ridiculous?"

The *J*s exchanged a cautious look; they knew, as did Sophie, that you had to tread carefully when stepping onto a mother–daughter battlefield. It could be laden with land mines that had been buried for years. Decades even.

"I'm vaguely familiar with the concept of hemp dresses," said Jill.

Nice dodge, thought Sophie, not really surprised that no one looked to her for an opinion.

"I remember seeing a few hemp dresses among the samples at the fall bridal expo in Boston," added Jenna. She gave Shelby a look of regret. "I have to say that, as I recall, they were all pretty dreadful."

Undaunted, Shelby flipped her long brown hair behind her shoulder. "Then you weren't looking at the right dresses."

Sophie's mouth curved into a smile. The kid was spunky, she'd give her that. Twenty-two was so young to be getting married, but there was a quiet, steadiness about Shelby Archer that made Sophie think she was more mature than lots of older brides she'd worked with . . . and that she could hold her own with her mother.

Smiling with professional excitement, Jenna leaned forward and tapped the photo of the bride. "What do you think of this style dress, Shelby? Naturally there's no guarantee that exact dress is still available . . . but I'm wondering what you think of the look."

"I think it's probably a great look for some people. But not for me."

"Don't be silly," said Jenna, entirely missing the point. "That dress would be beyond gorgeous on you. Look at you . . . those long legs, that tiny little waist. Do you have any idea how many brides would die to have your body and be able to pull off a gown with all those ruffles and flounces?"

"Just look at that big satin bow," urged Jill.

"And all the little bows made out of pearls and crystals."

"That is truly a dress fit for a princess."

Shelby nodded agreeably. "Exactly."

"It epitomizes the fairy-princess theme."

"Yes, it does," said Shelby. "Which is exactly why it's all wrong for me."

The *J*s frowned.

"I don't understand," said Jill. "Wasn't that the whole point of being married at Ange de la Mer . . . or the Princess House, as you call it? So that you could be a princess on that day? We thought it was your lifelong dream."

"Your vision," added Jenna.

"Your one nonnegotiable. Why else would we have gone to so much trouble to make it happen?"

Sophie had to roll her eyes inwardly at Jill's haughty tone and her use of the word *we*, considering that their only contribution to the venture was responsible for the blisters on her feet.

"It *is* my dream to be married there," acknowledged Shelby. "I just don't want a fairy-princess wedding. I never said I did."

There was the collective sound of three jaws dropping.

"Maybe not in so many words," Jill murmured.

"You didn't have to spell it out. The Princess House . . . that says it all," declared Jenna.

"I have to agree," said Helen. "Princess House, princess wedding . . ." Pointing at the open book, she added, "Princess gown. It just makes sense . . . and it will be beautiful." She gave Shelby's shoulder a squeeze. "You'll see."

"Mom, I love you, but I'm not the princess type. I know you wish I was, but I'm just not, and I never have been and you know it. And I'm not having some lame, fancy, fussy, prissy princessy wedding. I want to be married at the Princess House because of Dad, and because of the book, not so I can wear a dress that looks like what Scarlett O'Hara would have whipped up if the living-room drapes had been white . . . and had little crystal bows all over them. No offense," she said, casting a disparaging eye at the open book, "but Cordy wouldn't be caught dead in that getup and neither will I."

"Cordy?" Jenna queried.

"Princess Cordelia is the main character in *The Princess House*," Sophie explained. "And the most un-princessy princess there ever was."

"In fact she's known as the backward princess," Shelby added. "And she wears the name like a badge of honor . . . that's what makes her so wonderful. The only way Princess Cordy would ever wear that dress is at the point of a sword."

"And even then she'd probably insist on wearing it inside out," Sophie added, drawing a grin from Shelby.

The others appeared unamused, and a little confused. The *J*s liked being in control, or at least giving the appearance they were, and they disliked discussing things they didn't understand. But like any well-trained salesperson, their recovery time was negligible.

With her best the-client-is-always-right expression firmly in place, Jenna flipped shut the White Book and slid it off to the side. "All right, then, Shelby. Was there a particular theme you did have in mind for your wedding? Besides hemp, that is."

"Yes, do tell," urged her mother. "I can't wait to hear what sort of theme calls for the bride to walk down the aisle in a burlap sack. Old McDonald Had a Farm, perhaps? I can see it now, red-and-white checkered tablecloths and some sort of woven straw headpieces." She made a circular motion in the direction of her head.

Shelby appeared more bemused than bothered by her mother's comments. "Relax, Mom, I promise you there'll be no red and white checks anywhere . . . and no burlap. Matthew and I have given this a lot of thought and we want our wedding to have the feel of *A Midsummer Night's Dream*. The play," she added when there was no immediate reaction. She looked from one woman to another. "Shakespeare? Fairies? A magical forest?"

The *J*s exchanged a vague look and then Jill glanced behind her at the bookshelf. "I don't think we have . . ."

Sophie caught her attention and shook her head. "We don't. Shelby, I think this is a first for Seasons, and speaking for myself, I think it's a terrific idea. Romantic and whimsical and, my God, so full of possibilities."

"I know," countered Shelby, excitement rising in her voice. "And it's the perfect theme for us because it's how Matthew and I met, when we were both volunteering to help with an inner-city school's production of the play."

The final piece of the puzzle, thought Sophie.

"It is perfect," she agreed. "And I can see why you're thinking of a hemp gown; the designs I've seen in hemp are usually very simple and that would be in keeping with the play's sense of youth and innocence."

"You know about these hemp gowns?" Helen asked.

"A little," Sophie replied. "My mother was a dressmaker who specialized in wedding dresses, so I've always had a special interest in them and I like to keep up with what's current. Over the past few years hemp fabrics have come a long way, to the point where some top designers are starting to use them, especially the hemp silk or hemp cotton blends. They say they're every bit as good as the original in how they look and drape."

"Then why not just use the original?" Helen asked.

"Because no silkworms have to give their lives to make a hemp silk dress," Shelby explained.

The *J*s and Helen exchanged baffled looks.

Sophie explained. "It's a common practice for silkworm farmers—especially on large corporate farms—to toss the cocoons into an oven or boiling water to speed up the cultivation process. But a small group of eco-friendly farmers now wait and allow the moth to complete its natural life cycle even though it requires more time and more effort to harvest the silk fibers."

Nodding earnestly, Shelby said, "That's right. Did you know that over two thousand silkworms have to die to make one pound of silk?" She swept the table with a resolute gaze. "Feel free to laugh, I'm used to it. Besides being die-hard romantics, Matthew and I are also die-hard environmentalists, and we want our wedding to be as green as possible. Don't panic," she added, raising a hand to forestall her mother's protest. "Nothing heavy-handed, I promise; no speeches, no lectures. We did our research and I know our wedding can be both beautiful *and* green. It's really just a matter of making choices."

"What sort of choices?" inquired her mother, clearly wary.

"Well, for starters we want to use only local foods and wines, and for favors we'll come up with something organic, like maybe little trees, instead of monogrammed shot glasses or coasters. It will be done very elegantly." She grinned and squeezed her mother's shoulder. "You'll see."

Helen sighed. "Is this another first for Seasons?"

Head tilted to one side, Jenna smoothed the notebook page on which she had yet to write a single word. "We have had brides who insisted on biodegradable invitations or who wanted rose petals tossed instead of confetti, but an entire green wedding? That's a first."

Helen leaned forward, her eyes narrowing. "Will that present a problem? Especially given the time constraints."

"Not at all," Sophie assured her. "It sounds like Shelby has already done her homework; we'll do ours and I guarantee the end result will be everything you've ever dreamed it would be."

"I'm so glad you'll be handling the plans," declared Shelby. "I'll be away for most of July and I'll feel a whole lot better knowing you're running things here. Don't get me wrong," she added hastily. "I like working with all of you, but it just seems so obvious that Sophie . . . gets me."

"I'm sure she does," said Jenna. "But yours isn't the only event we're currently working on, or even the only wedding, for that matter, and we do things a certain way here at Seasons. We have our own system."

"A routine," said Jill.

"What does that mean?" Shelby asked.

"Simply that we work as a team. There are some jobs Jill and I are better at and others that fall to Sophie."

Jill elaborated. "Jenna and I will work directly with the designs in the books and put together an overall plan for your wedding . . . flowers, music, menu, everything. Subject to your approval, of course."

"But my theme isn't in your books."

"True. Which is why we'll have to take time to do some research of our own and get up to speed before we can present you with a detailed proposal."

"But Sophie is already up to speed," Shelby pointed out.

"Yes, but the way we work is that Jill and I deal directly with clients, cake tastings, dress fittings, all of that, and Sophie basically holds everything together behind the scenes," explained Jenna. "If we need someone to check on something—"

"Or find something," Jill interjected.

"Or make sure something gets where it absolutely has to be, Sophie's right on it."

"We literally couldn't survive without our Sophie."

Well, *they* might, thought Sophie, but she wouldn't place bets on the business.

Seeing Shelby's concern, Sophie smiled reassuringly. "Don't worry. I'll pass whatever ideas I have on to Jenna and Jill, and you can call me anytime you have questions or want to run something by me."

"I guess that will work," Shelby returned without enthusiasm.

Jenna smoothed the sleeve of her blouse and smiled. "It does work. Trust me; you don't get to be one of the most successful event planners in New England without teamwork. Ask any of the vendors we work with and they'll tell you, we get the job done in style." She broke into a smile. "There's even this one DJ, very hot commodity, who refers to us as 'The Divas and the Drone.' You know, like we're a rock group or something."

Shelby glanced across the table at Sophie, her eyes brimming with laughter. "Go, team," she murmured.

It had been three days since he made his deal with the devil. And make no mistake, that's what it was, even if it was hard to reconcile the image of Satan with his recollection of the way Sophia

Bennett smiled, or the light that danced in her soft green eyes when she did.

Owen paused midswing with the golf club extended behind his right hip and frowned at the imaginary golf ball on the carpet at his feet. Soft green. Was that even a color? Yes, he decided, and released his swing, managing to barely miss a nearby porcelain lamp; it was almost as if the unseen hand of his guardian angel intervened at the last second to nudge the lamp a few centimeters to safety.

Strangely, although he was unable to focus his mind on the work he was being paid a ridiculous amount to do, he could recall the precise shade of the intriguing little wedding planner's eyes. They weren't pale or light or grayish or bluish green; they were soft green, a calm, true green that made him think of fields of grass that went on forever, the kind of field where you could stretch out and rest your head without a care in the world, the kind of field that he was convinced didn't really exist.

Three days.

And for those three days he'd volleyed between wondering when he would hear from her again and asking himself the same existentialist question over and over. *Have you lost your fucking mind?* The answer varied with his mood.

On the one hand, there was nothing he wanted less than to allow a parade of complete strangers to traipse through the house, fussing and sprucing and doing God knows what in preparation for an onslaught of even more strangers, the main difference as far as he was concerned being that the second horde would be dressed formally and standing around sipping champagne and nibbling rabbit food off silver serving trays.

On the other hand, and at the same time, there was nothing he wanted more than to figure out who—or what—was sharing his house. He refused to use the word *haunting* because of the ghostly connotations, though he supposed that was splitting hairs once you acknowledged there was something there you couldn't see or touch or smell. Which raised another question he couldn't answer and couldn't stop asking: Was it Allie's spirit that was keeping him company? Was it possible he'd hit pay dirt when he followed through on the impulse to buy this particular house—the Princess House—in hopes of feeling closer to her and recapturing whatever scraps he could of all that he'd lost when he lost his only child?

The only thing he knew for certain was that he wasn't alone there. Things moved around, things went missing, windows and doors slammed in the middle of the night. Some of it he could chalk up to his own distractedness, but not all. The other night he climbed into bed and found a wet towel waiting for him. He might be preoccupied enough to misplace a beer, but why the hell would he bury a wet towel beneath the bedcovers when he could simply drop it on the floor as he usually did? It made no sense to him and he was becoming increasingly desperate to have it make sense. The fact that he didn't believe in ghosts only complicated the situation. He had no answers, and neither did Wikipedia or any of the other online sites he tried. He hadn't told anyone else about it for the simple reason that he was used to solving his own problems and he liked it that way.

He sure as hell hadn't gone looking for Sophia Bennett. She'd shown up on his doorstep uninvited and unwanted, but he'd known even before she set foot inside the house that whatever *it* was that was hanging around, she saw or felt or sensed it too. It was the only reason he'd let her in. There had been others in the house, of course: his agent, his lawyer, the guy who cut the lawn, the merry maids who came around once a week to pick up after him. And then there were the assorted delivery people who came bearing groceries or pizza or beer. But as far as he could tell, not one of them had ever tuned into anything out of the ordinary. Sophia Bennett had. And then she mentioned the Princess House, invoking all kinds of memories and leaving him no choice but to put aside his dislike of wedding foolery and his need to be left alone and agree to a wedding on his turf.

He'd assumed she would begin pestering him right away. He expected her to show up and be underfoot on a regular basis, which is just exactly where he wanted her and needed her to be if she was going to be any help to him at all. He wasn't sure yet how up front he would be about the sort of help he needed from her; he'd just take it one step at a time and see how it played out. Step one was getting her back there so he could keep her under surveillance.

When the first day passed with no contact, he wondered if she'd called while he was out. He tried to remember if he'd given her his cell number. Probably not; he hated giving it out because he hated getting calls when he was away from home even more than he hated getting them when he was home. Then he wondered if maybe he'd been so absorbed in work, he hadn't heard the phone ringing. Seemed unlikely, but just the same he went out and bought an answering machine. He checked regularly, some might say compulsively, for messages. Another day passed, and another. He started to worry that his complete ignorance of weddings had caused him to miscalculate how much advance preparation a wedding planner actually did. For all he knew, he might not hear from her again for weeks. And he'd go crazy if he had to sit around spinning his wheels, chasing down AWOL beers, and sleeping with wet towels for weeks.

When on the fourth day he happened to look out the front window and see her black SUV coming down the drive, it was like the answer to a prayer. Except that he didn't pray. Not anymore.

The sense of relief was so strong he didn't even pause long enough to calculate whether he ought to play it cool by waiting until she rang the bell. Barefoot, dressed in faded black jeans and an old T-shirt, he headed outside to greet her. It didn't occur to him that she might not be alone until the passenger doors started to pop open. Ignoring them, he circled to the driver's door just as a leggy blonde in a short skirt slid from behind the wheel.

"Who are you?" he asked, annoyed that she wasn't Sophie. Sophie. She'd told him that's what everyone called her, but it was the first time he'd thought of her not as Sophia Bennett, but as *Sophie*.

The woman wasted a thousand-watt smile on him. "I'm Jenna . . . "

"And I'm Jill."

Owen swung his gaze from the driver to the woman who slipped from the backseat and then back again.

"You two are . . ."

"Twins," the women confirmed, nodding in unison. "And obviously we're from Seasons."

They each waved an arm toward the car door, like a pair of game-show models revealing what was behind curtain number two. Written on the door, in script and pearlized silver paint, were SEASONS and a telephone number. It was all very classy and understated, which told him the business was successful enough that it didn't need a heavy hand with promotion and could send employees tooling around in luxury SUVs. Company cars. That explained why he'd mistaken it for Sophie's.

"And you must be Owen Winters," the driver twin went on, extending her right hand for him to shake. "I'm so happy to meet you and I'm really looking forward to getting to know you in the coming weeks. I work hard, but my motto is that you should always make time to make new friends. I can't tell you how thrilled all of us at Seasons are—"

"Thrilled and privileged," interjected Passenger Twin.

"—to be planning the first wedding ever held here at Ange de la Mer. Now come over here and let me introduce you to the bride, and her mother."

Owen's back teeth had begun to ache even before Helen Archer told him she had some ideas to make the landscaping along the front drive absolutely divine and asked if he would mind if they dug a small pond somewhere on the back lawn.

"Mom, I don't think it will be necessary to actually dig a pond," said the young woman beside her. "I talked it over with Sophie and she has a couple of ideas for creating the illusion of a pond."

"Illusion," drawled her mother, shaking her head. "It already sounds tacky."

"It won't be. It's basically a shallow pool with plants and lighting that make it look real. Sophie wouldn't suggest anything tacky."

For the first time he glanced at the youngest of the four women. Sophie mentioned that she'd just graduated from college. Which he knew would make her about twenty-one. Twenty-one. It was a great age. So full of . . . possibilities. He looked at her for a few seconds, thinking of someone else, and felt his throat tighten.

When she'd finished reassuring her mother, the young woman turned to him. "I'm Shelby Archer, Mr. Winters . . . the bride who started all this trouble for you. I really hope we're not inconveniencing you too much."

He liked the steady way she looked him in the eye even as he scowled at her; he'd had men in his command who couldn't do it so calmly.

"Why are you here?" he asked, wary.

"For the grand tour, of course," said Helen Archer.

"We really can't go any further with our plans until we see exactly what we have to work with in terms of layout," said one of the twins. He'd already lost track of which one was which.

"And also any special features the property has," added the other. "Is there a fountain by any chance? Please say there's a fountain . . . even a little one."

"Let me get this straight," he said. "You want to know where the johns are and if there's a fountain and so you just show up here unannounced?"

"Not unannounced. I left messages . . . the last one telling you I would assume it was all right to stop by this morning if I didn't hear otherwise. I'd have preferred a set appointment, but I also remembered that Sophie had better luck stopping by than she did calling."

"I'm glad you brought that up. Where is Sophie?" His annoyance with them for being there expanded to include Sophie for *not* being there.

"She's working," replied a twin.

"Back at the office," explained the other. "She's swamped with orders and paperwork—you know how June is—so she couldn't join us."

"But not to worry: we know you have your own concerns and Sophie's filled us in on all that. That's her thing, remembering picayune little details. Trust me, it's not a problem."

"For you maybe. The fact that you're standing here and she's not is a big problem for me."

"I don't understand."

"Then I'll spell it out. I never wanted a wedding here . . . no offense," he added with a quick glance at the bride.

"None taken. I completely understand why you would turn down our request . . . I'm thrilled that you didn't, but I understand."

"It was Sophie who changed my mind and it's Sophie I assumed I would be dealing with going forward."

"That's a completely understandable mistake," declared twin one, wasting another of those high-wattage smiles on him.

"Totally," agreed Twin Two.

"Sophie was the first one to contact you and it makes perfect sense that you would assume she would be the one to take the lead."

"But she won't be?" he asked

It was Shelby who answered. "No. She won't. I made the same mistake you did. I assumed I'd be working directly with Sophie since she's so obviously the best person for the job. I mean, she got the whole *Princess House* thing right away and then she was the one who convinced you to say yes."

"But as we explained to Shelby," said a twin, her smile becoming strained around the edges, "at Seasons we have our own system for planning an event. We work as a team."

"That's true," Shelby confirmed. "There's even a team name . . . what was it? Oh, right, the Divas and the Drone."

A look passed between the young bride and Owen.

The twins looked uncomfortable.

"That's just a joke," said one of them.

"Well, this isn't," Owen countered. "I expected to work with Sophie and that's what I intend to do."

"Oh my," murmured Helen.

Shelby bit the corner of her lip and Owen suspected it was to keep from grinning.

Both twins were suddenly clutching cell phones.

"Why don't I just call Sophie and see if we can't work this out?" suggested one.

"Good idea," he said, making himself comfortable on the low wall that ran along the front flower beds. It was as clear a signal as he could think of that he wouldn't be inviting them in for tea. "Just remember: no Sophie, no deal."

Five

S ophie was elated. And apprehensive. Cautiously optimistic and just a tiny bit worried. Maybe a tiny bit more than a tiny bit.

She felt the way she imagined Cinderella would have if there had been no fairy godmother to work her magic on the mice and the pumpkin and the spiderwebs. If, say, she were to have been suddenly plucked from the hearth midsweep and sent off to the ball "as is," barefoot and in tatters, no push-up bra, no breath mints, no glass slippers. Surely Cinderella would have had mixed feelings about what lay ahead. And so did Sophie.

On the one hand, how often does a plain Jane get the chance to go to the ball? On the other, if she was going to fail miserably, better to do so in the privacy of her own servants' hovel rather than before the royal court, to be immortalized in the society pages for all to see, thus providing her glamorous and ambitious stepsisters and stepmother with a reason to sigh and exchange long-suffering glances and ask one another whose bright idea it had been to let her out of the kitchen in the first place.

Once a drone . . .

One minute Sophie was happily, well, more or less, toiling away at her hearth . . . er, in her office, searching for a linen supplier who could handle a rush order for two dozen round translucent silver table covers to replace the two dozen square covers that had been delivered by mistake for a twenty-fifth wedding anniversary celebration only two days away, and the next minute she was on the receiving end of an emergency phone call from the *J*s. By the time the short, tense call ended, they'd been relegated to the backseat in terms of planning for the lavish, one-of-a-kind wedding to be held at Ange de la Mer in a little over six weeks' time and Sophie was the one in charge.

Holy shit, holy shit, holy shit were the words that kept running through her mind.

Needless to say, the *J*s were not happy to be usurped in their starring roles in such a high-profile project. That sort of thing just didn't happen at Seasons. But neither they nor Sophie had any choice in the matter. Owen Winters made that as clear as the expensive champagne they kept on hand for toasting new clients. Since they were already on the premises, he finally permitted them to go ahead with their walk-through of the house and grounds, but only after it was understood by all concerned that henceforth he would deal only with Sophie. The twins went down swinging, but to Sophie's amazement, their tag-team charm and talk of teamwork failed to put even a tiny ding in his resolve. Apparently there was just no arguing with the prince once he got something in his shaggy, stubbly-jawed head, and the image of the *J*s giving it their all and striking out brought Sophie a small, wicked smile as she hung up the phone.

She couldn't help it. Sweaty palms and trepidations aside, this was the most exciting thing that had happened to her in . . . maybe ever. Certainly the most exciting thing that was work-related. It was sort of like a backhanded promotion, albeit one she would never have sought, or expected. A woman had to know her limitations and Sophie knew hers. It was still thrilling and she only wished she had someone to call and share the news with. The one other person who was unreservedly thrilled to have Sophie take charge already knew. This is what Shelby Archer had wanted and lobbied for all along and Sophie was determined not to let her down.

For the next few days she went all out practically around the clock to keep up with her usual workload while pulling together her vision of a *Midsummer Night's Dream* wedding. As soon as she had the essentials in place, she arranged another meeting, which both Jill and Jenna were suddenly too busy to attend. Undaunted, she presented her ideas to Shelby and her fiancé using color charts and fabric swatches and sample sketches of specific areas within the enchanted forest that she proposed creating on the grounds of the estate. One sketch showed the illusion pond surrounded by petal-strewn paths leading to private nooks with cushioned benches and with a full-service bar nestled beneath a grape arbor at one end; another was of a dance floor illuminated by starlight—God willing—and white linen lanterns hung on brass shepherds' hooks. The overall mood was lush and elegant, but still natural and whimsical enough to suit the bride. Helen Archer was at the meeting as well, and before Sophie was halfway through her presentation, she could tell that the mother of the bride was now squarely in her corner, happy—not to mention relieved—to have found someone who understood what she considered her daughter's quirky notions and who promised to deliver on them without making her a laughingstock in front of her friends.

As the meeting was ending, Shelby brought up the subject of her wedding dress, specifically the trouble she was having in finding what she wanted.

"All I have to do is close my eyes and I can see my dress," she told Sophie. "It's simple, but not boring. It's light and airy . . . the kind of dress that makes you feel like dancing all night. And it's sparkly, but not weighed down with tons of crystals and beads. The kind of sparkle I imagine is more subtle . . . like fireflies on a summer night . . ."

"Like fairy wings," Sophie interjected softly.

Shelby nodded excitedly. "Yes. Yes, that's it exactly." She sighed. "I get it, and you get it, but I must not do a very good job of describing it to the saleswomen at any of the dozen shops Mom and I have been to. Either that or it doesn't exist."

"We ran out of local bridal salons last week," Helen explained. "And I think we must have hit every one in Boston yesterday . . . in fact, my poor feet are sure of it. I have to say that at this point I concur with whoever said that these hemp gowns are all dreadful."

"Mom," Shelby said.

Helen shushed her. "I'm not suggesting we give up . . . just that perhaps you should broaden your parameters a bit. What do you think, Matthew?"

At the first hint of mother–daughter tension, Matthew, a quiet, lanky young man with sandy hair and honest eyes, had become instantly fascinated with the photographs on the wall. Smart kid, Sophie thought, but Helen wasn't having it.

"Matthew, you don't think there's anything wrong with being open-minded about these things, do you?"

"I think . . ." His naturally slow drawl became slower as he searched for a way to avoid the trap. "I think Shelby will look beautiful in whatever she decides to wear . . . just like she always does. And I think that if you all are going to talk dresses, maybe I ought to go get the car. I know your feet got a real workout yesterday," he said, standing and aiming a solicitous smile at his future mother-in-law. "This way I can save you a few steps. And I can get the a/c cranked; I know how you hate having the windows open and the fresh air blowing your hair around."

"That would be lovely," Helen agreed, either oblivious to the fact that she'd been outplayed or enjoying it.

"Suck-up," Shelby mouthed as she caught Matthew's eye on his way out.

And then they did what Sophie had observed other engaged couples do, lucky couples: they exchanged what she thought of as "that smile," the one that only has room for two.

With Matthew gone, the talk returned to wedding gowns. Not only had none of those she'd tried on come close to Shelby's vision, but the message at every bridal shop had been the same: the designers they worked with required a minimum of six months for custom designs. Wheels were starting to turn inside Sophie's head even as she urged Shelby and Helen not to become discouraged.

"Shopping for the perfect dress is supposed to be fun," she reminded them.

"It has been fun, sort of." Shelby slanted a sheepish look at her mother. "What can I say? I'm not really the shop-till-you-drop type. And I'm getting worried about the time crunch."

"There is that," agreed Sophie. "I know of a couple of small salons off the beaten path where you might have better luck. Here, let me write down the names and addresses for you."

Shelby reached for the piece of paper Sophie slid across the table to her. "Thanks, Sophie."

"If you do find one—or more—dresses that you like and you want another opinion, you have my cell number."

"I'd love your opinion, but I know you've already taken on so much extra work for us. I hate to bother you."

"It's what I'm here for . . . and I can always squeeze in a quick fashion show. Call me. I mean it."

"I will . . . *if* I ever find something worth showing you."

"And if you don't," Sophie said, "if it turns out the dress of your dreams really doesn't exist, well, I just might have a solution. I'll check into it; you keep shopping. And we'll talk."

Their enthusiasm, as well as their confidence in her, was contagious. Sophie had gone into the meeting apprehensive and sleep-deprived, but she left feeling energized and raring to go. She didn't care what it took; Shelby was going to have the wedding of her dreams. If the diva division of the Seasons team chose to remain in a snit and provide only minimal help along the way . . . well, so be it. She'd just have to manage without them. And why not? She had no shortage of her own creative ideas and it was exhilarating to finally be free to present them to the client as a total package rather than trying to sneak one in here and there. As for the business side of things . . . who had more experience than she did at managing details and putting out fires? She'd proven she could coordinate schedules and oversee expenses and she had a good rapport with both outside vendors and the in-house staff. In fact, the more she thought about it, the more she thought it just might be a blessing in disguise if the *J*s sat this one out.

And then there was Owen Winters. A challenge of a different sort altogether.

The man was ornery and stubborn and clearly used to getting his own way, and yet Sophie had to admit that something inside her perked up at the thought of seeing him. It was funny how things worked out. She'd driven away from their first meeting wondering if their paths would cross again; now it looked like they would be crossing on a regular basis . . . and at his insistence no less. Something that continued to baffle her as much as it did the *J*s.

Baffling or not, it had felt good to be singled out by him that way, like being moved up to the head of the class and given a gold star while all the other kids looked on, wishing, for once, that they were her. She wasn't naive enough to think this meant only smooth sailing going forward. In fact she was braced for exactly the opposite, for the possibility that Winters had picked her because he thought he could ride herd over her more easily than he could the Js. Whatever his motive, he added another whole dimension of anticipation and excitement to what lay ahead.

Excitement of a professional nature. She certainly didn't expect anything to come of it on a personal level. She was far too self-aware and realistic to get swept up in impossible flights of fancy, and that's exactly what it would be to imagine anything happening between her and the brooding Mr. Winters. Not that she was an expert on men or relationships. The kindest way to describe her romance résumé was to say it was flimsy, consisting of lots of forgettable evenings and exactly one serious long-term affair that she had wholeheartedly believed would lead to white lace and promises of forever, and instead had ended in heartbreak and public humiliation. For her. But while she was no expert, she was an aficionado of both men and all things romantic, as well as a dedicated observer, on the job and off, and what she'd observed was that successful, über-wealthy men sexy enough to walk on water and blessed with a dark and enticing aura of mystery are invariably attracted to a certain type of woman. And she wasn't it.

The second time she made her way to Owen Winters's doorstep she went armed with assorted measuring tools, a notebook, and her camera. She planned to sketch the layout of the house and property and take measurements she would need when she met with landscape and lighting designers and with reps from the rental firms that supplied everything from tents luxurious enough to make royalty feel at home to floating dance floors to—should it come to it—the finest in portable powder rooms. Not to be confused with the familiar blue boxes found at rock festivals and county fairs. She was talking air-conditioned minitrailers complete with porcelain fixtures, marble countertops, and hot and cold running water.

At least this time she didn't have to bang on the door to get his attention, which was a good thing since she needed both hands to hold the case of beer she'd also brought with her. She'd called ahead to say she was finishing up at the office and would be there by late morning, but he appeared so quickly after she used her elbow to ring the doorbell that if she didn't know better she'd think he'd been watching for her.

She smiled as the door opened.

"Good morning. It's nice to see you again, Mr. Winters."

The greeting was out before she realized it was a lie. *Nice* didn't come close to describing what she felt standing face-to-face with him after rehearsing the moment over and over in her mind during the ride to his house. *Startled* was more like it, and a little lightheaded. The unexpected heat and rush of her response to him threw her. And for absolutely no good reason, because he looked pretty much as he had the first time she saw him—bare feet, ancient jeans, and a black T-shirt with that trademark fresh-from-the-ragbag look. But his effect on her senses was magnified a dozen times. Maybe it was because she was less preoccupied with other matters and free to focus on subtleties. All she knew was that his jaw looked squarer than she remembered, his cheekbones more chiseled, his mouth more distracting.

"Owen," he said.

She stared blankly at him.

"I have a feeling we'll be seeing too much of each other for formalities," he added.

"Oh. Yes . . . agreed. Please, call me Sophie."

"What's this?" he asked, eyeing the case of beer topped with a big red bow.

"An assortment of New England's finest microbrews . . . hand-picked by yours truly, who doesn't know diddly from squat when it comes to beer, so I hope they pass muster. The standard Seasons' thank-you is a bottle of Cristal, but I thought you might prefer your beverages a little less formal too."

"You thought right." He seemed about to smile, but stopped short of it. "Though you should be warned that gifts of any kind might be premature. I'm still not thrilled with this whole wedding thing, and I've been told I can be difficult to get along with under the best of circumstances."

"I'll consider myself warned. Maybe instead of a gift we could consider it a bribe . . . and it might already be working. You almost smiled."

"Don't get your hopes up." He injected a note of gruffness into his already deep voice, but she noticed that hint of a crooked smile lingered a split second longer this time. "Thanks for the beer. Let me grab it from you."

Stepping outside, he took the case of beer and hoisted it onto his shoulder as effortlessly as he would a box of cotton candy, and then extended his free hand in a silent invitation for her to precede him back inside. Sophie took a step in that direction, but before her foot landed on the threshold, the door slammed shut in her face with the same sudden ferocity it had swung open the last time she was there. A full second later she heard the lock click.

She glanced over her shoulder to see Owen glaring at the door. "Damn," he said.

Curious, she tipped her head toward the house. "Is there someone . . ."

He shook his head. "Just the wind."

"The wind blew the door shut *and* locked it?"

He shrugged the shoulder not weighed down with beer. "Old houses can be quirky. C'mon," he said as she wondered how those quirks might impact her work. "The back door should be open. If not, I'll give you a leg up to the kitchen window."

All thoughts of potential quirk complications shot to the back burner.

"A leg up . . . me?" She hurried after him, not liking the sound of that. "Now it's you who should be warned: I'm not very good at things like that."

"Like what?"

"You know, athletic things. Like climbing in windows."

"There won't be any climbing," he tossed over his shoulder. "Just lifting. And I'll be doing that. All you'll have to do is relax and enjoy the ride."

Yeah, right, Sophie thought. Like that would ever happen. She was already panicking just thinking about where he might have to put his hands to lift her high enough to climb in a window. Thank God for Spanx. But what about her thighs? What if he touched her thighs and thought they were too . . . squishy? At least she was wearing slacks and wouldn't have to wrestle with a skirt. Assuming he could lift her in the first place. If only she'd lost those ten pounds she'd bonded with over pineapple pizza and pints of Chunky Monkey ice cream, she wouldn't have to worry about his dropping her or throwing out his back. How embarrassing would that be? Talk about getting off to a humiliating start. The poor man already favored one leg when he walked; what if trying to get her off the ground aggravated the problem? Damn that stupid front door.

Sophie was literally dragging her feet as he led her across the patio and up a few shallow stone steps to the back door, which opened into the room where they'd sat last time. He tried turning the handle as she held her breath. His expression grim, he glanced over his shoulder at her and shook his head. Altogether there were four sets of French doors leading into the long room; the fact that he didn't bother to try any of the others told her he already knew they were locked. That didn't stop Sophie from trying them her-self. When she finished, she turned to find he'd put down the case of beer and was staring up at the house with a look that could only be described as perplexed.

"What are you thinking?" she asked.

Immediately his expression went blank. He looked at her and shrugged. "I'm thinking that you're going for a ride."

Again he loped off, leaving her to trail behind. His longer legs and her lack of enthusiasm combined to give him a good head start, and by the time she caught up, he was staring up at what she deduced was the kitchen window. He no longer looked perplexed, only purposeful, his dark eyes narrowed in assessment, his mouth edged with determination.

"Okay, here's what we're going to do."

"Don't say 'we,'" she protested, doing her best to sound pleas-ant, but firm. "Because there is no 'we' here. I wasn't kidding when I said I'm not good at stuff like this."

"Don't sell yourself short."

"Trust me, I'm not. I'm not being modest. Or coy. I know my-self. I know my strengths . . . and there are plenty of them. Well, maybe not plenty, but enough. If you need someone to oversee the details of a Jewish wedding ceremony, or Hindu, or Zulu, and to be standing by with her homemade Disaster Prevention kit in case at the last minute a bridesmaid's hem needs fixing or the best man needs a hangover remedy, and then to make sure the gifts end up in the right cars at the end of the day, I'm right on it. But being hoisted off the ground and climbing in windows? Not my thing."

"How do you know?"

"I just do." She waved her hand in his direction. "Look, you're obviously in great shape and can probably lift a refrigerator with one hand and do a gazillion push-ups. My hat's off to you. Really. But I know me, and I know that people like you don't know anything about people like me and what we can and can't do and just because you insist that anyone with half a brain can take an intermediate spin class without hurting herself doesn't make it true."

As she gathered herself with a deep breath, he raised one dark brow. "Issues?"

"Maybe," she allowed, shrugging. "I guess you could say that when it comes to fitness I'm the thorn in a family of roses . . . when it comes to a lot of things actually. But at the moment we're talking about fitness, so, yeah. Issues."

"That's tough."

Self-conscious, she brushed off his seeming concern. "Don't worry about it. I shouldn't have even mentioned it; it just sort of popped out when I was trying to make you understand why I can't do this."

He shook his head. "No. I didn't mean that's tough as in poor you. I meant that's tough, but you'll just have to suck it up."

"Suck it up?"

"Yeah. You could say that's the Winters family motto."

"How . . . inspiring."

"Damn straight. The first time I remember hearing my father say it I was five and didn't want to sit next to the Alligator Man in the back of the truck even though it was the only seat left and we were already two hours late setting up in Albuquerque."

"Issues?" she ventured because she really wasn't sure what else to say. Alligator Man? Albuquerque?

"Could be," he allowed, his tone indifferent. "I heard it hundreds of times afterward and I hated it each and every time. But it turns out it's not a bad motto, not to mention being the only thing the old man ever gave me that was worth a damn. I added the second half myself somewhere along the way: get it done. Suck it up and get it done. You'd be surprised how many problems can be solved using that approach. Such as being locked out of your house," he added. "So let's suck it up and get it done, shall we?" He backed up a few steps. "I'm going to stand here and—"

"And I'm going to call a locksmith," she interrupted, fishing her phone from her tote bag.

"Don't be ridiculous."

"I'm not. I'm acting on my own personal motto, which is 'when in doubt, call a professional.'"

"I am a professional," he shot back, his tone hard and dry.

Sophie's brows lifted. "Oh, really? In between your military career and your writing career you found time to become a locksmith?"

"Don't be naive. Locksmiths aren't the only ones who know how to get in—and out of—places without a key."

She held the phone without dialing, mulling over what that might mean.

"Think about it, Sophie," he urged, further distracting her by saying her name in that quiet, slightly rough way he had. "We could wait hours for a locksmith to show up. I have work to do and so do you. My way will have us inside and toasting our success with a cold beer in less than five minutes."

She couldn't argue with that . . . the work part, not the beer part. She had a couple of hours of work to do there and piles more waiting on her desk back at the office.

She gazed up at the window that was a lot of feet off the ground.

"Couldn't you be the one to climb in?" she asked.

"Not unless you can hoist me off the ground and onto your shoulders. Even if I could still jump that high, there's nothing up there for me to grab hold of."

Sophie was curious about his use of the word *still* and the telltale tensing of his jaw, but she resisted asking.

"What if you stood on something?" she asked.

"Such as?"

Hopeful, she looked around for a birdbath or wheelbarrow or stray lawn chair. Who doesn't have an old lawn chair hanging around? There was nothing in sight but a half-dozen empty and forlorn-looking majolica pots lined up at the patio's edge.

"Don't you have a ladder?"

"There might be one in the basement. I never looked."

She gazed up at the window and swore it was at least a foot higher than last time she looked. "Maybe I should just come back another day."

"And leave me stranded here alone?" he shot back. "Way to build a healthy working relationship."

Sophie sighed. "Oh, all right. It's your broken back I'm thinking of. If you're willing, so am I. Just tell me what you want me to do."

He ran through it step-by-step. It sounded impossible, but Sophie was slightly relieved to note that if things went according to plan, there would be no actual hand-on-thigh contact.

"Oh, one last thing." He pulled a knife from his jeans pocket and flipped it open with disquieting proficiency. "You won't be able to raise the screen because it latches on the inside, so you'll have to cut it in order to climb through."

He flipped the knife shut and then showed her how to open it using the small hidden pressure point on the side of the handle. Actually he showed her three times. She refrained from saying so and giving him another excuse to invoke his family motto, but the truth is she wasn't very good with knives either. Or with weapons of any kind, for that matter.

"All set?" he asked after she'd practiced a few times, but not as many times as she would have liked.

Sighing, she tucked the knife into her Spanx for safekeeping. *Suck it up and get it done.*

"No," she said. "But let's do it anyway."

Once they started, he talked her through it with more patience than she'd have credited him with. Sophie expected to be nervous and she was. The surprise was that she expected to be very nervous—hands-shaking, knees-knocking nervous—and after the first minute or so she wasn't. It was as if Owen's calm certitude radiated outward, like a force field of confidence strong enough to support her too.

He hunkered down and didn't flinch even a little as she climbed onto his shoulders, using the house to support herself as she slowly went from squatting to standing. There was only one slightly awkward, slightly remarkable moment when he cupped her butt with both hands to steady her as she found her balance. As soon as he sensed her control, he shifted his hands lower. Sophie was still afraid she was going to do something to screw it up, but she no longer had any fear of falling. She just knew with everything in her that Owen wouldn't let that happen. He felt like a rock beneath her and his grip on her ankles was absolute. Once her footing was secure, he stood, slowly, letting her continue to brace herself with both palms against the house, moving them higher a few inches at a time until she was able to reach the window with ease.

Still taking it slow, she pulled out the knife and used it to slice through the screen, following Owen's instructions so that the flap she created opened down and out of her way. Finally she listened as he coached her in a sort of sideways tumble through the window. The maneuver, while not the least bit graceful, was relatively painless.

"You okay?" he called to her as she sat with her butt in the kitchen sink, a silly grin on her face.

"Fine," she called back, feeling more swagger than tension now. She'd done it. And hey, it may not have been as demanding as an hour-long spin class, but it was just as far outside her comfort zone, and a hell of a lot more exciting. And she got to check out Owen's very impressive biceps and shoulder muscles in the process. For which she should probably feel guilty since she hadn't wanted him doing the same to her, but she didn't, not even a little bit. The man's shoulders were well worth a small moral transgression.

"Uh, Sophie?"

"Yeah?"

"About the door . . ."

"On it," she called to him, clambering from the sink. "Grab my bag for me and I'll meet you there."

She unlocked the door and held it open for him as he angled his way inside with the case of beer. He handed her the tote bag in passing.

"Thanks," she said, following him to the kitchen, still on a talky, adrenaline high. "I can't believe we did it. I guess I should say I can't believe *you* did it, since you did most of the work. Not to mention coming up with a plan in the first place. A *great* plan. I expected you to just sort of hoist me up like a sack of potatoes and shove me through the window, but I had a real Mary Lou Retton moment there."

"Who?"

"Mary Lou Retton. Olympic gymnast, gold-medal winner, face on the Wheaties box."

"Oh."

"That was something the way you lifted me onto your shoulders and then stood up. I mean, who can do something like that? Well, obviously you can. But where did you learn how?"

"The Winters Traveling Carnival and Show of Wonders," he replied without breaking stride.

Six

Sophie wasn't sure what she'd expected his answer to be, but that wasn't it.

"A carnival?" she repeated. "Seriously?"

"Seriously."

His earlier reference to the Alligator Man suddenly made more sense. "You said it was called the Winters Traveling Carnival; was it a family business?"

"Family? Not by a long shot," he said, his sneer telling. "My father ran it. He was a magician."

"And you were an acrobat of some kind?"

"No."

"Trapeze artist?"

"I was nothing. But I did dedicate a good chunk of my formative years to hanging around and watching the female acrobats rehearse. I guess I picked up a few moves by osmosis." He swung the beer off his shoulder and placed it on the floor in front of the open refrigerator.

"Wow. A traveling carnival," she mused out loud as he jockeyed bottles to make room for the new arrivals. "That sounds so . . ." *Exciting. Wild. Sexy.* "Interesting."

His response—a cross between a snort and a grunt—discouraged her from asking any of the questions that were bubbling inside.

She refused his offer of a celebratory beer, wanting a clear head for working, but hung around figuring that the kitchen was as good a place as any to start. Flipping open her notebook, she jotted down a few quick impressions. The kitchen was large by any standard, with plenty of open space for maneuvering. It had obviously been designed for entertaining. A plus. Double sinks. Long, deep, L-shaped counters. No center island. She also noted the adjacent breakfast nook with a large round oak table and double doors that opened to a humongous dining room.

She glanced approvingly at the more than adequate overhead lighting, and then winced at the circa twentieth-century appliances. Regardless of the menu choices, a caterer would need to bring supplemental ovens and cooktops. And most likely a generator to power them. The house was lovely and well maintained, but at first glance not much modernizing or remodeling appeared to have been done. The black-and-white tile floor and glass-front cabinets looked to be original. And while they were charming, an electrical system of the same vintage would not be.

After making a rough sketch of the kitchen, she pulled a laser measuring device from her bag.

"Need a hand?" asked Owen, finished stowing the beer.

"Thanks, but I think I've got it. This extremely cool laser tool makes measuring hard-to-reach places a snap."

"Does it really matter how deep the counters are?"

"Not to me personally, but I guarantee it will matter to the caterer who gets the job and has to set up in here. Caterers, tent makers, the guys who handle the parking . . . they're all the same; the first things they want to know are . . . how much space am I working with and how big is the budget? My mission here today is to measure everything that doesn't move."

"I'll keep that in mind should I feel a nap coming on," he said drily. He folded his arms, his expression thoughtful. "You know I hadn't given any thought to parking. How do you plan to handle that many cars?"

"Not by turning your front lawn into a parking lot, I promise. Obviously parking will be off-site and we'll need a small army of valets and some kind of relay system to get it done. On-site we'll need space to set up a valet station and enough room for guests to drive up and get out without causing a bottleneck at the beginning of the drive and tying up traffic all along Bellevue Avenue. Having that long circular drive is going to help a lot."

He looked reluctantly impressed. "I'm beginning to see why people hire wedding planners."

"Exactly. So they don't have to wake up at three A.M. worrying about traffic tie-ups or whether they remembered to tell the videographer to go to the groom's house first and then the bride's. Which reminds me, would it be possible to set aside a place upstairs, maybe a bedroom . . . or two," she added with a beseeching smile, "where the bride and her attendants can get dressed and do their last-minute primping?"

He shrugged, his hips resting against the counter behind him. "Sure, why not? My room is the last one on the left. The others are up for grabs."

"Thank you. While I'm up there I'd like to take some photos of the grounds; it helps to see it from a different perspective."

"Knock yourself out," he said, bringing the beer bottle to his mouth for a long swig. "You know it's funny, that kid . . . the bride . . . Shelby?" Sophie nodded. "She didn't strike me as the primping type . . . just way too damn young to be getting married."

"Trust me; every woman is the primping type on her wedding day. I think it's chemical or chromosomal or something. At any rate, it's inescapable. As for Shelby being young . . ." Her expression grew thoughtful. "Ordinarily I'd agree with you wholeheartedly, and as a general rule I still think that twenty-one or twenty-two is way too young to decide what you want to do for the rest of your life and who you want to do it with. But there's something about Shelby, and Matthew too for that matter, which makes me think it will work. You've heard the term 'old souls'? Well, those two strike me as very old souls."

"I hope you're right," he said, his skepticism obvious.

"I am." The conviction in her tone was heartfelt. "When it comes to romance, I have a sort of sixth sense. Trust me; Shelby and Matthew are in it for the long haul, all the way from clocks and pottery to silver and gold."

"Is that supposed to make some kind of sense?"

"It makes perfect sense," she replied, moving around to get the actual dimensions of the room itself. "Paper is the traditional gift for a first wedding anniversary, but clocks are the modern option. Pottery is for nine years married, either pottery or leather goods. Silver is twenty-five years, of course, and gold is for fifty. Shelby and Matthew are going for gold."

"Let me get this straight: each year is assigned a different gift?"

She paused to write a measurement along the corresponding side of her sketch before she forgot it. "Well, not assigned exactly. It's more of a tradition, along the lines of 'something borrowed, something blue.' "

"And these yearly gifts, you know what all of them are?"

"Pretty much."

"What's the proper gift for a twenty-fourth anniversary?"

"Opals are traditional. Musical instruments are the modern alternative."

"Seventeen years?"

"Furniture across the board."

"Nineteen."

"Aquamarine. Or bronze."

He shook his head. "That's pretty . . . absurd."

"Oh, I beg to differ. I have clearly pushed past the boundaries of the merely absurd." She said it with mock solemnity. "I am a living, breathing font of information on all things romantic. I didn't set out to be; it just sort of happened along the way. I think it might even be an occupational hazard. One day I woke up and realized my brain was cluttered with all kinds of useless trivia on the subject."

He looked amused in spite of himself. "You mean more useless than which gift goes with which year?"

"Pfff," she pronounced with a careless wave of her hand. "That's child's play. I know far more useless stuff than that."

"I know I'm going to be sorry I asked, but . . . such as?"

"Well, did you know that two out of five people marry their first love, or that only one in five men proposes on bended knee, but six percent of them do it over the phone? Or that there are more than nine hundred varieties of red roses?"

"No. And yet—brace yourself because this may come as a shock to someone with your hopelessly romantic sensibilities—somehow I've managed to eke out a life of sorts for myself."

"Only because ignorance is bliss. But now that your romance gene has been awakened, there'll be no going back. You'll find yourself wondering about the record for the most kisses in a movie . . . a hundred and twenty-seven, *Don Juan*, 1927. Or how many calories a kiss burns . . . nine, assuming it's passionate and not some lazy peck on the cheek. Or about the scientific name for the study of kissing . . . philematology."

"You might be right . . . *if* I had a romance gene to be awakened. I don't."

"Oh, you have one all right. Everyone does. It's standard equipment, like your funny bone. And goose bumps. Think about it: a person could live years and years without knowing they have a funny bone until one day they whack their elbow just the right way and it's like a lightbulb coming on. Same thing with goose bumps: years of blissful ignorance and then they take a sudden chill . . . or someone kisses exactly the right spot on the side of their neck, and *bam!* Life is never the same again."

She'd continued to work as they bantered and now, when he didn't respond, her attention instinctively shifted from the wall she was measuring to him. He was watching her; his gaze, intrigued and unwavering, made her feel flustered in a way she was much too old and too smart to let herself be flustered in.

"Tell me," he ventured in a deep, quiet drawl, still watching her in that thoughtful, heavy-lidded way. "This spot on the neck you alluded to . . . the one with such life-altering potential . . . does that knowledge come from personal experience?"

"Not exactly completely from personal experience. But I've heard . . . well, read—" She stopped and shook her head. "What I've experienced personally is irrelevant. I was simply trying to make the point that everyone has a romance gene, no matter how recessive it is or how much baggage it's buried under, and someday, some way, probably when you least expect it, it comes to life and—"

"*Bam*. Life is never the same again." He said it in an unapologetically mocking tone that she chose to ignore.

"Exactly."

He shrugged. "Interesting theory. Unfortunately it doesn't account for the possibility that some romance genes get switched on too soon and burn themselves out."

"That's because it's my theory," retorted Sophie. "And I refuse to give credence to that possibility. It goes against everything I believe in. Doing what I do, seeing what I see every day, I need to believe that when it comes to true love, it's never too late for anyone."

"To each his own." He downed the rest of his beer. "I should get back to work." Leaving the empty bottle on the counter, he started toward the door and then stopped and pulled a paper from his back pocket. "I almost forgot," he said, unfolding it and holding it out to her. "I meant to give this to you as soon as you arrived, but we got sidetracked."

Sophie took the paper and glanced at it, and then looked up at him, puzzled. "What is this? A list of demands?"

He lifted one shoulder in an offhand shrug. "You're welcome to think of it as a list of requests if it makes you feel more comfortable."

"A demand and a request having the same amount of wiggle room?"

"Pretty much."

"Then let's just stick with demands; it's more honest. Let's see. No work-related noise between eight A.M. and two P.M.."

"Those are my prime work hours," he explained.

Sophie nodded. "Also no loud music between eight and two. No rap or whiny-chick rock at any time." Biting back a grin, she glanced up. "Could you please define 'whiny-chick rock'?"

"No. But trust me; I know it when I hear it."

She gave a quick nod. "No unnecessary phone calls. No lengthy voice-mail messages. Weekly schedule of activity—including names and brief background details of anyone working on the property—to be submitted by the preceding Friday, oh-four-hundred hours."

She looked up, eyes wide and innocent. "Eastern Standard Time?"

Owen nodded, his expression inscrutable as he watched her refold the paper.

"You know," she said, "I think I'll just take this with me and go over the rest item by item when I can give it my full attention. If I have any questions, I'll get back to you."

She tossed the list into her tote bag.

"All right. I think you'll find it pretty self-explanatory . . . except maybe for that chick-rock thing. And even that could be negotiated, I suppose. I came up with the list because I wanted to make the process as easy as possible going forward, with no mixed signals. It seemed only fair since I'm the one who insisted on working only with you."

"I see. Well, since you brought it up, I do have a question. Why did you?" When he responded with only a quizzical frown, she elaborated. "Why did you insist on working only with me?"

"Oh. That." Owen ran his hand through his hair, considering his answer. He didn't want to lie to her, but it was too soon for the truth. He had no way of knowing how susceptible to suggestion she was and he didn't want his experiences to influence her.

"I suppose it was a case of the devil you know," he said offhandedly. "Also, it was obvious you were sent here to do the grunt work by getting me to go along with this crazy idea and then once you'd done the heavy lifting the A-team showed up with their matching smiles and matching bullshit, all set to slide into home plate and claim the win. That pissed me off in about a hundred different ways."

She'd been eyeing him with suspicion; now her expression relaxed, the wary glitter fading from her eyes and her mouth softening into something gentle and, from where Owen was standing, distracting.

"I don't think it was as calculated as you make it sound," she said.

"Really?"

Was she too trusting, wondered Owen, or too loyal? He knew something about both trust and loyalty, and as certain as he was that hers were misplaced, his admiration for her ticked up a notch.

"That doesn't mean I don't appreciate your concern," she told him. "It sounds like you wanted me to be put in charge because you thought I'd earned it. That was really sweet of you."

Sweet? No one had ever called him sweet; it was as unexpected and jarring as having a nail dragged along his spine. And as unwelcome.

"Don't get carried away," he warned, irked that something as simple as the slow dawning of her smile could play with his concentration. "It would be a mistake to ascribe altruistic motives to anything I do. I always act to suit my own purpose."

"Is that why you made Shelby's dream come true by agreeing to let her have her wedding here in spite of the fact that you claim to hate weddings?"

"No, it was because her mother's willing to pay through the nose for the privilege. And I don't just *claim* to hate weddings."

"I don't believe you," she declared, her small, knowing smile holding steady. She was like some green sailor, he thought, boldly steering her starry-eyed little boat straight into a gale. "I think you said yes to Shelby for the same reason you went to bat for me: to be nice. It just goes against your Big Bad Wolf image to admit it."

"I am the Big Bad Wolf," he told her. She'd earned that much truth at least.

"Oh yeah? Then explain to me how it could possibly suit your purpose to insist on working with me and only me."

"Easy. I wanted to keep distractions to a bare minimum."

*   *   *

His parting remark stuck in her head, replaying on a loop until she was halfway up the stairs and she hit the stop button to silence it. Her hand caressed the smooth white banister: the very banister she once imagined herself sliding up to all sorts of exciting adventures. Just being there was a childhood dream come true and she wasn't about to let some stupid remark keep her from savoring the moment.

So Winters didn't find her as distracting as Jill and/or Jenna. Hardly a news flash. Neither did any other man she knew. She'd been dealing with that ego-bruising truth most of her life and she'd deal now. Frankly she was more concerned with finding a way to keep herself from being distracted by *him*. She would have to exercise self-control and a perfect opportunity to practice presented itself as she reached the top of the staircase on her way to checking out the second-floor bedrooms. He'd said his room was the last one on the left. She hesitated, looking both ways as if getting ready to cross a busy street, and turned left.

Obviously she needed more practice.

She wouldn't set foot in his room, she promised herself, no matter how oh-so-tempted she was to poke around and maybe shed a little light on the mystery he presented. That would be nosy and unprofessional, not to mention totally humiliating should she get caught. No, she would limit herself to a quick, slightly less nosy, and unprofessional glance from the open doorway. It was the in-plain-sight rule of snooping. Whatever is in plain sight is fair game.

What she saw left the mystery intact. A treadmill, an unmade bed, a Bose stereo, and lopsided piles of CDs on the bedside table. So, he wasn't an iPod man. Interesting. She resisted the urge to check out his taste in music, but as she turned away she noticed something else on the table, something harder to resist. Half hidden behind the CDs was a picture frame. She glanced back toward the stairs, then at the frame, and drew the inevitable conclusion: if the universe hadn't intended for her to see the photo, it would have done a better job of arranging the CDs in front of it. Acting on behalf of the universe, she did a tiptoe sprint across the room and leaned down to see what it was Owen saw last thing at night and first thing in the morning, also known as the slapdash-no-touching rule of snooping.

The frame was simple and expensive looking; the photo it held was a composite of two shots. On the left was a much younger—and happier looking—Owen with a laughing little girl perched atop his shoulders. On the right was the same little girl . . . same wavy blond hair, same blue eyes—Owen's eyes—same sunny, look-out-world-here-I-come smile. But in the second shot the little girl was all grown up. The handwritten inscription across the bottom read: *Loved the view, loved you. Still do! Happy Father's Day, Dad. Allie.* Beside the name was a small open heart with the date.

So. Owen Winters had a daughter. A daughter he hadn't mentioned. Not that he should have necessarily. After all, they weren't friends who'd exchanged life stories, and they hadn't even spent that much time together.

Still.

Something about it didn't feel right. After all, they had been talking about a young girl getting married, and judging by the dated photo he kept by his bed, she'd guess that his daughter, Allie, was about the same age as Shelby. Wouldn't it have been the most natural thing in the world for a father to say "there's no way in hell I'd want my twenty-two-year-old daughter getting married."

It would be, she decided, hurrying from the room before her luck ran out, not at all happy with the fact that she'd risked her pride only to raise more questions than she answered.

It took real self-control to turn her full attention to work. Choosing the right rooms for Shelby and her attendants provided the perfect excuse for her to explore all seven remaining bedrooms. It was like wandering through the pages of *Town & Country* magazine. In each room, the silk wall coverings, bed linens, and window dressings were varying shades of a single color . . . rich colors like lavender and sage and periwinkle. The furnishings were old and solid, befitting one of Newport's grand summer "cottages," and there were touches of whimsy that convinced Sophie the woman who'd lived there had been blessed with both style and wit.

After playing Goldilocks and testing a series of overstuffed chaises and padded vanity benches, she finally settled on the two rooms opposite the stairs; the rooms shared a large bath and a panoramic view of the Atlantic. From the window of one of the rooms, the one she already thought of as the "Old Gold Room," she snapped a dozen or so photos of the grounds below and then couldn't help standing there for several moments watching sailboats drift on the open waters to the east and waves roll to shore on the crowded public beach in the distance. She would have lingered longer, lulled by the multimillion-dollar view, but she was startled by a sudden drop in the temperature of the air around her.

She turned from the window, instinctively folding her arms and rubbing her upper arms with her hands to warm up as she looked around to see if she was standing near an air-conditioning vent. She wasn't, but the change in temperature was that dramatic. The wind couldn't be blamed this time since there wasn't even enough of a breeze to stir the lightweight curtains. What was it Owen had said? That old houses could be quirky? Count her in the ranks of the true believers. Again she found herself wondering if these various and sundry quirks might interfere with the wedding. And whether she ought to warn Shelby. No, she decided quickly. If she mentioned cold spots and doors with minds of their own, Shelby would be on the lookout for strange occurrences; mix a runaway imagination with normal wedding jitters and anything could happen . . . or seem to. And for all Sophie knew, her own imagination was working overtime here.

But she didn't think so.

There was something different about the room . . . something besides the chill in the air. Something she couldn't put her finger on. Hoping to figure it out, she ignored the part of her that wanted to get the hell out of there and stayed to look around, peeking in the closet, where she found only a row of gold padded hangers, picking up and admiring the enameled hand mirror on the dressing table and putting it back. It was as she turned away that she thought she caught movement from the corner of her eye and she turned back to see the mirror resting about six inches from where she'd just placed it. She would definitely have thought that was her imagination at work but for the fine layer of dust on the table's mirrored top; it clearly showed where the mirror had slid across the surface to its original position. *Cue* Twilight Zone *theme,* she thought as she grasped the glass knobs on the table's drawer and yanked it open in search of wires or magnets or . . . something.

Nothing.

Okay. Her mind was still racing and coming up with nothing helpful when her gaze fell on the chest of drawers across the room and for lack of a better idea she walked over to check inside those drawers as well. Nothing. Nothing. Nothing. She tried to open the fourth drawer but it slid a few inches and then stopped as if stuck. No quitter, Sophie grabbed the front of the drawer with both hands to see if she could rock it loose. Instead the drawer slammed shut with her fingers inside . . . slammed shut so tightly she couldn't yank them free.

She shouted with surprise—and pain—and then clamped her teeth together as tightly as the drawer. What was she thinking? Did she really want Owen to come running upstairs to see what she was screaming about? And then have to explain what she was doing rifling through drawers in one of his guest rooms? Of course, if pressed, she could always blame her lapse in manners on the sudden chill in the room and the moving mirror, thereby confirming that she was a total airhead.

Then again, she might not have a choice. Her fingers were really beginning to hurt and she wasn't making any progress working them free. How the hell could this happen? Having her fingertips amputated would definitely put a crimp in her work performance. Visions of relying on the *J*s to drive her around and take notes for her amplified the tears that were already filling her eyes because of the throbbing pain. She bent her head and rested her forehead on the dresser's edge as if that might help her think.

"Go away," said a woman's voice.

The voice was clear and emphatic and chillingly close to her ear. Sophie jerked her head up and looked first over one shoulder and then the other, but saw no one.

"Go now," the voice said. "You don't belong here."

A couple of pounding heartbeats later, the drawer released her just as suddenly as it had trapped her and Sophie jumped back, cradling her bruised fingers against her chest. Anger and fear were tugging her in different directions; what she saw when she turned around made fear the hands-down winner. And she ran.

Owen heard the shout just as he gave up on skulking around downstairs trying to figure out what Sophie was doing upstairs all that time and headed back to his office.

Skulking; there was no other word for it. As an extraction specialist for a U.S. military dark ops operation, Owen had done more than his share of skulking, but today's undertaking presented a problem no terrorist or kidnapped foreign ambassador or psychopathic drug lord ever faced. There was always a risk of getting caught in the act, lurking in the shadows or crawling around on your belly like a slug, but in the past he'd never cared if he ended up looking foolish in front of anyone else. Or creepy. The past hour hadn't produced a scrap of information of the sort he was hoping for, but it had made one startling fact very clear: he never wanted Sophie Bennett to think he was creepy.

The instant he heard her scream, he turned and hurried back to the front of the house. He reached the bottom of the stairs just as she came barreling down, breathing hard, her eyes wide, her face pale. She landed in his arms and it felt like the most natural thing in the world for him to gather her close to him, stroke the back of her head, and whisper "it's okay, it's okay" against the sweet, fresh scent of her hair.

"Shh. It's okay."

After only a minute her breathing steadied; she lifted her head from his chest and looked up at him. She appeared slightly calmer, but no less alarmed. Mostly he was concerned for her, but a small reptilian part of his brain could focus only on the fact that she didn't pull away, and was pleased.

"Owen, you have to listen to me. Something happened upstairs. I know this is going to sound crazy, but you have to listen because I swear every word is true." She swallowed hard and said, "I think there's a ghost in your house."

He exhaled. "I think we need to talk."

Seven

T ell me again," he directed. "Everything that happened. Don't leave anything out."

"I told you everything. Twice," Sophie reminded him in an even and much calmer tone than when she'd come running down the stairs a few minutes earlier looking, quite rightly, as if she'd seen a ghost.

"I know, but sometimes during a debriefing a subject spontaneously recalls a detail in a later round of questioning that wasn't included in their first account. Or their second."

She tipped her head to the side and raised her brows quizzically. "Debriefing? I'm being debriefed now?"

"Sorry. It's a military term. Old habits die hard. This isn't an interrogation; I'm just trying to get a handle on what happened up there. Please, start at the beginning and take your time. Tell it any way you want to tell it."

They were sitting side by side at the kitchen table, which was actually located in an alcove off the main kitchen. He'd brought her straight there, took one look at her fingers, which were red and beginning to swell, and went in search of a remedy. He returned with ibuprofen, a bag of ice, a bowl of ice water for her to dangle her fingers in if the cubes were too rough, and the softest towel he could find. His military efficiency didn't surprise her, but his solicitousness did.

"Okay," she said. "The first really odd thing was the mirror moving—"

He broke in. "What about the temperature?"

"Oh. Right. I forgot . . . that came first. I was standing by the window and suddenly it was like someone had switched on a giant air conditioner. It wasn't the wind or an ocean breeze; the drop in temperature was too great for either. And it wasn't my imagination, although to be honest I wasn't one hundred percent sure of that until the rest happened."

"So the mirror was next?"

She nodded. "Once the cold set in, I got this funny feeling, like something in the room was different . . . something besides the cold, I mean."

"What was different?"

"I don't know. Nothing obvious. Nothing visible. It was just a sense I had . . . like a chill running up my spine, but it wasn't a chill exactly. Except for the chill from the cold, of course."

"More like a change in the energy in the room?"

"I guess."

"What happened next?"

"I just hung around for a few minutes. I wandered around the room, looked in the closet . . . and then I picked up the mirror. And when I put it back down, it moved. All by itself. I told you about the marks in the dust?"

"Yes. That's when you decided to examine the dresser."

"Right. I'm not sure why really. I think at that point I was equal parts spooked and curious. A big part of me was thinking I should just get the hell out of there, but I also wanted to see if something else might happen if I hung around. And boy, did it ever," she declared, grimacing as she lifted her fingers from the bowl and looked at them. "That is one strong ghost. Not to mention rude."

"Tell me about the ghost."

She tensed visibly. Without thinking, Owen reached over and stroked her arm. Her skin was warm and smooth, the smoothest thing he'd felt in a long time.

"Maybe I should make you a cup of tea or something," he said, at a loss as to what soothing measures were called for in this situation.

The corners of her mouth immediately lifted. "It's eighty-something in the shade," she pointed out. "Not my idea of teatime. But if that cold beer is still up for grabs, I wouldn't refuse."

"Cold beer coming right up." From the kitchen, he called, "Bottle okay or should I hunt for a clean glass?"

"Bottle's fine."

He came back with two beers, opened both, and handed one to her.

"Thanks." Sophie took a sip. "Mmm. That tastes so good, and the cold bottle feels even better on my fingers than the ice."

"Good. So. The ghost," he prompted.

"I heard her before I saw her."

"Her? You're sure it was a her?" He had to bank down hard on the urge to jump to conclusions. Not to mention the urge to bark questions at her.

"Positive. This whole thing is confusing and crazy, but that much I'm sure of. That and the outfit."

"Go on."

"The drawer slammed shut on my fingers and I yelled—because it really hurt—and I tried to get them out, but the way the drawer is designed they were sort of trapped under this ridge and . . . anyway, that's when I heard a woman's voice. It sounded really close, but I couldn't see anyone. She said, 'Go away. Go now. You don't belong here.'"

"That's it?"

"That's it. And then a second later the drawer opened and I got loose and turned around and . . ." She gestured with the hand not holding the beer, signaling amazement and disbelief. "And there was a bride standing right in front of me . . . gown, veil, jewelry, bouquet, the works. And it wasn't my imagination."

"You're sure?"

"Totally. She was as real as you and me." Her mouth quirked. "Except she wasn't. I mean, she was real and she wasn't . . . she was . . . different. I can't explain that part of it. I just sensed it."

"It wasn't an illusion? You couldn't see through her? And you weren't seeing her in the mirror?"

Sophie shook her head emphatically. "No. She was solid. Flesh and blood. Well, solid anyway. I'm not sure about the rest."

"And you said she was young?"

"Right. Young and pretty, beautiful really, but not happy. Not at all. There was no mistaking that. The phrase 'if looks could kill' would not be an overstatement."

"But young?"

"Yes." She pursed her lips. "Well, yes and no. She was youthful, but now that I think about it, she was . . . I guess dated is the best way to describe it. Her gown, her hairstyle, even her makeup . . . it was all very old-fashioned. I can't believe I missed telling you that before." She gave him a rueful smile. "I guess you military types know a little about debriefing after all."

"The bride . . . she didn't say anything else?"

"I didn't give her a chance. I bolted."

He stared at the floor, his forehead creasing as he tried to make sense of her story.

"What would you have done?" she asked.

The hint of defensiveness in her tone drew his attention from his own thoughts; he could tell from her expression that she'd interpreted his grim silence as disapproval.

"You did the right thing," he said to reassure her. "Retreat is always better than defeat. You had no idea what you were dealing with. We still don't."

"What would you have done?" she asked again.

Leaning back in his chair, he crossed his arms. "I'm not sure. I might have tried to communicate with her. But then I've had a lot more time to consider my options."

She looked puzzled. "What does that mean?"

There was no longer any question about telling her the truth about his own experiences since moving in, only about where to begin. And where to draw the line between what she had a right to know and things he didn't talk about.

"It means," he said, "that today's incident wasn't the first bizarre thing to happen in this house."

Again he saw her tense, and again he felt the urge to comfort her rise from somewhere deep inside him. He curled his fist around the bottle and took a swig to keep from touching her again. Touching her—or rather his response to touching her—was adding another layer of complication to an already confusing situation . . . one he didn't need or want.

"So this has happened before?" she asked.

Owen shook his head. "Not exactly. I never saw—or heard—any ghost. But there was other stuff."

He gave her a brief rundown of his experiences, telling of things being mysteriously moved from place to place, and things disappearing and reappearing, and of windows being slammed shut in the middle of the night. He told her about wet towels in his bed and coming downstairs in the morning to be greeted by the smell of Old English furniture polish.

"And with all this going on around you, it never occurred to you to call someone to look into it?"

"Who would I call?" he countered drily. "Ghostbusters?"

She made a face. "Very funny. There must be someone who deals with things like this."

"Sure. They're listed in the phone book under 'Quacks and Charlatans.'" He turned in his chair and stretched his legs out to ease the stiffness that came from sitting still too long. "There were a couple of times I came close to telling someone just to get a second opinion, but I was afraid they'd laugh in my face . . . or else think it was a cheap publicity stunt for my books. Then you came along."

Her green eyes lit with surprise. "Me?"

"That's right. I had no intention of opening that door no matter how long you stood out there banging on it and calling my name. It wasn't going to happen."

"Lucky for me the wind kicked up at just the right time."

He stared at her. "Did it?"

Even before he asked the question, understanding sharpened her expression. "Oh my God, she was the one who let me in that day. And today she slammed the door in my face and locked it to keep me out." Her brow furrowed. "I don't think she likes me."

She looked so dejected at the thought of being disliked by a ghost who slammed a drawer on her fingers that Owen had to smile.

"I wouldn't worry about it," he said, his smile disappearing as it occurred to him that this might not be the best advice. The truth was, they didn't know anything about this ghost or what she was likely to do. And in his experience, what you don't know about a situation is exactly what you need to worry about.

"I'm not worried . . . exactly. It's just that . . . I mean, what's wrong with me? I'm likable. I'm damn likable. And I like brides. No one is a better friend to brides than I am. It's in my blood, for heaven's sake. Sophie Bennett, friend of brides. That's me." She spoke emphatically, looking around as if hoping to be overheard. "Don't you think I'm likable?"

She looked so damned earnest that he probably would have lied if he had to, but he didn't have to.

"You're plenty likable," he said, his tone gruffer than he intended. "A little klutzy, and a total wimp when it comes to physical challenges, but likable."

"Gee, thanks." She sighed and sipped her beer before returning her fingers to the bowl of ice water. After wiggling them for a few seconds, she stopped and frowned. "So why did you invite me in?"

"As I recall, you invited yourself in."

"And you very rudely said no. But then you suddenly changed your mind. Why?"

"Because you saw something."

Her expression clouded.

"Behind me," he prompted.

She nodded her head, remembering. "Yes. Yes, that's right. I *thought* I saw something—or someone—behind you, and then it happened again a few minutes later, when I was following you through the foyer, but there was nothing there either time. Or so I thought." She met his gaze directly. "You don't think so."

"Of all the people who've been here since I bought the place, you were the only one who picked up on anything at all. I let you in because I wanted to see what else would happen."

"I get that," she said, nodding again. "Curiosity. It's the same reason I hung around upstairs to see what would happen next."

"For me it was a little more than curiosity. I thought . . . I thought that if there was a ghost or spirit behind the things that were happening here, that maybe . . ." He cupped his hands around his beer and stared into it. "I thought maybe it was someone I knew . . . and lost. I wanted to know for sure, and I hoped that maybe you would see something I didn't."

"It might be the person you're wondering about . . . I only got a quick look, but—"

She broke off as he pulled out his wallet and opened it to Allie's picture. "Is that her? Is that the girl . . . woman you saw?"

It felt like his heart was lodged in his throat and about to explode. For a second . . . two . . . he couldn't breathe. Then Sophie shook her head.

"No," she said softly. "That's definitely not who I saw. I am so sorry to disappoint you."

"You didn't," he said, looking away from the sight of her eyes welling up with tears. He didn't deal well with sympathy, or any other tender emotion for that matter. Black and white. Suck it up and get it done. That was his comfort zone.

"I'm not even sure 'disappointed' is the right word. I know she's gone. I've accepted that. I guess I wanted one more—"

He halted abruptly, uncomfortable. It wasn't like him to say even that much and he sure as hell wasn't going to blabber to this woman he didn't even know that what he wanted was the impossible: to turn back time.

"Yeah," she said quietly. "One more . . . one more moment, one more word. I know what you mean. I lost someone I loved and I've wanted that myself from time to time."

Owen didn't look at her. He couldn't. Instead he dragged his fingers through his hair, tilted his head back, and looked at the ceiling, then at the floor. "But all along there was something about it that didn't feet right. I mean, no matter how much I wanted it to be her, the energy, or whatever you want to call it, never felt like Allie."

He paused and she just sat. If she pressed him or comforted him or God forbid touched him, he could retreat back into his shell and batten down the hatches. But she didn't.

"The thing is," he heard himself say, "I couldn't figure out why she would be following me around playing housekeeper instead of . . . instead of saying . . ." He felt the corners of his mouth lift as memory collided with longing. "Instead of saying, 'Hey, dad, procrastinate much?' We had a kind of shorthand that came from doing most of our communicating through letters and e-mails. If it had been Allie, she wouldn't have wasted time picking up after me and polishing furniture; it would have been more her style to write her message in the dust . . . 'Deadline . . . Butt . . . Chair . . . Now.'"

"Well, if you ask me, that sounds like pretty good advice no matter how the message got through to you."

Meeting her gaze, Owen nodded. "You're right. It's probably just the kick in the ass I needed. Isn't there a song or a saying . . . something about not getting what you want, but getting what you need?"

"It's a Stones' song." She sang a couple of lines, very softly and off-key. *"But if you try sometimes . . . you just might find . . . you get what you need."*

Even off-key, her voice had the power to smooth some of the raw edges inside him.

After a minute she said, "I'm sorry about your daughter, Owen. She's a beautiful girl."

Her gaze moved to the picture he'd forgotten he was holding. He flipped his wallet shut and shoved it back into his pocket. "Yeah. She really was."

She didn't say anything and Owen understood that she was giving him time and space to talk if he wanted to.

He didn't want to. In spite of that, he heard himself say, "It's been three years, but sometimes it feels like it was just . . ."

"Yesterday," she said quietly when he faltered.

"Yeah. And other times it feels like she's been gone a lifetime. Like she was here one minute and gone the next."

"Was her death sudden?"

Owen nodded without looking up. "Car accident. The week before she left for college. Her freshman year. She was driving home from work and a drunk hit her head on. At the hospital they said she died instantly. From the impact. And so did he . . . the other driver. Which is just about the luckiest thing that could have happened to the son-of-a-bitch considering what I would have done to him." He heard the venom in his voice and it was nothing compared to what was in his heart. "If I sound bitter, it's because I am."

He flipped his wallet shut and shoved it back into his pocket.

"So," she said when it became clear he was done talking. "What happens now? It's obvious you only agreed to the wedding because you wanted information. Now you have it . . . more or less."

"And you want to know if I'm going to renege on our deal?"

"Yes, but first I'm going to remind you that you signed an agreement."

"Unwitnessed. Which I suspect makes it less than binding in the eyes of the law. And even if it is binding," he said over her attempt to protest, "I'm confident the right lawyer could keep the matter on a legal merry-go-round for years . . . long past the time when the happy couple should rightfully be either divorced or exchanging goat's heads or totem poles or whatever the proper gift is for doing that many years' time."

"Has anyone ever accused you of being a romantic?"

"No."

"I'm not surprised. Are you saying you're not going to honor the agreement?"

"No, I'm saying the agreement is crap. But I gave you my word and that's not crap. You can go ahead with the wedding as planned . . . assuming you still want to."

"That was going to be my next question; what do we do about . . ."

"The ghost bride?" he supplied.

Sophie nodded.

"Wrong question. The correct question is what are *you* going to do about her? I've got a book to write," he reminded her. "Until she slams a drawer on my fingers, I'm going to stick with the 'peaceful coexistence' approach that's worked so far."

"Thanks a lot." Shaking water from her fingers, she reached for the towel to dry them. "Unfortunately that doesn't seem to be an option for me."

"So what's your plan?"

"I have no idea. So," she said, sitting up a little straighter, "I'll just start there . . . with what I don't know. Which is just about everything. It seems logical that the ghost is connected to this house. So, working backward, what do you know about the old lady who lived here before you?"

"Next to nothing. No, make that nothing. Technically I bought the house from her great-nephew and all I know about him is that he lives on the West Coast and has no interest in anything back here."

"Okay, then forget him for now. I'm going to research the house itself, see who built it . . . who lived here . . . who died here . . . who might have gotten married here. The Newport Historical must have records on this place. I also have a friend who works in the reference department at the library," she said, thinking out loud. "I'm going to give her a call as soon as I get back to the office." She stood.

"Leave that," he ordered when she started to gather the towel and ice pack. "I'll get it later. Are you all right to drive?"

"Of course. Wimp though I am, half a beer is not enough to incapacitate me."

"I meant your fingers."

"They feel much better . . . thanks to you." She held them up and flexed them to demonstrate as she headed to the kitchen to collect her bag. "I'm okay to drive. And I can't wait to get back to the office and start Googling Ange de la Mer. There has to be something on record somewhere that will help us . . . help me figure out who the ghost bride is and what she wants."

"Or maybe," he said, reaching for the paper he'd just noticed stuck to the front of the refrigerator, "the answer is much closer to home."

After a quick glance at the paper, he handed it to Sophie. It was the list he'd given her earlier and that she'd tossed into her bag before going upstairs. There was now a thick black line drawn through what he'd written . . . no noise . . . no music . . . no long messages. And with the same heavy black touch, in letters large enough to cover the whole page, someone had written two words: NO WEDDING.

Ivy was not at all sorry to see Miss Sophia Bennett drive away; she only wished she was taking her leave permanently, but there was, unfortunately, still work to be done on that score.

It had been a long afternoon, with many interesting revelations, and she was exhausted. Not physically, obviously; that was one of the benefits of being dead. She was weary mentally and emotionally and glad to have her house to herself so she could relax and think. Owen Winters didn't count since she'd grown accustomed to him being underfoot all the time. In fact, in spite of his many faults and failings and his bad habits too numerous to count, she'd grown rather fond of the man. It saddened her deeply to learn that he'd lost a child . . . his only child, she was quite certain.

She'd seen the photo of his daughter, Allie, by his bed, and wondered about her. She'd thought perhaps they'd had a falling-out and didn't speak. Such things happened in the best of families; it had happened between her brother Archie and her after all, and lasted years. Or else, she'd thought, perhaps Allie lived nearby and he went to visit her on his infrequent forays out and that's why she never called or came there. She hadn't considered that the reason Allie never came around was that she was dead. To lose a child was a tragedy of the first order and it shed a new and very different light on Mr. Winters's brooding ways.

She had never lost a child and couldn't claim to know that particular pain. But she had lost the dream of having children, the children she and Joseph had wanted and planned for and had even chosen names for during long hours spent dreaming and talking about their future together; she'd lost the three girls and three boys who would have filled the bedrooms that instead became guest rooms, empty rooms. And, of course, she had also lost Joseph. So she understood loss and she understood how some losses cast a shadow across every minute of every day of the rest of your life, even the good days, even the happy times. Unlike a lump in your throat or a thorn in your side, some losses create only emptiness, a permanent, irreparable hole in your heart that you eventually learn to step around lest you fall in. She imagined that losing a child you'd actually held and nurtured and whose tiny fingers and toes you'd counted left a hole that was very deep and hard to avoid.

She would, she decided, go a little easier on Mr. Winters. For one thing, in the future, when she found a wet towel on the floor, she would put it in the bathroom instead of in his bed. The same latitude could not be applied to Miss Bennett. Stopping her was proving to be more of a challenge than Ivy anticipated. The young woman was plucky and as a rule she liked that. She liked that the wedding planner hadn't turned tail and run at the first hint of a ghost . . . even though that's exactly what Ivy hoped she would do. And she appreciated her kindness to Mr. Winters. The poor man could certainly use a friend. Ivy even admired the determined, no-nonsense way she went about doing her job; she simply wanted her to go do it somewhere else.

In another time and place, she might have liked Miss Bennett very much. Who knows? They might even have become friends. But this was not another time and place. It was the here and now, and her only interest was in putting a stop to the wedding Miss Bennett was planning.

Eight

Shelby and her fiancé were neither procrastinators nor ditherers, and for that Sophie was grateful. They understood that there was no time to waste choosing a caterer and deciding whether they wanted a harpist or a pianist to play during the ceremony and nailing down the multitude of smaller details that make up a wedding. It helped that they trusted her to narrow the field for them ahead of time so they weren't overwhelmed with choices.

Sophie counted herself lucky on the other end as well. No matter how diligent Shelby and Matthew were, if the vendors they selected were already booked solid for the date of their wedding, it would be back to square one. Incredibly that didn't happen. It turned out that the chance to be part of the first wedding ever held at Ange de la Mer was a temptation most local professionals couldn't resist . . . even if they were booked. For those on the fence, the fresh creative challenge of the *Midsummer Night's* theme was enough to push them over. So far, their first-choice vendors were all willing to juggle whatever was necessary to make room in their schedules.

The days flew by, and though it seemed as if Sophie always ended the day with a to-do list as long as when she started out, things were falling into place a lot more smoothly than she'd dared to hope. Except, of course, for that one pesky dark spot lurking on the horizon, gliding back and forth in her mind like the fin of a great white. The ghost of Ange de la Mer. Did it really matter if she got every detail of Shelby's wedding exactly right—the wine from local vineyards and table linens the perfect shade of lavender and the water lilies and beeswax candles floating in the illusion pond— did those extraneous details matter if the place itself was haunted by a ghost that was hell-bent on stopping the wedding from happening?

Sophie shook her head at what only a few weeks ago would have sounded like the most preposterous thing she'd ever heard. A few weeks ago she didn't believe in ghosts. Not really. Oh sure, like all teenagers, she and her friends had fooled around with a Ouija board and swore it worked, and she sometimes watched *Ghost Hunters* and wondered if the sounds and images captured with all that high-tech equipment could possibly be real. Well, now she didn't have to wonder. She knew they most definitely could be real and she had the scary firsthand knowledge to prove it. She just had no idea what she was going to do about it.

At one point she even considered appealing to Jill or Jenna for help. Fortunately she came to her senses in time. The Js meant well, usually, but one of the many things she'd learned about them through the years was that the safest way to handle any problem was to keep them out of it. It wasn't a major loss. If Sophie had to guess, she'd say their knowledge of the mystical and metaphysical was a muddle derived from urban legend and old *Bewitched* episodes. And she knew for a fact that their combined experience as wedding planners didn't include getting rid of a single ghost. If it had, she'd have heard about it. Several hundred times over. The Js weren't exactly poster girls for discretion. Another good reason not to confide in them. They might not mean to, but sooner or later one of them would let word of the ghost bride slip out and the local press would pounce on it and have a field day covering the wedding. And not in a way that either Helen Archer or Owen was likely to appreciate.

Solving the ghost problem was going to require serious, uninterrupted thought and at the moment that was a luxury Sophie couldn't squeeze into her schedule . . . at least not when she was still awake enough to think straight. Her days were filled with too many people and tasks clamoring for her attention right this very instant and so the problem-that-dare-not-speak-its-name kept getting shoved to the back burner. When she did have a few minutes to spare, she didn't have much to work with. Detailed information about the house's previous owner was proving to be as tough to come by as information about Owen himself. Her friend at the library promised to look into it and get back to her, but a call to the Historical Society had proven to be less than helpful. The place was understaffed and underfunded, and if she wanted to know what might be buried in their archives, she was going to have to make time to go there and dig for it herself. When she heard that, part of her wanted to immediately drop everything and go ghost hunting, but she resisted. She was an old hand at clamping down on her adventurous side in order to do what was right and responsible and expected of her.

In this case, the responsible thing was to focus on a problem she did know how to solve: Shelby's wedding dress. Specifically the fact that she still didn't have one. It's not that she was a prima donna or a picky fashionista; Shelby simply had a vision of herself on her wedding day and—to her mother's increasing frustration—she refused to give up on it. Sophie admired her determination, but the clock was ticking, and before she'd even rolled out of bed that morning, she'd decided her number one priority for the day was to make sure the bride didn't have to walk down the aisle naked.

Bella Bridal was among the area's leading bridal salons. In fact it was one of the first Shelby and her mother had visited on their hunt for Shelby's dream dress. She recalled Helen's exasperated recounting of how she had charged into the storeroom of the exclusive shop—an area strictly off-limits to customers—and personally gone through each and every dress, hoping to discover a designer whose work was similar to what Shelby described. She was certain she would be able to convince the designer to produce the wedding dress that existed only in her daughter's imagination. Sophie could have saved her the trouble. Even if Helen had found a designer whose work had the right "look," successful designers worked seasons ahead of time, always under pressure and always rushing to meet deadlines for the major industry shows. No matter how good Helen was at the art of persuasion—or bribery—no professional designer would be willing to drop everything and work like crazy to make one bride happy. But Sophie knew someone who might.

"My name is Sophie Bennett," she said to the tastefully dressed young woman seated at an ornate ivory-and-gold desk directly inside the entrance of Bella Bridal. "I'm here to see Lina Merchant." She spoke quietly because it was that kind of place. She also automatically threw her shoulders back and sucked in her stomach the way she found herself doing when her stepmother was watching.

"Is this your first fitting?" asked the young woman, her tone polite but businesslike as she slid the sales appointment book aside and opened the one marked *Fittings and Alterations*.

Sophie shook her head. "No. Actually I'm not here for a fitting at all. I just want to speak with Lina. I'm sure if you let her know I'm here, she'll squeeze me in."

We'll see about that, the pretty blonde's expression said as she closed the appointment book and reached for the phone. Clearly it was not routine for the head of alterations to see someone without an appointment.

While she waited, Sophie checked out the gowns elegantly displayed on dress forms in the shop's reception area. There were only a few, just enough to whet a bride's appetite. At Bella Bridal, all business was conducted by appointment only, in the plush private dressing rooms behind the tall paneled doors with brass fittings as shiny as sunlight on water.

It was through one of those imposing sets of doors that Lina appeared almost before the receptionist had time to relay the message that she was on her way. Angelina—Lina—Merchant had worked with Sophie's mother at Wedding Magic. "The magician's apprentice," she had jokingly called herself. Her mother had respected the sewing skills passed on to Lina from her Portuguese mother and grandmother, and had trusted her to share the work that was her pride and joy in a way she trusted no other living soul. After her mother's death, Lina had stayed on, working tirelessly and with a broken heart, to fulfill the shop's existing orders. Sophie knew that her father and Lina had discussed the possibility of her taking over the business, but as a single mother of two children who were under five at the time, her top priority had to be a regular paycheck.

They'd stayed in touch, however; Lina was the big sister Sophie wished she'd had. Lina would call just to chat and several times a year she would arrange for a babysitter and take Sophie to lunch, just the two of them. She would tell Sophie stories about working side by side with her mother, stories no one else knew, stories that nurtured Sophie's fascination with the world of weddings and all things bridal. And she would listen to whatever was on Sophie's mind at the time without telling her that if she would only slim down or wear a brighter shade of lip gloss or be more outgoing, all her problems would be solved.

Then came a new love and a new marriage for Lina and college for Sophie. As the years passed and their lives shifted and changed, the way lives do, their contact became more sporadic. Their professional paths sometimes crossed, but Lina's work hours were as long and as crazy as Sophie's; Sophie knew because they exchanged notes at Christmas and traded war stories when they ran into each other at some work-related event. It didn't matter. Turns out they had the kind of friendship that isn't about being inseparable, but about being separated and having nothing change.

When Lina appeared they hugged each other hard and then stepped back with big, matching grins. Sophie saw a soft, pretty woman about to turn fifty, with lively dark eyes that were even more striking with her salt-and-pepper hair cut in short, spiky layers.

"I love your hair," Sophie declared, still holding on to her.

"Yeah?" Lina shrugged, but looked pleased. "I got sick of running off to have it colored every time I turned around and finally decided, what the hell, let nature take its damned course."

"Well, it looks great. Very edgy." She ran her gaze over her old friend. "*You* look great, Lina."

"And you," Lina countered. She touched Sophie's cheek with one hand. "You have your mother's smile, and your mother's eyes. You're just as beautiful as she was."

The compliment had Sophie blinking back a sting of tears, happy tears. Nothing Lina said could have pleased her more.

"Enough of that," Lina pronounced, turning and linking arms with her. "Come on down to my office, where we can talk properly."

Her office was roomy and comfortable. Jars of beads lined one shelf and pretty snippets and swatches were scattered across the desk and worktable, creating an air of controlled clutter that reminded Sophie of her mother's shop and made her feel very much at home as they got caught up with each other's life and family.

Finally Lina threw up her hands, her expression eager. "All right, I can't take the suspense any longer. Spill it."

"Spill what?" countered Sophie.

"The beans . . . spill the beans," demanded Lina, the words rolling excitedly off her tongue with only the barest musical hint of the native language she'd spoken at home as a child. "I know you are far too busy to come to see me in the middle of the day unless there's a very good reason."

Sophie nodded, sheepish. "You're right. I'm here because I need your help, Lina."

"I knew it!" Lina exclaimed, clasping her hands together with delight. "It's happened . . . you've met someone special, someone wonderful, and you've come to me for the most beautiful, absolutely perfect dress in all the world."

"Well, as a matter of fact, yes," confirmed Sophie, laughing because she should have anticipated the conclusion Lina would jump to. "I *have* met someone special, and I do want your help coming up with the perfect wedding dress, but not quite the way you're thinking."

As concisely as she could, she explained to Lina about Shelby and Matthew and the Princess House, about how they would be leaving for Ecuador in September, and about Shelby's youthful idealism in opposing the senseless slaughter of silkworms.

"My goodness, the Peace Corps," Lina said when Sophie had finished. "Both of them?"

Sophie nodded.

"Sounds like those kids have good hearts."

"They really do. That's why I want Shelby to have the dress of her dreams. I've sent her and her mother to every bridal shop I could think of and we've come up empty. The dress just doesn't exist . . . not in the fabric she has her heart set on. Not yet, that is. That's why I came to you." She leaned forward. "Lina, this is the sort of work you and my mother did all the time . . . it was your bread and butter back then."

"Yes, but that's because your mother was a creative genius."

"She would say the same about you," Sophie argued. "I know she would. And I know that you've done custom work on your own from time to time, for family and friends. Amazing work."

"Mmm-hmm. And now you're thinking maybe in my spare time I can design and make a custom wedding dress for this girl in . . . what? Five weeks?"

"Give or take," Sophie acknowledged, her expression sheepish. "Yes, that's what I came here to ask you . . . but before you give me an answer, let me show you the sketches Shelby made of her dress. They're rough, but you can get an idea from them."

Lina took her time studying the sketches Sophie put in front of her. "Mmm. The lines are very good . . . clean and simple," she noted. "That's a plus. No complicated tucking or pleating. If she wanted poufs and flounces and ruffles, I'd say no, can't be done in so little time . . . it's not just the extra labor, it's the number of fittings required to get it just right. But this . . ." She looked at the sketches again and shrugged. "This is doable."

"In hemp silk?"

Lina gave a careless wave of her hand. "Of course. The fabric is no problem."

"It might be," Sophie said, and relayed Shelby's ironclad requirement of fairy-wing sparkle without heavy-handed beading or crystals.

"I know just the thing," Lina responded without hesitation. Sophie was encouraged by the hint of excitement that had filtered into her tone. The seamstress tapped her finger on the sketch. "The bodice will be entirely lace, with only the teensiest, tiniest crystals and seed pearls accenting the design. If I agreed to this—and I'm not saying I will—I'd do all the beading myself to make sure it was nestled into the lace so all you see is that soft glimmer when she moves. Now the skirt—you wouldn't think so, but that's the tricky part. We want flow and draping, but we also want movement—"

"And fairy-wing sparkle," Sophie interjected. "Don't forget the fairy wings."

"I'm getting to the fairy sparkle . . . and it so happens I know the right fabric to create exactly the effect you're describing. We'll use it in layers as an overlay for the hemp silk."

She got up, moved a few piles on her worktable, and came back with a sample piece of sheer fabric with a subtle but unmistakable sparkle. She held it out to Sophie, who rubbed it between her thumb and fingertips.

"It's so light," she said.

"But it drapes beautifully, which a lot of lightweight fabrics don't. It could even be used alone for the veil. It's strictly special order, and I do mean special. I've only worked with it once."

She placed the sample on top of a length of soft white silk and the sparkle came alive . . . like flickering candlelight . . . like fairy wings.

"Now, just so you know, it's not hemp," Lina continued, "but it's also not silk. It's a synthetic blend especially designed to take the paint that gives it that luster."

Sophie's brows shot up as she touched the fabric again. "Paint? Are you kidding?"

"No. Crazy, huh? The supplier is a small company . . . very small. The paint is a special organic formulation created by two sisters who basically run the business single-handedly. Artsy, creative types, the pair of them. The painting is done by hand with tiny little brushes. Very labor-intensive. And thus very expensive," she added on a warning note.

"Trust me. Not a problem. But time might be. Can you order this fabric and have it in time?"

"Not a chance," Lina returned, sinking Sophie's hopes. "It would only be possible if we already had a goodly amount of it on hand. Which it so happens I do." At Sophie's incredulous smile, she shrugged. "I ordered it for my niece when the plan was for her to marry the boyfriend who turned out to be a dirtbag." She gave a careless wave. "A story for another day. The important thing is the fabric is tucked safely away in my workshop at home. And finding a fine grade of hemp silk to work with it won't be any problem at all. Hemp is not exactly in demand."

"Does that mean you'll do it?" Sophie asked.

"You mean will I stay up all night, pulling out the hair I have left, to make a one-of-a-kind dress for a special bride . . . like in the old days?" Lina smiled. "Try and stop me."

The last thing Sophie did before meeting with Lina was turn off her cell phone. The first thing she did once she was back in her car was check for missed calls. There were five. Three from Owen.

Only two words came to mind: *uh-oh.*

Three calls in less than an hour? Something was wrong. Never before had he made first contact and . . .

First contact? Sophie rolled her eyes. Sheesh. Stealth speak. That's what she got for staying up till all hours reading graphic novels about a tough and brooding super-being who—at least in her increasingly fertile imagination—bore a deep resemblance to his creator. Owen might not have an eye patch or a pair of magnificent black wings to unfurl, but to her he was every bit as fascinating a creature as the darkly mysterious Osprey. More fascinating, in fact, because he was real. Flesh-and-blood real. And gifted. His work was a surprise. She began

reading the first book out of curiosity and finished it in one sitting. The next day she was at the bookstore in search of the
earlier volumes in the series and she tore through those with
the same fervor. Josh was right; Owen was a damn good writer.
The graphic format had taken some getting used to, but it didn't
stop the novels from being exciting and complex and
intriguing . . . and the more she read about Osprey, the harder
it was to get Owen off her mind.

It was a sure bet he wasn't thinking about her that much, or at
all, for that matter. That's how she knew that his repeated attempts
to get in touch with her could only mean trouble. The landscape
designer was scheduled to send a crew to do some preliminary
work today, but she'd made it clear there was to be no noise and
absolutely no interrupting Owen during his work hours. At least
she thought she'd made it clear. Bracing herself to be chewed out,
she dialed Owen's number. It took only a few seconds for it to start
ringing and even less time for him to pick up.

"Hi, Owen, this is Sophie Bennett. I'm returning your call."

"About time."

He sounded irritable. Which wasn't so unusual, she reminded
herself, trying not to jump to dire conclusions. She flash-froze her
smile in place, having read somewhere that just smiling when you
speak on the phone can make you sound more upbeat and confident. The best defense is a good offense and all that. "Is there a
problem?"

"Several. Get here as fast as you can."

"Well, let's see," she replied, conjuring up her schedule for the
rest of the day as she tried to keep her sinking heart from dragging
her smile down with it. "I have an appointment at two and—"

"Cancel it," he snapped. "We need to talk. I'll expect you here
in thirty minutes."

"Thirty minutes? There's no way I can—"

"Where there's a will . . . you do want this wedding to happen, right?"

"Of course I do," she told him, upbeat giving way to feeling cornered, and then resigned. "Oh, all right. I'm not guaranteeing thirty minutes, but I'll be there as soon as I can."

Somewhere deep inside, Owen knew he probably ought to feel guilty for dragging Sophie away from her work in the middle of the day because of a problem he'd already solved. But that place was buried very deep inside, beneath a lifetime of identifying a target and going after it. In the world of dark ops, the end always justified the means. Guilt didn't enter into it and rules of etiquette didn't apply. So he was understandably a little rusty when it came to playing fair. True, there really was something besides the disastrous events of the morning that he wanted to discuss with her, but that easily could have waited until she was done with her two o'clock appointment or even until later that evening.

He grimaced, slouched deeper in his deck chair, and stared out at the ocean, impatient for her to arrive. He was the one who couldn't wait and he wasn't sure why.

Scratch that; he knew why. He knew exactly what was driving his persistent need to see her. He'd figured it out when he was around thirteen and one of the college kids who'd signed on as a carnival roadie for the summer showed him a magazine with photos of Madonna dressed in fishnet stockings and a skimpy black leather thing that laced from crotch to tits. To his hormone-addled brain, those laces were the gateway to heaven and he'd done extra duty for weeks, mucking out the Prancing Palominos' trailers, to scrape together the exorbitant price the college kid wanted for that dog-eared magazine. Yeah, he knew what those rapid-fire phone calls he made to Sophie were really about. What baffled and annoyed him was that he was having these feelings for Sophie Bennett of all people.

To say that she was not his type was to say the ocean was a little wet. He'd bet his next royalty check that the no-nonsense little wedding planner had never owned a pair of fishnet stockings or a black leather thingamajig. A damn shame really, because she ought to. He'd revised his original assessment of her once he had a chance to take a longer, closer look and saw that the woman had the kind of curves that begged for leather laces . . . among other things. He considered that a compliment, but he was pretty sure she wouldn't. That was the problem in a nutshell.

And, hey, it went both ways. He sure as hell didn't meet her specifications for Mr. Right. As soon as she'd opened her mouth about love and marriage and fiftieth-anniversary pottery, it was clear she was looking for a forever kind of guy, and he was only interested in one kind of woman . . . the kind who came with no strings attached. It was a match made in hell.

So why in God's name had he pounced on the first flimsy excuse that came his way to call her? Why did he wake up every morning wondering if she would be stopping by to check on something? And fall asleep wishing she had?

Boredom, he decided. Boredom and frustration. It had to be that. The writing wasn't going well—another world-class understatement—and he was ripe for a diversion . . . any diversion . . . even one as blatantly, laughably wrong as Sophie. He was an idiot. A lucky one. At least he'd come to his senses before any real damage was done. He never should have agreed to the wedding. The whole thing was becoming way too complicated and trying to scratch this sudden itch for Sophie would only add to the mess.

What's done was done, he thought. The only thing he could do now was to avoid her as much as possible and keep things strictly business between them when he couldn't. When she showed up he would make it clear to her that his end of their business deal didn't include ghost busting or family-tree research or emergency medical treatment of any kind. The meddling ghost bride and blown electrical system and bee-stung workmen too spooked to hang around and work were her problems and she was welcome to them. With any luck she'd soon see for herself that having the wedding at Ange de la Mer was more trouble than it was worth.

When the doorbell finally rang he went to answer it filled with righteous resolve. Through the sidelight he could see Sophie standing on his doorstep, looking worried. Her hair was caught up in a clip, revealing the line of her throat. He came to a stop a few feet from the door.

Not good.

Among other recent, unsettling signs of insanity, he seemed to have developed an inexplicable fascination with the side of Sophie Bennett's throat, specifically the spot where it curved into her shoulder. When she was around he had to force himself not to stare, and when she wasn't all he had to do was imagine himself putting his mouth to that spot and his thoughts disintegrated into a tangle of soft, honeyed skin and long, lazy kisses. And heat, waves of heat, around him and inside him, pulling him in deeper and deeper. The way they could pull him in now if he wasn't careful.

It was ridiculous. The black leather fantasy was something he understood and could deal with. But this . . . this was something else entirely. His first instinct was simply to shrug it off, but the soldier in him knew that it was often the seemingly small and innocuous threats that prove most deadly because they slip beneath your radar.

Not this time, he decided.

Knowing your enemy was half the battle. He knew what he

was up against here and he would deal with it. His mission was the same as always: get in and get out alive. He'd gotten himself into this and he was about to get himself out. He reached for the doorknob, his target in sight, his objective clear.

He would bring Sophie up to speed on the situation and then hand her the reins and walk away. Mission accomplished.

Nine

I got here as fast as I could," she announced, stepping inside without waiting to be asked. Given their history with the front door, Owen thought that was probably a wise move.

"What happened?" she asked, glancing around in a slightly wary manner. "Did the Gentle Gardener crew show up? Did they interrupt your work? Because I swear I made it clear there was to be no intrusive activity or noise before two. Now that I think about it, I guess the term 'intrusive' was a little vague and could be open to interpretation. So if that's what you're upset about, I'll call them right now and be more . . ."

She talked nonstop all the way from the front door to the kitchen and didn't show any sign of slowing down. Finally Owen broke in.

"I'm not upset."

"You're not?" She stared closely at his expression and he tried not to do the same to the graceful curve of her throat.

The silvery-blue dress she was wearing made her eyes look greener and it had some kind of ruffle thing at the neck that was cut just low enough to show a hint of shadow between her breasts, and because it was merely a hint . . . a suggestion . . . a mystery . . . it was irresistible. Somehow he managed to resist staring there as well, though the effort made his mouth go dry. His mission to put distance between them had seemed a lot less daunting when she was on the other side of the door and the subtle, flowery scent of her didn't drift his way whenever she moved.

"Because you sounded pretty upset earlier," she pointed out matter-of-factly. "On the phone . . . when you insisted I be here in thirty minutes if I wanted to go ahead with the wedding plans."

"Yeah. Right. About that whole thirty-minute thing. I can be a little impatient at times."

She arched her brows.

"And other times I can be damn impatient . . . obnoxiously impatient, I've been told . . . and I'm sorry."

She nodded. "Okay. So if you're not upset about anything, why did you call me three times? Why did I cancel my two o'clock meeting? Why am I here?"

He thought about how best to answer. Obviously not with the truth. It would be counterproductive to admit that when you stripped all the bullshit away she was there because he wanted her there . . . because he wanted to see her badly enough to grasp at straws to get her there . . . and that now that she was there, he really wasn't at all sorry, but rather was perversely glad he'd done it. He was an idiot.

"What's a Gentle Gardener?" he asked. He'd first learned the art of misdirection from his father. It was a magician's stock and trade. It was later, while working special ops, that he discovered how useful it could be when trying to save his own ass.

Sophie blinked, shifting gears. "The Gentle Gardener is the name of the landscape design firm working on the wedding. They're ultra-earth-friendly, which makes the bride and groom happy, and their unobtrusive approach means there'll be less work to do after the fact to restore the property to its original condition . . . which should make you happy."

"Earth-friendly, huh?" He nodded and crossed his arms as he leaned back against the counter. "That probably explains why they didn't approve of my method of dealing with the bees. Pesticide and plenty of it, that's my strategy."

"So they did show up." Her relief was short-lived. "But there was a problem with bees? No one was stung, I hope. They were only supposed to check out the area I chose for the illusion pond to make sure it was suitable, and then to place markers so whoever does the actual digging will know where to dig. Did they do that?"

"They made a start," he told her. "Did you know the illusion pond is going to have underwater lights? Real, nonillusion lights. The kind that require real power. Which is why one of the Gentle Gardeners was on a ladder checking out the power lines running to the house when the beehive fell on his head."

Wincing, she clasped her hands over her mouth. "Oh no. How awful. Is he all right?"

"Pretty much. The EMTs said—"

"EMTs? You had to call for help?"

"Just to be on the safe side, since he wasn't sure if he was allergic to bee venom. They said that considering the size of the hive and the fact that he was standing on a ladder and couldn't run, it was a miracle he wasn't stung more than eight times."

"Eight bee stings? That poor man."

"Lucky man is more like it. If he had been allergic he might be dead now. They gave him a shot of adrenaline as a precaution, but they were more concerned about his buddy, Gentle Gardener number two. The one who fell down the cellar stairs."

Shuddering, she squared her shoulders and let her hands drop to her sides. "Tell me everything."

Owen obliged, relating how it was the bee-sting victim's bloodcurdling shouts that had drawn him from the guesthouse, where, as luck would have it, he had a can of insecticide handy. He explained how when the guy jumped from the ladder, it fell sideways and knocked the meter box from the house, breaking wires and setting off a shower of sparks that sent his coworker racing to the basement to throw the circuit breakers. Three steps from the bottom the guy tripped over a golf club that just happened to be lying there, stumbled, and slammed his head against the concrete wall. He concluded with his own contribution: rushing in with a giant can of Raid and fending off the disgruntled and marauding bees long enough to drag the guy from the ladder into the house.

"Afterward I was all set to hit what was left of the hive with gasoline and torch it, but they insisted on taking a"—he smirked—"gentler approach. They called a bee specialist they worked with before to come and cart it away for a proper burial or relocation or whatever the politically correct procedure is for dealing with displaced hives."

"What a nightmare. That's worse than anything I imagined as I was driving here and I thought I imagined the worst. Are both men all right? Did anyone end up in the hospital?"

"They're okay. The guy who hit his head is going to get checked out by his own doctor. Their boss told them to take tomorrow off too and I promised them both tickets to see the Red Sox play the Yankees next week."

"You did?" Her startled expression softened into one of wonder. "You didn't have to do that. I mean, this really isn't your problem and . . . well, thank you. That was really sweet."

Sweet?

He shrugged one shoulder, almost as uncomfortable being called sweet as he was with the look she was beaming his way. He was no Galahad and he didn't want her thinking he was. "No big deal. The law firm I use has a private box at Fenway. All I did was make a call. Cheaper than a lawsuit."

"Thank you," she said again. For a few seconds neither of them said anything. Then she shook her head wearily. "I still can't believe all this happened. A damn beehive. What are the odds? Where was it to begin with? I mean before it fell."

"It looks like it was wedged beneath the crown molding on a window right above where the ladder was braced."

"Of course, it would have to be the window directly above the ladder. He probably hit it with the ladder and knocked it loose."

"He insists he didn't. And I have to agree. If he had bumped it, those bees would have started buzzing around right away; no one in his right mind would climb a ladder with that going on overhead."

"Why else would it suddenly fall at that precise moment?"

"Why do you think?"

Sophie groaned. Dropping her voice, she asked, "Do you really think she had something to do with it?"

"I think she had everything to do with it. I know for a fact that the golf club the other guy tripped over was by the back door earlier this morning and that I didn't move it. Face it: that note we found stuck to the fridge was Ivy's official declaration of war."

"Ivy? You're on a first-name basis with her?"

He gave a philosophical shrug. "We have to call her something and that is her name."

"I can think of a few things I'd like to call her right about now," she grumbled.

As soon as she said it, the ceiling fan above her head started whirling faster than any fan he'd ever seen. If a fan could be said to be pissed, this one was. Owen shot forward and grabbed Sophie by her shoulders to move her aside.

"Considering everything that happened today, I don't think it's such a good idea for you to be standing under rapidly spinning blades," he explained. "In fact, I don't think it's a good idea for us to have this conversation here at all." He thought for a few seconds. "Come with me."

His hand was still resting on her shoulder; without thinking, he dropped it and took hers to tug her along with him as he headed out the back door. It was only as they reached the side of the house that he considered the fact that he was still holding her hand and she hadn't pulled it away. It felt . . . nice, he decided. And strange. Women came and went in his life, some faster than others, but he couldn't recall the last time he'd held hands with one of them.

"Where are we going?" she asked.

"Somewhere we can talk without being overheard. You have an important decision to make about whether or not it's practical—not to mention safe—to go ahead with this wedding, and I have information that might help you make it."

They reached the section of the drive that ran in front of the garages that had been added sometime after the original house was built. Parked there was a black Harley with enough heft and horsepower to satisfy Owen's inner caveman.

Sophie looked from the motorcycle to him and shook her head. "No way. In case you didn't notice, I'm wearing a dress."

"I noticed," he replied, swinging his leg over the bike. He turned his head and met her gaze. "Believe me, I noticed. That's how I know that skirt is loose enough for you to hike it up or do whatever you have to do in order to climb on." He held out the helmet the law required passengers to wear. "So climb on."

Sophie took the helmet and stood staring at the motorcycle, which he revved to life and which now sat roaring impatiently at her. This was ridiculous. Owen stared straight ahead, either oblivious to her dilemma or choosing to ignore it. He was right: her skirt was loose enough to scrunch up without risking a charge of indecent exposure. The real problem was that she'd never ridden a motorcycle before and wasn't exactly sure how to climb on gracefully and stay there. She had seen it done. In movies. And back in high school when some girl would run out and hop on a waiting motorcycle, riding off with the wind in her hair and her arms wrapped tightly around her boyfriend's waist while Sophie watched and wondered if that could possibly feel as exciting and liberating as it looked from her vantage point at the bus stop.

Here was her chance to find out. She could stand there shouting over the roar of the engine to suggest they be sensible and take her car instead or she could climb on.

She climbed on.

Her inner thighs were still vibrating.

It was not, she decided, an unpleasant sensation. Nothing about riding behind Owen on a motorcycle was unpleasant. Not the wind or the feel of his abs beneath her clenched fingers. The man had a serious six-pack. Not the soft brush of his hair against her face or the way the muscles in his back tensed and shifted as he leaned into a curve and then eased out of it, making Sophie press closer to him until she felt as if she was one with him and the bike. She liked all of it. A lot. She especially liked the fact that he took the long way to get where they were going. They raced the entire length of Ten Mile Drive, a winding road known for its spectacular ocean views, and wound up back at a small cove close to the end of Bellevue Avenue where his house was located.

So, thought Sophie, now she knew what she'd missed out on all those times she was left standing at the bus stop and on the sidelines, watching and wishing. Except, oddly enough, at that moment she didn't feel like she'd missed out on anything at all, not a single thing. Nothing else could possibly have measured up to this . . . to the excitement of leaping out of her comfort zone and being swept away . . . of tossing caution out the window and doing the very last thing she expected to be doing when she climbed out of bed that morning. And, let's face it: nothing she imagined could compete with the unfamiliar thrill of doing it with a man like Owen. There was also the edgy anticipation of what could happen next. From the moment his front door whipped open and she first stood face-to-face with Owen, nothing had gone quite as she expected. Without trying, he tilted her careful and orderly world off balance. And part of her liked that too.

The cove was tucked out of sight from the road above, but it was plain he knew exactly where he was going. Sophie kicked off her sandals and allowed him to take her hand for the climb down to a wide flat rock by the water's edge. When they came to a good-size gap between boulders, she hesitated, gathering herself to make the short leap, but before she could jump, he surprised her by placing his hands on her waist and lifting her, wordlessly, effortlessly, his casual gallantry and the rustle of her skirt in the wind making her feel like the wispy heroine of a Merchant-Ivory film. It took all of four seconds and left her slightly breathless and secretly giddy. The heady sense of stepping into another, slower and simpler age was enhanced by the quiet beauty of the setting. Seagulls swooped and drifted across the cloudless blue sky. The strong, midday sun warmed her bare legs and the occasional fine spray from the surf rolling and frothing against the rocks cooled her. Breathing deeply, she tasted the tang of the ocean air and was content. Schedules and stress and the long list of things she could be doing and should be doing seemed a thousand miles away.

"How did you find this place?" she asked once they were settled.

"I used to come here to fish."

"Catch much?"

"I seem to recall doing all right. But it was a long time ago."

She nodded. She'd never been fishing, but the peaceful, isolated spot seemed ideal for it. "Did you grow up around here?"

"No. I grew up in a trailer, driving from one place on the map to the next."

Like her, he was staring out at the horizon, where a sailboat was drifting south, but from his tone alone Sophie could tell that his jaw had tightened and his gaze had become narrow and unreadable, the way she'd noticed it did when the conversation turned too personal for his liking.

"Of course. You must have done a lot of traveling with the carnival. I just thought maybe your family stayed put around here during the school year."

"We didn't," he said simply. "We didn't stay put anywhere."

"I can't imagine what that life was like," she told him, saying the first thing that came to mind to fill the awkward moment. "The freedom from the same boring old routine and the excitement of waking up in a new place. I'm sure it had its drawbacks, but I have to confess that like lots of kids I dreamed of running away to join the circus." She paused. "Mostly after my mom died and my father remarried. Life with my new stepmother and stepsisters made walking on stilts and taming lions look like child's play."

He nodded without looking at her. "I can understand that. Not having your mother around . . . well, it changes things. And just to prove that it's true what they say about the grass always being greener somewhere else, running *away from* the circus is what I used to dream about."

"Any particular destination in mind?"

"I wasn't picky." He reached for a small piece of driftwood lying on the rock beside him and turned it over in his hands. "Sometimes when I saw a family walking down the midway, I'd follow along and I'd watch how they talked and laughed together. I'd watch the father play the rackets—that's what we called the games—sticking with it until he'd shelled out six times the price of whatever crap prize his kid wanted. But the fathers never seemed to care. They always looked happy, even proud, to be pissing their money away trying to land a ring on a bottle or sink a basketball.

"And the mothers, they were even . . . weirder. I'd watch a mother wipe the ice cream dripping down her kid's chin and then wrap the ice-cream cone in a napkin and hand it back to him. Smiling the whole time. Not mad that the kid was making a mess or getting in the way of something she'd rather be doing. I'd watch and I'd wonder what it was like to be a kid in a family like that. A real family." He tossed the driftwood aside and hunched forward, resting his forearms on his bent knees. "I guess that's what I dreamed of running to . . . someplace that felt real."

Someplace that felt real.

His tone was haunted, his words like a vise around Sophie's heart. Her mother's death had shattered her small family, but at least until then she'd had a family. A *real* family. And because of that, she had her memories, memories real and happy enough to get her through even the toughest days.

What if she'd hadn't? What if she'd never known a place in the world where she felt completely safe and completely loved, adored in fact, not for anything she had or anything she did, but simply for being her? What if she'd never had the chance to know what that felt like? If she had only glimpsed that kind of love from the outside looking in, could she even be certain it existed? That it was real?

It was a chilling thought, enough to make her feel a little desperate even at her age, and her heart broke for the lost little boy lurking inside Owen's words. She longed to comfort him, but didn't dare. Owen was no longer a little boy; he was a loner and a very private man. Something about being there, in that out-of-the-way place from his past, had lulled him into opening up just a little, but she was sure he'd clam up and get all prickly if he caught even a whiff of what he'd consider pity.

"I was eleven when my mother died," she revealed after a short pause, her tone casual. "How old were you?"

"Six. But she didn't die." He turned his head and met her gaze. "She just left."

She just left.

Owen felt every muscle in his body tighten at hearing the words said aloud and quickly turned away. They tore the scab off a chunk of the past he preferred not to think of and would rather rip his tongue out than talk about. Too late for the thinking part. Images popped up faster than he could block them. As fast as that, he was back in that tin can of a trailer, curled up under the table in the spot that had served as his makeshift bed, a blanket over his head, his heart pounding as he waited for his parents' shouting to reach its nightly crescendo.

He knew the routine. They'd argue and his father would stomp out, slamming the door behind him. His mother would light a cigarette and pour herself a glass of wine, and after a while his heart would stop hurting with every beat and he would be able to fall asleep. Except that night was different. A few minutes after his father left, his mother did the same. She'd never done that before and he scooted to the window and watched her cross the dusty parking lot to the phone booth.

He didn't know it then, but she was calling for a taxi. He didn't even know what a taxi was or that one could suddenly appear in the night and swallow up the person you loved most and take her away so that you never saw her again. He didn't know about any of that, but he did know something was different and wrong. He smelled it in the extra perfume his mother put on when she returned to the trailer and he heard it in the impatient *click-clack* of her high heels on the metal floor as she rushed around stuffing things into a suitcase.

"Please, Owen, not now," she said no matter what he asked her. He didn't ask much, nowhere near all the scary questions that filled his head watching her. He didn't dare. She'd said "not now, Owen" in the snappish, rushing voice he knew meant not to pester her too much or a slap would be coming his way.

When he saw lights and heard a car pull up outside, he looked out the window again; that's when he found out what a taxi was.

His mother didn't say anything when she went out the door, dragging the big suitcase behind her, but at least when he ran after her, barefoot, across the dirt and cracked asphalt, and asked her one last question, she didn't just brush him off with another "please, Owen, not now." She gave him a real answer, one that grew bigger and more complicated just like he did in the years that followed. The more he thought about them afterward, the more her words shed light on life and love and the way things fall apart when you least expect it.

Can I go with you? That was the last question he ever asked her.

"No," she said. She only half turned to look at him over her shoulder when she said it. Mostly he remembered her looking past him at the trailer with its crooked steps and dented chrome and the sign with a black top hat and white rabbit and THE AMAZING WINTERS written on it. Her eyes were hard and bright as she said, "I've had all I can take of this freak show. I'm done with all of it."

He understood what *no* meant. It had taken him a while to figure out the rest and that the "all of it" she was done with included his father and him. He never did get a hundred percent clear on how a mother could just take off and leave her own kid and never come back; he just gave up and stopped thinking about it, like it was a mathematical equation he would never be able to solve because he didn't have the right formula. If one existed, she'd taken that with her too.

It was a while before Sophie spoke to him. If she thought silence would get him to open up and say more, she was wrong.

"Is that when you came to Rhode Island?" she asked eventually. "After your mother left?"

She touched his shoulder tentatively. He knew it was intended to be a friendly, reassuring pat, but instead it sent heat rushing through him. And this time, when he turned his head to look at her, her mouth curved into a smile as soft and gentle as her touch, and he was swept by the sudden, fierce, and totally inexplicable need to kiss her. Long and hard. He wanted to kiss her the way he had a nagging feeling Sophie Bennett, for all her romantic notions and bravado, had never been kissed, and should be.

Damn.

Still smiling at him, she tucked her hair behind one ear, baring the side of her throat. His fingers itched to touch her and he was no damn good at resisting that kind of temptation. Especially not when it came out of nowhere and went off like a Roman candle in his gut. The reason he was no good at resisting was simple: he never had to. Not because of any special appeal or talent or charm on his part. It was because he always made sure the women he crossed swords with were interested in the same outcome he was, and nothing more.

Sophie wasn't one of those women.

But somehow it suddenly didn't matter.

He was dangerously close to giving in to the craving to kiss her when he remembered there was a reason he'd brought her to this place and it wasn't to find out if she tasted as good as she looked at that moment.

"No," he said, barely managing to recall her question from a moment ago. "I ended up here later . . . after my father was shipped off to prison."

Her startled expression quickly turned questioning. Owen

didn't give her a chance to say anything. He had no intention of answering questions about his family history, about how dancing the fine line between what was legal and what was a scam to cheat people out of whatever was in their pockets had finally landed his old man a few years in jail, or about how his aunt had reluctantly taken in his surly, fourteen-year-old ass and arranged for him to attend the private school where she was assistant to the headmaster. It had been a turning point in his life, an important one. All the highs and lows of his life could be traced back to that.

"I didn't bring you here to talk about me," he said. "We're here to discuss Ivy, and how you plan to make sure we don't have a repeat of what happened today . . . or worse."

He was clearly intent on changing the subject and Sophie didn't blame him. God knows there were things in her past she'd rather not dredge up or dwell on. And besides, he was right: after today, it was clear she couldn't waste any time coming up with a way to stop Ivy from interfering with the wedding plans.

"That's a good question," she acknowledged. "Wish I had a good answer. Do you happen to have any suggestions?"

"As a matter of fact I do."

"Great. I'm listening. You said you had information about her that I'd find useful. Which means you've had better luck than I did. I have a friend looking into the history of the house, but I wouldn't describe anything we've come up with so far as being especially useful. I really appreciate your help."

He shrugged. "I had some free time the other day, so I dropped by the Historical Society to see what I could find out. I wasn't helping so much as I was curious."

"That's on my to-do list," she told him. "Currently somewhere around item one hundred and sixteen, if I'm not mistaken. And now that I have to juggle things around and reschedule the landscape design team, it will get bumped even lower. I did try checking with them by phone, but the woman I spoke with insisted I had to show up there and do the research personally."

"Yeah, she told me the same thing. I didn't have *that* much free time, so instead I just hung around until they took their break and treated the entire staff to Starbucks. I was hoping if I got them talking, someone might loosen up and drop something helpful about the property or the previous owners."

"And did they?"

"Sort of. The assistant director gave me the name of someone she thought had been a friend of Ivy's and who might be willing to answer a few questions. She even made a call to arrange for me to speak with the woman. Evidently Mrs. Theodora Todd Whitman was once a fixture on the Newport social scene and she still loves entertaining. She lives at an assisted living facility called Seaside Villa; we're talking five-star cuisine, health spa, indoor pool . . . the place is swankier than a lot of resorts I've seen. And lucky for me, the assistant director also remembered that she's a big fan of handmade chocolates with raspberry filling."

"Starbucks . . . chocolates . . . is bribery your go-to fix for everything?" she teased.

"Whatever works," he replied with a matter-of-fact shrug. "Lately I have more money than I do time . . . or patience. Mrs. Whitman got her chocolates and I got some useful information about our psycho ghost bride."

"Please tell me you didn't actually mention anything about a ghost."

"I didn't. Trust me; I don't want that getting out any more than you do. Less, in fact, since it's my doorbell every kook within a hundred miles will be knocking on in hopes of a sighting."

"Then we're agreed: we'll keep that strictly between the two of us. So," she continued as soon as he nodded agreement, "what did she tell you about Ivy?"

"It turns out Mrs. Whitman is quite a bit younger than Ivy Halliday was, at least twenty-five years. They met at a handful of charity functions through the years, but they only spoke in passing."

"I don't see how that helps."

He shot her a quelling look.

"Sorry."

"It was actually her mother who was friendly with Ivy Halliday at one time. Seems they were both debutantes and made the same rounds of balls and parties when they were in their teens and twenties. In fact, her mother was supposed to be a guest at Ivy's wedding."

"Supposed to be?"

"Right. Here's where it gets interesting. The wedding was planned for Ange de la Mer. And from Mrs. Whitman's description, it sounds like it was exactly the kind of fancy, overpriced, over-the-top affair you specialize in," he added with no effort to hide his disapproval.

"I prefer to think my specialty is making couples happy by giving them the kind of wedding they want, not the kind someone else thinks they should have . . . it is their big day after all. But do go on."

"So her mother was invited to be there on Ivy's *big day*, along with several hundred others. Evidently the guest list read like a Who's Who of Newport, circa 1920-something, which means it likely included more than its share of famous names and society heavyweights. That wasn't long after the Gilded Age. Must have been wall-to-wall Bentleys and Rolls out front . . . and all for nothing, as it turned out. The wedding never took place."

"Why not? Did she tell you what happened?"

"Oh, she told me all right." His mouth slanted in a long-suffering grimace. "In excruciating detail. Who wore what, who said what, what they almost ate. Like it happened yesterday. Nothing I enjoy more than the play-by-play of a wedding story. This one was the talk of the season and Mrs. Whitman's mother never got tired of retelling it. Every time the Halliday name came up, she was off and running at the mouth. She told the story so often and so well that Mrs. Whitman said she sometimes forgets she wasn't there herself and that she only knows what happened secondhand."

"So what did happen? You might have been bored by her story, but the suspense is killing me." She swung around so she was facing him, her legs curled to the side. "Why would a bride who went to all the trouble of planning a big splashy wedding call it off at the last minute . . . in front of hundreds of guests?"

"She didn't."

Sophie threw her hands up, impatient. "Then what—" She winced as the other obvious possibility occurred to her. "Oh no."

"Oh yeah, you guessed it. The bride was willing and able. The groom was the no-show."

"Poor Ivy. That has to be every bride's worst nightmare. I've only seen it happen once, but . . ." She shuddered and shook her head, remembering. "Once was more than enough. It's humiliation on top of heartache on top of betrayal . . . on top of more humiliation." She sighed. "So what was this jerk's excuse? A simple case of cold feet? Or did he suddenly fall head over heels for some bimbo he just met and decide he'd only *thought* he was in love with the woman he'd known and who he'd been professing to love for years and years and who had quite rightly assumed they would be spending the rest of their lives together, except that only now, *après* bimbo, did he understand what it meant to be truly in love?"

Not until she ran out of steam did she realize that Owen was watching and listening with greater-than-usual interest, his expression somewhere between amused and speculative.

She gave an awkward shrug. "Sorry. Pet peeve. You were saying . . . about the groom's reason for not showing up?"

"No one knows. The guy—Joseph something—just disappeared, never to be seen or heard from again."

"Never?"

"Never."

"Not by anyone? Not even his own family?"

"Didn't have one, according to Mrs. Whitman. She seems to recall that he came from somewhere down south and met Ivy while he was in the navy and stationed here in Newport. Ivy was your average, everyday society princess volunteering as a USO hostess and he was your classic kid from the wrong side of tracks, no family, raised in an orphanage, not even close to what the Hallidays had in mind for their beloved only daughter. But apparently what Ivy wanted Ivy got. Eventually her father came around and gave his permission for them to marry. He even offered the guy a position with the family shipbuilding business. And he had Ange de la Mer built to Ivy's specifications as a wedding present. So not only was it to be her wedding day, it was also the grand unveiling of her dream house."

He reached into his pocket. "I almost forgot . . . this is from Mrs. Whitman's late mother's collection." He handed Sophie a photograph. "It's a copy so you can hang on to it if you like."

She studied the black-and-white photo, tipping it to see more clearly in the bright sunlight. It was a formal pose, obviously taken by a professional. An engagement photo was Sophie's guess. It probably accompanied the official notice that appeared in the society pages. The young woman's sweater and jewelry appeared dated, but her beauty was timeless. She had high cheekbones, a confident, almost cocky smile, and sleek shoulder-length blond hair. Except for the haircolor, a young Lauren Bacall, thought Sophie.

"That's her all right," she said. "The ghost bride. That's the woman I saw."

"The woman who nearly broke your fingers," Owen reminded her.

"She was very beautiful, don't you think?"

She looked up in time to see him shrug.

"She was all right, I suppose. If you don't mind all the trouble and complications that go along with that stuck-up, spoiled-princess type."

Tilting her head to the side, she regarded him curiously. "Once burned? You sound like a man who speaks from experience."

He averted his gaze, his tone gruff. "Let's just say it's a mistake you don't make twice."

She nodded and took another look at the photo. "Okay. So a kid from nowhere, with nothing, scores a beautiful princess and a brand-new castle and then just walks away? That doesn't make sense."

"That's what Ivy said. She refused to believe he would leave her and insisted that something must have happened to him. Something bad. Her father agreed. He'd come around to thinking his future son-in-law was a decent guy, and he had enough clout to force a large-scale police investigation into his disappearance and to get the FBI—or the BOI, as it was known at the time—involved."

"BOI?"

"Bureau of Investigation. When the official search came up empty, he hired a team of private investigators. They didn't have any better luck. After that, Ivy took on the mantle herself. Local legend has it that she had a team of investigators on retainer to do her bidding right up until the day she died. She moved into the house on the day they would have been married, lived there alone, and never gave up hope."

"Maybe that's because Ivy knew something no one else did . . . or could. She knew that he—Joseph—was her soul mate . . . her forever love. That's how she knew he would never leave her . . . and that something had happened to keep him from coming to her."

"Well, regardless of what she knew or didn't know, at least

now we know why she's pissed at us. Me because she doesn't want me messing up Ivy's dream house with wet towels and beer bottles, and you because she doesn't want anyone else getting married there."

"I can't blame her on either score. It's only natural she has such strong feelings about that place. It's not just her home; it's a shrine to what might have been . . . to what *should* have been."

"A shrine? Maybe. Her home? No. She's dead, remember?"

"She's dead, but her love for Joseph isn't. For Ivy, those feelings are as alive and real today as they were on her wedding day. True love is very powerful . . . a force to be reckoned with."

"True love? Sounds more like true lunacy to me. But I'll bow to your expertise on the subject. The important thing is that we agree our headstrong ghost bride won't be giving up the fight anytime soon."

"Definitely not."

"It could get ugly," he warned. "Someone could get seriously hurt. She's shown she's willing to play rough. Who knows how far she'll go? A woman scorned and all that."

"It's a very delicate situation," agreed Sophie. "We obviously can't force her to behave. And it's not as if we can call the police or threaten her with legal action if she doesn't cooperate."

"Face it: we don't have a lot of options."

"She definitely has us at a disadvantage."

"A major disadvantage. So I think we know what we have to do."

Sophie nodded and they spoke at the same time.

"Back off."

"Reach out to her."

Ten

"ack off?"

Owen nodded emphatically. "That's right. Back off. Walk away. Find someplace else to have the wedding."

"Why on earth would I back off?"

"Why in God's name would you reach out to her? So she can hand you a homemade Molotov cocktail?"

Sophie's mouth curved slightly. "Don't you think that's being a little overly dramatic?"

"No," he snapped, exasperation evident in the way he dragged his hand through his hair. "I think you're being overly naive if you have some touchy-feely notion that you can deal rationally with a whack-job ghost." He shook his head. "I can't believe I'm even sitting here having a conversation about a ghost."

"Ditto. To the last part," she hastened to add. "Not the rest. For your information, I am not naive . . . or touchy-feely. And I also don't think Ivy is a whack job. Exactly. I think she's a . . . a romantic." She lifted her chin as she said it, ignoring his muffled snort. "I admit that at first I was at a loss as to how to handle this whole thing, but I feel much better now. Thanks to you."

He went from looking annoyed to aghast. "Me? What did I do?"

"Exactly what you said you'd do: you gave me information that helped me decide what to do."

"Only because I assumed you'd make the right decision."

Frowning, Sophie drew back a little. "Is that the reason you told me about Ivy's background? Because you *wanted* me to give up . . . to back off?" Her surprise turned to suspicion. "Is that why you were so helpful and went to the trouble of looking into it in the first place?"

"I never claimed I was trying to be helpful. And I told you because I thought you were smart enough and levelheaded enough to know when you've run into a brick wall, and to realize that having this wedding somewhere else would be the best—not to mention the safest—thing for everyone involved."

"Not for Shelby," she retorted. "Being married at the Princess House means everything to her. And not for me; I keep my promises and I promised Shelby the wedding of her dreams."

"And you did your best to deliver. Sometimes things happen that are beyond your control."

"Sometimes," she allowed. "But not this time. There's no way I'm giving up now that I know the whole story. Ivy Halliday and I share common ground. We're—"

"Kindred spirits?" he interjected in a sardonic tone.

"Bad pun aside, yes. I understand what she went through and how she must have felt that day . . . and I understand why she doesn't want some stranger barging into her house and having the beautiful, happy wedding day that should have been hers."

"And exactly what are you planning to do that will change any of that? You can't turn back time. You can't wave a magic wand

and make her missing groom reappear. What can you possibly say or do to change feelings she's nursed for the better part of a century?"

She tilted her head to the side, her mouth quirking with indecision. "I'm not sure . . . yet. Truthfully, I'm not sure I *can* change the way she feels." Before his triumphant grin had a chance to form, she folded her arms in front of her with serious determination. "But I just might be able to change her mind about the best way to deal with those feelings."

"How?" he challenged.

"Like I said, I'm not sure yet." She hesitated, thinking. It wasn't easy to do in the face of his disgruntled glare. "For starters, I might try telling her about Shelby. You mentioned that Ivy was a USO volunteer; I think she'll admire Shelby and Matthew's decision to join the Peace Corps. And then there's the house itself. Ange de la Mer was a gift to Ivy from her father and Shelby's father took her sailing near there because he knew how much she loved it. There's a strong emotional link there. If I can get Ivy to feel a personal connection to Shelby, it may be easier to get her to listen and to convince her that ruining Shelby's wedding won't change what happened to her . . . it will only add to the negative karma of the house she loves."

He looked coolly unimpressed.

"Look, I understand your concern," she said, wanting him in her corner. "Believe me; I don't want anyone to get hurt any more than you do. And I promise you I won't let it come to that. Please, just give me a chance to try to bring Ivy around. I've talked dozens of brides through bouts of cold feet and last-minute jitters."

"Ivy doesn't have cold feet," he pointed out. "She has a raging case of 'get the hell out of my house or I'll hurt you and break your stuff.' "

"Well, yes. True. But she's still a bride . . . at least I think she thinks she is. And brides can be emotional and irrational, and that's where I come in. I'm good at what I do. When it comes to brides, I've learned to trust my instincts and my instincts are telling me I can get through to Ivy. Who knows? This might turn out to be the best thing for her too. She can't be happy rattling around all alone in that big house. Maybe I can help her work out whatever is holding her there so she can move on in peace."

He almost smiled. "Yeah, right, you're not at all the touchy-feely type. So that's your grand plan? Two happy brides for the price of one?"

"Go ahead and laugh. But I can do this. You'll see. As soon as we get back to the house, Operation Befriend a Ghost goes into full swing."

She made a move to stand and instantly he was on his feet to offer her a hand up. With him supplying the muscle, Sophie rose gracefully, but as she turned away, instead of letting her go, he tightened his grip on her hand.

She glanced back to find out why, half knowing already. Not in words. This wasn't about words. She knew from the telltale heat and sizzle where his palm was pressed to her own, and in that wordless place deep inside, that place where she had somehow always known it would come to this, where she'd yearned for it from the start and welcomed it even now as her pulse skipped and her breath went still as glass in her throat.

He gazed at her without smiling, his dark blue gaze turbulent as it moved unhurriedly from her eyes to her mouth and back.

"Is something wrong?"

"Yes," he said. The frown lines at the corners of his mouth deepened. "No." And then, muttering, "Oh, what the hell . . ."

The instant of indecision behind him, he took her shoulders and pulled her to him.

There was ample time for her to resist, to say no, to say they should be sensible and go back to the house and back to work, and not do anything reckless that her heart would almost certainly regret.

Instead, curious and impatient, she leaned closer to him, lifting her chin so that their gazes met and held and heated, and then his mouth was on hers in a searching, drugging kiss that made her senses spin and her knees buckle. He held her and she clung to him with both hands on his back, her fingers curling into the soft, sun-warmed cotton of his T-shirt. He tasted smoky and intoxicating. His flesh was hard, his touch urgent, and with her eyes closed, it was like hurtling through the blackest of nights, no lights, no caution, just heat and excitement.

Her lips parted under his as his possession of her mouth grew harder and deeper. It started something burning between them . . . and inside her. It was a flame licking at her core, rushing in her blood. As unfamiliar as it was to her, it didn't feel new; it felt . . . awakened. Unleashed. Like a part of her had always been waiting for this . . . and for him.

The kiss ended abruptly with a cold shower, courtesy of a rogue wave that crashed hard against the rocks and sent spray cascading twelve feet in the air. They broke apart, breathing hard.

"Looks like true love isn't the only force to be reckoned with," Owen said after a minute, in that low, rough tone that made her shiver.

At first Sophie thought he was referring to the incoming tide, but then he lifted his hand to her face, rubbing his thumb along her jaw and trailing his fingertips down the side of her throat.

"You seem to have become an irresistible impulse for me." He said it softly, with a faint undertone of amazement. "I'm going to have to work on that."

Work on it how? Sophie wondered. Work on resisting the impulse? Or on getting better at giving in to it? With her lips still throbbing, she really didn't think that was possible. She managed to say nothing, which was probably for the best. She felt a little dazed, like one of those cartoon characters that walk off a cliff and end up with a merry-go-round of stars and chirping birdies circling their heads. Her most eloquent comment would be along the lines of "Wow."

Owen either recovered more quickly or he hadn't been nearly as blindsided as she was. She didn't want to think about that right now. Strong and sure-footed in spite of whatever had happened to his leg, he led the way back to his bike, helping her over the rough spots. There might have been another Merchant-Ivory moment along the way, but she couldn't be sure. She was distracted, consumed with thoughts of The Kiss, amazed that she, die-hard romantic and starry-eyed champion of love and passion, could have lived her whole life without knowing that that feeling existed.

"I don't get it," Sophie said. "Now that I want to talk with Ivy, she's gone all MIA on us. When I wanted her to go away, she was all about making contact."

"Was she?" countered Owen. "I'm not so sure."

He was comfortably sprawled in a big cushy chair in the sunroom at the back of the house, where he'd waited while Sophie methodically made her way through each and every room in the place, doing and saying anything and everything she could think of to entice the spirit of Ivy Halliday to appear. Candles, soft music, polite requests, and impassioned pleas, thinly—and not so thinly—veiled threats: she'd tried them all. And she hadn't elicited so much as a glimpse or whisper from the house's resident ghost.

With a discouraged sigh she dropped into the chair facing him.

"Let's see, squashed fingers, spooky bride vision, hostile warning, beehive assault." She ticked them off on her fingers. "The way

I see it, all the above qualify as making contact, and that's not even counting what's been happening with you."

"I think 'assault' might be the key word there. Ivy's shown she's willing and capable of lashing out and attacking on her terms, but I wouldn't classify piling wet towels in my bed or planting a golf club for someone to trip over as efforts to make contact with the natives. The way I see it, she hasn't shown any interest in a two-way dialogue, much less playing nice."

"You're probably right. But I'm too damn tired to think about it. I give up."

His dark brows shot up.

"For today," she clarified. With a sigh, she rested her head back against the seat cushion. "There has to be a way to get her attention; I just need to figure out what it is."

"Maybe I can save you some time." He stood and headed out of the room. Reluctantly, Sophie scrambled from her comfy perch to follow.

"Where are we going?"

She got her answer when he stopped in the formal living room at the front of the house and stood looking around. It was a huge room, big enough for several furniture groupings, with a white marble fireplace at one end.

For no particular reason Sophie found herself wondering if this was where Ivy put up her tree at Christmastime. She was envisioning the room decked for the holidays, with twinkling white lights and handblown glass ornaments and a towering, fragrant pine tree at the center of it all, when it suddenly occurred to her to wonder if Ivy had even bothered with a Christmas tree. Or with a Thanksgiving turkey or Fourth of July fireworks and barbecues. Had she bravely gathered family and friends there to celebrate holidays, the way she must have dreamed of doing when the house was being built and her future looked so rosy? Or had she put all that on hold and allowed her life to dwindle down to simply waiting for Joseph to return? She wasn't sure if knowing the answer would help her in her quest, but she was curious just the same. She wanted to believe that in spite of everything, there had been Christmas carols and champagne toasts and laughter in that house . . . and in Ivy's life.

"This'll do for starters," Owen announced. He was standing in front of a tall, narrow, enamel curio cabinet. She watched, first puzzled and then alarmed as he yanked open the door and began grabbing pieces of crystal and blue-and-white Wedgwood off the glass shelves and tossing them onto a pale gold velvet chair a few feet away. There was the sound of breaking glass.

"What are you doing?" Sophie demanded, hurrying to his side.

"Getting this junk out of the way." He removed the last item from the bottom shelf, a slender crystal vase perfect for holding a single bloom.

Sophie snatched it from his hand before he could toss it. "Why? Out of the way of what?"

"Out of my way. So it won't be as heavy when I drag it out-side." He swung the door shut and bent his knees slightly as he positioned his hands on the sides of the cabinet, preparing to lift it.

"Stop." She grabbed his forearm. "What the hell do you think you're doing?"

"What does it look like?"

"It looks like you've lost your mind," she blurted.

"Trust me, I haven't. You wanted to get the attention of your ghost pal? I promise you this will do the job. She gets in a snit when I put a glass down on one of her precious tables; what do you think she'll do when I start tossing her stuff out with the trash? One fancy-ass piece at a time."

"Stop," she said again. "I mean it, Owen. You are not going to toss anything anywhere."

He didn't let go of the cabinet, but she felt his muscles relax as he turned his head to look at her. "I'm telling you: this will work. Sometimes you have to get tough and fight fire with fire. Do you think she'd shy away from breaking something of yours in order to get her way?"

"I don't care. That's not how *I* work. It's cruel."

"So was slamming a drawer on your fingers. Maybe two wrongs don't make a right, but it can still be damn effective."

She shook her head. "No. Maybe Ivy felt she didn't have a choice, that she had no other way of dealing with what she perceived as a threat. But I don't feel that way. I don't want to hurt Ivy; I want to try to help her. I know this can be resolved so that everyone is happy . . . or at least content . . . and without causing any damage. I just need some time to think about my next move."

For a long moment he scowled at the cabinet without saying anything. He didn't need to; his frustration fairly crackled in the air between them. Finally he took his hands from the cabinet and straightened. "Fine. That's just fine. We'll play it your way. On one condition. You do your thinking here."

"I didn't mean I could come up with a solution tonight, on the spot," she clarified.

"I'm not talking about tonight. I'm talking about you being here twenty-four/seven from now until the wedding day. I'm talking about you being the one to deal with whatever crap she dishes out. Because I'm done with it."

She gave a feeble laugh, eyeing him in disbelief. "You can't be serious."

"I'm nothing but. This whole thing has turned into a giant pain in the ass . . . my ass. My vote is to throw in the towel and cut our losses. You're the one who wants to keep banging your head against the wall. So it's only fitting that you be the one standing by, ready to stick your finger in the dike whenever your kindred spirit feels like poking another hole in it."

"That's ridiculous. Not to mention impossible. I have other clients . . . and a life. I can't possibly be here around the clock."

"Then you can't go ahead with this wedding. It's as simple as that."

"This wasn't part of our original *signed* agreement."

"Lots of things weren't part of our original agreement. Do you really want to air them in a public courtroom?" He paused. "I didn't think so."

He went on, saying something about being sorry he had to play hardball with her and about his deadline and ghosts with bad attitudes. Sophie only half listened. What he was proposing was beyond ridiculous. It was outrageous and unfair and out of line. And she had no doubt he meant it and wouldn't be backing down. He had her cornered. She couldn't disappoint Shelby and she couldn't just take a hiatus from the rest of her life and camp out there for the next few weeks. Forget about the overall inconvenience and the havoc it would play with her work schedule, she would be living alone in a house—granted, a very big house—with a man she hardly knew. As for the fact that the prospect concerned her and excited her in about equal parts, well, she wasn't sure how to factor that into the mix.

"Look, if you're worried about what happened earlier, on the rocks," he said, immediately commanding her full attention. "You don't need to be."

"You mean the . . . our . . ." She gave a little wave of one hand.

"Kiss," he supplied.

For an instant, amusement lifted the corner of his mouth, and suddenly she couldn't seem to move her gaze from that spot. With that wicked glint in his eyes and the dark whiskers shadowing his jaw, he looked like an advertisement for whiskey, or sin. The feeling of being in his arms shivered through her, undermining her concentration.

"Like I told you," he continued, "that kiss was just a momentary impulse. What I'm proposing now is about business. Period. It has nothing to do with my little lapse in judgment earlier. You can trust me to see to it that it doesn't happen again."

"Well, good," she said, disappointment a small, hard knot in her chest at hearing that he considered kissing her to be a "lapse in judgment." "That's good. And reassuring. Very reassuring. It's certainly not a mistake I would want to repeat."

So there. He wasn't the only one who could plead a lapse in judgment.

"Good. Very good. So we're clear."

"Very clear."

"Then it's settled, and the ball's back in your court. So . . ." He folded his arms, watching her. "What's it going to be Sophie? Wedding or no wedding?"

It had been a most interesting day, reflected Ivy as she watched Sophia Bennett return the objects removed by Mr. Winters to their rightful place in the curio cabinet. Most interesting indeed.

She wasn't certain what she would have done if he'd actually hauled the cabinet outside and tossed it in the trash. But whatever she did would have made a few bee stings pale in comparison. If Mr. Winters thought she had been a "pain in his ass" thus far, he didn't know what real pain was. It was her belief that she had exercised remarkable restraint under the circumstances.

The obvious recourse would have been to retaliate by destroying something of equal value to him. Except she couldn't think of what that would be. As far as she could tell, his worldly belongings consisted of little more than the silver frame holding his daughter's

picture—which she would never touch, the clothes on his back—
which were not worth the effort, and that horrible, noisy
motorcycle—tempting, but alas, out of the question. What sort of
grown man rode around town looking like a common hoodlum
and didn't have a stick of furniture to call his own?

There was, of course, the computer he used for his supposed
writing. Surely it was of some value monetarily, but her sense—
based on the many times she'd heard him cursing at it—was that
it was merely a necessary evil in his life, not something he cared
about, and certainly not something comparable to the curio cabinet that had stood in the corner of her mother's dressing room
when she was a girl. Back then it held her mother's silk scarves and
her hair ornaments adorned with jewels and silky feathers and
exotic beads; she still recalled the hours she spent sorting and rearranging them and posing with them on in front of the dressing-
table mirror.

Those memories came back to her strongly as she watched Sophia Bennett carefully arranging the Waterford crystal and Wedgwood pieces on the shelves, and she felt herself smiling. Which was
silly, because at the moment she wasn't even really there. Not in a
physical sense. It had been a long day and she was too weary to
gather the energy required to appear. No physical presence, no
smile, but she felt herself smiling nonetheless and she wondered at
it. The feeling itself was strange to her. It had been so very long. So
long that she couldn't recall the last time she'd smiled.

It suddenly occurred to her that it was taking the young Bennett woman an inordinate amount of time to return the items to
the cabinet and she realized why: she was trying to return each one
to its original position and, Ivy noted, she was doing an impressive
job. The fact that she had intervened and stood up to Mr. Winters
was impressive. But this, the extra care she was taking to make
things right again, touched Ivy in a way that had become as unfa-

miliar to her as her own smile. The show of kindness made her feel
a trifle sorry for the way she had ignored the young woman earlier,
and it almost made her want to gather herself to make an appearance and listen to whatever Sophia wanted to say to her.

Almost.

As moved as she was, she had no patience for lost causes. Nor
was she a proponent of suggesting there was hope where there was
none. She didn't have to actually hear her say it to know what the
young woman had to say. She knew very well what Sophia Bennett
wanted from her . . . and why she would attempt to curry favor to
get it. She wanted a truce of some sort; she wanted leave for her
wedding plans to go forward without interference. She wanted Ivy
to step aside and let another bride take her place.

And that, thought Ivy as she withdrew from the room, was
never going to happen.

Sophie got lucky and found both Jill and Jenna still in their offices
when she arrived back at Seasons shortly after seven. It meant she
would only have to tell the tale once and not have to rely on either
twin to get it straight in the retelling.

She waited until they finished their meeting with a new client,
using the time to catch up on her own work and put her desk in
order. She joined them in Jenna's office. Like the twins themselves,
their newly redecorated offices were nearly identical: white tex-
tured wall coverings, black lacquer furnishings, and photographs
of Seasons' events in brushed silver frames. A pop of color was
provided by the carpeting and a few carefully chosen accent pieces:
turquoise in Jenna's office and lime in Jill's.

"Hey, you two," she said with a quick rap on the open door.
"Got a minute?"

From her seat behind the desk, Jenna waved her in. "Sure. Grab a chair."

"Thanks, but I have to get home. I just want to fill you in on a problem that's come up with the Archer wedding."

She gave them a quick, sanitized, strictly need-to-know run-down of the day's events that did not include any mention of Ivy.

When she finished there was a second of silence.

Jill, looking bewildered, spoke first. "You can't be serious."

Sophie almost laughed. It was the same thing she'd said when she heard Owen's ultimatum.

"Nothing but," she said, borrowing his reply.

Jill's eyes grew comically wide and for a second Sophie thought she might slip from her perch on the corner of the desk. "You're moving in with Owen Winters?"

"No," said Sophie. "I'm—"

Shaking her head as if to clear it, Jill chuckled and cut her off. "Of course you're not. I knew that couldn't be right. But it sounded like that's what you said." She glanced at Jenna. "Didn't it sound like that's what she said?"

"That is what she said," Jenna snapped. "Sophie, what's wrong with you? You can't just move in with a man you hardly know. Especially not a man like Owen Winters."

"What kind of man is that?"

"Wealthy," Jenna said without hesitation. "Good-looking . . . at least he could be if he made any effort at all. Successful, famous, charming . . . when he wants to be. And at times rude and self-absorbed. Need I go on? Unless I miss my guess, and I seldom do when it comes to men, he's the kind of man who prefers his women young and hot."

"Twentysomething eye candy," Jill added, nodding with conviction. "No doubt about it."

"I really wouldn't know," Sophie responded, managing to keep both her amusement and her annoyance from her voice. "But what does his taste in women—or lack thereof—have to do with this? I'm not moving in with Owen Winters. I'm simply doing what I have to do to make sure there is someone on-site at all times to supervise the wedding preparations."

"Of course. I understand that's all there is to it. I just want to make sure you're okay with that . . . that you're not, well, reading something more into his request."

"It wasn't a request; it was an ultimatum. And the only thing I'm reading into it is that he has a deadline and doesn't want to be dragged away from his work and forced to do damage control the way he was today . . . which he is entirely within his rights to demand. There's a lot of work to be done to get ready for this wedding, a lot of complicated setup, and not a lot of time to do it. I'm going to have crews working overtime and weekends. Problems are bound to arise and it will be to our advantage timewise if someone is on hand to deal with them as soon as they do. A lot of thought and time went into coordinating this job to run like clockwork. If one work team runs into trouble, it could have a domino effect, forcing others to wait around or reschedule in order to get their work done. I called in a lot of favors to get vendors to squeeze us in at the last minute, during their busiest time of year; rescheduling will be a nightmare."

Jill gave an impatient wave of her hand. "We get all that. We have planned a wedding or two ourselves, remember? All Jenna was trying to say is that we don't want to see you get your heart broken."

"Again," added Jenna.

Jill nodded, her delicate features forming a sympathetic frown. "Do you remember how horrible it was when Keith dumped you?"

Sophie drew a deep breath. "Yes. Yes, I do remember."

"You were devastated," Jill recalled.

"Crushed," said Jenna.

"A mess. For weeks. Maybe months. I don't remember exactly, but it seemed like you were moping around forever. And we just don't want to see you get taken again."

"I wouldn't say I was taken," Sophie protested. "Keith and I dated for over three years—"

"Nearly four."

"Yes, nearly four. And for most of that time things were fine."

"So it seemed." Jill's tone was lilting and skeptical.

"I was in love with Keith and I trusted him. People change. It happens."

"And it's nothing for you to be ashamed of," Jenna assured her. "You were in love with love and that's just so you. You have this whole fairy-tale thing going on and it's adorable, and it probably made you see things in the relationship that weren't there."

"That's not quite . . . you know what? It doesn't matter. I got over Keith ages ago.

"And, more importantly, the situation with Owen Winters is entirely different. It's business: period." Her fingers were curled so tightly the tips were numb. A reflex. She felt like punching something. Maybe herself, for being stupid enough to try to justify her past to the *J*s. She knew better, and yet every once in a while she suddenly found herself feeling fifteen again and trying to convince them—and herself—that she really wasn't a completely clueless dork who needed their endless advice and guidance.

"And you're okay with that?" inquired Jenna. She smiled indulgently. "You're not moving into the castle with stars in your eyes and visions of Prince Charming dancing in your head?"

"Not at all," Sophie replied, loosening her fists before she drew blood. "But it's really sweet of you both to be so concerned about *my* feelings." Even if it meant dredging up one of the most painful and humiliating events in her life and rubbing her nose in it. Of course the subtext was lost on them, as she'd known it would be.

Jenna beamed her most benevolent smile. "Hey, what are big sisters for?"

Lips pursed, Jill spoke with a hint of petulance. "You know, I understand why someone has to be there to keep an eye on things, but all this talk of castles and princes has me wondering why that someone has to be you. I wouldn't mind spending a few weeks in an oceanfront mansion. No kids. No housework." She glanced at Sophie. "He does have a housekeeper, right?"

Hmm, thought Sophie, *tricky question.* She settled for a shrug.

"He must," Jill decided. "And probably a cook, too. I could live with that for a while."

"Now that you mention it, so could I," said Jenna. "God, can you imagine? My friends would be green when they found out I was living in a mansion on Bellevue Avenue. Do you think Winters would let me have people over once in a while? Nothing fancy. Strictly drinks and hors d'oeuvres."

"Maybe he'd like to join in," suggested Jill.

Jenna nodded. "I'll bet he would. He seemed kind of recluse-y. He probably doesn't know too many people here." She glanced at Sophie. "He's not from around here, is he?"

Another shrug. "I don't know where he's from exactly."

"I think having a famous author in the mix would make for some interesting conversation," ventured Jenna.

"Absolutely," agreed Jill. "And if we hit it off he might even let us handle his next book launch."

"That would be a real coup."

"Maybe we should take a vote on who gets to play princess," suggested Jill.

"Great idea," said Sophie. "Except that the only vote that

counts has already been cast." She did her best not to sound smug as she said it.

For a second or two the *J*s appeared stumped. Then Jenna grimaced.

"Shelby," she said.

Jill heaved a sigh of disgust. "Oh, right. You know, she turned out to be a lot more trouble than we bargained for."

"First, none of our wedding ideas are good enough for her. Then she wants to pick and choose her planner. And now there's not a dress to be found anywhere that meets all her requirements."

"A *hemp* dress."

"Right . . . and she wonders why none of them are flattering."

"Actually, the dress problem is solved," Sophie told them. "So you can cross that off the list of things you have to lose sleep worrying about."

Jill scoffed.

"As if," muttered Jenna.

"You don't get off scot-free however." Stepping forward, Sophie slid the list she'd prepared across the desk.

"What's this?" asked Jenna.

Jill moved so she could read it over her twin's shoulder.

"That's a list of the things I ordinarily take care of, but won't be able to for the next few weeks. I downloaded the files I need and set it up so that I can access my office computer from my laptop. Most of my work I can take care of by phone or e-mail. I'll shoot you a status update of current jobs every morning, but someone will have to update the Big Board in my office so you can keep track of everything. And at the bottom of that list are appointments I won't be able to keep. One of you will have to either fill in for me or reschedule. Oh, you'll also have to reschedule the appointment with the flower wholesaler that I had to cancel this afternoon."

The *J*s exchanged a look.

"This is a lot of work," Jenna said. "And a lot of running around."

"And that's on top of all the work we already do," added Jill. "I'm not sure we can handle all this."

"Oh, don't sell yourselves short." Sophie's smile was wide and genuine. "After all, you've planned a wedding or two in your time."

"Yes, but we don't usually get involved with background stuff."

"Or all these picayune details."

"Or the Big Board."

"That's right. You don't do any of that. But look on the bright side: anything I can do, you can do better. Think of this as an opportunity to get in touch with your Inner Drone."

Eleven

It was late by the time she made it back to Newport and arrived on Owen's doorstep, bag and baggage. Or rather, bag and bag and bag and baggage. There are people in the world who travel light, content to wander from home with a wing and a prayer and a favorite pair of flip-flops. Sophie wasn't one of them.

As much as she loved to visit new places and meet new people, she was a homebody at heart, into cocooning long before it became trendy. There were things she just liked having around, familiar things that made her feel safe and happy. When her father remarried and her stepmother moved in and gradually put her stamp on the house, Sophie's room became her sanctuary. She decorated it with castoffs that had been relegated to a box in the garage and that she rescued before Goodwill came to haul them away. Relics of happier days, those favorite things went with her to college and then to her first apartment and to the condo where she lived now. A few small treasures, mostly photos, always found their way into her suitcase when she was away from home, but three bags full were a little much even for her.

It couldn't be helped. She had a gut feeling that between dealing with Ivy and dealing with the feelings Owen stirred up inside her, she was going to need as many stress busters and creature comforts as she could get. First she'd decided to bring along her own pillow, then her favorite mug and the ginger-peach tea she liked, and it just sort of snowballed from there.

Owen met her at the door.

"You look surprised to see me," she observed. "We did agree that I would be back tonight?"

"That was the plan," he confirmed, nodding. "But I wondered if you'd have second thoughts."

"About moving in? Oh, I've had second, third, and fourth. You have to admit, the situation is more than a little unorthodox. And awkward."

"And yet . . ."

She sighed. "And yet when you come right down to it, I'd rather deal with unorthodox and awkward than have to look Shelby in the eye and tell her the reason she can't have her Princess House wedding is because I'm a quitter."

He didn't comment, but since he'd already made clear his feelings about love and marriage and happy-ever-after, Sophie figured it had to be pure cynicism that she saw glitter in his eyes. Naturally he would think she was wasting her time.

"Here, let me take that for you," he said, reaching for the handle of the suitcase resting on its wheels beside her.

"I've got this one, but there's more in the car if you want to help."

She wheeled the suitcase into the hall and then followed him back outside. By the time she reached the car, he had one bag on his shoulder and one under his arm.

"How about handing me that duffel bag?" she said.

"I'm all set."

"Yeah, but I don't want you to hurt yourself."

He stopped and glanced at her over his shoulder. "You think I'm going to hurt myself carrying luggage?"

"I just meant that maybe with your leg you shouldn't—"

He cut her off sharply. "Let me worry about my leg."

"Oops," she murmured under her breath, trailing slowly.

He grabbed the suitcase in the hallway with his free hand and waited for her at the bottom of the stairs. She decided not to point out that he was being ridiculous. Carrying all the bags single-handedly had clearly taken on some sort of testosterone-laden significance she couldn't hope to understand. She knew just enough about the primal instincts of the male of the species to be certain that there was no reasoning with a man having an MSS—Macho Shithead Syndrome—moment. In hindsight, she could see that she obviously shouldn't have tried to help him with the bags, or implied that he might need help in the first place, and especially not because of a physical infirmity. She made a mental note not to avoid taking a sensible approach to such matters in the future, but for now all she could do was stand by, ready to call 911 if his leg gave out and he came tumbling down the stairs in an avalanche of tea bags and down feathers.

"Do you want to go on up ahead of me and choose a room?"

"I already have," she told him. "Last room on the right, overlooking the water. It's the one with—"

"Yeah, I know which one it is," he growled, already turning away. "Last room on the right. Your bags will be inside the door."

Something was different. Not necessarily wrong. He didn't have enough to go on to make that determination yet. But definitely different.

His senses had been honed to detect the slightest change in his environment because there was a time when it had meant the difference between survival and that other thing. Bad luck and bad intelligence could screw up a man's leg and end his military career, but once developed, his spider senses remained ever vigilant. They interacted with life on a fundamental level: scent, sound, motion, temperature. And right now they were telling him that something about this morning was different from other mornings.

For starters, he was fully awake and it was still dark. He lay still, staring at the ceiling above his bed and listening intently, and then it came to him . . . the realization that he wasn't alone in the house. Of course. It wasn't some*thing* that was different about this morning: it was some*one*.

Sophie.

Owen held his breath, listening to the sound of water running and then the whisper of slippered feet at the other end of the hall. All the way at the other end. In the room farthest from his own.

There was a message in her choice of rooms. *Keep your distance, Winters.* It was a message he wholeheartedly agreed with and intended to heed. For both their sakes, he would keep his distance.

That didn't mean he had to like it.

There was a light on over the kitchen sink, a cool breeze coming through the half-open window and the rousing aroma of coffee in the air. Which turned out to be a big tease since the coffeepot was as empty and dry as it was every other morning. There wasn't even a jar of instant coffee in sight, although he did notice a few jars of other stuff neatly arranged at the back of the counter. Honey. Apricot preserves. Some sort of grinder with raw sugar crystals and chunks of cinnamon inside.

Sophie was exactly where he recalled her telling him she would be the first time they met: out back waiting for the sun to rise.

She was sitting on the wide steps leading from the patio to the lawn, the lacy yellow shawl pulled around her shoulders a beacon in the darkness, an oversize coffee mug cradled in her hands.

She glanced up as he approached, her pleased smile too quick to be feigned.

"Good morning," she said.

"Private viewing?" he inquired, angling his head toward the ocean, where the sun was still only a soft orange streak on the horizon. "Or would you like some company?"

"I'd love company." Still smiling, she patted the step beside her.

The warmth of her welcome was something of a surprise considering that last night she couldn't get far enough away from him. And in light of his own less than gracious response.

"You're not a coffee drinker?" she ventured as he settled in beside her, leaning back on his elbows with his legs stretched out in front of him.

"I am. I'm just not a coffee maker . . . not coffee worth drinking at any rate. I usually take a ride out to a coffee shop downtown, but I didn't want to miss the show. And I'm not sure they'd even be open yet. I'm not usually up this early."

He yawned as he said it and she slanted him a guilty look. "I'm sorry. Did I wake you? I tried to be quiet."

"You were quiet. I'm a light sleeper."

"Let me make it up to you with a cup of coffee."

"Then you'll miss the show . . . the pot's empty. I checked."

"Oh, I didn't use that. I brought my own single-cup brewer. I'm kind of a creature of habit. I like having my stuff around." As evidence, she sheepishly raised her mug and tugged on the edge of her shawl.

"Well, that explains why you needed a dozen suitcases."

"It was only three . . . it probably just felt like there were a dozen because you were lugging them up the stairs all by yourself."

He shrugged, ignoring the undercurrent of amusement in her tone. "They got there."

"Yes, they did. And I appreciated it. Another reason I owe you a cup of coffee. It will only take a minute. Less than actually. That's the beauty of brewing one cup at a time: it's fast . . . and you can have whatever kind you like. I brought along a full array of flavors . . . caramel crème, island Kona, mocha java . . . what will it be?"

"Hot. Strong. Black."

"Midnight Magic coming right up," she said, getting to her feet and heading inside.

It was fast. It was also the best-tasting cup of coffee he'd had in a long time. Maybe the best ever. Then again, it was entirely possible his judgment was clouded by the foolish rush of pleasure he got from knowing that Sophie had gone to the trouble of making it and bringing it to him. He added that to the growing list of feelings and motives he was being careful not to explore too deeply.

At the very top of that list was his reason for insisting that Sophie move in with him. The explanation he gave her and continued to cling to was perfectly plausible. This powder keg of a wedding was her problem, and by rights, if it was going to blow up in someone's face, it ought to be hers. Ivy Halliday was also her problem. End of story. Whatever else he might have been thinking or feeling when he got the idea to issue that ultimatum didn't matter and didn't bear thinking about.

Keep your distance, Winters.

"Good coffee," he said after several minutes. "Thanks."

"My pleasure. I knew you'd be a Midnight Magic man."

They sat quietly, watching the sun inching its way higher in the sky. The sky itself went from black to gray to blue as night melted into day.

"It really is beautiful, isn't it?"

"It is," agreed Owen.

It *was* a beautiful sight. The stuff of poetry. And he felt suitably boorish over the fact that he was finding it nearly impossible to keep his gaze focused on the magnificent ball of fire rising from the ocean with Sophie sitting only inches away. When he'd first wandered out there to join her, all he could see well was her yellow shawl. As the darkness around them lifted, he gradually saw her more clearly. It was like watching a Polaroid snapshot develop. Or peeling the wrapping paper off a present. And the more clearly he saw her, the more difficult it was to look away.

She was barefoot, wearing a snug, pale gray ribbed tank top and gray knit pants, like sweatpants and yet not at all like sweatpants. Sweatpants were baggy: the top and pants she had on clung to the soft curves of her breasts and thighs and hips in a way he found more fascinating than a thousand sunrises. Her face was scrubbed free of makeup and her hair was haphazardly gathered in a clip on the top of her head. She looked guileless and fresh and vulnerable, and he wanted her more than he'd wanted any woman in a very long time.

Which was just one more crazy incongruity of the sort that had been sneaking up on him ever since Sophie Bennett steamrolled into his life. He shouldn't want her for the very reason he did . . . because she looked guileless and fresh and vulnerable. She was the antithesis of what he looked for in a woman. He looked for polish and sophistication. He looked for long legs and nice tits and a distinctive air of self-absorption that told him the woman was so into herself she'd never notice if he was into her or not. He counted on that high-priced, high-velocity glamour to provide emotional cover and keeps things uncomplicated. You could sleep with a woman like that a hundred times and never get truly close to her. And that's just the way he liked it. To be honest, Sophie's sisters, as annoying as they were, were more his usual type than she could ever be.

He hurriedly shifted his attention back to the horizon as she stretched her arms over her head and turned to him. That smile again. That quick, strange tug on his insides.

"I'm going to give this morning's performance a nine on a scale of one to ten," she announced. "Only so I'll have something to look forward to. It was definitely worth hauling myself out of bed for. And to think I nearly hit the snooze button and skipped it."

Owen paused before taking a gulp of coffee. "So you managed to get some sleep after all."

"Sure. After the day I had yesterday? Why wouldn't I sleep?"

"I just know you were a little uneasy." He sat up so they were shoulder to shoulder. "Last night, I mean."

She shrugged. "Like I said, it's an unusual situation. That's not enough to keep me awake. Especially not when I have my own pillow."

"I meant that you were uneasy around me." When she appeared puzzled, he added, "Why else would you choose the smallest room in the house just to put as much distance between us as possible?"

"Are you kidding? Is that really what you think? That I chose that room because it was the one farthest from yours?"

"Didn't you? I gave you my word that I wouldn't put my hands on you again, but that obviously wasn't enough to put your mind at ease."

"You're wrong. I wasn't uneasy. Trust me," she said, her mouth curving into a rueful smile, "I don't consider myself so irresistible that you'd be driven to jump my bones in the middle of the night.

Unless you were deranged. In which case I wouldn't have accepted your ultimatum in the first place."

"Then why choose a room that small? It seems an especially odd choice for a woman who drags everything she owns around with her."

She heaved a small sigh. "If you must know, I chose it because of the bed."

"All the bedrooms have beds . . . a lot bigger beds than that one."

"Not canopy beds. That's the only room with a canopy bed. A *white* canopy bed. With a white ruffled eyelet canopy and matching dust ruffle . . . and white eyelet-trimmed sheets. Although I didn't know about the sheets when I made my choice."

"I don't know what the hell eyelet is," he countered. "But you're telling me the reason you picked that room was because you wanted to sleep in a bed with a hood over it?"

"Yeah," she admitted, sheepish and defiant at once, something he wouldn't have thought possible. "I mean think about it, how often do you get a chance to sleep in a fancy canopy bed in the Princess House?"

Owen shook his head. He didn't get it.

"It's all because of that stupid Sears catalog," she said.

He shot her a look of confusion.

"When I was a kid, around seven or eight . . ." She gave a small, defensive shrug. "And nine and ten, and maybe eleven, one of the most exciting days of the year was in the fall when the new Sears catalog arrived. I'd commandeer it right away, take it to my room, and open it to—not the toys, although I eventually spent a lot of time on the Barbie doll and bride-dolls pages too—but to the furniture section. Specifically to the white canopy bed with the matching dresser and vanity table and a full-length, oval freestanding mirror. Just like the one in *Snow White*. And I cannot believe I'm admitting any of this out loud," she groaned, rolling her eyes and shaking her head.

"It was my fantasy dream bedroom," she explained. "My vision of the ultimate in luxury and style. When I wasn't dreaming of running away and joining the circus, I was dreaming of being a princess and sleeping in that bed. It never happened, of course, since I already had a perfectly good, sensible bedroom set. So when I saw that canopy bed upstairs, I figured what the hell and I went for it."

It was the damn bed, thought Owen. She hadn't been trying to get as far as possible away from him. Not that it mattered, he reminded himself. She could be sleeping in the room next door . . . hell, she could be sleeping in the same bed and she would still be off-limits to him.

"So tell me," he said, "did it live up to your expectations?"

She grinned with delight. "Pretty much. I guess you're never too old for some dreams."

"Or too young for them," he said without meaning to, and then felt obliged to explain. "I was . . . thinking about Allie. She was three the first time I read *The Princess House* to her and from that day on it was her favorite book. I read somewhere that this place had been the artist's inspiration for the house on the cover, so I brought her here to see it."

"She must have been thrilled to see it come to life . . . I know I was."

"She was," he said, remembering that day. "After that, we came here a lot. Her mother and I had split by that time and it became a weekly routine when the weather was good. She was my fishing buddy. We'd fish at that little cove I showed you and then hike along Cliff Walk to get here."

"You made her walk all that way?"

"Well, it's not like I could pull into the front drive and park.

Besides, I did the walking: Allie rode on my shoulders most of the way. I'd pack a lunch and we'd sit in the shade of those huge bushes and have a picnic." He pointed to a spot at the very edge of the property.

"You never ran into Ivy?"

Owen shook his head. "Technically we were trespassing, so I did my best not to get noticed." He smiled briefly. "Of course, Allie wasn't nearly as concerned about that as I was. She'd eat two bites of her peanut butter and jelly sandwich and then be off running in circles, picking daisies so I could make her a princess crown . . . which she then insisted on wearing until the next week when I made her a new one. I imagine if she could have seen that canopy bed, she'd have wanted to sleep in it too."

"I'm guessing that it's no accident that you ended up living here."

He hunched forward and stared at the bushes, seeing instead something that happened a long time ago. "No, not exactly an accident. More of an impulse buy. Now I own the whole damn place, enough daisies to make a thousand crowns, and Allie's gone."

"But you made her those daisy crowns when it counted, and you'll always have the memory. I know it's not enough, not nearly, but it's something. And sometimes that's all you get."

He nodded and felt her hand rest briefly on his arm.

"Okay," she said, her tone taking a no-nonsense turn. "I confessed a deep, dark, and totally humiliating secret from my past to you. Now it's your turn. Fair's fair," she added as if to forestall any argument.

He eyed her warily. "What kind of secret?"

"The juicier the better," she drawled.

"I just confessed to trespassing."

"Tch. That's not even close to being juicy enough." She laughed at his sudden frown and knocked her shoulder against his. "Don't panic; I'm teasing. I want you to tell me . . ." She chewed her bottom lip, thinking. Her eyes brightened. "I know: tell me how you hurt your leg."

"I wouldn't call that juicy," he said. "It's not even much of a secret."

"It doesn't have to be an actual secret secret." She slanted him a look of amused exasperation. "The whole concept of friendly bantering is lost on you, isn't it?"

"It's just that getting injured isn't something I usually talk about."

"You think I go around sharing my embarrassing canopy-bed fantasy with everyone I meet?"

He hunched forward, fingers laced, saying nothing.

Sophie touched his shoulder lightly. "Look, it's no big deal. If you really don't want to talk about it—"

"It's not that. I guess I'm just not used to talking about myself at all." He stretched his leg out and stared at it. "I got hurt in the military. While I was still on active duty. It's what put an end to active duty for me."

"Were you in the army?"

"I started out there. Worked up to being a Ranger and eventually I was assigned to a multiforces unit."

"Is that like special ops or something?" Sophie asked. "And I should probably warn you that everything I know on the subject I learned from action movies."

He smiled at that. "Special ops covers a lot of territory. My unit specialized in off-the-books extractions. Missions of Last Resort, we called them."

"Sounds dangerous."

"The military is a dangerous place. You know that going in and you're trained to deal with whatever they throw at you."

"So what exactly is an off-the-books extraction?"

"Off-the-books means we operated under the auspices of the JSMC—Joint Special Mission Command—and that there was a minimal paper trail for whatever we did. Extractions . . . well, bad guys have a nasty tendency to take things that don't belong to them . . . weapons, classified documents, the occasional diplomat. Sometimes they make demands in exchange for their return: sometimes they don't. It doesn't really matter since official policy is that we don't negotiate with scumbags of any kind. We also don't like losing weapons and documents and diplomats to them. That's where I come in. It's my job to get whatever—or whomever—they took back by whatever means necessary. *Was* my job," he amended.

"And that's what you were doing when you injured your leg?"

Owen nodded. "The military especially doesn't like losing its own. We got the call after a reconnaissance chopper went down in Afghanistan. It was a two-man crew: only one survived and we had good local intel that he was being held in a mountain cave on the Pakistan border. It's never easy, but this was a pretty standard extraction for us. We were air-dropped in and then it was a four-and-a-half-hour climb to the cave."

"My God, this really is like an action movie. A four-and-a-half-hour climb would kill me."

His mouth quirked. "It would be shorter, but you can't go all out at that altitude or you'll be spent. When we got close to the cave, we set up our ORP—that's objective rally point—and the two of us making the final approach to the target went into full assault mode. It was late and it was cold and there were only three captors on watch. We . . ." He hesitated, glancing sideways at her as she hung on every word as raptly as if she were watching a film. "We dealt with them, grabbed our guy, and got out. He was in real rough shape and it wasn't until we were on our way back to the pickup zone that he suddenly looked around and asked us where his partner was."

"I thought . . ."

"Yeah. So did we. But the local intel got it wrong. Or maybe they wanted to double-dip and get paid twice. Both guys survived the crash and one was still in that cave. There are two things you don't want to do on a mission: veer from the plan, and linger too long. I had to make the call on the spot."

"And?" she demanded.

"I went back. Those caves are like damn wormholes; they twist and turn and keep going deeper. I finally reached the second guy and he was in even rougher shape that his buddy. I got him out, but there was no way he was going to make it to the pickup zone under his own power. So we found a spot with enough clearance—barely—for a Chinook to come in and drop a line for him. Not an easy thing to do in the mountains. It takes time, and it's loud. Damn loud. Loud enough to attract exactly the kind of attention we didn't want.

"I strapped him into the harness and grabbed the line and we were about twenty feet in the air when we started taking fire."

Her eyes filled with concern. "They were shooting at you? You got shot?"

Owen shook his head. "No, but they hit the chopper and sent it reeling. We lucked out because the pilot really knew his stuff. He got it back under control, but not before we got slammed into a solid wall of rock. A couple of times, as I recall."

"That's how your leg got hurt."

He gave a short, humorless chuckle. "Believe me, everything hurt, every last bit of me, but my left leg and hip got the worst of it . . . shattered femur, torn everything. I've got pins holding together parts I didn't know I had."

"You poor thing. I can't even imagine how much pain you must have been in. How long were you in the hospital?"

"Four months. Six operations. And then a whole lot of rehab to get me back on my feet . . . literally."

"That must have been a really tough time. I can understand why you don't like talking about it."

"It was tough," he admitted, "but it also had its bright spots. Allie, for one. For a couple of those months she was out of school and she came and stayed with me. It was the first time we'd lived together since she was two." He stared straight ahead. "Now I'm . . . well, I'm thankful I had that time with her, no matter the price."

"I'll bet she felt the same way. My God, she must have been so proud to have a hero for a dad. You saved that man's life . . . both men."

"I didn't do it alone."

"You went back alone!" she exclaimed. "You went up on that rope thing with people shooting at you alone. If you ask me they should have given you a huge bonus and the biggest medal they have."

He couldn't help chuckling at her vehemence. "No bonus. No medals. No paper trail: no fanfare. That's how the game is played."

"Well, that sucks. And it's not fair. If it were me, I'd want everyone to know how brave I was."

"I doubt that."

She folded her arms across her chest, looking torn between suspicion and indignation. "What's that supposed to mean?"

"It means you don't give yourself credit or demand credit for a lot of the things you accomplish. It means that since I've gotten to know you and watched you work I've broadened my definition of bravery and loyalty and honor."

"I'm not sure why. I've never climbed a single mountain," she reminded him. "Or rescued anyone from a cave."

"And I've never talked a single bride off a ledge."

She made a face. "That's not quite the same thing."

"I'm not saying it's the same. I'm saying I've seen the way you work. What you do isn't just a job to you: it's a mission . . . and it's an important one because of how much the outcome matters to the people involved. You do what it takes to get it done right for them. And I respect that."

"Well . . ." She shrugged, looking both pleased and flummoxed. Was she so unaccustomed to compliments? Owen wondered. Or simply surprised it came from him? "Thanks. I just hope you don't revise your opinion when this is done. I did some tossing and turning last night. I'm worried Ivy may be tougher to win over than I hoped. I have a tendency to tackle problems by looking on the bright side and running with it."

"No kidding. I've gotten mowed down trying to play defense against a couple of your looking-on-the-bright-side plays."

"If only it worked that well on Ivy. So far she seems a lot less susceptible to my approach. Hell, I can't even get her to come out of hiding and hear me out."

"I'm still available if you want to try the tough-love approach."

"You mean toss out the stuff she loves? Thanks, but I'm not desperate enough to declare all-out war. Yet."

"Then I'd say you've got your work cut out for you. As far as I know, there's no course in how to communicate with wayward ghosts."

She swung her head around to look at him, her eyes widening slightly. And then she laughed, an all-out whoop of excitement that had him smiling even as he braced himself for what might be coming next.

"You're a genius," she told him. "You just gave me a great idea."

"Again?" he countered. He really had to stop inspiring her to make his life more difficult.

"Yep. I can't believe I didn't think of it before now. It just so happens I know someone who could teach that course. And she's the perfect person to help me connect with Ivy."

"I'll bite. At the risk of knowing more than I want to, I have to ask. How?"

"Easy. One word. *Séance*."

Twelve

There was no guarantee the séance would work, but it was way ahead of Sophie's next-best idea simply because she had no other ideas. The Queen of the Backup Plan had hit a wall when it came to communicating with Ivy . . . as she now found herself thinking of her, rather than as "the ghost bride." Owen was right: she had a name . . . and a past. Complete with hopes and dreams and heartaches. And it was now Sophie's hope that the séance would remove some of the baggage from the past and pave the way for a happy ending for all of them.

As soon as she made up her mind to give the séance a shot, she was eager to get on with it. Unfortunately, Carla Bonnet, the one person she trusted to make it happen, wasn't available for a week. The delay translated to seven long days of small disasters and petty annoyances. Not to mention the ongoing challenge of explaining random weird noises, sudden temperature changes, and other various and sundry odd occurrences to whoever happened to be around at the time. Ivy took top honors in both persistence and innovation and every day brought a new challenge.

On Tuesday, the instructions for the landscapers that she'd left pinned to the back door mysteriously disappeared, replaced by alternative instructions that mentioned nothing about the wide stretch of daisies growing wild at the far edge of the lawn, the daisies that WERE NOT UNDER ANY CIRCUMSTANCES TO BE DISTURBED. The daisies were important to Owen: they were a link to the past, and to his daughter, Allie. Sophie understood and she was fine with leaving the daisies untouched. They added a whimsical touch that was in keeping with the enchanted forest of the wedding's *Midsummers Night* theme. Unfortunately the guys on the ride-on mowers weren't so tolerant; where Owen saw something worth protecting, they saw only blight on the green velvet turf they were being paid to maintain. A melee ensued. She rushed outside and managed to calm Owen's fury over the daisies that had already lost their heads, and then she stood on the lawn and supervised as the crew created a natural-looking line of demarcation to establish a no-mow zone going forward.

On Wednesday, she was catching up on paperwork when the window-washing crew went ballistic because they suddenly found themselves squeegeeing jet-black water from the windowpanes. It was as if, in the words of one man, someone had come along and squirted black ink into all their buckets. But who would do something like that . . . who *could* do something like that without being seen?

Who indeed?

Grumbling and unhappy, they emptied their pails and started over, but naturally the ink turned out to be oil-based, so that when it dripped from the glass onto the white window frames it had stained them, adding another job to the to-do list from hell.

Day after day her cell phone disappeared and reappeared minutes or hours later. It happened so many times—resulting in dozens of missed calls and messages as she searched for it—that she finally went MacGyver and jimmied a way to hang it on a cord around her neck. It wasn't pretty, but it worked . . . at least it worked when Ivy wasn't screwing around with the reception.

And then there was the ongoing, random cacophony of slamming doors, falling objects, and strange noises in the walls and ceiling. They spooked the work crews and they also finally drove Owen and his laptop out of his office to work in the guesthouse.

Sophie missed him.

She missed bumping into him here or there as they both went about their days. She missed that little tickle of anticipation she felt just knowing she might bump into him. She missed seeing him smirk and shake his head over Ivy's latest stunt. She missed that drift of fresh, sort-of-soap and sort-of-pine scent she smelled whenever he was close.

At least he continued to join her for coffee at sunrise. She secretly thought of that as "their time." Time to talk about how the wedding plans were progressing and about the day ahead. Time to laugh over yesterday's disasters, which never seemed at all funny at the time, but somehow became less nerve-racking and more amusing when she was sharing them with Owen. Time to become friends.

Sometimes they ended up in the same place at the end of the day too, sharing a sandwich or a bowl of popcorn in the small den with the humongous, man-cave-worthy TV that had been Owen's contribution to the decor. He was turning her into a fairly knowledgeable Red Sox fan and she'd introduced him to the wonderful world of cooking shows. Although he'd disparaged them at first, the shows must have been growing on him because he kept coming back to watch. Sophie had to laugh at his disgruntled announcement that not only did he now understood what ceviche was and how a pressure cooker worker, he could even name a few of the *Top Chef* contenders.

As much as possible he stayed out of Ivy's way and left all damage control to Sophie. That was his reason for wanting her there around the clock after all. It seemed to Sophie that the séance was an exception, however. He didn't talk about it. In fact, outwardly he maintained a bemused skepticism about the whole thing, but as the day of the event grew closer she could sense his anticipation mounting along with her own.

"She's late," he said, wandering into the kitchen at approximately four minutes after eight on Friday evening.

Sophie glanced up from the pitcher of iced tea she was making, not at all surprised that he'd remembered that tonight was the night or that he was also watching the clock. "She called to say she'd hit traffic and would be a few minutes late." She held up the glass pitcher. "Iced tea?"

"Sure."

"You said this woman is a friend of yours?"

"Not really a friend," she replied as she grabbed a tray of ice cubes from the freezer. "Seasons handled her sister's wedding last year, so we spent a lot of time together at dress fittings and the like, and I remembered that she did this kind of thing . . . séances, consultations. And I trust her to be discreet."

Shouldering the freezer door shut, she got a lemon from the fridge, where the wall-to-wall beer bottles had slowly but surely given way to real food: fresh fruits and veggies, Greek yogurt, sliced turkey and lobster salad from the great little deli she'd discovered not too far away. Prior to her moving in, Owen had lived on drive-through fare and whatever he could have delivered. He didn't seem to mind the change at all; in fact he even mentioned picking up a couple of steaks and firing up the grill on the weekend. Sophie repeatedly reminded herself not to read too much into the offer, or anything else he said or did. It would be so easy for her to get carried away with . . . possibilities. In spite of what she'd told the Js about knowing exactly what she was getting into, there were times when she wondered what the hell she'd gotten herself into. Handsome man, killer smile, two lonely people marooned together in a fairy-tale castle under precarious and emotionally charged conditions. She'd read enough romance novels to know how that story ended. But life wasn't a romance novel. At least hers wasn't: she had to remember that.

Owen ambled over to take the lemon from her. He tossed it in the air and caught it a few times and then stood beside her to slice it while she poured the tea. Instantly Sophie was engulfed by him. Not only by his familiar scent that made her want to inhale deeply, putting her in danger of hyperventilating; she felt swamped by *him* . . . his nearness . . . his *thereness*. Her brain might know better, but as far as her senses were concerned, when he was in the room . . . when he was that close, he was all there was.

He put down the knife.

She reached for a slice of lemon.

And their hands brushed.

Sophie's pulse jumped and her gaze shot to meet his.

His blue eyes were dark, his expression somber and guarded, but there was no hiding the feeling of explosive awareness that suddenly thickened the air between them. There were no words. Only the *tick, tick, tick* of the kitchen wall clock.

And then, the sudden trill of the doorbell.

Damn!

She pulled her hand back.

Owen cleared his throat. "Must be Clara."

"Carla," she corrected automatically. "Carla Bonnet. I'll go let her in."

She practically jogged to the front door. Hopefully Carla would assume it was because she was rushing that she was breathless, instead of guessing the embarrassing, adolescent truth . . . that she had gotten all flustered because a cute guy had touched her hand. Sheesh. *Snap out of it,* she told herself. Then she told herself she ought to be thankful and not annoyed that Carla had arrived when she did. For good measure she reminded herself that she was there to work, and that she didn't have time for distractions. No matter how good they smelled.

Her *self* listened to all of it without enthusiasm.

"That's her?" inquired Owen, frowning as he glanced through the sidelights at the woman standing on the front steps. "That's Clara the hotshot psychic?"

"Carla."

"Sorry. Clara just sounds like a more fitting name. Like Clara the zany sidekick. Or Clara the wacky neighbor."

"Be that as it may, her name is Carla. And yes. That's her. Why," she demanded when she saw his dubious expression. "What's wrong with her?"

He shrugged. "She's just not what I pictured. I expected her to show up wearing . . ." He gestured toward his head. "You know, big hoop earrings and some kind of red silk turban thing. Maybe a cape."

"I think you have her confused with Ali Baba . . . or Harry Potter."

"Let's just say I expected her to look more like a psychic and less like a lawyer."

"She's not a psychic. Not exactly."

"I just assumed . . . what is she exactly?"

"A college professor. She teaches Anthropology of the Occult at Brown, and she writes about all things paranormal. Séances and consultations are something she does for research purposes, and also because she's genuinely interested. She downplays having any special psychic gift, but she does describe herself as an empath. That means she's especially sensitive to—"

"I know what an empath is." He was still peering through the sidelight, looking unconvinced. "I thought she'd at least bring a Ouija board. No way is that bag big enough to hold a Ouija board."

"Maybe they've downsized them," Sophie retorted, shaking her head as she opened the door and welcomed Carla inside.

Slender, with short dark hair and pretty dark eyes, she did appear a little lawyerly in a simple black suit and heels, the look only slightly softened by a pale blue silk T-shirt under the jacket. But then she had said she'd been busy all week with curriculum planning sessions. That probably explained the suit.

"Thanks for coming, Carla," Sophie said. "I'm really in a jam here, and when the idea of a séance came up, you're the first person I thought to call."

"I'm so glad you did. Just from the little you told me, it sounds like a fascinating case." She gazed around. "Wow. This is quite a place."

"Isn't it amazing?" agreed Sophie. "And this is the man who owns it . . . and who has graciously agreed to let my client be married here. Owen Winters, this is Dr. Carla Bonnet. Carla, Owen Winters."

Carla's brows lifted as she offered her hand to shake. "*The* Owen Winters? Author of *The Fane Chronicles*?"

"Guilty as charged," he replied. "It's a pleasure to meet you, Dr. Bonnet."

"Please, just Carla. And it's a treat to meet you. I'm a big fan of your books."

He gave a small nod. "Well, it's flattering to know I have an Ivy League professor of the occult as a reader."

"Are you working on a new book now?" she asked.

"I am."

From her eager expression it was clear she would love to have him elaborate. And it was also clear—at least to Sophie—that he wasn't going to. He didn't talk about his work. At first she thought that was just more of the same since he wasn't comfortable talking about himself in general. Lately, however, she'd come to suspect it wasn't his work, but his work progress he didn't want to discuss . . . and that there might be more getting in his way than either Ivy or the wedding.

Silent, he regarded Carla with what looked to Sophie like interest bordering on speculation. She wasn't surprised. Even in drab business attire, Carla had a sultry, exotic look that turned heads. Men's heads in particular. And both being writers, they shared a common bond. It was only natural he'd be interested. Then he spoke and she realized it wasn't Carla's writing or her sultriness Owen was thinking about.

"So," he said, folding his arms across his chest. "No Ouija board?"

Smiling, Carla shook her head. "I'm afraid not. I've never had much luck with them. I did bring along a few crystals," she added, tapping the black leather bag slung over her shoulder. "Those and some candles are about as high tech as I get." She turned to Sophie. "The candles are because I prefer to work without overhead light and I never know what will be available where I'm going. The crystals I arrange on the table in front of me to help gather and focus the energy in the room."

Sophie nodded. "I'm all for doing whatever makes you comfortable . . . and whatever works. While we're on the subject of high tech, I wanted to ask if you have any objection to the séance being recorded." She quickly explained. "I just don't want to miss anything and I thought it might be good to have a record of everything that happens to review later."

"I have no objection at all, though in the past I've found it's usually better to have a third party do the recording. That way you can focus your energy on making a connection with whoever shows up."

"I thought of that, and I'm also not particularly tech savvy myself, so I had one of Seasons' assistants come out and set up the equipment ahead of time. Josh is a whiz with everything electronic and he fixed it so it's completely out of the way and all I have to do is hit one button and we're up and running."

"That sounds fine."

Noticing Carla's curious glance at the cell phone hanging on a cord around her neck, Sophie gave her a rueful smile and shrugged. "It's been a long week, filled with ghost tricks like the disappearing cell phone."

"You poor thing. I'm sorry I couldn't get here sooner."

"I'm just glad you're here now. You mentioned choosing a central location, so I had Josh set the camera up in the dining room. I can't wait to get started."

"We will," said Carla. "But first I'd like to do a walk-through so I can get a feeling for the house itself."

"All right. Let me show you around: it will give me a chance to fill you in on what we've found out about the woman who used to live here."

"Actually," Carla said as she fell into step beside her, "I'd rather get a clean impression of the house first. No preconceptions. Then you can share with me whatever background information you have. And *then* we'll see if we can persuade your elusive ghost to join us."

The walk-through didn't take long. Most often Carla stopped a few steps inside a room and glanced around. The only place she lingered was in the room at the top of the stairs where Sophie had first encountered Ivy. While Sophie waited at the door, she walked slowly around the room, pausing to rest the fingertips of both hands on the dressing table without saying anything and then moving to the bed and curling her hands around the rail at the foot of the bed, as if the old, polished wood had secrets to tell.

"This was her room," she announced finally, her tone matter-of-fact. She moved to the door connecting with the adjoining room and opened it. "And this was designed to be the nursery. It was never used."

She closed the door very gently and gazed around the room again.

"There's great heartache here," she told Sophie. "And great longing."

She spoke with quiet certitude and tears pricked the back of Sophie's eyelids. She bit her lip to hold them back.

Great heartache and great longing.

Since moving into the house, she'd been doing a lot of thinking about Ivy. In spite of all the aggravation she caused, Sophie found herself feeling a kinship with her. They had things in common. Not the made-to-order castle or the family fortune obviously, but both Ivy and she had had their hearts broken by men they'd loved and trusted and they had both survived and gone on to make satisfactory lives for themselves. At least on the surface.

Had Ivy been satisfied to live in that big, beautiful house alone? Carla's insights made her wonder. After being left at the altar, she had traveled extensively and dabbled in horticulture and photography, as well as being involved with several charities. But she had never married. Never had a family. Only a nephew who had been disinterested enough to dispose of her beloved home, part and parcel, from the other side of the country.

After standing by the window for a moment, Carla moved to the center of the room, took a deep breath, and closed her eyes. When she opened them she met Sophie's gaze and nodded.

"I'm ready," she said.

* * *

They were seated in the dining room. Carla sat at the head of the long table with Owen and Sophie on either side of her. She had listened intently and without comment while Sophie ran down the pertinent details of Ivy Halliday's life. Fairly certain that Ivy was in the vicinity and would not take kindly to either pity or amateur psychology, she chose her words carefully.

When Carla finished listening, her expression was somber and thoughtful. "It's easy to see how the idea of having a wedding here could be a sore point for her."

"I understand that, believe me. I don't blame her for being upset. That's exactly why I want to reach out to her and try to make her see that this isn't just any wedding. I want to explain to her what a great kid Shelby is and how much it means to her to be married here. To her this is *The Princess House* and she's loved it since she was a little girl. It's something she shared with her dad when he was alive. I think if I can appeal to Ivy's kindness and generosity—"

Somewhere upstairs a door slammed.

The three of them exchanged looks.

"Kindness and generosity," Owen repeated. "Good luck with that."

"It could have been the wind," Sophie insisted.

He snickered.

"I understand what you're hoping to do," Carla told her, "but as I explained when we spoke on the phone, this isn't a science. There's no guarantee it will work. And even if we do succeed in connecting with a spirit in this house, it could happen in a number of ways."

"Such as?" Owen prompted.

"I've conducted séances where the only response was the vibra-

tion of the table, or random noises. There could be a silent appari-
tion, or even some form of psychography . . . automatic writing.
That's why I always have a pen and paper handy." She indicated
the notebook in front of her. "What I'm saying is that I can't promise you there will be a dialogue, or that she'll even listen to anything you have to say."

"What can you promise?" inquired Owen.

"That I'll do my best."

"That's good enough for me," declared Sophie. "What's next?"

Carla took several items from her bag and arranged them on
the table in front of her. "This is my own interpretation of a traditional séance. Some of the elements date all the way back to Nos-
tradamus. Sandalwood oil," she explained, placing a small
earthenware bowl on the table and pouring a small amount of oil
into it. Next she placed three white candles around the bowl and
lit them.

"The oil and candles create a welcoming atmosphere of light
and warmth. The crystals help ward off negative energy and gather
the positive."

With the crystals in place, she turned to Owen. "I know that
your interest here is divided. There's someone else, another spirit,
someone close to you, someone you've lost, whom you're hoping
to make contact with." He started to shake his head, but she
stopped him. "There's nothing wrong with that, but I have such a
strong sense that what you're hoping for is not going to happen
that I felt I should say something. It will be better if you're not
distracted by other thoughts." She seemed to hesitate before adding, "When there's no unfinished business, a spirit moves on." She
smiled. "That's not a bad thing."

"I understand," he said quietly. "And . . . thanks."

Allie, thought Sophie. Of course Owen was thinking about the
daughter he'd lost. Thinking and hoping. She hoped he took com-

fort from Carla's insight that Allie could move on because she was at peace.

"So do you think unfinished business is what's keeping Ivy here?" she asked Carla.

"Pretty much. Or perhaps she just thinks there's unfinished business and she's keeping herself here. Whatever the cause, I'm as certain as I can be that she's tethered to this house . . . and that her energy is directly linked to her strong emotional connection to this place."

"Does that mean that if she was to go out into the yard or down the street, she wouldn't have the same power or ability or whatever you want to call it . . . that she couldn't move things around or—"

"Slam a drawer on someone's fingers," interjected Owen in a dry tone.

Carla nodded. "That's right. I think if she left this house, her energy would slowly dissipate, and she would most likely have to move on . . . ready or not. Be that as it may, within these walls, she's a power to be reckoned with. She has a strong and turbulent history here . . . it's like a tapestry of emotions that have built up over a lot of years. Lots of different colors and textures."

"And that's what she draws energy from?"

"Yes. Either consciously or not," Carla replied. "And the stronger the emotional connection, the more energy she'll pull. Usually a ghost uses gathered energy to either manifest or to manipulate their surroundings . . . slam a drawer shut, move a vase. One thing at a time. But you told me that Ivy has done both at the same time."

"Yes. That first day in the bedroom. I saw her and heard her *and* she moved things around. Since then I haven't actually seen her . . . although she's sure done plenty of manipulating," Sophie added, her mouth curving in a wry smile.

"She obviously has the power to materialize at will. Let's hope she sees fit to appear tonight. Shall we get on with it?"

While Carla lit the candles, Sophie started the recording equipment Josh had set up on the mahogany buffet. She and Owen followed Carla's example and placed their palms flat on the table, with the tips of their pinkie fingers just touching the person beside them. Carla gently guided them in taking a few deep breaths and relaxing their muscles. In a soft, soothing tone, she urged them to focus their thoughts on connecting with Ivy. After several quiet moments she began with a blessing.

"We invoke the Power of the Sword of Michael and the Angels of Protection to surround and protect us. We invoke the Power of the Light and we align ourselves with the Love of the Universe. We come together with open hearts and pure intentions, to learn and to better understand every stage and aspect of life. We seek harmony with all and harbor malice toward none. May our circle and our efforts be blessed."

She paused for a few seconds and then, in a warm and friendly tone, said, "Ivy Halliday, will you please honor us with your company and join our circle?" She spoke slowly and calmly, pausing between sentences to wait for a response. "Sophie and Owen and I have come together this evening especially to speak with you. We're eager to hear whatever you have to share with us about this beautiful house which was once yours."

Immediately the temperature in the room plummeted.

Sophie was pretty sure it was the "was once yours" that Ivy objected to. Something told her it was going to take more than a deed or a death certificate to change Ivy's view that the house was hers and always would be.

"Deep breaths," Carla reminded them. "Relax your shoulders. Focus."

Sophie tried to relax her muscles, but it wasn't easy to do while shivering. It was *that* cold.

"Ivy, are you here with us now?" Carla asked. "I sense another presence in the room, but we can't be sure it's you unless you communicate with us. Please share your thoughts with us."

Silence. Ivy wasn't biting. Sophie noticed that when she exhaled she could see her breath. She wished she'd worn something a little warmer, but of course, she'd had no idea when she chose a gauzy cotton skirt and tank top that she'd be risking frostbite. Was it possible to get frostbite indoors? she wondered. In August? And if she did, how would she explain it to the folks at the ER?

Carla tried again.

"Ivy, if you can, please give us a sign that you understand."

She'd barely uttered the last word when the candles sputtered out, leaving the room in near darkness. The only light came from a lamp in an adjoining room.

"All right, Ivy. Thank you for that sign. Now I have another request." Carla's tone was steady and unhurried. "Sophie would like to speak with you about the wedding that she's—"

That's as far as she got before the video camera came flying across the room, causing all three of them to duck. It whizzed past them and crashed hard against the opposite wall before landing in pieces on the floor. So much for reviewing the action later.

"Well, that was close," Sophie said, straightening cautiously.

"Too close," growled Owen, running a concerned gaze over Sophie. "That damn thing missed you by an inch. Who the hell does this woman think she—"

He broke off as the candles reignited on their own, the flames flaring high in the air and then cascading onto the table in a puddle of fire while the candles remained standing.

Immediately Owen was on his feet and using a linen place mat to smother the flames. As he did, a loud whooshing sound drew their attention to the white marble fireplace at the end of the room, where another blaze ignited. Both Sophie and Carla scrambled to their feet.

Owen swore as he headed in the direction of the kitchen, nearly tripping over a chair in the process. There was no longer any light coming from the other room. *Great,* thought Sophie. In addition to the pyrotechnics, Ivy was playing with the circuit breakers again. There was no moon in the sky and the house was set far back from the streetlights of Bellevue Avenue. She flipped open the cell phone hanging around her neck: the screen light was better than nothing, but not by much.

Owen was back quickly, bringing a small fire extinguisher from the kitchen. He sprayed the embers on the table in passing and then turned it full force on the fireplace, where the fire was roaring without benefit of firewood or any other fuel.

When the candles reignited a second time, Sophie grabbed the place mat and went to work.

"Oh no. This isn't good," muttered Carla. She no longer sounded relaxed or patient, but it was too dark for Sophie to see her expression clearly.

Sophie was still slapping at the flames—which were a lot more resistant to being squelched this time around—when Owen came over and grabbed the candles. "I'll take care of these."

Before she could ask just how he intended to do this, there was a loud crash in the hall as the front door flew open. It was quickly followed by the high-pitched wail of a car alarm. Correction: two car alarms.

"My car," Carla exclaimed as she bent down and began feeling around on the floor beside where she'd been sitting. "My bag . . . my bag. Where's my damn bag?"

Sophie moved through the darkness to find her own keys and she and Carla ended up on the front steps together, aiming and clicking their remotes to turn off the alarms. The sudden quiet was a relief, but her heart continued its frenzied pounding. The calm might simply be the eye of the hurricane.

Owen joined them and they waited, silent and stiff and edgy, like cats poised to pounce at the drop of a feather.

When a minute passed, and then two, and nothing happened, Carla heaved a deep sigh and turned to Sophie. "Well. That was . . . scary as all hell. God, Sophie, I'm so sorry for all this."

"Don't be. It wasn't your fault."

"Something I did—or said—provoked her."

"She was already provoked. And besides, the séance was my idea. You were only trying to help."

"I'm afraid I only made things worse. You really have your work cut out for you here. Have you considered moving the wedding somewhere else?"

Sophie shook her head, ignoring Owen's quiet snigger. "No." She crossed her arms in front of her. She didn't like conflict, but something about being bullied and threatened with fire and flying video equipment had brought out the stubborn in her. "Shelby has her heart set on being married here. And I have mine set on not seeing the time and effort I've already put in go to waste. The wedding is going to be here and that's that."

The front door slammed shut.

The lock clicked.

Séance over.

They had no trouble getting back into the house thanks to the keys Owen had hidden outside.

Fool me twice, shame on me.

The problem apppeared once they were back inside. The lights were still out and Ivy had been busy rearranging things so that making their way to the kitchen, where Sophie recalled seeing a flashlight, was like tackling an obstacle course blindfolded. Owen led the way: he whacked his shin a couple of times and singed the air with a string of suitably uncomplimentary observations about Ivy. Going second gave Sophie an advantage and she made it most of the way before being blindsided by an open door and ending up with an egg on the side of her head.

"You okay?" he asked when she cried out.

"Yeah. Stupid door. Stupid ghost."

"No argument here," he retorted. "I still say it's time to get tough."

"Maybe," she allowed. "My approach was certainly a spectacular failure. I mean, the séance literally crashed and burned."

"It was still worth a shot," he allowed in a gruff tone. "Now you can say you tried and you don't have to feel guilty when I haul a Dumpster out front and start chucking her crap into it."

Sophie listened for some reaction from Ivy . . . a slamming door, a rattling window, an explosion in the middle of the living room. Nothing. Maybe she'd worn herself out. Or maybe she was afraid she'd gone too far and that this time Sophie might not stop Owen from carrying out his threats. Sophie rubbed her head where it hurt. She was right to worry: at that moment not only would she not stop him, she just might join in. Hurling china and crystal would at least burn off some tension.

She was tired and stressed and time was running out. She'd tried to reason with Ivy and failed. Owen was right: the time for diplomacy was over.

It was time to get tough.

Thirteen

✳

"Y ou're sure the flashlight was in this cupboard?"
Owen's question pulled her from her thoughts. She heard
the clink of china and glass as he felt around in the cupboard next
to the refrigerator.

"I think it was that one." She thought more and added, "Or
else maybe the next one over. No, it was definitely the next one. I
remember now: I saw it when I was looking for a container for the
strawberries."

He yanked open the door of the adjacent cupboard and was
immediately caught in an avalanche of various-size plastic storage
containers and lids. They bounced off him and scattered noisily
across the floor of the kitchen.

"Booby trap," she murmured.

"That's it," Owen snapped. Roughly kicking aside containers,
he started toward the door to the basement.

Sophie hurried after him, catching her toe in the handle of a
plastic bowl and shaking it off. "Where are you going?"

"To do what I should have done to begin with . . . I'm going down to throw the damn breaker so we can see what the hell we're doing."

"Wait. You can't go down there without a flashlight."

"We don't have a flashlight."

"We do. I saw it. We just have to figure out which cupboard it was in."

He stopped and turned to her. "Right . . . *was* in. Past tense. Don't you get it? She knew we'd go looking for the flashlight, so she hid it. It could be anywhere. A different cupboard. My sock drawer. The roof."

"I wish I could say you're being paranoid, but the fact is you're probably right. Except for the part about the roof. Her power only exists inside this house, remember?"

"That didn't stop her from triggering your car alarm."

"True," she conceded, sighing unhappily. "You know, when Carla said she was tethered to the house, I almost began to get my hopes up. I figured, hey, outdoor wedding, it could work in spite of her meddling. And then she goes and strikes in the driveway." She shook her head. "Carla said it only proves she can project a certain distance from the house. We just don't know precisely what that distance is . . . and I don't want to find out the day of the wedding with a hundred and fifty guests in the line of fire."

"I don't care what the distance is. She can project all she wants. And she can keep the flashlight," declared Owen. "I'm done letting her yank my chain."

Sophie grabbed his arm as he started to turn away. "I still say going down there in the dark is too risky."

"I'll go slowly."

"Go slowly? That's your grand plan for avoiding whatever other booby traps she has waiting for you?"

"Sophie, I've crawled on my belly through a football field's worth of land mines: I think I can handle whatever one old lady—

one *dead* old lady—can throw at me." There was more than a hint of animosity in his voice and he raised it so it was loud enough to be heard throughout the house.

"Don't be so sure," she told him. "I'm not questioning your ability, but let's face it, Ivy is very resourceful. And highly motivated. And while we have actual lives to distract us, she has all day to sit around plotting her next move. Maybe all night too. For all we know ghosts don't sleep."

"I don't care if she sleeps. No one is going to jerk me around in my own home. My own home," he repeated, again raising his voice to make sure he was heard.

"Fine. Go play conquering hero . . . but if you fall on the stairs I'm not going down there in the pitch dark to rescue you."

"Fine."

"I mean it. You could trip and bang your head. Remember the Gentle Gardener? You could be knocked unconscious. Or worse. Last time she planted a golf club on the stairs: tonight it could be a machete."

"I'm not going to trip."

"You do realize you're being stupid? Pigheaded and macho and stupid."

"Anything else?"

She wished she could see his eyes. Was he laughing at her? Offended? Serious about going down to the cellar unarmed? She tightened her hold on his arm.

"I mean it, Owen. I . . . I just don't want anything to happen to you, okay?"

Silence. His head angled to the side. In the darkness, Sophie couldn't see his surprise, but she sensed it. She felt him considering her words carefully.

"Because of me," she blurted. "I just meant I don't want anything to happen to you because of me. God knows, I don't need the added stress of having your prolonged coma on my conscience."

"So now I'm not just unconscious, I'm in a coma . . . a *prolonged* coma? Will I eventually come out of it?" There was definitely amusement in his voice now.

"The doctors aren't sure. But they have warned that you could wake up drooling, and suffering from amnesia . . . and impotent," she added for good measure.

"Wow. That's some badass coma I got my stupid, macho, pigheaded self into."

"It certainly is. And I'll be to blame for all of it since if I hadn't insisted on the séance we wouldn't be standing here right this minute."

"To tell you the truth," he said, angling his body closer to hers ever so slightly, the distance small but unmistakable. And unsettling. Good Lord, he was unsettling when he was so close. "I like where I'm standing just fine. If you have a problem with that, now would be the time to say so."

In a heartbeat the whole world shifted. Sophie felt worry give way to awareness. That electrified, skin-tingling kind of awareness when every fiber of your being is energized and every sensation amplified. Her knees felt weak, her breath heavy and slow. She shook her head. "No. No problem."

"So," he said, running his hand down her hair. "Did you have a better idea in mind than a full frontal assault on the circuit breakers . . . one that will avoid a prolonged coma and impotence and still get the lights back on . . . and while you're at it, the coffeemaker."

"There's wine," she offered, too distracted to provide the details of the thought chain that had led her from coffee to wine.

"Thanks. But I've gotten used to getting the best cup of coffee around right here at home every morning. I'm not sure I could start the day without it." He paused a second, still touching her hair, and added, "I'm not sure I'd want to."

"Well," she said, melting inside as she realized he might be talking about more than coffee. "I guess my suggestion would be that we look for a few candles and—"

"And hope they don't turn into industrial-strength flares and burn the place down?"

"Right. Good point. Candles might be a little risky, all things considered. Option Two: We go to bed early and wait until morning to deal with the whole restoring-power issue."

"We could do that," he said, taking hold of her with both hands, his palms warm and rough on the smooth skin of her shoulders. "Or . . ."

His thumb caressed her jaw. Sophie could feel his eyes on her. Expectancy pulsed in the air between them and the darkness only heightened the excitement.

"We could . . . do this . . ."

His pulled her against him, hard, with the agility and finesse of a man who'd crawled through a field of land mines and lived to tell the tale. Pushing his hand into her hair, he tipped her head back.

He kissed her just beneath her ear, his low-pitched voice caressing. "I want you, Sophie. I've been wanting you all night . . . and all last night and the night before that." He kissed her again, and incongruously the damp heat of his mouth made her shiver. "Hell, it feels like I've wanted you from the instant that door blew open and I saw you standing there . . . and the list of things I want to do to you just keeps getting longer . . . and harder to resist."

"Don't," she whispered. "Don't resist."

He sucked in a sharp breath.

Sophie fisted the front of his T-shirt with one hand and grasped the back of his neck with the other.

He turned his head and their mouths crashed together. Both needing. Taking. Demanding more.

The fury of his kiss forced her jaw wide and he explored her mouth with deep, relentless sweeps of his tongue. Sophie clung to his shoulders, her urgency a match for his own. This felt so right, and long past due, and she had no qualms about taking as much as she gave.

He spun her so her back was to the refrigerator and pressed her against it. His hands, big and warm and rough, dragged down her body in a slow and detailed caress. When he lingered at her breasts, Sophie bit her lip to keep from whimpering. When those clever hands slipped beneath her loose cotton skirt and stroked her thighs, first the outside and then the soft, sensitive flesh inside, bringing him perilously close to the part of her that was already damp and needy for him, she did whimper.

With one hand still under her skirt, he used the other to strip off her tank top. Running his tongue along the top edge of her strapless bra, he reached around her for the clasp.

Sophie slowed his progress only long enough to turn the tables and tug his T-shirt over his head.

She ran her hands over his smooth chest.

He unhooked her bra.

She unzipped his jeans.

As his mouth closed over the tip of her breast, her trembling fingers slid beneath the denim and found him hot and hard.

She quivered and held her breath as his fingers at last moved high between her parted thighs and cupped the very core of her. Curling her fingers around him in a long, upward stroke, she arched into his touch, letting him know she wanted him the same way she could tell he wanted her . . . fast and hard and right . . . that . . . instant.

Sophie was ready, beyond ready, and when the darkened room suddenly exploded into light, it was as jarring to her careening senses as being hit in the face with a snowball. She was so startled by the light it took her another fraction of a second to register the sound of someone clearing their throat . . . pointedly and very close by.

She looked up to see Ivy—not dead-old-lady Ivy, but lovely and youthful-looking Ivy—seated prettily on the counter across from where Owen still had her pinned to the refrigerator door. Dead or not, the woman's timing was horrifyingly perfect, designed to deliver the maximum amount of surprise and humiliation. Half dressed, face flushed, senses reeling, Sophie couldn't feel more vulnerable or more embarrassed.

It took Owen, his eyes closed, his face buried between her naked breasts, a second longer to pick up on her reaction and realize they weren't alone. When he lifted his head to glance over his shoulder, he didn't appear at all embarrassed to find Ivy playing voyeur, only angry. Very angry.

"You," he growled, remnants of passion mixed with the disgust in his rough tone.

"Yes. *Moi*," countered Ivy, tossing back the shiny, shoulder-length blond hair that dipped over one eye. "But I must say, when you begged for the honor of my company, I had no idea this is what you had in mind." Her own tone—pitched just an intriguingly bit low for a woman—somehow managed to sound both breezy and sultry.

"Trust me, I didn't," he retorted. "And the only thing I'd ever beg for is a way to get rid of you."

"Ah, the ever-gracious Mr. Winters." She ran a withering glance over his naked back. "Your lack of charm is exceeded only by your lack of decorum. And now, since my presence here is obviously neither required nor desired, I shall—"

"No," Sophie blurted, and then cringed inwardly as Ivy turned and fastened her critical stare on her.

She looked glamorous, and bored. Her pale peach satin dressing gown and matching high-heeled, fur-trimmed mules made Sophie think of 1940s movie stars, and made her feel severely lacking by comparison. She felt like a teenager caught making out with her first boyfriend. Ivy was intimidating and she knew it. The only thing saving Sophie from being embarrassed beyond speech was that even though Owen had swiveled to face Ivy, she herself was still mostly shielded by the solid wall of his body. Now, if only she could think of a graceful way to get her top on and her skirt unbunched . . .

Feeling around on the counter for her top, she said, "We . . . that is, I . . . definitely want to speak with you. I've been trying to contact you on my own without any luck, so I asked a friend who's more knowledgeable in . . . these things, to come and help."

Ivy's look was icy. "Did you really think I would come when summoned like a pet poodle? As you can see, I appear when and how I choose."

"Yes, I can see that. And you're here now: that's what matters. Obviously the timing is a little . . . awkward." She nervously smoothed her skirt. "So if you could just give us a minute to pull ourselves—"

"No," said Ivy.

Sophie blinked. "No?"

"No. My time is valuable. I won't hang around cooling my heels so you can be spared the embarrassment of your own imprudent behavior. Say whatever it is you have to say to me and be done with it."

"Well . . . let's see. I . . ." She fumbled, her clever, well-rehearsed arguments nowhere around. Surprise, surprise. Being disheveled and half naked threw her off her game. "I guess, what I most wanted to speak with you about is the wedding."

"I believe I've made my feelings on that subject abundantly clear. If not, then I'm sure I can—"

"No. No, your feelings are clear. Very clear. There's no need to prove anything to us. But I can't help thinking that if you knew more about the couple being married, you would feel diff—"

"Knew what? That the would-be bride is a lovely girl with a heart of gold who's marrying a paragon of virtue and honor, and that the charmed couple will be running off to save the world together? That she looks on this house as part of a fairy tale and believes that's what her wedding day should be? That she and her doting father shared a fondness for sailing and pretending that she was a princess? That being married here is her fondest dream? I know all that and it does not change my stand on the matter in the slightest."

Sophie desperately plodded on. "I hoped you might feel a kinship with Shelby . . . that's her name. Shelby Archer. After all, your father had this house designed and built just for you . . . to make you happy. I'm sure you shared a special bond with him the same way Shelby did with her father. For them, this house was a part of that bond . . . from the time she was a little girl, it was their special place. And then when Shelby was only fifteen—"

"He died," Ivy interrupted brusquely. "Please. Everyone's father dies eventually, Miss Bennett. Does that mean I should let everyone who wants to traipse through my private property and—"

Bristling, Owen cut in. "Lady, you have a twisted take on the concept of private property . . . among other things. Let me straighten you out: to own property you have to be alive. You're not. Ipso facto."

Ivy regarded him with a gaze like broken glass. "I once thought your slovenly housekeeping was your least attractive attribute. I see that I was wrong."

Noting the combative glitter that came into Owen's eyes, Sophie spoke before he could.

"Trust me, Miss Halliday, I understand why you feel the way you do about Ange de la Mer. I understand that it has nothing to do with deeds or legalities. That it's beyond all that mundane, everyday stuff. It's even beyond being a matter of mere life and death."

Ivy gave a regal, one-shouldered shrug, but she didn't disagree.

"This house isn't only a part of your past . . . or even a part of your heart. It represents something bigger, something intangible. It represents a life that should have been, a dream that never came true. And I know it sometimes feels like it's all there is left of that dream . . . and that you're the only one who even remembers the dream existed, and that makes it very hard to give up and walk away."

Ivy was looking past her, wearing that same slightly bored, ice-queen look, but Sophie caught a small tremble at the corner of her mouth and knew her words were getting through.

She took a deep breath. "I understand because it happened to me too."

Ivy's flawless brows lifted as she looked Sophie up and down with surprise and increased interest. "You were . . ."

When she hesitated, Sophie shook her head. "No. I wasn't left on my wedding day, if that's what you're asking, but . . ."

Ivy flinched. "Neither was I *left* on my wedding day," she declared. "Joseph would never have left me."

"No, no, of course not."

"Something happened. Something kept him from coming that day."

"I'm sure that's true," Sophie told her.

"Are you? Really? Because you'd be surprised how many people choose to believe the opposite."

"I wouldn't be surprised by what anyone thinks . . . or says. Like I said, it happened to me. I may not have gotten as far as the actual wedding day, but I fully expected to. Everyone expected it. We were together for years. We were the perfect couple. Everyone thought so. Even me." Her mouth quirked in a small, self-deprecating smile. "Especially me. It's what I wanted to believe. But later, afterward, I knew. I knew that I had wanted so badly for it to be right that I refused to see anything else. Looking back, the signs were so clear, so easy to read, they burned my eyeballs."

"What sort of signs?" asked Ivy.

"Oh, the fact that we were together for years, but he didn't want to live together until we were married . . . so that when we did it would be perfect. And he didn't want to get married—or even engaged—until he got all the things he'd always wanted to do out of his system . . . also so it would be perfect. Rock climbing and backpacking across Europe and getting his damn MBA. It was like a bucket list, only instead of listing things to do before kicking the bucket, these were things he wanted to do before marrying me. You'd think that alone would have told me something about his feelings on the subject." She paused for another quirky smile and a sniffle. Damn. She was so over this. Why on earth did talking about it still make her fill up? Obviously for the same murky reasons Ivy clung to her house.

"Anyway, when my thirtieth birthday rolled around, he made reservations at a very fancy restaurant and told me he wanted it to be my best birthday ever. 'This is it,' I thought. 'The Proposal.' I told myself he'd finally realized that he wanted me more than he wanted to do all the things left on that list. I went all out. Why the hell not? I'd waited long enough. A new hairstyle, a new, blow-the-budget outfit, new shoes." She shook her head at her foolishness. "They were these silly, glittery Cinderella shoes that screamed 'celebration': I fantasized about how I would wear them every year on the anniversary of our engagement, and about how someday I would show them to our kids and tell them about the wonderfully romantic night when their daddy proposed and their mommy said yes. Ridiculous, I know."

She felt Owen recoil because it was so ridiculous, but mercifully he refrained from comment.

"The worst part is I was so excited I couldn't stop grinning. For days I went around with this big sappy I've-got-a-secret smile. Of course, everyone surmised something was up . . . my sisters, my stepmother, all our friends." She shuddered, remembering the aftermath of that night, the shock . . . the pity. She crossed her arms even more tightly in front of her. "When the big night finally arrived, we met at the restaurant, and when I walked in, my present was already on the table. It was a package about the size of a book and I thought, 'How adorable. He put the ring box inside a bigger box to throw me off.' He was so nervous, and I thought that was adorable too."

She knew she was rambling and tried to rein in her thoughts. Baring her soul hadn't been part of her plan. Her prepared spiel was all about Shelby and Matthew. They were her secret weapon, her way to win Ivy over. But that hadn't worked and now she was desperate . . . desperate enough to dredge up her own unfortunate past.

"You've probably already guessed the ending," she told them. "There was no proposal. There was, however, a big surprise. He'd met someone else. A woman at work. They'd fallen madly in love . . . so madly she was pregnant with his baby. He'd only found out about the baby that afternoon. He'd planned to let me down easy by getting through my birthday before coming clean, but—to his credit I suppose—he discovered he couldn't sit there and look me in the eye and lie."

There was an uneasy silence. Sophie understood. What was there to say?

Ivy spoke first.

"What was in the box?"

Sophie smiled cynically. "A book. *The Romantic's Guide to Paris*. He knew I always wanted to go there. I'm not sure he even remembered I wanted to go there on our honeymoon. At that point it seemed pointless to ask."

Owen cleared his throat. God, he had to be thinking she was the biggest dope ever.

"Anyway," she said, feeling even more awkward now that it was all out there, "I guess the reason I told you all this is because I understand that dreams don't die. Even when they don't come true and we've made peace with the fact that they never will, they're still a part of us. Even if we're the only one who remembers them or who gives a damn about what might have been and should have been . . . well, I still have my Cinderella shoes tucked away on a shelf and you still have this house."

"So to speak," Owen said under his breath.

Ivy said nothing.

"But I don't think it would tarnish that dream or my memory of it if I let someone borrow the shoes for a special occasion of her own. In fact, I think it would honor my dream to help someone else's come true. What I'm trying to say—"

"I know what you're trying to say, Miss Bennett. I am not the village idiot." There was no hint of warmth or softening in Ivy's voice now. "Nor do I have time for pointless conversations."

"Really?" Owen challenged as she slid gracefully from her perch on the counter. "Afterlife that busy, is it?"

She shot him a look that would quell another man. Owen smiled coldly.

"It so happens I have a great deal to do. It turns out that stopping a wedding is as much work as planning one."

She spun away from them in a swirl of peach satin and was gone, literally melting into the air.

Owen shook his head and looked disgusted. "Well. That was a waste of time."

"Maybe," allowed Sophie, clinging to the hope that Ivy might think about what she'd said and soften her stance. "But on the bright side, at least the lights are on. And no one is in a coma, and we can make coffee in the morning."

"Yeah," he said, grabbing his T-shirt without meeting her eyes. "I'll see you then."

Fourteen

He overslept.

That's what happened when you spent the night tossing and turning, caught in a battle between conscience and desire.

In this corner: desire. He wanted Sophie: he hadn't exaggerated when he told her how much he wanted her. And for how long. But he didn't want the same things she wanted . . . hell, he no longer even believed in the things she wanted. And that complicated matters.

He might not have a "bucket list" like her jackass ex-boyfriend, but he was just as wrong for her. Any idiot could see that. Unfortunately, it wasn't any idiot's perception of things that concerned him: it was Sophie's. He couldn't shake the memory of the small, almost imperceptible quiver in her voice when she admitted that she had wanted so badly for her ex to be Mr. Right that she'd been blind to the giant neon Mr. Wrong sign flashing above his head. She might be a little older and a little wiser now, but the woman was still a die-hard believer in true love and happy endings and she still wanted both just as badly.

Her story may not have touched Ivy's heart, but it had punched a giant hole in his. At first he was furious with Ivy for showing up when he was so close to having all his fantasies of ravishing Sophie become real. Now he was thankful for her no-doubt-intentionally-lousy timing. She'd stopped him from making a big mistake.

What he had to offer Sophie would never be enough. She deserved more than he had left to give. She deserved to be happy. She deserved someone who shared her dreams and was willing to do whatever it took to make them come true. Once, a long time ago, he'd deluded himself into believing he could be that kind of guy. He knew better now. And his conscience was telling him that under the circumstances the right and honorable thing to do was to back off. Doing the right and honorable thing mattered a great deal to him, enough to keep him awake all night coming to terms with the inevitable. Unfortunately, knowing what he had to do didn't make it any easier . . . and it didn't make him want Sophie any less.

The question was . . . could he do it? Could he manage to keep his hands off her when she was so close . . . living in his house . . . sleeping right down the hall . . . smelling like wildflowers and possibilities whenever she came close . . . making him want to chuck everything and follow her forever? Could he keep from touching her when the longing to do that and so much more was like an open wound inside him?

Owen would like to think he had that kind of self-control. But then, he'd also like to think the fact he hadn't had a cigarette since Sophie moved in meant he'd never backslide again. The truth was that he wasn't sure. Both were one-day-at-a-time jobs. But he'd been smart enough to take the precaution of tossing his last pack of smokes in the trash. And he knew that if there was to be any chance of him doing the right thing for Sophie, he would need to keep as much distance between them as possible at all times.

* * *

She was a thirtysomething woman.

She'd started nearly every day of her life—hundreds, no, make that thousands of days—without the benefit of Owen Winters's company or conversation or attention. And she could count on her fingers the number of mornings he was around.

So why the hell did it feel like an indispensable part of her being had gone AWOL just because he'd stopped joining her for coffee at sunrise? It made no sense. And that's what scared her. It meant her heart was trying to take control of matters best left to her head.

The first time he didn't show up was the morning after the séance and the awkward encounter with Ivy that followed. His abrupt good-night had left her bewildered, and a little hurt, but she'd still looked forward to seeing him in the morning. When he didn't appear, she chose to believe he'd simply overslept. But he didn't show again the next day and he also stopped coming around in the evening and he never offered an explanation. It would be easy to chalk up his sudden coolness to the obvious, ego-crushing theory that he'd been hot for her in the dark, but had second thoughts as soon as the lights came back on. After all, on a bad day she could do paranoid insecurity with the best of them. But in her heart she knew that wasn't it.

Again, she was a thirtysomething woman: not—in spite of her nervous babbling after nearly being caught in the act by Ivy—a clueless teenager. She was experienced enough to know when a man was interested. Owen was interested. She'd sensed his desire. She'd seen it in his eyes. Lord knows, she'd felt it. He'd meant it when he told her he wanted her. The problem was that he didn't want to.

His reasons didn't matter. She ought to count herself lucky he hadn't tried to pick up where they left off when Ivy interrupted them. She'd never been into one-night stands and he obviously wasn't the kind of man she wanted to share her life with. She didn't want another man who ran hot and cold or who held back. Hadn't she learned the hard way that it was better to be happy alone than to pretend to be happy with a man who didn't want to be there? She wanted a man who *wanted* to be with her . . . a man who wanted *her* beyond all reason . . . a man who didn't come to his senses when the lights came on.

With both Owen and Ivy avoiding her, their living situation took on a surreal quality. The three of them inhabited the same physical space, but rarely—if ever—crossed paths. It was as if they existed in different dimensions or moved in separate, nonintersecting orbits, and in a way, she supposed, they did . . . each of them concerned with his or her own agenda and deadlines.

For Sophie, that meant keeping a sharp eye on the wedding preparations, checking daily on her other Seasons responsibilities, and never forgetting that, seen or unseen, Ivy was a very real threat. There had been no major catastrophes since the séance, but as the days ticked away she continued to make her presence and her opposition known in small ways.

The gauntlet had been thrown down, and picked up. Sophie had declared her intention to go ahead with the wedding no matter what and Ivy had warned her to cease and desist or face the consequences. The fact that Ivy was no longer openly sabotaging her work made Sophie worry that Ivy had refined her strategy and was now biding her time and saving her firepower for the big day itself. It was not a comforting thought.

She wished she could talk it over with Owen, but he was never around. She had no choice but to follow her own instincts. And in spite of her thus-far-dismal track record, her instincts told her not to give up on the possibility of changing Ivy's mind about the wedding. The more she thought about it, the more convinced she was that she was right in thinking Shelby was the key to winning Ivy over. She was sure that if Ivy got to know Shelby, she would like her. And if she liked her, it would be harder for her to do anything to ruin her wedding day.

Sophie refused to believe that Ivy was really as bitter or vindictive as she seemed on the surface. She certainly hadn't started out that way, she thought, recalling the engagement picture of Ivy looking so young and so happy. The woman in that photo had not been bitter or vindictive. Maybe she had to build walls to protect herself . . . to survive the heartache and loneliness. But walls didn't change who a person was deep inside. And walls could be breached. You just had to know how.

What Sophie needed was for Ivy to see Shelby not as some generic bride looking to take her rightful place there, but as a real flesh-and-blood young woman, a young woman with hopes and dreams and plans . . . the same sort of hopes and dreams and plans Ivy herself had had at the same age. And since Ivy was hell-bent on not hearing what Sophie had to say about Shelby, Sophie would just have to find a way to show her.

Ivy now knew how the Confederates felt when the Yankee army stormed Atlanta.

Ange de la Mer was being invaded by chattering, garment-bag-wielding women, young and old alike. If she'd had some advance warning, she could have organized a proper defense, but she'd had no warning, no inkling, no glimmer of what was coming.

Touché, Miss Bennett, she thought. *Touché.*

The first woman to arrive carried two bulging white garment bags and assorted smaller satchels that required making two trips from the car. Sophia Bennett hurried to greet her with a warm embrace and help her carry it all to the room at the top of the stairs. *Her* room. The very same room where she'd dressed the morning she and Joseph were to be married.

She was not happy about this. Not happy at all.

Next came the mother of the bride, a chirping sparrow of a woman whom Sophia greeted with a polite smile and somewhat less enthusiasm. With her was an ample woman with luminous skin and a southern accent . . . Charleston was Ivy's guess. The mother of the groom, she decided.

All of them traipsed up the stairs as if they had every right in the world to be there.

It was well over a half hour later when a sleek red convertible came careening into the drive. Whoever was at the wheel drove too fast and parked haphazardly, blocking the other vehicles, as if the driver had no time for common sense or good manners.

Three young women in shorts and those rubber flip-floppy things piled out and hurried up the walk. Their legs were tanned and their long hair gleamed in the sunshine. They laughed and talked excitedly, bumping shoulders and interrupting one another, utterly confident in their friendship and in their world, and Ivy envied them so much her heart wrenched in a way she'd believed no longer possible. She remembered that feeling. She remembered laughing with her best friends and the sunshine on her face as she ran along that same path.

The girls entered the house without knocking.

One of them—the one with rhinestones and silly-looking white flowers on her flip-flops and a white T-shirt reading THE FUTURE MRS. WINSTON—held her cell phone to her ear.

"Sophie, Shelby. We're here," she said into it, and then paused, listening. "Yes, we all remembered to bring our shoes. Well, one of us forgot and had to go back for them . . . that's why we're late." She laughed. "Yup. The right underwear too, so you can tell Lina to relax. Okay, we'll be right up."

Of course, thought Ivy, *by all means, go right up.* Why stop with three interlopers storming through the house when you could have six? What next? A ticket booth out front and tourists mucking about? Well, she, for one, had had enough. And she knew just how to put a stop to it.

Sophia Bennett must believe herself to be very clever. She no doubt thought that bringing Shelby Archer and her bridesmaids there for a dress fitting was a stroke of genius, that the sight of them looking so young and fresh and beautiful in their gowns would work some kind of magic and Ivy would be moved enough to allow the wedding to go ahead as planned. Well, this time the crafty little wedding planner had outfoxed herself. Instead of changing Ivy's mind, she had just presented her with a way to stop the wedding at the source.

Sophia Bennett was a professional, and so far she had been admirably resolved and resilient in championing her client's interest. Now Ivy had a chance to deal directly with the client herself. And she was about to find out how the young bride felt about having her fairy-tale wedding take place in a haunted house. They were all about to find out.

From her vantage point halfway up the stairs, she considered her options. She could go for pure shock value and suddenly materialize before the young women, but the séance woman had been right: materializing consumed a lot of energy. And focus. And she wasn't in the mood to muster up enough of either. Besides, the silly things were sure to go around babbling about the ghost they'd seen and that could lead to complications in the days ahead. She wasn't interested in publicity or notoriety, only to be left in peace in her own home. Far better to pass on the dramatics and take a more subtle, roundabout approach.

Unseen, she surveyed the front hall below and quickly zeroed in on the crystal chandelier above the girls' heads. Perfect. She'd start there. It saddened her to damage the house itself, of course, but she really didn't have time to sit around rattling windows and flicking lights to get the message across. Desperate times called for desperate measures.

She drew the equivalent of a deep breath, gathering energy. As she did, she was outraged to see one of Shelby Archer's friends open the glass door of the Danish tall-case clock in the hall and reach for the hour hand.

"What are you doing?" exclaimed Shelby, hurrying over to stop her.

Excellent question, thought Ivy.

"I wanted to see if I could make it chime," her friend explained. "It probably does it on the hour."

"Well, then just wait for it to get there on its own. Don't go touching anything."

"That's right," agreed the third girl, joining them. In a teasingly stern tone, she added, "No one messes with the Princess House. Right, Bridezilla?"

"Right. And I am not a Bridezilla."

"True." Her friend poked her with her elbow. "But you are a dork."

"I don't care," said Shelby, smiling happily. "I love this house. And I consider myself very lucky to be getting married here. And I don't want anything to mess it up or make Mr. Winters change his mind . . . such as a broken clock."

"Okay, okay." The girl who'd opened the clock door closed it carefully, and then considered the clock with a small frown. "You know, a white clock with those carved curlicue things is kind of girlie looking for a guy . . . especially a guy who writes that rock 'em, sock 'em paranormal crap."

"It's not crap," Shelby countered. "And he probably didn't choose the clock. Sophie said he bought the house already furnished by the previous owner."

"Oh, that makes more sense. Come on; let's go squeeze me into that dress so we can go out to lunch afterward."

"Which will only make it harder to squeeze you into it on the big day," the other girl pointed out.

"No, because after today I'm going on the cabbage-and-rice-noodle diet until the day of the wedding."

"Sure you are."

"I am. And I'm going to wake up early and get on the treadmill every day."

"I'll help you get a head start . . . race me up the stairs."

Laughing, they hit the stairs and took them two at a time, running right through Ivy. Literally. It was a feeling she didn't think she'd ever get accustomed to, though technically she didn't *feel* anything anymore. It was unsettling to be run through just the same.

Shelby Archer laughed along with her friends, but she lagged behind, gazing around as she slowly climbed the stairs. When she reached the step where Ivy was seated—unseen—she suddenly turned and sat beside her.

She looked out over the hallway below.

Ivy looked at her, taking note of the expression of wonder on her face. She was startled to see tears well up in the girl's eyes in spite of the faint smile on her lips.

"Thank you," she whispered, leaving Ivy to wonder just whom she was thanking. Her father? Her lucky stars?

She supposed it didn't matter. What Shelby Archer thought or did or wanted was of no import to her.

Just the same, as Shelby went to join the others, Ivy found she'd suddenly lost her enthusiasm for throwing a good old-fashioned ghostly scare into the girl. Let her have her dratted dress fitting. It was the wedding Ivy was determined to stop and stop it she would.

In the meantime she would go keep an eye on what was happening in her room. Forewarned is forearmed. She would have to remember that going forward. And besides, she'd always been a bit of a clotheshorse. It couldn't hurt to see for herself just what passed for wedding fashion these days.

The dress fitting was a success on all fronts.

Lina had worked her magic and created for Shelby the wedding dress of her dreams. When she walked into the room wearing it, jaws dropped and Helen's eyes filled with tears.

"Oh, baby, you look beautiful," she whispered.

"I feel beautiful," exclaimed Shelby, laughing as she did a twirl and sent the frothy layers of skirt fluttering.

Lena had personally supervised the earlier fittings of the bridesmaids' dresses and they too were perfect. Simple and strapless and a soft shade of amethyst, they were perfect for the late-summer wedding.

And to Sophie's relief, Ivy did nothing to ruin the moment . . . or the expensive and irreplaceable dresses. She'd taken a big risk by arranging to have the fitting there. It could have backfired even more spectacularly than the séance had . . . and this time in front of witnesses. It hadn't. But had it succeeded in softening Ivy's no-wedding stance even a little? She'd just have to wait and see.

When the oohing and aahing was over and the dresses safely back in their garment bags, Shelby invited Lina, Sophie, Helen, and Matthew's mother to join her and her friends at a café on Bowen's Wharf for what locals agreed were the best lobster rolls in town. Matthew's mother was quickly on board, but both Lina and Sophie had previous appointments. Helen also had to decline, explaining that she had a lot of running around to do to take care of last-minute details for a fund-raiser for the private school both she and Shelby had attended.

"I should have stepped down from the planning committee when I realized the date for the ball was only a week before the wedding, but I like to keep busy and I'm always convinced I can do it all." She sent Sophie a small, regretful smile. "I'm just sorry I wasn't available to pitch in and do more to help you to fine-tune the wedding plans."

"No, no. Believe me, Helen, you've done more than enough."

Shelby grinned and Sophie knew it was because she understood exactly what she meant. Shelby knew her mother very well. That was the only thing that gave Sophie solace when she woke up in the middle of the night worried over Helen's most recent bit of fine-tuning. Technically her job as a wedding planner was to make the bride and groom happy, but she couldn't completely discount the fact that in this case it was the bride's mother who was paying the bills. So far Helen had *tweaked*—her word—the guest list, the menu, the seating arrangements, and the music. She would have tweaked more if Sophie had allowed it. Most often her changes were actually additions, which she intended to be a wonderful surprise for her daughter and future son-in-law. Sophie wasn't so sure, and the surprise element prevented her from checking with Shelby about adding an extra dozen out-of-town guests or an elaborate vodka-and-caviar station during cocktail hour.

Helen lingered after the others left and Sophie steeled herself to hear her latest "scathingly brilliant idea."

"Fireworks," Helen said, quite pleased with herself.

"Fireworks?" echoed Sophie, struggling to see how fireworks fit in with the whimsical, magical-woodland wedding theme.

"Yes. Isn't that a fabulous idea? Shelby loves fireworks," she added. "She'll be so surprised."

"Fireworks have become very popular, especially for outdoor weddings," Sophie allowed. "Which is why I doubt it would even be possible to arrange for them at this late date."

Helen waved off her concern. "Oh, it's all taken care of. A friend of a friend helped me and it's all set . . . technicians, permits, a barge, everything."

"A barge?" Sophie repeated, getting a mental image that made her shudder.

"Right. They're going to be set off on a barge out at sea. Let's go around back and check out what the view will be like, shall we?"

She was off without giving Sophie a chance to agree or time to say, "No, there's no need to check the view because your daughter has her heart set on a simple, understated, unpretentious celebration and a professional fireworks display is neither understated nor unpretentious".

Instead Sophie followed her to the back of the house and all the way to the edge of the lawn, where a path now provided safe passage through the daisies.

"Oh my God, the view from here is amazing . . . Shelby will be so surprised."

"Yes, I'm sure she will be. But you know, Helen, your wedding day isn't really a time for surprises. I think we should run the fireworks idea by Shelby and Matthew before we make a final decision."

"Oh, I've made the final decision," Helen countered with another of those careless waves of her hand, the practiced gesture of a woman accustomed to getting her way. "And I take full responsibility in the event Shelby doesn't love it. But she will. You'll see." Leaning slightly to her right, she looked past Sophie and her expression brightened. She shook her three-hundred-dollar haircut into place and moistened her lips.

Sophie recognized the preening reaction and didn't need to turn her head to know what, or rather who, had sparked it.

"Oh, look, there's Owen," announced Helen. "I'm just going to dash over and say hello."

Owen was coming out of the guesthouse; he stopped when Helen called out to him.

Let Helen dash all she wanted, Sophie thought. There's no way she herself was going to rush over there and give Owen the impression—the mistaken impression—that she was eager to talk with him after he'd made an avocation of avoiding her. She headed straight for the house, giving a quick wave in passing, but apparently Owen found Helen's company even more odious than hers because he moved quickly to head Sophie off and corral her in their little group.

At least she didn't have to come up with something to say. Helen was entirely capable of keeping the conversation going all by herself. She talked about the girls' dresses and the fireworks display and the engraved sterling-silver bubble wands and matching tiny crystal decanters until Owen's eyes glazed over and his expression implored Sophie to save him. Of course, she did nothing of the sort.

Instead, she waited until Helen at last showed signs of winding down, then said, "Tell me, Helen, have you finally decided on your outfit for the wedding?"

"Well, yes and no. You know the hideous problem I was having finding something in the right color palette that was flattering on me. People just don't understand how difficult it is when you're as petite as I am," she said in a coy aside to Owen. "Anyway, after months of searching for just the right dress, I found two. Can you believe that? And now I can't decide which one to wear."

Sophie gave a commiserating nod. "Feast or famine; isn't that always the way? Why don't you describe them and maybe we can help you choose?"

She followed up the suggestion with a sweet smile aimed directly at Owen, just to make sure he understood that shoving him from the Helen frying pan into the Helen fire had not been accidental. His gaze immediately went from glazed and imploring to lethal. Game on.

They continued to trade pointed glances as Helen wound her way through painfully elaborate descriptions of both dresses. Silk dupioni and silk shantung and slit skirts and covered buttons and lace appliqués . . . not a thing was left to their imaginations.

"So what do you think?" she asked at last.

"The bronze," said Sophie at the same time Owen said, "The green." He glanced at them cautiously. "One of them was green, right?"

Helen rolled her eyes dramatically. "Oh, you two; you're no help at all. I'll just have to muddle through on my own and hope for the best."

"I'm sure you'll be stunning in whichever dress you decide on," Sophie told her.

"How sweet of you to say so." Helen sighed, again with great drama. "I still have over a week to think about it. At least I know what I'm wearing to the ball this weekend." She reached out and briefly rested her fingertips on Owen's arm. "Owen, I know you'll get a particular kick out of this. The ball is a fund-raiser for the new library at Madison Academy . . . my alma mater," she added with obvious pride. "And we're calling it the First Annual Book Lovers' Ball. Book lovers. Library. The name was my idea. We're encouraging guests to dress as their favorite fictional character. My favorite book is *Gone with the Wind*. Need I say more?"

"No," Owen said bluntly.

"I think he meant to say, 'No, Scarlett,'" suggested Sophie.

Helen smiled broadly. "That's right: Scarlett O'Hara. At your service." She did a little curtsy and then gave a small gasp. "Oh my goodness. I just had the most scathingly brilliant idea. There's going to be a silent auction at the ball." She looked directly at Owen. "How great would it be if we auctioned off a complete set of your books and you were there to personally autograph them for the lucky winner? Please say you'll do it, Owen . . . for me? It would be such a coup."

He looked like a cornered mountain lion: fierce and unhappy. Sophie had to bite the inside of her cheek to keep from grinning.

"I'm sorry, but I really don't ever—"

"Say no to a worthy cause," Sophie jumped in helpfully when he hesitated and gave her a split-second opening. "And what cause could be more worthy than the Madison Academy library?" She smiled at Owen. "Just think, you'll get to meet your fans and probably pick up a bunch of new readers while you're at it. Now that's what I call win-win."

"This is wonderful!" exclaimed Helen. "I can't wait to tell the rest of the planning committee. And I'm so glad I ran into you and the idea just popped into my head that way. So it's settled. I'll get the books for the auction and you'll be there to sign them."

"Or better yet, I could just sign them in advance," suggested Owen.

"You silly," Helen retorted, again resting her hand on his arm. Longer this time. "That wouldn't be the same as you being there to meet the winner and write a personal inscription."

"Of course it wouldn't," agreed Sophie. She smiled at Owen. "You silly."

He looked decidedly unenthusiastic at the prospect. In fact, if she wasn't mistaken, behind the grim line of his mouth, his teeth were clenched. Poor little recluse, poked from his cave, and all for the pleasure of spending an evening with Scarlett O'Hara and her pals. She almost felt a little sorry for him.

In a terse tone, he said, "All right, I'll be there. But I'll need to bring someone else along with me."

Helen's smile froze in place, boosting Sophie's suspicion that

the idea of inviting Owen to the ball wasn't quite as spontaneous—or altruistic—as she'd have liked them to believe. "Someone
else? You mean like a date?"

"More like an assistant," he told her. "Whenever I do a book
signing, I have someone there to open the books and hand them
to me."

"Well, I'd be more than happy to assist you myself," said Helen.

He quickly shook his head. "You'll have your hands full making sure everything runs smoothly. You did say you're on the planning committee?"

"Yes. The chairman actually."

"Then you definitely won't have time for this. I'm sure Sophie
won't mind pitching in for a cause as worthy as the Madison
Academy."

"Oh. Sophie." Helen shrugged. "That's fine. Bring her along, if
you like."

Sophie bristled. "Actually, I—"

That's as far as he let her get. "Good. It's settled. We'll be there."

"Fabulous," said Helen. "I'll e-mail directions and all the other
information you'll need. And I'll be sure to leave word at the reception desk that you're there as my personal guest." She shifted
her rapt gaze from Owen long enough to glance at Sophie. "Both
of you. I'd love to stay and brainstorm costumes with you . . . I
have some marvelous ideas, but I have to dash to the bookstore for
those books and then I have a million other errands. TTFN," she
called over her shoulder as she left.

Owen's brow furrowed. "TTFN?"

"Ta-Ta For Now."

He shook his head. "That woman is . . . exhausting."

"She's also smitten. With you," Sophie clarified when he shot
her a quizzical look. "That's why she was so upset when she
thought you wanted to bring a date. And so relieved when she re-

alized it was just me you wanted to drag along. I'm not exactly Helen's idea of competition."

He gave a short, harsh laugh that could mean anything.

Sophie shook her head disgustedly. "I can't believe she roped us into going to her stupid ball."

"Thanks to you and how quick you were to throw me under the damn Book Lovers' bus," he retorted, but without any real rancor.

"Right back at you, Mr. I-need-an-assistant-to-hand-me-the-books." She shot him a look. "And just so we're clear: I am not wearing a costume."

"Thank God. I was afraid you'd want to go as Romeo and Juliet."

"I was afraid you'd want to go as Batman and Robin."

"I'd make a damn good Batman."

"Oh," she said, straight-faced. "I sort of assumed I'd be Batman."

He grinned and knocked his shoulder against hers playfully. "Sorry, Robin. The Batmobile is all mine."

They both gazed out at the water, not knowing what to say to fill the sudden silence and not wanting to walk away.

"So," said Sophie. "How's the book going?"

"Good. It's going good. Well, it's going all right."

"I'm glad to hear it. I'm really looking forward to reading it . . . especially after the way you left us hanging at the end of the last one."

"That's right. I forgot you're a big sushi-western fan."

"Go ahead. Laugh. I deserve it. I admit I tried to flatter you by saying I'd read your books when I hadn't. But I'll have you know that since then I have read them, all of them. And not for any ulterior motive. I'm hooked. Osprey is a great character . . . dark and brooding and yet intrinsically noble. And with that quiet, dry humor that comes from out of nowhere. I'm sure you've heard this many times, but he really reminds me of you."

"Actually I haven't."

"You're kidding," she countered, surprised. "It seems like a no-brainer to me. And I know you're going to accuse me of being a single-minded romantic, but I can't wait for him and Valene to get together." She caught the flicker of surprise in his eyes. "They are going to get together, aren't they?"

"I'm not sure. I've toyed with the possibility, but it's nothing firm."

"Toyed with it? That's crazy. They have to get together. It's the key to everything: Osprey's quest for redemption, his search for a family, his longing to find someplace where he belongs." She shook her head. "I knew Osprey was blind to all this, but I was sure you had it all figured out. Now I can see that you two are even more alike than I thought. Don't you get it, Owen? They have to get together. She's the missing piece of the puzzle. Valene is the dream that Osprey is afraid to dream."

Her comments took him by surprise and kicked his creative juices into overdrive. He was inundated with what-ifs. It was pure reflex at work when he muttered, "Osprey's not afraid of anything."

"Prove it," she said.

Fifteen

It was with trepidation that Sophie opened her eyes to check out her image in the full-length mirror in her room. It had been a busy day, but between meeting with the pastry chef who was baking the wedding cake and the landscape designer in charge of transforming the grounds of Ange de la Mer into an enchanted forest, she'd managed to stop by her place and grab three evening gowns she could conceivably wear to the ball to-morrow night.

The first two were instant strikeouts. Obviously it had been longer than she realized since she'd had occasion to dress up. Which was ironic. As a wedding planner, she attended more than anyone's fair share of formal events, but not as a formally-attired guest. The first dresses she tried weren't current enough to be trendy or vintage enough to be charming. They fell into that dread-ful middle ground known as the Land of Blah. She knew she could do better than that.

The third dress was dark blue silk with wide shoulder straps, a band of beading at the edge of the bodice, and a sort of inverted pleat down the front that she distinctly recalled the saleswoman telling her would be flattering to her curves. Lips pursed, she studied the way the pleat opened at the widest part of her hips and decided the woman had lied. It didn't matter. The dress wouldn't win her a spot on anyone's best-dressed list, but it wouldn't make the worst-dressed list either, and since she didn't have time to shop, it was going to have to do.

She just wished the *J*s weren't going to be there to pass judgment. When she mentioned the ball to Jill, she discovered they were also going. Madison Academy was notoriously difficult to get into, and although both Jill's and Jenna's children were still a few years away from applying, it was never too soon to start lobbying on their behalf. Attending the school's high-profile fundraisers was one way to do that. Currying favor with influential alumni was another, and it was another reason why the *J*s were so eager to please Helen Archer.

The *J*s definitely would not approve of her gown, but with the right jewelry, and if she remembered to keep her shoulders back so it didn't sag at the neckline and her stomach tucked in so it didn't do that pouchy thing in front, she'd get by. To reassure herself, she sucked in her stomach and threw back her shoulders and took a final look.

"Close enough," she muttered.

"Surely you jest."

Startled, Sophie spun around to find Ivy sitting on the bed behind her.

The movie-star dressing gown was gone. Instead she had on a crisp white cotton sundress from the same era. She sat dangling one leg, hands thrust in the pockets of her full skirt.

With one hand pressed over her rapidly beating heart, Sophie chided her. "You know, you really ought to quit popping in without warning. It's impolite. And it's not good for my heart."

"Sorry," Ivy said without sounding it. "I'm not accustomed to knocking in my own house."

"Fine. Pop in all you want. And I'm too busy to argue with you about whose house this is."

Ivy fluffed a pillow and slid it behind her. "Do you really intend to wear that to the ball tomorrow night?"

"How do you know about the ball?"

She shrugged her bare shoulders. "I have my ways."

"Meaning you eavesdrop. Also impolite."

"The dress," Ivy prodded. "Is that what you intend to wear?"

"So what if it is?"

"It doesn't flatter you in the least. You're quite lovely. Stubborn and impertinent, but lovely. Your figure is an asset, but instead of playing to your strength, you choose to dress in a . . . a . . ." She waved her hand. "A shroud. Also, that color washes you out." She stood. "Come with me."

She walked to the door of the room, graceful even in platform sandals, and turned to see if Sophie was following. She wasn't.

"I said come with me."

"Why?"

"Just come along, Miss Bennett." Ivy ran a disparaging eye over the blue gown. "You really don't have time to waste being petulant."

"'Just come along,'" Sophie mimicked. "On command . . . like a pet poodle."

"And stop muttering," Ivy called over her shoulder.

Sophie rolled her eyes, but she followed. She was too curious not to. Besides, she still had the wedding to consider. She couldn't afford to miss out on any opportunity to bond with the competition. Assuming this wasn't a trap of some kind, it could work to her advantage.

Ivy led the way down the corridor to a door that opened to

stairs to the attic. Like everything else about the house, the attic was roomy and in impeccable order, with boxes neatly stacked and labeled. It hadn't occurred to Sophie that when Owen bought the house "as is," it included not only furniture, but also whatever other worldly goods Ivy had acquired over her lifetime that her nephew didn't want.

A wall had been built down the center of the attic and on the other side of it was the longest closet Sophie had ever seen. Multiple sets of heavy, sliding metal doors opened to reveal a long row of garment bags, also neatly labeled.

"Let's see," Ivy murmured, fingering through one group of bags and then moving on to those behind the next set of doors. She clearly knew what she was looking for, so Sophie just stood back and let her have at it . . . even though her own fingers were itching to unzip those bags and see what goodies were inside. Shopping wasn't her idea of fun, but this felt more like a treasure hunt, and that she did find exciting.

She'd already learned something new and interesting about Ivy: she loved clothes. It was obvious not only from how many she owned, but from how carefully, even lovingly, she treated them.

"Aha," she exclaimed at last, pulling a dark green garment bag from the closet and handing it to Sophie. "Do be careful, Miss Bennett. That's a Pierre Balmain original, from the early fifties. And now for the Chanel."

She went back to work, and when she located the second bag, she handed it to Sophie as well.

"We could try more, of course, and if need be we will. But if I do say so myself, I have a flair for these things and I'm certain both these dresses will be perfection on you, and that, Miss Bennett, is what you must aim for: perfection. Always."

"I have an idea," Sophie said. "How about if you call me Sophie and I call you Ivy? I mean we are practically roommates."

"No. Come along."

She led Sophie to a three-way mirror at the far end of the room. On the wall beside the mirror there were hooks for the garment bags. Sophie carefully unzipped the first bag and her breath caught in her throat when she saw the dress inside. She'd seen beautiful dresses before, gorgeous, to-die-for dresses, starting with those her mother made, but at that moment she couldn't remember seeing one that compared to the dress before her. At first glance she thought it was ivory, but it was actually the softest shade of gold imaginable. Even on the hanger it glimmered like fine gold: she could only imagine what it would be like to wear . . . to move and dance in. It was strapless, the top subtly accented with tiny gold and crystal beads. Tightly shirred on an angle through the bodice and hips, the full skirt fell in soft gathers from a rosette of the same fabric on the left hip.

"This is . . . beautiful," she said softly.

"Yes. It is," agreed Ivy. "Well, go on . . . try it on."

"I'm afraid to. I'm almost afraid to even touch it. It must be fragile after all these years of being packed away."

"Nonsense. Everything was cleaned and professionally treated before being stored, and the closet is climate controlled. Some people collect art; I collected fashion, and I treated it with the same care and attention."

"Well, lucky for me. I would have looked odd wearing a Picasso to the ball."

Amazingly, Ivy laughed along with her. Easily. As if, thought Sophie, they weren't on opposite sides in the wedding war.

Ivy sat on an old trunk while Sophie slipped out of the blue gown and then very carefully put on the gold Pierre Balmain . . . who she'd never heard of, but who was suddenly her favorite designer of all time. When she looked at herself in the mirror, the dress took her breath away for the second time.

It suited her perfectly, as if it had been made just for her by someone who really knew their stuff. The fit was perfect, the drape of the fabric was perfect, and in the waning light through the attic window the soft, warm color made her skin glow with a faint apricot tinge.

"Well? What do you think?" asked Ivy.

"I love it," Sophie replied, not able to take her eyes off her reflection. She turned first one way and then the other to see the dress from all angles. "I love it, I love it, I love it." She spun around to face Ivy. "Can I really wear it to the ball?"

"Of course you can wear it. That was the whole point of coming up here. But don't you want to try on the Chanel before you decide?"

Sophie shook her head and turned back to the mirror, as taken up with her own image as a kid with a new toy. "No. I already know it couldn't possibly compare to this. I love this dress. And I love it even more with me in it. That's never happened to me before."

"I shouldn't wonder if that"—Ivy pointed at the blue gown—"is indicative of your fashion sense when left to your own devices."

Sophie barely heard. She couldn't stop grinning. She was thinking out loud when she said, "I can't wait for Owen to see me in it."

"Well, if pleasing Mr. Winters is your goal, then we have wasted our time for nothing."

That she heard. The words struck her like a dart.

"I know," she said, her shrug awkward. "I know he'd never be seriously interested in me. I just thought that in this dress I'd be a little harder to dismiss . . . or ignore."

"You misunderstand me. When I said we wasted our time, I meant that you don't need a fancy designer dress to impress or captivate that man. When you're in the room, you're all he sees.

And judging from what I observed of you two together the other night, he's very seriously interested."

Sophie shook her head as their gazes met in the mirror. "I think he's physically attracted to me, at least a little, enough for a one- or two-night stand. But not enough for anything more. And to his credit, I think he's gentleman enough not to lead me on. Either that or he just doesn't want any messy complications as long as we're living under the same roof."

"You listen to me. Just because I never married doesn't mean I don't know a thing or two about men. I do. And I can tell when a man is falling so fast he doesn't even know it."

"It wouldn't matter if he did fall. He'd refuse to admit it even to himself. He doesn't believe in true love."

"Horsefeathers. The man might as well say he doesn't believe in gravity. Or hurricanes. He can say what he likes. When he stops talking, his big feet will still be firmly planted on God's green earth, and when those hurricane-force winds start to blow trees and park benches around as if they were Tinker Toys, he'll run for cover just like everyone else. Let him talk all he wants, Sophie, but pay closest attention to what he says with his heart."

"You know, if I weren't wearing an irreplaceable Pierre Balmain original from the early fifties, I'd hug you."

"Whatever for?"

"You just called me Sophie."

A smile tugged at Ivy's lips. "So I did. Well, as you said, we are practically roommates. Now I think you should take off that gown before anything happens to it and we should go downstairs so I can show you what I have in mind for your hair. And I have thoughts about the right makeup as well. You need to work on your brows. And then there's the matter of the right jewelry. I'll handle that too."

"Okay, but at the risk of ruining things just as we got to the first-name stage, I have to ask. This isn't all some kind of trick, is it? To get me to lower my guard? Is this dress booby-trapped? Maybe rigged to disappear at midnight so I'm left standing in the middle of the ballroom stark naked?"

"I'm a ghost, not a magician. Even if I could do a thing like that, why on earth would I?"

"To embarrass me and throw me off-kilter and make me all frazzled so I can't focus on the wedding."

Ivy looked crestfallen. "Do you really think I would do something like that to you?"

"Well, you have done lots of other stuff."

"Yes, because I don't want a wedding here. I've done what I had to do to get that message across. But I wouldn't do something malicious just to hurt or embarrass you. If fact," she said, tossing back her hair, "I hereby propose a truce. Until after the ball."

"That sounds good to me. A truce it is, starting now."

"Fine. Now come along. The dress is perfection, but we have a ways to go before you are."

It was on the way out of the attic that Sophie noticed the doll-house sitting on top of a stack of boxes just inside the door.

"Wait up," she called to Ivy.

Crouching down, she undid the center latch and swung the front panels open to reveal the rooms inside, complete with the split staircase at the center. "It's the Princess House," she said to Ivy, who had walked back to stand beside her, holding the garment bag. "The windows, the colors . . . it's just like the book." She looked around. "Were there ever people and furniture to go with it?"

"I have no idea," replied Ivy. "It doesn't belong to me. Owen brought it with him when he moved in. I assume he made it."

Sophie nodded. "For his daughter. For Allie." She thought for a moment and then closed and latched the panels and lifted the doll-house. It was heavy, but she'd manage.

"What are you doing?" Ivy asked.

"Taking it downstairs. I'd tell you why, but I'm afraid you'd try to trip me and that would violate our brand-new truce." She grinned over her shoulder as she maneuvered the dollhouse through the doorway. "And I really need help with my hair."

"Among many other things."

"Now who's muttering?"

They both laughed. Sophie couldn't explain why, but for some reason she was already more comfortable taking advice from Ivy than she ever was from the *J*s.

Owen finished working for the day and walked out of the guest-house with a smile on his face.

He was writing again.

That in itself was akin to a miracle. It was an even bigger miracle that when he reread what he'd written at the end of the day, he didn't hit delete and walk away angry and disgusted with himself.

Sophie's comments on his work had been like a live grenade tossed into the giant pile of garbage he'd been wrestling with as he sat at the computer day after day. But somehow—miraculously—when the debris from the blast settled, the story he was telling made sense to him in a way it hadn't in a very long time.

He was writing.

He was still taking with a grain of salt her romanticized vision of Osprey and Valene together. And her comment that Valene was the dream Osprey was afraid to dream was way off base. Like he'd told her: Osprey wasn't afraid, just rational. It had gotten him thinking, however, thinking about his hero, and about the things men dream about, and the things they fear.

He was writing again, but he was losing the battle to control his feelings for Sophie. Years of experience with sheer, white-knuckled self-discipline worked to keep her from commandeering his thoughts during the day, but at night his dreams were another world entirely. In his dreams there were no rules, no limits, and usually no clothing. There was only a megadose of Sophie, under him, riding him; in his dreams she was all he could feel or smell or touch. He woke up sweating and shaking . . . shaking with pent-up desire and with the awareness that everything he craved was sleeping just a few steps away.

As he lay awake in the dark, his dreams slid into fantasies, keeping sleep at bay for long, frustrating hours. Sometimes, lying there, he imagined he could smell her all around him, hear her breathing and whispering his name.

It didn't help that he chanced to walk by at just the right moment and caught a glimpse of her wearing only a slip, a filmy, strapless thing that clung all the way to her ankles and was somehow almost more arousing than his fantasies of her naked. Almost.

Ivy had been there too. She'd caught him looking, rolled her eyes, and swung the bedroom door shut in his face. Afterward, he heard them on the other side of the door, talking and giggling like a couple of teenage girls.

It wasn't the only time he'd seen them together in the past few days. Something was definitely up. But after he'd so abruptly—all right, rudely—taken himself out of the loop, making it clear to Sophie that Ivy and the wedding were her problems to solve, he didn't feel right asking her directly about what was going on. And when he tried to be subtle, casually observing that she and Ivy were at least finally on speaking terms, Sophie had simply flashed him an enigmatic grin and gone on her way. Humming. In an irritatingly cheerful way that made him think she wasn't losing any sleep over him.

Why was he making this so complicated? He wasn't a damn

monk. He'd dated and gone to bed with plenty of women. The process wasn't rocket science. He wanted her. She wanted him . . . at least she had at one point, and the fact that she hadn't flat-out refused his backhanded invitation to go to the ball with him and that she'd hung around to talk with him the other day suggested she was still at least a little interested. He ought to just let nature take its course and not worry about the rest.

It wasn't as if he'd lied to her about who he was or what he wanted. He'd been honest. She was an adult, and a shrewd businesswoman, capable of sizing up a situation and making up her own mind. So what the hell was his problem?

Nothing, he decided.

Tomorrow night he would be taking Sophie to the ball. It's not something he'd chosen to attend, but now he was almost glad Helen Archer had roped him into it. He was even happier that he'd succeeded in roping Sophie into going with him. He was really looking forward to spending the evening with her. He'd never been a great dancer and he was sure to be worse now, but one of the things he was most looking forward to was holding Sophie in his arms as they danced.

Thinking about it had him smiling as he walked into the kitchen and headed straight for the refrigerator, hoping he'd find a pitcher of iced tea with slices of lemon floating in it and the perfect amount of sugar. Instead he stopped short when he saw the dollhouse sitting on the counter. His smile disappeared, along with the past twenty or so years of his life.

Seeing it ripped the lid off memories and emotions he kept buried. He would have quickly shoved them back down deep inside and dumped a load of denial and distractions on top if Sophie hadn't distracted him by strolling into the kitchen at that moment. His first thought was that Ivy had put the dollhouse there, that it was just one more of her attempts to get under his skin. But the cat-that-swallowed-the-canary expression on Sophie's face told him that this time Ivy wasn't to blame.

"What the hell is this?" he demanded.

Her smile deepened, which only pissed him off more.

"Don't you recognize it?"

"Yeah. I recognize it. I meant what the hell is it doing here?"

"I found it in the attic. Ivy brought me up there so I could borrow a dress for the ball," she explained before he could ask what the hell she was doing poking around in his attic. "Shades of Cinderella," she went on, her self-effacing shrug putting only the slightest dent in his ire. "At first I assumed the dollhouse belonged to Ivy, but she told me that you brought it with you when you moved in. Did you build it yourself?"

"Can't you tell?" he retorted and for the first time she seemed to register the fact that he was royally irked. "Check out the uneven roof shingles and the botch job on that second floor window. I must have ripped that sucker out and re-set it a dozen times and I still couldn't get it square. A smarter man would have taken that as a sign and thrown in the towel, but back then, an abundance of smarts wasn't my biggest problem. Not by a long shot."

"Are you kidding me? I think it's beautiful just as it is. You did an amazing job. The wrought iron trim on the windows, the curving staircase, the chandeliers . . . it's perfect. Allie must have loved it. I'm assuming Allie is the one you made it for?"

"For her fifth birthday," he told her, not sure why. He was torn between wanting to talk about it and wanting to grab the damn thing and smash it, to make the memory go away once and for all. The urge to smash he understood and could deal with. The urge to talk was new. He suspected it had something to do with the fact that it was Sophie standing there, stirring up these feelings, and he didn't like it.

"I'll bet she went crazy when she saw it," she said.

He shifted his gaze from the dollhouse to meet hers. "I never gave it to her."

"You didn't give . . . why on earth not?"

He shrugged and crossed to the sink, settling for a glass of water instead of the iced tea he'd hoped for. He stared out the window at the daisies dancing in the sunlight, neither of them speaking for what seemed like a very long time. Long enough for a particularly painful stretch of his life to pass before him in slow motion.

"I'd never built anything before," he said finally, his back still to her. "It took me months to finish it. That window wasn't the only thing I ripped out more than once. It didn't matter. I didn't care how long it took or how much I had to cut corners to pay for parts and tools. The whole time I was working on it I kept imagining the look on Allie's face when I walked into her party carrying it. Rachel—my ex-wife—and I had been divorced for nearly four years by that time and she was remarried to a guy who was everything I wasn't . . . rich, successful, Ivy League–educated . . . a guy who met all of her—and her parents'— requirements. Sometimes while I worked on it I pictured the look on their faces too: I was going to show all of them that even though I'd been a lousy husband and provider, I was a damn good father."

"I'm sure you weren't a lousy . . ."

"No. I was," he acknowledged, turning and leaning against the sink. "By almost anyone's standards, but especially by Rachel's and her folks'. Hell, I was eighteen when Rachel got pregnant and we got married . . . against her family's wishes, needless to say. The son of an ex-con carnie wasn't what they had in mind for their little girl. I was so sure they were wrong. I was convinced that love and hard work would make everything all right in the end. It took me a while to figure out that it didn't matter how much I loved her, or how hard I worked, or how many backbreaking jobs I juggled to pay the bills. I would never be able to make Rachel's dreams come true. We wanted different things."

"I'm sorry. I'm sure that wasn't an easy decision to make. You had a baby you loved to think of, as well as your own future. Whatever you did was bound to be painful."

"Yeah. It was painful, all right. Painful not to be able to see Allie whenever I wanted to. Painful to see her with a new step-father . . . just the word alone made me want to punch a hole in something . . . a step-father who could give my little girl all the things I wanted to give her and couldn't." His jaw hardened as he looked at the dollhouse. "But I was going to fix that. Just one time I was going to give her something no one else could . . . something that would top everything else. I kept telling myself that and I believed it, right up until the moment I drove up and saw Allie riding up and down the driveway of their big fancy new house in her brand-new, fully motorized miniature pink convertible, just like the one her favorite Barbie dolls drove . . . a custom-made present from her step-father. I looked at the dollhouse and suddenly all I could see were flaws and amateur mistakes . . . and what a fool I'd been to ever think I could one-up them."

"What did you do?"

He shook his head, his short laugh harsh. "I took off with it still in the back seat and skipped the party. The next day I went to Toys "R" Us and bought Allie something else . . . I can't remember what it was. It took me another day to get up the nerve to go back there and give it to her . . . thereby securing my reputation as a screw-up and all-around failure."

He didn't need to look at Sophie: he could feel the pity oozing from her. He could have told her the rest of the story. He could have told her that things changed after that. But he didn't. He was sick of talking.

But things had changed. Because he changed them. He'd decided he was probably never going to be filthy rich—and how about the irony there?—but he could be the kind of man Allie was proud to have for her father and he made up his mind that he was going to do whatever he had to do to become that man. He enlisted and discovered there were things he was good at. Very good, in fact. There were things he could do that very few men could. Important things. Over the next few years he tasted real success for the first time. He earned the respect of men he respected, men willing to trust him with their very lives, and he learned to respect himself. He became the father that Allie deserved.

But he never gave her the dollhouse and he wasn't sure why he'd held onto it all this time. It represented a time he'd rather forget and brought back memories of feeling inadequate and disappointed. Disappointment in himself, and in love. He'd grown up watching his parents fight and saw their marriage wither and die. It made him wary. But still, when he met Rachel, he fell hard and fast and forever. Or so he thought. That was before he learned that nothing is forever, least of all a fragile emotion like love.

Suddenly impatient with the feelings and memories it triggered, he grabbed the dollhouse and headed for the back door.

"What are you doing?" Sophie called after him.

"What I should have done years ago," he told her, grunting as he shouldered the door open. The damn thing was heavy. "Getting rid of it for good."

"No. Wait. I brought it down here so I could ask you if it would be all right for me to use it as a focal point in the sunroom during the cocktail hour."

"No."

"No? Just like that?"

"Just like that," he said, and let the door slam shut.

Sixteen

＊

Ivy turned out to be the mother of all fairy godmothers and Sophie was profoundly grateful to be taken under her wing. Dress, hair, makeup: Ivy had a knack for pulling it all together. She even revealed a secret compartment in the drawer of her dressing table where she'd tucked away several of her favorites pieces of jewelry and she came up with the perfect finishing touch: a necklace of three twisted strands of small, luminescent pearls and matching earrings that seemed to have been designed to complement the dress. Having heard stories of Ivy in her prime, Sophie thought they very well might have been. Either that or a gift from some besotted foreign ambassador or globe-trotting adventurer. She'd seen the old photo albums that were also in the attic closet. Ivy had stolen the hearts of a string of interesting men. And had any one of them ever measured up to her Joseph, she told Sophie, she might have married after all. No one ever had.

At last it was time to look in the mirror to see how it all came together. Ordinarily Sophie's first reaction to the beautiful, sophisticated woman she saw reflected there would be that it couldn't possibly be her, but not tonight . . . tonight she felt beautiful from the inside out. Tonight she gazed at her reflection and felt very much at home in her own skin.

She was convinced it was the most astounding makeover ever . . . until she saw Owen waiting for her at the bottom of the staircase. Gone were the battered T-shirt and jeans. Tonight he was tall, dark perfection in an impeccably tailored black tux. His hair was cut short, all the sun-bleached streaks gone, and he was clean-shaven, emphasizing the strong angles of his handsome face. She had to stop for a moment because she was finding it hard to walk and breathe and control the sudden explosion of lust all at the same time.

First things first. Lust. Breathe. Walk.

He smiled when he saw her.

Ivy's final words of advice played in her head.

"Now about Mr. Winters. Never underestimate the power of playing hard to get. Trust me, I know the type. A warrior, born to conquer. Men like that value most what they have to fight and sweat and struggle to win. So let him sweat. Let him eat his heart out. It will do him a world of good, I promise you."

Sophie would have found the advice hard to follow even before she saw him standing there looking like the incarnation of every fairy-tale prince fantasy she'd ever had. She wasn't good at playing games. And she didn't want to be. After devoting entirely too much thought to the problem of Owen Winters, she'd made up her mind to simply take things as they came. Tonight she was going to let down her guard and enjoy the evening for what it was, a gift, a fluke, a rare and unexpected opportunity to step outside herself and be the confident, beautiful, adventurous woman she'd like to be. For once she was going to relax and go with the flow . . . without planning an alternate route in case of emergency, without expectations or stipulations.

He came toward her as she reached the bottom step, took her right hand in his, and slipped on her wrist a corsage of ivory roses and baby's breath, the dark green leaves lightly dusted with gold.

"I've been advised by someone who should know that this is customary for a lady attending a formal ball."

"Hmm," she murmured, smiling as she glanced up and around. "Something tells me we have the same fairy godmother. Thank you. It's lovely."

He smiled at her. "You're lovely, Sophie. Beautiful, in fact. Beyond beautiful. I feel like I need another thousand or so words to do justice to the way you look tonight, but instead I'm suddenly speechless . . . a rarity for a man who makes a living with words."

"That's probably for the best, actually. I'm already feeling very belle-of-the-ball-ish. At this point compliments would go straight to my head and push me over the line into being obnoxious." She ran her gaze over him approvingly. "But I must say you look amazing. It's like we wore costumes after all, because I feel like a princess and you make a very dashing Prince Charming. No, not costumes. Prom night. It's like prom night all over again, except this time it's not a disaster waiting to happen."

"Let's hope not."

She slanted a look of concern from under her newly lush lashes. "You're not planning to tell me halfway through the night that you're in love with my sister and only invited me because she promised to repay you by going to see a movie with you next weekend, are you?"

He winced a little as he shook his head. "A resounding no to all of it."

"Then we definitely have the prom beat hands down." He was looking at her intently with what could either be fascination or bafflement about what he'd gotten himself into.

"Did I mention that when I get overexcited I have a tendency to babble?" she asked him.

"You didn't have to. This isn't a blind date, Sophie."

"Meaning?"

"I've already heard you babble."

She sighed. "That's what I was afraid you meant."

"You didn't let me finish . . ."

"Because I was babbling."

"I've heard you babble, and I like it." He offered his arm. "Shall we do this?"

"Yes." His arm felt solid beneath her fingertips. "But this time we're definitely taking my car. You can drive if you like, but there's no way I'm getting on a motorcycle . . ."

He opened the front door and she saw the black stretch limo parked in the drive. The uniformed driver slid from behind the wheel and held the door open for them.

His smile rakish, Owen held out his hand. "Your pumpkin awaits, Princess."

The ball was more fun than Sophie would have thought possible. It helped that the most handsome man there stubbornly refused to be pried from her side all evening . . . which was saying something considering the effort Helen Archer put into trying to commandeer him. In the end Helen seemed content to drag Owen, who in turn dragged Sophie, around to meet the other board members, which allowed her to bask in the glory of having landed the biggest celebrity there.

The auction was a huge success. A doctor from Barrington bought the collection of Owen's books for an outrageous amount and Sophie played her part by handing them to Owen to be signed, which also allowed her to soak up a bit of reflected glory in the process. It was clear he had a lot of fans in the crowd.

For Sophie, the only flaw in the evening was that it went by too quickly. She kept reminding herself to take mental pictures of the highlights so she could relive them later. Highlights such as the moment when she and Owen were leaving the dance floor and she bumped into Jill . . . literally. They exchanged apologetic murmurs and then Jill looked directly at her and did a double take straight out of a Hanna-Barbera cartoon.

"Sophie?" she blurted. "Sophie?" She dragged her stunned gaze down to the sparkly new stiletto-heeled shoes on Sophie's feet and then back up to her face, which was still flushed from dancing and from the incredible feeling of being held tightly in Owen's arms. "My God, Sophie, you look . . . gorgeous."

"Thanks. So do you."

"Where did you find that fabulous dress?"

"Long story. I'll fill you in later," she promised, knowing Jill would be on the phone first thing in the morning wanting details.

The night went by too fast and ended too soon. Feeling like Cinderella, she was back in her chauffeur-driven coach by midnight. With one important improvement on the fairy-tale version: she was riding with the prince. They were soon home, but Sophie wasn't ready for the night to end and Owen appeared to feel the same way.

"Nice night," he said as they stood in the front drive, neither making a move to go inside. He tipped his head back to gaze at the sky. "A lot of stars up there tonight."

Sophie looked up and nodded agreement. "I think I see the Big Dipper."

"Want to take a walk around back where we can get a better look?"

She very much wanted to . . . she wanted it even before he took her hand in his and closed his fingers around it possessively and made her heart thump harder.

It felt good to be walking hand in hand with him. It felt right.

The only light in back came from the stars and a sliver of moon. They followed the path that led to the cliffs. Off to the right Sophie could see the shadowy outline of the recently completed illusion pond and the bushes and small flowering trees that were the beginning of the surrounding fantasy woodland. Remarkably she didn't squander a single brain cell wondering if it would all be ready on time or what Ivy might do to interfere once their truce was over.

Tonight her mind was on other things. And obviously Owen's was as well. They didn't make it halfway to the ocean's edge before he stopped and dragged her into his arms. Not that any dragging was necessary. She'd been his from the first deep "shall we dance?" hours ago, and her yearning for more . . . for this . . . had grown each time his hand caressed her back or molded to the curve of her hip.

Oh yeah. Definitely better than the prom.

Eyes closed, she gave herself up to his kiss and to the waves of shimmering pleasure it sent rolling through her. She reached up to cup his face with her hands and kissed him back. He tasted of whiskey and desire, and the midnight hint of stubble along his jaw made his skin feel deliciously rough against her softer skin as his mouth raked impatient kisses over her throat and bare shoulders.

Warmth bubbled through her as the effect of several glasses of champagne collided with the electrifying effect Owen had had on her from the instant they'd met. She felt energized and reckless, and she liked the feeling.

He slid his palm down her arm and took her by the hand once more, his quiet voice even rougher than usual. "Come on."

As soon as she sensed him trying to pull her off the path and toward the guesthouse, she resisted. "Owen, I can't."

"Huh. What?" He gave his head a small shake, staring at her in the darkness. "Damn it, Sophie. Okay. No is no, but . . . damn it, Sophie."

"No, no. I meant I can't because I'll get the bottom of my dress wet in the grass. It's one of a kind. Irreplaceable."

Comprehension—and quite possibly relief—gleamed in his eyes as he reached for her. "One of a kind and irreplaceable? Damn it, Sophie, so are you."

Seemingly without effort, he scooped her up in his arms, another of those freeze-frame Merchant-Ivory moments to savor later, and carried her to the guesthouse and over the threshold. Kicking the door shut behind him in the time-honored tradition of Rhett Butler, he kissed her long and hard, not stopping until he'd made his way to the next room and gently lowered her to her feet beside the bed.

Owen Winters could claim he wasn't a romantic all he liked: Sophie knew differently.

Reaching behind him, he turned on the small bedside lamp and the room filled with soft amber light.

"I want to see you," he explained.

Taking her by the shoulders, he turned her so her back was to him and slowly lowered the zipper on her dress. His fingers brushed against each inch of newly revealed skin and Sophie swore she felt his hands tremble. With the dress loosened, he slid it down her legs and helped her step out of it, taking time to drape it across the back of a chair.

She and Ivy had debated the need for a slip beneath the dress and the slip lost. Now she stood before him in only her lacy panties and strapless bra and it would be a lie to say she hadn't thought about just such a moment when she was putting them on earlier.

Owen bracketed her waist with his palms, pleasure and approval radiating from him as he slowly stroked over the soft curves of her hips and thighs. Again she felt his hands tremble.

He sought her gaze, his expression rueful. "It's been a while for me."

"And me," she whispered.

"I want to take my time, but I'm not sure I can."

Sophie swayed closer to him. "I'm not sure I want you to."

He sucked in a sharp breath and dragged his palms higher to cup her full breasts. Sliding one hand around to the clasp at the back, he unfastened it with a minimum of fumbling and leaned back to look at her.

Her breasts lifted with a deep breath and the tips hardened under his heated gaze even before he bent his head and found them with his mouth.

She gripped his shoulders and threw her head back as his tongue sent shivers of excitement racing through her. A fierce feminine hunger rose up in her. She wanted the hot, damp pleasure to go on forever and she wanted more . . . wanted all of him . . . right . . . that . . . instant.

Owen's urgency matched her own. Pressing her hard against his hips, he lifted his head to kiss her mouth again and again.

They were both out of breath, chests heaving in an effort to get it back, when he stopped and stepped back just enough to see what he was doing as he hooked his thumbs at the side of her panties and slowly, deliberately, peeled them off.

Her knees like jelly, Sophie braced one hand on his chest as she stepped out of them. The fact that she was naked except for the crystal-studded stilettos—and that he was still *GQ* perfect in his tux—made her feel sexy and slightly wanton. The effect wasn't wasted on Owen: he growled low in his throat as his gaze moved over her slowly, a sound that was part need, part pleasure. Excitement and impatience flared darkly in his eyes.

"Lie down," he urged, his fingertips stroking the V between her thighs.

"Not yet." She reached to undo his bow tie and pull it off. His shirt required more work: all those studs and cuff links. When she reached for his belt, he kicked off his shoes. And then in a rush of movement and tangled, impatient hands, his trousers were unzipped and gone and his naked body was pressing hers down onto the mattress.

"Not fair," she whimpered as he caressed her belly before sliding his hand between her legs, where she was hot and wet and ready. "You got to look at me."

He might have laughed, or groaned, but he rolled slightly to his side so that she could see him. The light gilded the flat planes and sculpted muscles of his body. Her gaze slid greedily over his chest and flat belly to the visible proof of how badly he wanted her. He was hard, and magnificent.

Usually she would be thinking too much to enjoy the moment, analyzing and second-guessing and worrying what her partner was thinking. Not tonight. Owen's touch shattered her ability to think. This was all about raw sensation. Without shyness or hesitation, she reached for him, curving her fingers as she slowly stroked him. She watched his eyes close and his muscles shudder. Another slow movement of her hand and sweat glistened on his forehead.

"Enough," he said roughly, grabbing her hand and kissing the inside of her arm from wrist to shoulder as he rolled back on top of her.

He nudged her thighs apart and Sophie spread them to welcome him. She felt him, hot and hard, poised against her sleek entrance.

Bracing his weight on his hands, he found her gaze and held it. "Next time we'll take it slow," he promised.

Sophie smiled and lifted her hips. "Maybe."

With one sure stroke he was inside her. He rocked against her, slowly at first, silk against silk, and then faster, harder, deeper, both of them already dangerously close to the edge of control.

Sophie wrapped one leg around his hips and then the other, and felt a whole new rush of sensations, and then came the first fluttery contraction of muscles she couldn't control if she wanted to.

She clutched at his shoulders.

She closed her eyes.

She gave herself over to the pleasure building inside.

She'd heard the expression *drowning in sensation*, but Sophie didn't feel like she was drowning. She felt like she was flying . . . soaring . . . her arc sure and true as she raced through the brilliant white light that filled her with heat. And Owen was with her. She felt his arms tighten around her and heard his rough cry echo her own as they rocketed past the edge of everything, together and alone.

Usually, if Owen spent the night having sex with a woman and then woke up alone, his overriding reaction was relief. It meant he wasn't obliged to hang around and have "the talk." He didn't make pregame promises he had no intention of keeping, and the postgame wrap-up that so many women required always struck him as pointless. Sex was what it was. Fun while it lasted. It wasn't something that had to be dissected and analyzed.

This morning when he awoke, saw where he was, and remembered how he got there, he was instantly hard and hungry all over again. Smiling, he rolled over and reached for Sophie . . . and found her gone. Along with her one-of-a-kind, irreplaceable dress and every other visible sign that she'd been there. Had last night been just another of his fantasies?

No. Impossible. There was no way he could have imagined last night. For one thing, he didn't have the raw material to work with. And for another . . . He just knew, that's all. Last night had been different from any other night . . . different and new in a way he couldn't explain. And now Sophie was gone and he didn't feel relief. He felt . . . something else. It wasn't a pleasant feeling. It was more like a hundred pounds of crushed stones had been dumped on his chest and settled right over his heart. Disappointment: that was it. And then, before he'd even come to terms with the disappointment, came another novel morning-after feeling: worry.

Had she left because she was upset about something? Or maybe she'd also awoke feeling disappointed, but for an entirely different reason? Maybe she'd wanted to get out of Dodge without having to explain or pretend. An uncomfortable heat crept up his neck to his face. What if the sex hadn't been as much fun for Sophie as it was for him? *Crap,* he thought. Was this why women wanted to talk about it afterward? To make sure everyone was on the same page and was going away happy?

He folded his arms behind his head, staring at the ceiling and seeing quick flashes of images from the night before. She'd seemed happy enough afterward. Hadn't she? Happy and satisfied. She'd smiled drowsily and curled up in his arms before falling asleep, but they hadn't actually said much. He tried to recall exactly what they had said, and couldn't. He tried harder, but no matter how hard he focused, the memory that kept pushing to the forefront of his mind, the one he knew he would carry away from last night and never forget, was of looking into Sophie's eyes at the moment their bodies joined for the first time and feeling an explosion of warmth and wonder unlike anything he'd ever felt before.

Had she felt it too? He wasn't even sure what it was or what it meant. But suddenly it seemed crucial to know if she'd felt it too.

* * *

As soon as he stepped outside the guesthouse he noticed something different. Something besides the people scurrying about with ladders and shrubbery and giant rolls of electrical wire. Workers had been coming and going for weeks, but suddenly there were more of them and their movements seemed more purposeful. There was a new energy in the air.

He drew a few curious looks and sly grins as he made his way to the house barefoot and wearing half a tux. He considered showering and changing before looking for Sophie, but only for about a second and a half. He was much too anxious to see her to waste time. From the sounds of it, the kitchen was ground zero, and that's where he found her, clipboard in hand, papers strewn across the counter beside her. He glanced at them in passing and saw an oversize calendar and a diagram of the house and grounds marked with scribbled notes and large red Xs.

Sophie smiled at the sight of him and he felt a trickle of relief begin to flow. But when he moved closer and leaned in to kiss her, she put a hand up to stop him and quickly stepped out of reach.

"Sorry," she said, her quiet tone rueful. She indicated the pair of burly men carrying in worktables from the truck parked out back. "It's tough enough to get union laborers to take orders from a woman seriously. I don't want to give them any idea that I'm not a hundred percent business."

"Of course," Owen agreed, also taking a step back. He shouldn't have had to be told that, but to be honest, when he walked in and saw Sophie, he forgot that she was working and that there were others around. "I'm surprised they're even working on Sunday. Don't unions have rules about that kind of thing?"

"Yeah, it's called the time-and-a-half rule. This is costing plenty. Another reason I want them hustling, not ogling."

"You couldn't have waited until tomorrow for those tables?"

She shook her head, her eyes on her clipboard. "No, because tomorrow the portable ovens and cooktops and the refrigerator cases arrive. And the tables have to be in place in order for—" Her attention was caught by a man across the room. "Those are going straight out back," she called to him. "By the patio. I'd like to keep the shepherd's hooks together with the lanterns so that when the electrician comes to wire them he won't have to waste time hauling them around."

"He better not haul them around," said one of the men carrying tables, his tone only half joking. "Hauling is laborers' work."

"And there's plenty of it, so keep moving," said Sophie. She looked at Owen with an apologetic shrug. "Sorry I'm so crazed, but today begins the six-day countdown and I need everything to go like clockwork. I'll be lucky if I have time to breathe between now and the wedding . . . and that's without any spontaneous mystical interference," she added pointedly.

He nodded, understanding. "I'll let you get back to work, then. I just wanted to . . . About last night . . ."

"What about it?" she countered distractedly, her attention split between him and the activity swirling around them.

"It's just that I know women like to discuss those things afterward . . . to know where they stand."

"Don't worry, I know where I stand. Last night was fun for me," she assured him, and then gave a quick frown. "For you too, I hope?"

"It was. Definitely . . . though 'fun' isn't the first word that comes to mind to describe it."

"I guess maybe . . . no, no, don't force it," she called to the men struggling to wedge a worktable next to the stove. "If it won't fit there, put it in the dining room for now." She turned to Owen with a rueful look. "Sorry. Where was I? Oh, right . . . last night. Look, if you're worried that I'm reading more into it, or that now things between us will be complicated or awkward, don't be. I'm not . . . and they won't."

"Well, good. It's just that when I woke up, you were gone . . ."

"Not by choice. The crushed stone for the pathways was being delivered at seven and I had to be there to greet it and make sure it was the right size and color. I would have mentioned it last night, but I was a little . . . preoccupied."

"Yeah. Me too." His face warmed at the memory. "Anyway, I just wanted to make sure you were all right."

"Thank you. I'm fine. I can see how you might wonder about the fallout . . . me being a self-proclaimed die-hard romantic and all. Usually I am more emotional about these things. But this was different."

Owen didn't know why, but he wasn't sure he liked the sound of that. "I don't see how different it could be. Romance is romance."

"Except last night wasn't about romance. Oh, it was plenty romantic, with the gown and the dancing and the chauffeur-driven limo, but it wasn't about the serious, forever kind of romance. You made it clear where *you* stand when it comes to that sort of thing and because of that I went into last night with my eyes wide open and . . . what happened happened. It was a great evening. End of story."

"What's that supposed to mean?"

She shrugged. "It's just an expression." She peered more closely at him. "But you know, seeing that grim look on your face makes me wonder . . . could it be *you're* the one with a serious case of the morning-afters."

Owen felt obliged to scoff.

Her green eyes sparkled mischievously. "Maybe that latent romance gene I warned you about is finally kicking in."

"Don't be ridiculous."

"Maybe you're worried about falling head over heels in love and having to surrender your role as Chief Cynic and Skeptic."

"Never happen," he retorted.

She cocked her head to the side. "Do I detect a new note of uncertainty in your bravado and bluster?"

"Not at all." He swung his tux jacket over his shoulder and hooked it with his index finger, hoping the nonchalant George Clooney impression would compensate for any lack of confidence in his tone. "You can't fall in something that doesn't exist."

Seventeen

Bemused, Sophie watched Owen leaving the kitchen. It was sweet of him to come looking for her in case she had any morning-after regrets. Only suddenly she was wondering if that's all there was to it.

She'd been teasing when she suggested his latent romance gene might be kicking in, but something about his reaction had her thinking her words might have struck a nerve. Could it be that Owen had been bothered when he woke up and found her gone and that perhaps *he* was the one in need of a little morning-after reassurance?

She shook her head and reached for her clipboard. Impossible.

She had no idea how many women there were in Owen's no-doubt-adventurous past, and she didn't think she wanted to. Suffice it to say that the man knew his way around a bed. And not only had he not fallen in love with any of those other women, he hadn't even come close enough to be swayed from his belief that love was nothing more than . . . how had he put it? Ah yes, a hormonally driven mutual fantasy. A fantasy that, according to him, one partner inevitably tired of first. The fact that the theory went against everything she believed in didn't stop it from being the Gospel according to Owen. To even entertain the possibility that making love to her had somehow managed to melt his cynical heart overnight was the kind of wishful thinking she knew all too well. She'd spent an embarrassing number of years wishful thinking that her relationship with Keith was something it wasn't.

That kind of thinking led to disappointment and heartache. But she was older and marginally wiser now and she was going to stick with her new modus operandi, the one she'd adopted prior to the ball, free of the influence of both fairy dust and hormones. Live for the moment: that was her new approach. And last night's test drive had exceeded her wildest expectations. Sex with Owen had been uncomplicated and amazing, and she woke this morning feeling great. No regrets. No second thoughts.

She wasn't normally the type to throw caution to the wind. Far from it, in fact. But that's exactly why it was the right approach for right now. *Normally* she didn't live in an oceanfront mansion and attend balls on the arm of a handsome and famous millionaire. She didn't wear vintage designer gowns and she sure as hell didn't walk around turning heads and causing jaws to drop when she entered the room. The past few weeks had been like a dream. And dreams were finite. She had only a short while left to live "the Princess House life," and most of that time would be taken up with work. She didn't want to waste a single moment caught up in a spiral of what-ifs and if-onlys. This was one adventure she was going to live to the fullest without worrying about what might happen tomorrow and the day after and the day after that. Coffee at sunrise or sex at midnight: she was open to it all, to whatever temptation fate saw fit to drop in her path.

She might leave Ange de la Mer with regrets, but for once they weren't going to be about things she wished she'd done.

Her musing was interrupted when the floral designer called her outside for a huddle with the lighting technician concerning the pair of seventeen-foot-high distressed-wood columns to be built around the tent's center poles. They would each be wrapped in a garland of wild-grape-and-bare-honeysuckle vines, and at random points wrought-iron brackets would be added to suspend antique white silk lanterns filled with white candles. They wanted final approval on the number of lanterns to be hung from each pole— twenty-one—and Sophie double-checked to make sure the materials being used were fire retardant. Then she was called away again, this time to confirm the exact dimensions and placement of the white dance floor.

They were using white wherever possible . . . dance floor, tent draping, bleached white table linens. Soft shades of white blended well with the abundance of natural and organic elements and all that white would also provide a neutral, light-absorbing surface for the elaborate custom lighting that would create the ambience of an enchanted forest. The effect of the lighting would be lush and rustic at first glance, evolving over the course of the evening into wild, shifting tones of magenta, cobalt blue, and emerald green. The designer in charge assured her it would be fantastical and breathtaking, and Sophie had seen enough of his work to trust he would deliver.

She was in constant motion throughout the day, working with the vendors on site and repeatedly updating her lists and diagrams so she knew exactly what was done, what was in progress and what would be happening tomorrow and the next day and the next. Countdown week was always a killer and this wedding had a lot more going on than most. Oddly, though, instead of feeling weary or frazzled, Sophie felt energized. And happy. An inside-out, whistle-while-you-work, silly-smile-for-no-special-reason kind of happy. She should have tried throwing caution to the wind years ago.

Around noon she escaped to the quiet of her room to call Shelby with a status report and also to remind her that the minister was expecting the final version of the vows she and Matthew had written by the end of the day. Afterward she took a minute to splash water on her face and comb her hair.

"Have you lost your mind?"

She glanced over her shoulder in time to see Ivy strolling into her room as if she owned it, which of course she believed she did. And it was exactly that—her passionate connection to the house—that supplied the energy for her to just materialize whenever she damn well pleased.

"I thought we discussed the whole popping-in-unannounced thing and you promised not to do it," Sophie reminded her.

With a long-suffering sigh, Ivy retraced her steps and knocked dramatically on the door.

"Better?" she asked, sashaying back in without waiting to be asked and flouncing down on the bed. "Now where was I? Oh, right. Have you lost your mind?"

"No," Sophie countered. "But the very fact that you feel the need to ask makes me wonder if I'm the right person to judge. Why did you ask?"

"You were singing."

"And that makes me crazy?"

"No. It's what you were singing. Christmas carols. In August. When it's so hot even I'm on the verge of sweating and I never, ever sweat."

"Ghosts don't sweat?"

Ivy arched her brows and paused briefly in the act of fanning herself with her hand. "*Ladies* don't sweat."

"Oh . . . horsefeathers . . . to quote a friend of mine." She hadn't realized she was singing and now she wrinkled her brow as she tried to recall the song. "What carol was it, anyway?"

Ivy sang a few lines from one of Sophie's favorite carols, all about *mistletoeing* and hearts that are glowing.

"It's the most wonderful time of the year—" she sang and stopped suddenly, her eyes wide. "Oh my goodness," she exclaimed, "that's it. Of course. I should have guessed it straightaway this morning when you went on and on about his dancing and his manners and the cleft in his chin . . . you've fallen in love with Mr. Winters."

"What? Don't be silly. I mean, sure, I may have commented on his manners," she allowed. "He happens to have very nice manners. And a very nice cleft in his chin. But I certainly didn't go on and on . . ." She paused, remembering, and frowned. "Or if I did, it was only because you came barging in here before I was even dressed, demanding to hear every single detail of what went on last night."

"Not all of which were forthcoming," Ivy pointed out, referring to Sophie's refusal to discuss what happened after they returned home. She was so glad the guesthouse was outside Ivy's free-range zone.

"Forthcoming or not, none of it, including the singing, means I've fallen in love. Which, for the record, I haven't."

Ivy looked doubtful. "You're certain?"

"Very certain. I have everything under control," Sophie added, mostly to reassure herself of that fact. "And what do Christmas carols have to do with falling in love, anyway?"

Ivy lifted one shoulder with a negligent sigh. "It's not the carol specifically; it's more the mood . . . that whole chirpy, hap-hap-happiest mood. Let's just say I have a sixth sense about these things." She hesitated, glanced at the window, and then said hurriedly, "But that's not what I'm here about."

Sophie was suddenly aware of the sound of a siren, close by

and drawing closer. Much closer. She looked at Ivy's catbirdlike expression and a shiver of apprehension ran along her spine.

"*That's* what I'm here about," Ivy said, pointing toward the window as she stood, the rustle of her rose chiffon skirt almost drown out by the fire engine now speeding up the drive with siren blaring. "I wanted to remind you that our truce is over."

By the time Sophie got downstairs, firefighters in protective clothing and with ventilation masks at the ready were swarming around the first floor. The captain explained to Sophie that they'd received a call about a suspected gas leak. As soon as she heard that the 911 call had come from inside the house, she had a few suspicions of her own . . . none of which she was about to share with the firemen.

Instead she had no choice but to go along as they took the precaution of evacuating the house and nearby grounds, cooling her heels as her temper simmered and the time she was losing ticked away second by infuriating second. It was a big house, with many nooks and crannies, and the "wild gas chase" as Josh, who was working overtime as her assistant and all-around errand runner, dubbed it, cost her nearly two hours. And all for a false alarm. She didn't want to think about how long they'd be twiddling their thumbs if the firefighters had actually found something.

She wouldn't have been surprised if they had found a small leak somewhere. Ivy was nothing if not resourceful and she'd also demonstrated that she had a reckless streak. But Sophie had come to know her well enough to believe she wouldn't intentionally hurt anyone. In fact, the more time she had to stand outside, baking in the midday sun and stewing about the senseless interruption, the more the false alarm made perfect sense to her.

Today had been a warning to her . . . a preview of what *could* happen if she didn't back off. If the same thing occurred on Saturday, perhaps with an actual leak thrown in to up the ante and drag out the entire process, it would be a wedding planner's nightmare. She shuddered as she pictured hundreds of people, guests and staff alike, being herded away from the house and made to stand around for hours while back in the kitchen, food in various stages of preparation went untended. If they were lucky, the outdoor ceremony might be salvaged, but the reception would be a shambles . . . if not completely ruined.

She was trying to prepare for whatever happened, but in all the disaster scenes she'd conjured up in the past few weeks, she'd never considered a gas leak. It was so simple . . . so diabolically, deceptively simple. Obviously whatever bonding had taken place between Ivy and her during the truce hadn't softened Ivy's resolve any: she was still dead set against the wedding. And Sophie still felt honor bound to do whatever she could to follow through on her promise to Shelby. It was going to take a lot of creative juice to come up with a contingency plan in case of sudden evacuation, but she was going to give it her best shot. If Ivy had expected her to give up, she was in for a surprise. She still had five days after all. In that way the false alarm had been a gift . . . she'd gotten a quick peek at the cards Ivy was holding.

And that, Sophie suddenly realized, is precisely what Ivy had intended. The truce hadn't been a total waste after all. In her own screwball way, Ivy was trying to play fair.

The knock on the guesthouse door would have interrupted his writing had there been any writing going on. But after a string of highly productive days, Owen was back spinning his wheels and staring at the blinking cursor and a blank drawing board. This time, however, it wasn't entirely his fault. He'd done his part. He'd labored over the plot, fine-tuning it until it unwound as precisely as a Swiss watch. And he'd peppered it with fresh twists guaranteed to surprise faithful readers and hook new ones. Or so he thought. Instead he was the one surprised. Shocked, in fact.

He'd thought he knew Osprey. He'd thought he could predict his every move . . . his every thought process. Not because the character was that boring; because he was that solid. That stalwart. That dedicated to duty and to doing what had to be done without being sidetracked or swayed by personal considerations. Osprey had no personal considerations, damn it. Owen had intentionally created him that way because he knew it would make Osprey's life simpler and his mission easier. He would never have to worry about screwing up or having someone he trusted walk out when he needed them most. Unencumbered and straightforward and free of any messy emotional crap that tore you up inside and left you reeling . . . that was Osprey. Designed to be totally independent and efficient. He had a job to do and he did it. Period. He never made compromises because he never had to. The world around him might fall apart or implode or erupt into a fiery inferno, but Osprey's world remained steady and inviolate.

At least that's how it was supposed to work.

Instead, just as the final plot dominoes were beginning to fall and he needed to be at his most vigilant and focused, Osprey was suddenly distracted and preoccupied. To put it another way, he was a brooding mess. And why? Because in a moment of weakness, he'd lowered his guard and given in to sweet temptation.

Okay, Owen was willing to admit that that part might be mostly his fault, or more accurately Sophie's fault, since she was the one who'd planted the idea that his books could stand a bit of romance. *It's the key to everything,* she'd said. The key to disaster was more like it. *Valene is the dream that Osprey is afraid to dream,* she'd said. Now the dream had turned into a nightmare. For Owen anyway. Osprey had swilled so much whiskey it was impossible to know what he was thinking. The bottom line was that at the moment Owen's clever plot had ground to a halt and neither he nor Osprey had a fucking clue what to do about Valene.

When he heard the knock on the door, his first thought was that it was probably one of the gardeners or carpenters or other invaders who were hard at work making noise and turning his once-peaceful sanctuary into a three-ring circus. The instant he touched the door, however, he knew it was Sophie who waited on the other side. All day he'd had a restless, edgy feeling that he couldn't put into words, a nagging sense that he had misplaced something, but he wasn't sure exactly what. Something important. Something crucial. It was as if a part of him had gone missing. He hadn't felt that way in a very long time, and as soon as he touched the door, the feeling went away. Suddenly he felt whole again and he knew it was because the missing piece was Sophie.

That could be a problem, since in less than a week she would be gone, but when he opened the door and she smiled at him, everything else—including the warning light flashing in the very back recesses of his mind—ceased to matter.

"Hey there," she said, her eyes very green and lit with excitement. Her hair was caught up in a clip except for a few escaped curls of bronze and gold around her face. Her cheeks were flushed and she was wearing a yellow dress that left her shoulders bare, and as impossible as it seemed, she looked even more beautiful to Owen now than she had last night.

"Feel like taking a break?" she asked.

"Sure. Why not?" He didn't bother to mention that so far his whole day had been one long, frustrating break. He didn't mention it because it didn't matter. He could have a midnight deadline and be writing the book's climactic scene at a breakneck pace and he would stop everything for Sophie. Another warning sign that he didn't have time to think about right now.

She took a few steps inside and then turned to face him as he closed the door, twisting her fingers together in front of her. Anxiously, it seemed to Owen.

"I tried to think up a good reason for barging in and interrupting you," she said. "Like asking if you had an extra notebook I could borrow or bringing you a glass of iced tea."

He smiled appreciatively at the mention of her iced tea.

She rolled her eyes. "I know. Lame."

She thought he was laughing at her.

"But I decided I don't have time to be bothered with props or excuses," she went on before he could explain about the lemonade. "I'm on union time here, which means this is a twenty-minute break. So I'm just going to cut to the chase and come right out and tell you what I'm here for."

"You want to talk about last night," he said.

She looked startled. "What? No. A thousand tons of no. Last night was . . ."

"Confusing?"

"Wonderful. Amazing. Spectacular. Last night was the most romantic night of my life. The last thing I want to do is spoil it by doing a postmortem."

"Then what—"

"This," she said, her breath catching as she launched herself forward and grabbed the front of his T-shirt with both fists to yank him closer. "I came for this."

Her open mouth crashed against his. She kissed him hard and greedily, leaning against his body in a way that left no doubt that when she'd said "I came for this," she was talking about more than a kiss. A lot more.

Owen hardly needed convincing. Wrapping his arms around

her, he gave as good as he got. His heart drummed inside his chest and the memory of her naked and under him roared to life in his head.

When they ran out of air, they levered back just enough to look at each other. Their gazes locked, both of them breathing hard. He loved the way she was looking at him . . . with a kind of intense, bottomless longing. The simple fact that she wanted him made him feel like he could walk on water and conquer nations and hang the moon in the sky.

Unconsciously she slid her tongue across her swollen lower lip and fresh desire ripped through him, pushing him to touch and taste and take. He tried to tether it because he thought he should. Then her hand drifted lower to touch him intimately and he understood that Sophie wanted what he wanted.

He tugged on the tie behind her neck and the front of her dress tumbled down.

She shoved his T-shirt up and over his head and they were skin to skin. . . . the contact hot and damp and erotic.

His mouth roamed over her throat and shoulder, and when he stroked the side of her bare thigh, she bent her knee and rubbed her leg against his side.

He whispered close to her ear. "Only twenty minutes, huh?"

"Less," she said, running her hand down his back. "I lost a few minutes getting here because I couldn't cut across the dance floor."

He raked his thumb back and forth across her nipple. "How many is a few?"

"Too many. Time is definitely"—she shivered delicately—"of the essence."

"In that case . . ."

Owen caught her up in his arms and in a rush of strength propelled her a half-dozen feet across the room until her back was pressed to the wall. Supporting her weight with one arm, he swept beneath her skirt with his other hand, pushed her panties aside, and found her wet and ready for him.

With trembling hands, Sophie reached to open his belt and his zipper, touching him and guiding him. She held him where she wanted him and rubbed against him, her head thrown back, her pleasure revealed in a soft rough purr that wound its way deep inside, to the very core of him.

He wasn't even inside her yet and she was burning him up . . . consuming him. He was reeling from the taste and feel and scent of her. Everything about her was all new and deeply familiar at the same time and he wanted more. He wanted all of her.

Hungry and impatient, he shoved her a few inches higher, angling for entry. Sophie was eager to oblige, wrapping her legs around his waist and lowering herself to meet him.

Owen cupped her bottom as he thrust inside her, making love to her against the wall, the sweetness and madness of it running together, as she clung tightly to him and said his name over and over.

She wasn't kidding about the twenty minutes.

She left him spent, but not satisfied. It would take a hell of a lot longer than twenty minutes for him to come even close to being satisfied that he'd done all the things he wanted to do to Sophie Bennett. It would take more like twenty years, he thought, already missing her.

Or twenty lifetimes.

Eighteen

✴

Late Friday evening Sophie stood alone at the edge of the stone patio overlooking the grounds that had been transformed into an enchanted woodland and wondered if it was too soon to breathe a sigh of relief. Just a tiny one. Surely she'd earned that much.

The gigantic, oh-my-God-it's-finally-over-and-I-can-sleep-for-a-week sigh of relief that she was planning would have to wait until tomorrow night, of course, after the actual wedding and reception had taken place and the last guests had been sent safely, and hopefully merrily, on their way. For now she was content to savor the small success of having the rehearsal and the dinner that followed go off without a hitch. There had been no gas leaks or falling beehives and the only flickering lights were the candles inside hurricane globes on the buffet tables in the sun-room. The wedding party and a few of Shelby's and Matthew's close friends and family members had dined under the stars on the patio, while in the background Sophie kept a constant and uneasy vigil.

"Sophie, I checked to make sure everything in the kitchen is squared away. The caterers packed up their stuff and I loaded those boxes of extra linens in my Jeep like you wanted me to. I'll drop them off at Seasons first thing tomorrow and be back here by nine. Maggie and Deanna said they're leaving now too, if that's okay with you. Oh, and I told Shelby and Matt you're waiting out here to talk with them as soon as they're done finding rides for tipsy bridesmaids." Josh paused in his run-on spiel to grin at her. "Pretty hot bridesmaids, huh?"

Sophie feigned a puzzled expression. "Are they? I honestly didn't take note of their hotness factor. I did, however, notice that they're bridesmaids, which means they fall under the broad heading of clients, and therefore they are—"

"I know, I know. Strictly off-limits. Just saying." He shrugged, unbothered by the reminder. "So is it okay if we take off?"

"Yes, go. Thanks for your help, Josh. I know it was a long day. Tell Maggie and Deanna thanks for all their hard work too and that I'll see them tomorrow."

Maggie and Deanna were part of a large team of experienced Seasons employees that worked events only and were worth their weight in gold. For tomorrow she'd booked them plus four other assistants in addition to Josh, who could be counted on to be wherever she needed him to be to do the inevitable last-minute running and moving things around. It was a big crew, considering the size of the wedding, but under the circumstances she believed the extra pairs of eyes and hands were warranted. She'd worked her butt off all week and done everything she could to forestall disaster and ensure that everything would run smoothly tomorrow. Food, flowers, music, transportation, photography, and on and on, right down to the engraved menus and eco-friendly favors: she was on top of every detail and confident that everything under her control would come together flawlessly. And if by chance there was a glitch, she or one of her team would be right there to catch it and fix it with an absolute minimum of fuss and fanfare.

It was the things *not* under her control that worried her. Worried, schmorried. Who was she kidding? She was beyond worried. The thought of what Ivy might be planning to do to ruin the day scared the hell out of her.

Several times in the past few days, every chance she got in fact, she'd attempted to talk to Ivy and change her mind, but her reasoning and pleas seemed to fall on deaf ears. Deaf and stubborn. And she hadn't had that many opportunities. Ivy wasn't around much, and while Sophie didn't miss the spooky noises and the disappearing-cell-phone trick, she discovered she did miss Ivy. In spite of her grumbling, she'd gotten used to having her pop in unannounced. For a while it was almost as if they were roommates, and more than once it struck her that *The Ghost and the Wedding Planner* would make a pretty good sitcom, with Ivy being the beautiful and irreverent star with a gift for making her mousy, workaholic roomie laugh and showing up just at the right moment to dispense wise advice on matters of fashion and affairs of the heart.

Besides missing Ivy, she was worried about her. The last few times she had appeared, she hadn't been her usual glamorous, insouciant self. She'd seemed distracted and weary. And, as odd as it sounded, she looked older. Remembering what Carla said about ghosts' emotions fueling their ability to appear and to affect their surroundings, Sophie couldn't help wondering if the changes she saw were a result of Ivy's having second thoughts about the wedding and if her emotions were suddenly pulling her in two different directions. She was pretty set in her ghostly ways; it couldn't be easy to suddenly find herself questioning what she'd been so sure about.

If that's what was happening. It was an interesting theory, but seeing as Ivy hadn't actually said anything to indicate she was wavering even a little, Sophie didn't dare lower her guard. As the big day approached she felt almost as if they were playing a high-stakes game of chicken. Her troubled gaze moved over the vista before her, from the reflecting pond to the winding tree-covered paths surrounding a white tent luxurious enough to entertain royalty, and she thought that seeing all that, Ivy must surely realize that there was no possible way Sophie was going to blink first.

The sound of approaching footsteps drew her attention. She turned to see Shelby and Matthew headed her way, smiling and holding hands, the way they usually did when they were together.

"Mission accomplished," Shelby announced. "I just hope Kristy sobers up in time to walk down the aisle."

"Relax. She'll be fine," Matthew assured her in a quiet, solid tone that struck a chord in Sophie.

He sounds like Owen, she thought. Oh, the accent was different and his voice wasn't as deep, but more than once in recent days Owen had eased her qualms and bolstered her confidence with that same sure and steady tone. It was magical in its ability to make her believe everything was going to be all right. Owen was the only one she could speak freely to about Ivy . . . and about Helen's meddling, which she also feared could blow up in their faces. Brides could be very unpredictable, which is why last-minute surprises were never a good idea. And although Sophie had limited Helen's input, there would still be more hoopla than Shelby and Matthew wanted or expected. She was anxious on both fronts, and being able to unburden herself to Owen was like having a shelter in the middle of a raging hurricane. It was plain to see that Matthew would be Shelby's shelter no matter what life threw at them in the years ahead. Sophie was happy for her . . . and envious at the same time.

"Josh said you wanted to speak with us," said Shelby.

Sophie nodded. "I do. I'm breaking Seasons protocol a bit here and I want to explain. Usually, after the wedding ceremony is over and before the bride and groom greet their guests, I steal the couple for a few moments and take them into the reception room for what we refer to as 'the big unveil.' It gives them a chance to see the room completely and perfectly decorated, before anyone spills wine or rearranges the chairs."

They both laughed.

"But your situation is a little different. For one thing, there's more to it," she said with an expansive sweep of her arm. "It's all kind of interwoven and not the typical grand ballroom that I can keep under wraps until the last minute. After the ceremony here on the patio, your guests will head that way for cocktails." She gestured toward the sunroom and the extended stone patio that ran the entire length of the back of the house. "The sun will just be setting and the lights will slowly and gradually come on. I could probably arrange a private moment to show you the inside of the tent, but that's only a small part of what we've done. So I decided that after everyone else left tonight, I would give the two of you a preview of the overall effect . . . that is, if you'd like to see it ahead of time."

"We'd like," Shelby exclaimed, grinning with excitement and bouncing on the balls of her feet as she squeezed Matthew's arm. "We'd very much like. Wouldn't we?"

"Definitely," he agreed, pulling Shelby in front of him and encircling her with his arms.

"I just wanted to make sure," Sophie explained. "Some couples would rather be totally surprised on the day itself."

"Oh, I think there'll be more than enough surprises to make the day itself interesting," Shelby observed drily. Her mouth curved into a rueful smile. "Do you know my mother arranged for a cigar roller? A man who sits at a table and rolls cigars on request. Have you ever heard of anything so ridiculous?"

"I think she just wants you to have everything that could conceivably make your day special."

"Well, that would certainly explain the vodka ice luge . . . what little girl doesn't dream of having that at her wedding?"

Sophie's eyes narrowed. "Vodka ice luge?"

"Oh, so that one's a surprise for you too."

"In a manner of speaking," Sophie said. "We did discuss the possibility of a pyramid-shaped ice luge and I told your mother it didn't fit with your theme."

Shelby scoffed. "As if a little thing like that would get in the way of her trying to make this the most overblown, over-the-top wedding of all time."

She sounded irritated, but not—to Sophie's relief—on the verge of a bridal meltdown.

"So the luge is definite?" Sophie asked.

"'Fraid so," Shelby replied, smiling as she rolled her eyes at Matthew.

"Well, I'm just glad you're smiling about it instead of letting it upset you."

Shelby shrugged. "It's hard to be upset or angry when I know she's doing all of it because she thinks it will make me happy. I just keep telling myself that at least it's making her happy, and that's something."

"Good. That's a great attitude to take, because you never know, there may be even more surprises in store. Some bigger than others, and it would be a shame to end a perfect day on a sour note . . ."

"Are you talking about the fireworks?" Shelby asked.

"Oh, thank God. You know about them?"

"Oh yeah."

Matthew explained. "One of my groomsmen knows the guy Shelby's mother hired for the job. He tipped me off and I told Shelby. I figured forewarned is forearmed and all that."

"Smart man. You're both very lucky."

"We are lucky. That's another reason I can't be upset about anything," said Shelby. "I'm marrying the most wonderful man in the world and I get to do it here . . ." She gazed around with an expression of wonder. "It's exactly where I always dreamed of being married, but I never believed it would really happen. I have the perfect dress . . . the perfect everything . . . thanks to you," she added with a smile at Sophie. "It would be pretty petty of me to throw a hissy fit over the cigar man or some fireworks."

"I'm kind of looking forward to the fireworks," Matthew admitted.

"I'm looking forward to seeing what you want to show us tonight," Shelby said to Sophie.

"Then let's do it." Sophie flipped over her phone and hit speed dial. "Owen, we're ready on this end."

When she first asked him if he'd be willing to give her a hand by manning the light panel in the garage, she thought Owen might balk at having anything to do with "wedding crap," as he referred to it. Instead he surprised her by agreeing without any pressure or pleading; he didn't even complain about spending over an hour that morning getting instructions from the lighting engineer so he wouldn't mess up.

"I'm heading down to the garage now," he told her. "Give me two minutes."

They waited in silence. Shelby's excitement was palpable . . . and contagious. Sophie had already seen the setting fully lit when they did the final check last evening, but she was eager to see the young couple's reaction to having their fantasy come to life before them.

Owen didn't let her down. The lights came on gradually, and although the timing would be extended during the reception itself, the effect was just as spectacular. The first to twinkle on were thousands of amber and white fairy lights embedded deep within the branches of the newly planted "forest." Next came the copper-and-brass lanterns hung on wrought-iron shepherd's hooks that lit the pathways and secluded alcoves. It was a careful building of subtle layers of illumination and color, culminating with the rotating up-lights that lent energy and movement and created the ambience of an enchanted woodland.

Except for a couple of sharp intakes of breath, Shelby and Matthew watched in silence. But their rapt attention told Sophie all she needed to know about how much they loved it.

"Oh my God," Shelby said finally. "It's even better than I imagined it would be . . . a zillion times better than I ever *could* have imagined. It's perfect. It's amazing. Oh my God, Sophie, *you're* amazing. I love you so much."

She hugged Sophie hard.

"Thank you so much for making it happen," she went on. "And for giving us this moment tonight. It's all exactly what I hoped it would be."

"It is really cool," agreed Matthew. "Check out the way the color crisscrosses the dance floor, Shel."

"I can't wait for our first dance," Shelby exclaimed, reaching for his hand.

Sophie laughed. "Well, that you will have to wait for . . . some traditions even I don't mess with."

Her wide-eyed gaze still on the transformed grounds, Shelby rested her head back on Matthew's chest and sighed quietly. "I just wish . . ."

"What is it, Shel?" he prodded. "What do you wish?"

"I love how quiet and peaceful it is right now. It's magical. Tomorrow there'll be so many more people here . . . so many people I hardly know, thanks to my mother's magically expanding guest list, and I almost wish we were getting married now, tonight, right this minute, when it feels so perfect. No fuss. No one snapping pictures. Just us."

Chuckling, Matthew gave her a quick squeeze. "Nice fantasy, Shel, but your mom would have a total meltdown, after which she'd kill both of us."

"Not if she didn't know about it," Sophie heard herself say.

The couple stared at her in surprise and confusion.

She didn't blame them. Ordinarily the wedding planner in her would be appalled at the very idea of them jumping the gun and marrying tonight when so much had gone into making sure that everything would be perfect tomorrow. But from the very beginning, when Shelby lost her way and happened upon Sophie's office and saw the picture of *The Princess House* book hanging on her wall, nothing about this wedding had been ordinary. Why start now?

Far from being upset, Sophie saw the bride-to-be's impulsive wish as a possible answer to her prayers, and she seized it. If they were to exchange vows tonight, privately, it would mean that no matter what madness ensued tomorrow, courtesy of Ivy and/or the mother of the bride, the young couple would have a perfect memory of their wedding . . . not to mention a hell of a story to tell their grandchildren.

"Who's to say you can't get married tonight if you want to?"

"My mother, for one," Shelby replied immediately. "Matthew's right. She was born to play the role of mother of the bride and she'd never forgive me if I cheated her out of it."

Sophie shook her head. "No, no. I didn't mean you should do it tonight instead of tomorrow . . . I meant in addition to tomorrow. Two ceremonies for the price of one. You have the license, the rings, witnesses . . . me," she said, pressing her hand to her chest. "And I'm sure Owen would be thrilled to be part of it."

Thrilled was a real stretch, but she was pretty sure she could get him to go along with the plan.

"And I'll bet Reverend Allard hasn't even made it home yet. I happen to know he has a romantic streak and I'm sure he'd come back if you asked. You could have a small private exchange of vows tonight and still go through with the ceremony as planned tomorrow in front of all your guests."

The couple was staring at each other, smiles tugging at their lips. Sophie didn't say what she was thinking, that tonight would be an insurance policy in case disaster struck tomorrow. And she certainly didn't use the words *preemptive strike*. She didn't want to frighten or worry them. If they decided to do it, she wanted it to be because they were carried away by the romance of the moment. Tonight or tomorrow, the most important thing was that they have their perfect moment.

"What do you think?" Matthew asked Shelby. They were facing each other now, arms outstretched, hands clasped together.

Shelby nibbled her lip thoughtfully for a couple of seconds and then broke into an excited grin. "I think yes . . . let's go for it." She threw herself into his arms. "Oh my God, in a few minutes I'm going to be Mrs. Matthew Winston."

Sophie's mind was already processing what needed to be done as she saw Owen approaching.

"How'd they like the show?" he asked her.

"They loved it. In fact . . ."

She quickly filled him in on what was happening. She didn't mention Ivy. She didn't need to for Owen to understand why she was so enthusiastic about the sudden change in plans, and he volunteered to do whatever she needed even before she had a chance to ask. Sophie squeezed his hand and made a mental note to thank him properly later, when they were alone.

Handling last-minute crises was something she was good at. She took charge and within a few moments everyone had been given an assignment. Shelby was to get dressed. Matthew was to call the minister and get him back there ASAP. And since the flowers weren't being delivered until the morning, Owen was sent to gather daisies for an impromptu bridal bouquet.

"Your dress is 'something new,'" Sophie told Shelby. "We'll consider the daisies as 'something borrowed.'"

Shelby touched her ear. "My earrings are sapphires."

Sophie nodded. "Something blue."

"That leaves only—"

"Something old."

"The lace from my grandmother's veil," Shelby reminded her.

Sophie nodded, remembering the heirloom lace that Shelby's grandmother had refused to entrust to the mail and had instead insisted on bringing with her when she arrived from California earlier that day.

"Did your grandmother remember to bring it?"

"Yes, and in the nick of time. I was still sewing on the cuff link when Matthew came to pick me up for the rehearsal."

"Cuff link?"

"It was her father's," Matthew explained as emotion swept Shelby's face. He put his arm around her gently.

"I gave them to him for Father's Day when I was six," she explained. "They weren't real gold, of course, but I thought they were and my dad acted like they were. He wore them all the time. I thought that sewing one onto the lace that I tie around my bouquet would make him even more a part of this day."

"I think it's a lovely gesture. Did you bring the lace with you tonight?"

"Yes, thank goodness. I was afraid I'd forget it at the last minute. It's in a small bag on the buffet in the dining room."

"I'll get it. You go get ready. You can use the guesthouse; Lina had your dress delivered this afternoon and I put it there to keep it safe."

"Safe from what?" asked Shelby.

Sophie had to think quickly. "Oh, you know . . . spills, that kind of thing."

Owen whacked her on the back and grinned at Shelby. "Who knows the workings of the mind of an obsessive wedding planner?"

"Thank God she is obsessive," Shelby countered. "If I had to remember half the stuff Sophie does, I swear we'd be getting married at city hall, in jeans and T-shirts."

"Well, you're not. You're getting married right here in just a few minutes. Now all of you get to work."

There was no bag on the buffet or anywhere else in the dining room. Sophie checked the table in the front hallway and then ran upstairs to look in the rooms the girls would be using the next day. No bag. No lace.

She tried calling Shelby, but the call went straight to voice mail and she decided it would be faster to run down to the guesthouse and ask her in person. She was on her way out of the room when a familiar voice brought her up short.

"Is this what you're looking for?"

First she jumped, same as she always did when Ivy caught her unawares. Then took a few seconds to gather herself before turning to acknowledge her. Ivy was standing by the window holding the lace in her hand.

"And don't tell me I should have knocked," she snapped before Sophie could speak. "I'm not in the mood."

"Hello, Ivy."

"Don't 'hello, Ivy' me. You're up to something. I know you are and I demand to know what it is."

"You already know what it is," Sophie said calmly. "Tonight was the rehearsal dinner."

Ivy waved her hand impatiently. "That's over. This is something different . . . something new you cooked up. I saw you out there, conspiring."

"We weren't conspiring. It's no big deal. A slight change in plans is all. Why don't you go lie down? You look . . . tired."

"What you mean is that I look old. That *is* what you were thinking, isn't it?" She pressed her hands to her cheeks and Sophie had the sad impression of someone trying to hold herself together.

Ivy was right. Sophie had been thinking she looked older. Oh, the changes were subtle. Ivy still looked damn good for a dead woman . . . a dead woman who'd died in her nineties no less. But she was not the same vibrant beauty she appeared to be not so long ago.

"Are you feeling all right?" Sophie asked, gently sidestepping the age question.

"All right? No. I'm feeling . . . old," Ivy replied. Her soft laugh drifted off in a sigh. "I'd forgotten how exhausting it can be to be young."

"Are you sure you wouldn't like to lie—"

"No," she snapped. "I do not want to lie down. Nor do I care to be patronized. What I want is for you to tell me what you're up to."

Sophie drew a deep breath and held it, thinking. She considered trying to stall. She thought about lying. She even considered simply refusing to discuss it and walking out. Ivy would keep watch at the window, of course. She would see the minister return and figure it out for herself soon enough. But it was a reasonable bet that she wouldn't be able to wreak much havoc outside the house on such short notice.

When she met Ivy's gaze, however, something about the look in Ivy's eyes wouldn't let Sophie lie or play games with her. This mattered too much.

"Shelby and Matthew have decided to be married tonight . . . quietly and—"

"No," Ivy bellowed.

Sophie winced and glanced out the window, hoping Matthew and Shelby weren't in earshot.

"I said there would be no wedding here and there will be no wedding. Did you really think you could fool me by sneaking around in the dead of night?"

"Oh, for pity's sake, Ivy, if I was sneaking around or trying to fool you, why would I have told you about it?"

Ivy's usual regal shrug held a new edge of desperation. "How should I know what tricks you have up your sleeve?"

Hoping to calm her, Sophie smiled and held out her bare arms. "No sleeves. No tricks. Ivy, please try to understand."

"Oh, I understand perfectly."

"Then please try to be happy for them. Put yourself in Shelby's place. I know you remember how it feels to be so excited and so filled with hope for the future."

"How could you possibly know how I feel?"

"Because I know you. But I don't have much time. The minister is already on his way back here. Ivy, please give me the lace so I can tie it around Shelby's bouquet. It's from her grandmother's bridal veil, and the cuff link she sewed to it belonged to her father. What happened to you on your wedding day was a tragedy, but Shelby had nothing to do with it. Ruining her happiness won't change the past."

"It's not the past I intend to change. It's the future. And if you insist on ignoring my wishes and charging full steam ahead, then you shall be the one accountable for the next tragedy. There isn't going to be a wedding here. Not tonight. Not tomorrow. Not ever. Not in my house."

"This is not your house," Sophie shouted, forgetting she might be overheard as the weight of all the worrying and long hours crashed down on her. "It hasn't been your house for years. You just refuse to do what any normal dead person would do . . . accept it and move on."

Ivy drew herself up. "I do refuse to accept it. And I shall move on when I am ready. Not a moment sooner. I certainly shall not be hurried along by an interloper who goes around planning other people's weddings, but is afraid to close the deal for herself."

"Me?" Sophie slapped her hand against her chest. "I'm the interloper? You're talking about me being afraid? What about you? You make me look like . . . like . . . like goddamn Wonder Woman."

"There's no need for profanity."

"Oh yeah, there is. I need it . . . otherwise my head might explode from trying to deal with you."

"Or theatrics."

"Look who's talking. I'm not the one who goes around rattling my chains and playing with the lights to get attention."

"I'm not the one who has fallen head over heels in love and yet goes around pretending to be deliriously happy and satisfied with so much less than she deserves."

"For your information, I am deliriously happy and satisfied, and I'll thank you to . . . never mind. I don't have time for this." She spun around and made it halfway to the door.

"You're right."

Sophie stopped. She turned back around. Ivy stood with her arms tightly wrapped around herself; she seemed suddenly smaller and frail.

Sophie took a few steps toward her and asked quietly, "Right about what?"

"Me. I am afraid."

"Afraid of what, Ivy?"

"Of everything, it seems sometimes. Mostly I'm afraid of leaving this house, and I'm afraid that another wedding here will break the spell or whatever it is that has kept me here and I will have to leave. And I am not ready for that. Not nearly. I am not ready to be somewhere else."

"But, Ivy, someplace else might be so much better. You must be lonely here. This is no kind of . . . well, life."

Ivy gave a snuffly laugh. Ghosts might not sweat or sleep, but they did cry. Sophie walked closer, but when she went to put an arm around her, Ivy flinched.

"No," she said. "Don't touch me. I'm . . . barely here. It's so hard lately. So hard to stay."

"Then why do it? Why keep fighting? Is there something keeping you here?"

"Joseph. I feel him here, all around me. I've always felt him here, close by, watching over me. It wasn't the life together that I'd envisioned, but it was . . . something. And it was all I had, so it was enough."

"But, Ivy, don't you think that Joseph may be waiting for you . . . somewhere? That you could go to him and be together at last?"

"Yes, I do think that. Sometimes. But I don't *know* it. I do know what I have here. What if I leave what I have and . . ." She pressed her lips together tightly. "What if I was wrong all those years? About something happening to Joseph on our wedding day. About him loving me as much as I loved him. Oh, Sophie, what if I was wrong about him? I'm not afraid of finding out that I was a fool. Lord knows, most people thought I was a fool for clinging to a pipe dream. I don't care about that. I think I'm afraid of finding out that I was wrong and feeling my heart break all over again."

"It won't," Sophie said with all the conviction she could muster. "That is not going to happen. My God, Ivy, you are one of the strongest and wisest women I've ever known . . . dead or alive. No man could ever have duped you so completely. There's a reason you fell in love with Joseph. And a reason no other man ever measured up to him in your eyes . . . and in your heart. That's because he was the one. It was meant to be. You never lost faith in him or in the love you had for each other while you were alive. You can't give up now." She looked at her sternly. "I won't let you."

They heard footsteps on the stairs and suddenly Owen stood in the doorway. "Sophie, what's taking you so—oh. Sorry to interrupt. I just wanted to let you know that the minister is here. So . . . whenever you're ready . . ."

"Go," said Ivy. "Go do your job."

Nineteen

Back outside, Shelby and Matthew had decided they wanted to exchange vows beside the softly lit pond. Shelby looked ethereal in her wedding gown and Matthew was handsome and beaming in the dark suit he'd worn for the rehearsal party.

Shelby received calmly the little white lie that one of Sophie's assistants had mistakenly left with the bag containing the lace and would return with it in plenty of time for the ceremony the next day. As a substitute, Owen produced an old penny to slip in her shoe.

They were arranging themselves in front of Reverend Allard when Shelby suddenly glanced over Sophie's shoulder and gave a small surprised smile.

"There's someone here," she said just as Sophie turned in that direction and saw Ivy walking toward them.

She had left the house and was walking down the wide, shallow steps from the patio to the lawn.

She had left the house.

Sophie struggled to come to grips with the implications of

that. Not certain whether to cheer or panic, she would have moved to head Ivy off but for Owen's calming hand on the small of her back.

"Hold on," he said, so softly only she could hear.

Smiling, Ivy walked closer. "Forgive me for intruding, but I saw all these beautiful lights and I . . . well, I was . . . curious and couldn't help myself. I used to live here, you see, a very long time ago."

Shelby's smile deepened and there was an added note of excitement in her voice. "Seriously? It must have been so wonderful to actually live here. Was it wonderful?"

"It was," Ivy confirmed. "I always felt very lucky to be living in such a beautiful house . . . the most beautiful in the world, in my estimation."

"And mine," Shelby countered with a nod of solidarity. "I feel so lucky just to be getting married here."

"It is a beautiful place for a wedding." Ivy's expression softened as she gazed at Shelby's dress. "And you do it justice, my dear. You make a beautiful bride."

"Thank you."

"But I believe you're missing something." She held the lace in one hand and with the other gestured vaguely. "I found it there."

Shelby turned to Sophie, confused. "But I thought . . ."

"I fudged a little," Sophie explained. "I didn't want you to panic when I couldn't find it. I was sure it would turn up."

"May I?" asked Ivy, holding the strip of lace by the ends.

Shelby smiled and held out the bouquet of daisies so Ivy could tie the lace around the stems.

"There," she said when she was done. "The perfect finishing touch. I wish you both a lifetime and more of love and happiness. And now I should leave so you can—"

"No, don't go" said Shelby, reaching out to touch Ivy's arm.

She laughed awkwardly, a little surprised by her own vehemence. "I'd really like you to stay . . . that is, if you'd like to."

"I would like that very much indeed," Ivy told her.

"Then shall we get started?" asked the minister. "I'm not sure if you know this, but I have another wedding tomorrow and it looks like I'm the only one here who needs his beauty sleep."

He waited for their laughter to stop and opened his prayer book.

"Dear friends, we are gathered here tonight in the sight of God and angels to celebrate one of life's greatest moments and greatest gifts. As we give recognition to the worth and beauty of love, we add our best wishes and blessings to the words which shall unite Matthew and Shelby in holy matrimony."

The ceremony was brief, and after a champagne toast, the newlyweds were understandably eager to be alone. Reverend Allard was almost as eager to get some sleep.

As soon as they were gone, Sophie turned to Ivy with the question burning inside her.

"Why?"

Ivy did not need her to elaborate.

"Because it was the right thing to do," she replied. "And because it is time. Past time, some have said."

"Ivy, I didn't mean—"

"Hush. I needed a swift kick in the behind and you gave it to me. I understand that's what good roommates do for one another." She looked more closely. "And now tell me what's bothering you? I saw it on your face as they exchanged their vows."

Sophie shrugged. "So I get teary-eyed at weddings. Occupational hazard."

"This was more than that." She folded her arms across her chest. "I shall not be moving from this spot until you tell me, and I don't think any of us want that."

"For God's sake, tell her what she wants to know," urged Owen, only half teasing.

"Oh, all right. But it's silly. It was the lace, that's all. It reminded me of my mother and of a piece of lace from her wedding dress that I had, but that I don't have anymore, and it just made me sad for a minute. That's all."

"What happened to it?" asked Ivy.

"Long story."

Ivy folded her arms a little more snuggly and said nothing.

"I think," said Owen, "that the term 'long' could be relative in this case and that you might as well just tell the story."

Sophie found herself explaining how her mother's dress and veil had been lost in a house fire before she was born. All her mother had managed to salvage was a piece of the lace edging, and after she died, Lina had helped Sophie to frame it. While she was away at college the prized possession fell prey to one of her stepmother's redecorating frenzies and Sophie blamed herself for not being there to rescue it in time.

"You never found it?" Ivy asked.

She shook her head. "No. I'm not even sure if it went to Goodwill or ended up in the trash." Even now there was a tremor in her voice as she said it. "My stepmother isn't a bad person, but she doesn't have a sentimental bone in her body . . . especially when it comes to decorating. If it doesn't fit the new look, it goes."

"Still, you must never give up hope of finding it," Ivy told her. "It could reappear when you least expect it."

Sophie gave her a droll look. "Thanks, Ivy, but I've been out of college a long time. The house has been sold. I'm pretty sure it's gone forever."

"Don't be. Stranger things have happened. You should know since you've seen some with your own eyes. Thanks to me. And I can tell you that things, like people, can magically appear when you are most in need of them. Don't look so cynical," she chided. "Haven't you heard the expression 'leap and the net shall appear'?"

"Sure. I've heard it, but . . ."

"Then remember it. And do it." Smiling, she reached out and placed her hand on the side of Sophie's face. "Leap, Sophie. Leap when the time is right."

"And just how am I supposed to know when the time is right?"

"You'll know," Ivy assured her with a laugh. "I'm sure of it."

She took a deep breath and looked back at the house for a moment and then turned to Sophie. "I'm leaving now. It has been a pleasure to be your roommate, Miss Sophia Bennett."

"It's been an honor to be your friend, Ivy Halliday," Sophia countered, forcing the words past the sudden ache in her throat. "It really has."

"Don't sniffle," Ivy chided in her most superior tone, helping Sophie to smile instead of succumbing to the tears that threatened. "Also, promise me you'll remember to keep your shoulders back, especially when wearing strapless attire."

"I promise," sniffled Sophie.

Ivy turned her attention to Owen and Sophie would swear he threw his shoulders back.

"Mr. Winters," she began.

He cut in. "I promise to use coasters and not to drop wet towels on your wood floors or leave golf clubs tossed around all over the place. Anything else?"

"More than we have time for, I'm afraid. So I will only say this: fate saw fit to deliver to both of us a great blessing when she arranged for Miss Bennett to appear at our door. Try not to be more of a dolt about it than absolutely necessary. I should hate to have to come back because you mucked up and made a muddle of things."

With that final arch warning and no formal good-bye, which Sophie thought would be more than she herself could bear without getting weepy, Ivy walked away, moving briskly toward the circle of light that appeared in the distance.

"Can she do that?" Owen asked when she was far enough away not to hear. "Come back, I mean?"

Sophie smiled, her throat still aching. "I wouldn't bet against it."

As they watched, Ivy seemed to hesitate for just a heartbeat. Sophie understood why when she saw the figure of a young man in uniform deep within the circle of light. She reached instinctively for Owen's hand at the same time he was reaching to put his arm around her.

"Do you see . . . ?"

"I do," he said, his tone incredulous as he drew her close to his side.

The fog over the ocean made it difficult to gauge how far away the light was, or how far Ivy had walked. But the distance was not so great that they couldn't plainly hear the note of wonder in her voice as the young man opened his arms wide.

"Joseph?" she said.

Just that one word. And then she was running toward him, and was gone.

Owen had been no fan of big fancy weddings even before he learned that they were as much of a pain in the ass after the fact as they were to plan. Maybe more. It seemed to him that Sophie was even busier and working harder now, two days after the wedding— make that *weddings*: the impromptu first round and the second, public ceremony—than she was during the mad rush leading up to it. Everything that had been hauled in or constructed on-site dur- ing the weeks of preparation now had to be packed up, broken down or uprooted, and hauled away. And Sophie was once more at the helm, her lists and schedule in hand, steadfastly creating order out of chaos. It seemed like every time he tried to talk to her, she was either dead busy or dead tired.

He'd thought—foolishly, he could see now—that they would have more time together as soon as the wedding was over and done with. Not to mention some privacy. With the house now one hundred percent ghost-free, he had all kinds of plans for how to put their time together to good use. Instead, work crews were still showing up and traipsing through the place at all hours of the day and into the night. Like the cleaning crew that was there this morning, scrubbing and polishing every inch of the kitchen. From his office window he could see Sophie outside giving directions to the men about to lay down fresh rolls of sod to replace the turf that had been dug up in the interest of the multitude's being able to dine and dance in style.

When he complained about the ongoing ruckus, she reminded him that returning the house and grounds to their original condition was part of their deal. It was her responsibility and she intended to see that it was done right.

Personally, he'd be willing to put up with a fake pond and a dance floor in his backyard if it meant getting to spend time alone with Sophie . . . the awake and alert Sophie, that is, the woman who made him smile just by showing up unexpectedly, the woman who sought him out for midday trysts and could keep him awake and hard and wanting her long into the night . . . the first woman in years . . . maybe ever . . . whom he couldn't get enough of.

He couldn't even take solace in counting the days until the cleanup was finally done because he knew it would mean Sophie was done there too. There would be no reason for her to hang around. At least none they ever talked about . . . or that he even knew how to begin talking about. Theirs was supposed to be a business arrangement and her business would soon be finished. She would pack up her coffeemaker and her favorite pillow and those ridiculous butterfly and hummingbird hair clips she left all over the house and she would leave. Status quo restored. Deal done. Everything would be just the way it was before she came.

Well, almost, anyway. One thing had changed. The house was no longer haunted by Ivy's ghost. Thanks to Sophie, Ivy had finally gotten her happy ending. That was something he wouldn't have believed possible, and frankly he still couldn't quite process what had happened even though he'd seen it with his own eyes. Sophie once told him that everyone was good at something and that what she was good at was making other people's dreams come true. And damn, she wasn't kidding.

In a perfect world, someone would do the same for her. But Owen knew for a hard, cold fact that this wasn't a perfect world. And he sure as hell wasn't a perfect man.

Would she stay if he asked her to?

Did he have any right to ask?

Did it matter?

Lately he had a lot more questions than answers and those answers he did have were about as solid as words carved in beach sand. For a man trained to see the world in black and white, his world suddenly had an unsettling amount of gray. There were moments when he thought the best thing for both him and Sophie was to be grateful for the time they'd had together, quit while they were ahead, and get back to living their own separate and very different lives. And there were also moments, too many of them, when he didn't think he was physically capable of watching her walk out the door without doing whatever he had to do to make her stay.

It would be easier all the way around if Sophie could wave her magic wand and make his dream come true the way she did for others. The only problem was that he didn't have a dream. Not anymore. And as much as he might want to for her sake, he wasn't able to buy into hers.

What he did have were survival skills. The army had seen to that. If you find yourself trekking across dangerous terrain with a hundred pounds of essential equipment on your back and you get hit by a sniper, you have to stop and reassess the situation. First, you appraise your injuries and then you look at that hundred pounds of equipment and redefine the word *essential*. You hang on to only what you absolutely need to survive and you ditch the rest. Quickly and ruthlessly. You don't let things like comfort cloud your judgment. And when it's done, you don't look back and second-guess yourself or bellyache over what you had to leave behind.

Suddenly he was seeing a whole lot less gray.

He should have looked at the situation in a way he understood a whole lot sooner, he thought.

He didn't know squat about romance or the scientific study of kissing or those other things Sophie was so well versed in, but survival was something he did understand.

He was a survivor.

And he knew what he had to do to survive.

Sophie looked at the gaping mud patch where the pond had been with sadness. A wedding planner knows going into a project that no matter how hard she works or how creative she gets, the result of all her planning and fussing is only temporary. Inevitably the cake gets cut and devoured, the rented chairs are stacked and returned to the warehouse, and the confetti is swept up and tossed in the trash. But knowing it and actually seeing the scene stripped of its magic are two different things. And this particular project had been special and closer to her heart than others. For a lot of reasons.

With a philosophical sigh she turned away from the mud, which was already disappearing beneath strips of healthy new sod. Various rental companies had come and collected the furniture and linens. The caterer had removed the extra cooking equipment from the kitchen and carted off dozens of plastic crates filled with china and flatware. The tent, the lights, and the sound system were all gone, along with the trees that had never actually been planted, but simply strategically placed, with mulch used to hide the burlap that was wrapped around their roots lest they grow attached to the soil and think they had found a home, only to be ripped out when the time came, leaving bits and pieces of themselves behind. That was messy and not good for the trees.

She noticed the sky overhead beginning to darken and recalled the weather forecaster's warning to keep an umbrella handy for late-afternoon downpours. It was barely September, but already there was a change in the air, and as much as she griped about the heat and humidity, she felt a sudden urge to hold on to summer for a while longer.

As she headed back inside, she automatically checked along the way for anything she might have overlooked, but there wasn't so much as a crumbled napkin or wilting bloom to be seen anywhere. This must be how a producer feels after a play's final performance, when the actors have left the stage, the costumes all packed away, and the sets taken apart. With one significant difference: at best, a play is an illusion. When it finishes its run, all that's left are memories. But a wedding is only the beginning of the magic; it's just the start of something new and real and important. Together, Shelby and Matthew would go on to make a new life and a new family, and though Sophie couldn't come close to explaining Ivy and Joseph's situation, she had the comforting sense that in some way, in some better place, they were picking up where they left off so long ago. Just thinking about it renewed her faith in love and life and whatever comes next. She was proud and thrilled to have played even a small part in both love stories, and she chose to believe that someday she would know how both turned out.

The house was quiet. The cleaning crew had left it spotless and smelling like lemon furniture polish. No one walking into the kitchen now would guess what a high-pressure hub of activity it had been just a couple of days ago. Her first solo wedding had been an unqualified success from start to finish. Shelby and Matthew were happy, Helen was happy, even the fireworks had been a spectacular hit, and Seasons already had several new referrals. What more could she ask for?

Nothing, she told herself. Because if you had to ask, it wasn't meant to be.

It was time to go. The cleanup was just about done and there was no need for her to be on-site to supervise what remained. To be honest, she could have been out of there yesterday and handled the rest of it by phone. She'd only stretched it out and stuck around because . . . either because hope springs eternal or she was a hopeless idiot. Take your pick.

Although she hadn't consciously planned it ahead of time, she'd stayed at least in part to give Owen some extra time to . . . to say . . . something. Oh, she wasn't a big enough idiot to expect him to make a declaration of any kind or extend an invitation for her to move in permanently. She wasn't even sure she was ready for either. But she thought he might mention the possibility of continuing to see each other or maybe casually suggest she leave a toothbrush behind for future sleepovers: just some small acknowledgment that what they shared was more than a convenient sexual fling.

But he didn't. And it wasn't.

And she was all right with that. Just as with the wedding itself, she'd known the parameters going in. It was never meant to last forever. And she'd been diligent about reminding herself of that each step along the way. She looked herself in the eye in the mirror each morning and told herself it was only temporary and just for fun, and she tried to remember to do the same at night . . . right before she fell asleep in Owen's arms.

It was time to go.

She purposely hadn't mentioned to Owen that she'd be leaving today. Just as she'd made a point of staying busy and out of his way the past couple of days. Maybe she was overly cautious, but announcing her departure ahead of time struck her as contrived, as if she was trying to force the issue and back him into saying something he didn't feel. That was the last thing she wanted. For that same reason, she'd waited until he headed off to his office that morning before gathering her things and packing, and she decided to bring her bags out to the car herself now before saying good-bye. No awkward, dragged-out leave-taking for her.

She managed to get only one bulging duffel bag stowed in the back of her SUV before there was a rumbling overhead and the rain started. *Downpour* was the right word, she thought. *Über-downpour* was an even better one, and *mother of all downpours* also wouldn't be an exaggeration.

It was raining so hard it hurt, and within seconds she was soaked to the skin. Wishing she'd taken time to move the car closer to the house, she ran back up the drive with her hands covering her head and nearly collided with Owen where the front walk merged with the one leading from the side of the house.

"What are you doing out here?" he asked, running his gaze over the cotton shorts and T-shirt plastered to her body.

"I was trying to get the car packed before the rain started. But as you can see . . ." She gave up trying to use her hands as an umbrella and threw them in the air in surrender.

"Packing?" Frowning, he glanced at the car. "Why?"

"Why? Because I'm leaving."

"You're leaving? Now?"

"Yes."

"Why?"

"Why? Because . . . because the wedding is over. And the cleanup is pretty much done. I have work piled up back at the office and a life to get back to."

They were both already speaking loudly to be heard over the rain and the rumbling, which had grown closer and more ominous sounding. Now his voice shot up another few notches in volume.

"A life to get back to? What the fuck does that mean? You're leaving? Just like that? Moving out? Without telling me? Without saying a fucking word? Without even—" He broke off, looking furious, and swept his hand across his face, sending big drops of water flying. "Tell me something: Were you planning to leave me a note? Or is that expecting too much too?"

"Wow. That's a lot of questions . . . and I'm not really sure why you're so upset. Do you think we could go inside out of the rain and talk about it?"

She intended it as a rhetorical question, but for a couple of seconds he had the look of a man who wasn't going anywhere until he got answers. Finally he gave a grudging nod and grabbed her arm as if afraid she might make a run for it if given a chance. As uncomfortable and confused as she was, she had to admit that there was something satisfying about his over-the-top reaction.

She struggled to keep up as he hurried her along the walk and up the steps to the front door. Still holding her arm, he reached for the door handle, and through some kind of eerie blend of intuition and déjà vu, Sophie knew what was going on even before he turned to her in glowering disbelief.

"You locked the door?" he shouted.

"No . . . I didn't mean to, anyway," she said. "I always check before I close it."

"Obviously you didn't this time."

"What can I say? I was . . . preoccupied."

"Either that or in a damn big hurry." He scrutinized her wet clothing. "Please tell me you have your keys on you."

She shook her head. "I didn't think I'd need them; the car was unlocked. You?"

"No," he said, even as he patted the pockets of his wet jeans. "Wait here."

She huddled against the door, as far under the overhanging roof as she could get. He wasn't gone long, and when he returned he didn't look happy.

"The back door?" she asked hopefully, shivering.

"Locked."

"The spare key?"

"Gone."

"All of them?"

"Both of them," he corrected. "I used the one under the brick planter and forgot to put it back. It's upstairs in my room."

"But we hid three. Who could have taken the other two?" Their eyes met. "Ivy."

"She's gone, remember?"

"She could have moved them days ago."

His jaw clenched. "If she was here, and she wasn't already dead, I'd wring her neck."

"Cheerful thought . . . but we'd still be stuck out here in the rain."

He looked around and reached for her hand. "Come on."

"I'm not climbing in any windows," she warned, keeping her feet planted. "I'm tired and wet and—"

"You don't have to climb in the window. You said your car is unlocked, right?"

She brightened. "Yes."

"Then let's go. We won't be able to run the heater, but at least you'll be out of the rain. Once it lets up, I'll take a look around for the spare keys."

Unfortunately the bag she'd brought out didn't have any dry clothes in it, but it did have the warm throw she liked to curl up with at night when she was watching TV. She offered to share it, but Owen declined, either out of gallantry or because he was too annoyed with her to do anything that even resembled cuddling.

"Look," she said, once her teeth stopped chattering. "I think you have the wrong idea. When I said I was leaving, I didn't mean right that very minute. I would never just take off without saying good-bye to you. On the other hand, I didn't know my lease demanded a two-week notice."

The feeble attempt at humor fell flat. Never mind force a polite smile, he didn't even stop staring at the rain pelting the front windshield to look at her.

"I'm sorry if I upset you," she told him, "but the wrap-up here went more smoothly than I expected and I really do have a lot of work to get back to. I have a couple of new assignments waiting. One of the brides heard about Shelby's wedding and requested me personally. Also Lina is interested in working together again and has a few projects lined up. We've even tossed around the idea of combining our talents and starting our own business . . . not right away, of course, but it's worth thinking about, and working together now will be like a risk-free trial run. The point is, I've got a pretty full plate waiting for me, and we both knew I'd be leaving as soon as—"

"You can't leave." Now he did turn to look at her and the expression of grim resolve on his face brought her up short. "There's something I have to say to you and I'm not sure how to do it. Hell, I never thought I would be saying it, to any woman, but I've looked at this from all angles and I don't have a choice."

He looked so troubled; Sophie instinctively pulled the throw closer, bracing herself for whatever bad news he was about to deliver. Could he be dying? Fear tightened like a vise around her midsection. *Please, God, don't let him be dying.* She could go away. She could live without ever seeing him again if she had to. *But please, God, don't let anything bad happen to him.*

"First off, I'm sorry for the way I flew off the handle a few minutes ago. It's just that . . . hell, you just took me by surprise when you said you were packing the car to take off. You're right, of course: I've known all along that once your work here was done, you'd be leaving. I thought I could handle it, but . . ." A small, grim smile shaped his mouth. "But it turns out I can't."

"What do you mean . . . you can't?"

He hesitated, scrubbing his fingers across his lips. The small smile disappeared. In the scant light inside the car, his eyes looked very blue, and very unhappy. He looked wet and cold, and even without knowing what was bothering him, Sophie wanted to wrap the throw around him and hold him and tell him everything was going to be all right.

"I have a confession to make," he said after a minute. "I didn't give you that ultimatum about moving in because of Ivy. I did it because of me, because I liked having you around. It was stupid, I know. I knew even then we were all wrong for each other, but I wanted to spend time with you, to get to know you better. I figured whatever happened, happened, and it would run its course and be over. But that didn't turn out the way I planned either. Obviously."

"Obviously? Maybe to you, but I'm really not sure what you're getting at."

"Look, there's something between us, all right?"

His words, as gruff as they were, set off a little twang of excitement deep inside her. She immediately cautioned herself not to jump to conclusions. "Something between us" could mean any number of things. Not all of them twang-worthy. For all she knew he was about to tell her he'd contracted malaria on one of his supersecret military missions and had passed it on to her.

"You can't deny it," he told her. "I know because I tried. This thing . . . it's real. It's the first thing I think of when I wake up in the morning and it's hovering around me all day, and at night . . . at night it's the reason I can't stay away from you. It's the reason I can't keep my hands off you when we're together. It's gotten so everything I see or hear reminds me of you in some way . . . and nothing that happens seems real until I share it with you." He shrugged and crossed and uncrossed his arms and rearranged his long legs, looking uncharacteristically uncomfortable in his own skin. "Weird, huh?"

"Not so weird," Sophie said gently and without even a small smile, lest he misread her amusement. "Not really. Because I feel the same way."

"You do?" Disbelief and then relief flickered in his eyes.

Inside Sophie, the small twang of excitement was growing stronger, the vibrations spreading through her in little waves, like ripples in a pond.

"That's good," he said, nodding. "That's exactly what I hoped you'd say. Whatever the hell this thing is, I don't trust it. And I damn sure don't trust myself. But I trust you. Sophie, you're the most loyal and giving person I've ever known . . . not to mention stubborn. And sexy as hell. There's no one I'd rather be in a foxhole with."

It wasn't poetry, but she didn't need poetry . . . or fireworks or to live in the Princess House. She only needed him. She'd been afraid to admit that even to herself, but it was true.

"If I have to do this thing, there's no one else I'd want to do it with."

Sophie tucked her wet hair behind her ears, not sure she'd

heard him right or if she was imagining the reluctance lurking in his tone. "This *thing*?"

He nodded, unsmiling. "Like I said, I didn't plan for it to happen. I didn't want it. And I don't trust it. But I don't have a choice. It's come down to a matter of survival."

"Survival." It wasn't a question. She just wondered if the word would make better sense if she said it aloud instead of letting it bounce around in her head.

"What I'm trying to say is that if you're willing to take a chance on me, I'm willing to take a chance on whatever this is. We could give it a year, if you want. That's longer than my first marriage lasted."

She was stuck on the "whatever this is" part until she heard the word *marriage* and a whole new array of conflicting emotions flooded her system.

"Owen, are you by any chance proposing to me?"

Now he looked confused. "Well, yeah. That's what this is all about. I don't have a ring to give you." He looked guilty, or embarrassed. She couldn't tell. "I didn't have time, and anyway, I figure you'd rather pick it out yourself. You know all about that stuff. Whatever you want is fine with me. Except . . ."

"Except?"

"Except I don't want a big fancy wedding."

"Not a problem." She pushed the throw aside, suddenly feeling a rush of heat, most of it headed straight to her face.

"It's not?" He gave a sigh of relief and the tension creases across his brow relaxed ever so slightly. "I thought for sure that after planning so many weddings for other people, you'd want the same hoopla and showboating for your own."

"Oh, I might . . . when the time comes. Or I might not. I meant it's not a problem because I can't marry you, Owen . . . with or without hoopla."

"But you said . . . why the hell not?"

"Because I'm in love with you."

"That's why you can't marry me? Because you're in love with me? That doesn't make any sense, Sophie."

"Maybe I shouldn't have said I *can't* marry you. I should have said I *won't* marry you."

"There's a difference?"

"There is to me. I settled for less than I deserved once before. When it ended, he told me something I didn't fully understand at the time. I couldn't possibly have. Not then. He told me that you can think you're in love and be wrong, you can tell yourself and everyone around you that you're in love and be wrong, but when you meet the right person, the person you're meant to love and to be with, you just know. He was a jerk. But he was right about that. I know that now. I know because of you. Just the way Ivy knew. All her life she knew Joseph was the man she was meant to love and nothing anyone else said could change that. Ivy knew, and as young as they are, Shelby and Matthew know too. I look at you and I know. But you don't."

She put up her hand to keep him from speaking.

"Did you hear yourself? The words you chose to propose to me? You talked about having no choice and survival and being in a foxhole together."

"Okay. I'm not the most romantic guy in the world. You already knew that."

"I'm not talking about romance, Owen. I'm talking about love. You didn't. It's like you can't even bring yourself to say the word. I deserve more than that. And so do you."

Twenty

Owen couldn't believe how badly he'd fucked up.

He understood immediately what a lousy job he'd done. He knew it long before the rain stopped and they got out of the car and he found the key to let them back into the house. Once they were inside, Sophie had been adamant that she wanted to leave right away.

Who could blame her?

Just the same, his first instinct was to protest and try to buy some time by convincing her to wait until morning. He managed to restrain himself. Pride forced him to behave with at least some of the grace and dignity and kindheartedness with which she was dealing with the situation, a situation he knew must be as difficult for her as it was for him.

She'd said that she loved him. She hadn't said "I love you" in those exact words, but she had admitted that she knew he was the man she was meant to love and to spend her life with. Logic told him he should be mad crazy with happiness right now. But one of the things he'd learned today was that love didn't give a damn about logic.

There were other things she said that were even harder to get out of his head. They confirmed what he'd known all along, that Sophie was more than he deserved and that he could never measure up and that if he tried he would only end up failing and hurting her.

I can't marry you, Owen. I won't. I won't make the same mistake again. It hurts too much to love someone who doesn't love you the same way.

While she changed into dry clothes he'd carried the rest of her stuff to her car. It took him two trips, and with every step, his wet boots squished out a message that to his ears sounded like *jackass, jackass, jackass.*

His damn boots could have done a better job than he had done.

He now understood what Ivy was talking about. He had most definitely mucked everything up and made a muddle of things, exactly what she had warned him not to do. She was right: he was a dolt. He almost wished she would make good on her threat to return. He obviously needed help.

Unless it was already too late.

Clearly he was no authority on the subject, but it seemed to him that a marriage proposal wasn't one of those situations where you could ask for a do-over. It wasn't like parallel parking or a friendly game of minigolf. Once Sophie had pointed out his mistakes, he couldn't very well ask her to let him take it again from the top. That would be like proposing using cue cards that she'd written for him.

He'd tried to explain, of course. About how he panicked when he thought she was going to take off before he had a chance to say what he wanted to say. About how he hadn't had time to practice or think about buying a ring or coming up with a more romantic setting than the inside of a car with them both soaking wet. He used to laugh at those dumb schmucks who thought it was cool to propose via the JumboTron in a football stadium. He wasn't laughing now.

He stayed outside for a long time after she left. Sitting on the patio steps, afraid to go into his own house. Fear wasn't something he was accustomed to feeling and he hated it. The thought that he might have lost Sophie forever was like something lodged in his chest, making it hard to breathe, and he had a feeling it would only get worse when he went inside and she wasn't there. It wasn't only Sophie that would be gone. He knew there would be empty places and things missing everywhere he looked. Reminders of all he had lost. There would be no red, heart-shaped coffee mug on the shelf beside the sink, no sparkly flip-flops by the back door, and no piles of bridal magazines near the sunroom chair where she liked to sit to read. Somehow, in just a few weeks' time, she had made the house feel like a real home. *His* home. During the time she lived there with him, he'd felt more at home than he'd ever felt anywhere.

Reminding himself that he'd lived in the house alone just fine before she came along didn't help. He was wiser now. About a lot of things. Wise enough to know there was no going back to the way things were before.

It was like if you lived your whole life in a cave without running water and then suddenly you got to spend a few weeks in a five-star hotel, in a deluxe suite where the bathroom had a sunken marble tub and one of those room-size walk-in showers with a dozen jets pulsing water at you from all directions. When the time came to go back to your cave, you didn't suddenly forget running water existed. Or decide life was just as enjoyable without it.

You woke up every morning knowing that running water was out there somewhere and that at that very moment people were brushing their teeth with it and making tea with it. You missed running water and cursed yourself for being so blind to possibilities that you'd settled for living in a damn cave for so long. You began thinking of all the things you were prepared to do and all the things you were willing to sacrifice to have running water in your life again. And if you had any sense at all, you began praying to every god there was that you'd get the chance.

Not until he was certain he was tired enough to sleep did he go inside and then he went straight to his room, avoiding the empty spaces along the way. He dropped onto the bed without bothering to undress. His T-shirt and jeans had dried, but they felt stiff and uncomfortable and his eyes refused to close. Instead, as he lay there in the darkness, he made out the shape of something on his dresser, something boxy and unfamiliar that shouldn't be there.

He flicked on the lamp by the bed and at first he wasn't sure what it was. Then his eyes adjusted to the light and he recognized the dollhouse he'd built for Allie, the dollhouse he'd tossed in the trash because it reminded him of all the things he wasn't good at . . . all the things he'd failed at . . . all the reasons he wasn't the right man for Sophie.

He got up and put on the overhead light to take a closer look. It hadn't been there that morning; he was sure of that. If Ivy were still haunting the place he'd suspect she was up to something. But Ivy was gone. And the dollhouse appeared as good as new. Which was odd because he had a vivid memory of throwing it into the trash can and of the roof coming off. In fact it was better than new, he realized, noting that the window he had never been able to get quite square was now perfect.

Sophie. It was the only explanation. She must have put it there before she left. Probably while he was taking her bags to the car. He didn't understand. With everything else she had to do in the past couple of weeks, when had Sophie found time to fix a damn dollhouse? He didn't have to dig deep for the answer. She hadn't *found* time; she'd made it. Probably by staying up nights when she should have been sleeping and stealing moments here and there throughout the day. That's who she was. Someone who found a way to have a wedding dress custom-made for a bride who couldn't find the dress she envisioned any other way. Someone who would befriend the cranky ghost threatening to wreak havoc on her well-laid plans. Someone who, instead of becoming bitter when her own romantic dream crashed and burned, found pleasure and satisfaction working her ass off to make other people's dreams come true.

Someone who had fixed the broken places inside him in the same quiet way she had rescued the dollhouse.

Someone he'd be a fool to let go.

He wasn't going to let her go. He decided that even before he noticed the small wreath of daisies stuck on the front door. He hunkered down to get a better look at it, smiling when he saw that the stems were wound together the same way Allie used to do it. He remembered opening up to Sophie about how he and Allie used to trespass and picnic on the lawn out back; it wasn't something he'd ever talked about with anyone else. He told her about Allie gathering daisies to make a princess crown. And she remembered. And understood.

He had no idea how, but somehow he had to find a way to make Sophie understand what he now realized, that people can change if they have a good enough reason to . . . he could change. He could be the man she needed, the man she deserved . . . a man who could love her without holding anything back.

He wasn't going to let Sophie go. Not without a fight.

The first package arrived on Monday morning.

Shortly after nine, the receptionist called Sophie to let her know there was something for her at the front desk. She was expecting some fabric samples, but as soon as she saw the package leaning against the receptionist's desk, she knew it wasn't fabric samples. The plain, heavy-duty brown box was about three feet square and about six inches deep. And heavy, she discovered when she went to pick it up to take it back to her office. Curious, she borrowed a letter opened and sliced through the wrapping tape right there.

"What's that?" asked Jill, wandering out of her office, coffee mug in hand.

"I'm not sure," Sophie told her, opening the side flap in order to slide out whatever it was.

Jill came closer. "Who's it from?"

"Don't know that either. There's no label on the box."

"No return address?"

"Nope. Nothing."

"I hope it's not a bomb."

Sophie slanted a quelling glance her way. "Gee, thanks."

"Well, these days you can't be too careful."

"Jill, it is not a bomb."

Jenna arrived for the day just in time to hear the end of the exchange. Shoving her sunglasses to the top of her head, she asked, "What's not a bomb?"

"Whatever's in that package. According to Sophie, anyway. I still wouldn't stand too close," Jill advised.

Jenna and the receptionist both took a step back.

As if that would save them if a three-square-foot bomb went off, thought Sophie, grunting as she struggled to work the Styrofoam packing loose without chipping her new nail polish.

It had been a rough few days since she returned to her own place, a place she was finding it hard to think of as home. Crazy as it seemed, when she thought of home she thought of a sweeping staircase and an ocean view and a guesthouse with the cushiest feather bed in the world. Her condo had none of the above. But that's not why she was finding it difficult to settle back in or why she had resorted to pampering herself in every way she could think of, including a massage and manicure and a steady supply of hand-made dark chocolate truffles from the little shop down the street. All that was an attempt—a desperate and thus far completely unsuccessful attempt—to distract herself from the fact that the condo also lacked the one thing she missed the most. Owen Winters.

On the dismally insignificant bright side, at least her struggle to open the package was burning truffle calories.

"Here, let me hold the box while you pull," Jenna said, daring to get close enough to grab it with both hands.

That did the trick. Sophie slid the contents out and peeled off the protective wrapping to reveal a framed print.

"Wow. Nice," admired Jill, coming around to look over Sophie's shoulder at the painting.

It was a signed and numbered print done in warm shades of yellow and orange and red; the work was simply rows of different-size, interconnecting boxes. Sophie didn't know a lot about contemporary art, but she understood that the artist's command of color and ability to make a simple design so compelling were the marks of a major talent.

Jenna bent down and squinted to read the signature. "M. L. Lark. I knew it. Nick and I fell in love with one of her paintings in a gallery in Boston, but it was too rich for our blood. Who sent it to you?"

"She doesn't know," Jill replied for her.

"Well, read the card. Duh."

Sophie checked the box, and the wrapping. "There is no card."

"Call the gallery," suggested Jenna.

"What gallery? There's no label anywhere."

"I know. You can call the delivery service and have them check their records. Tell them the card must have gotten lost."

It was a good idea, but Rae, the receptionist, couldn't recall what company had delivered the package. In fact, the more she thought about it, the more she thought the man who carried it in hadn't been wearing a uniform and that there also hadn't been any writing on the van he drove off in. Ignoring Jill's suggestion that she call the FBI, Sophie carried the print back to her office and leaned it against a wall where she could see it every time she looked up. It was an expensive painting. Eventually whoever sent it would check to make sure she'd gotten it. Either that or it had been delivered to her by mistake and someone would come looking to take it back.

It did cross her mind that Owen might have sent it, but then thoughts of Owen were constantly crossing her mind. Or else pitching a tent and hanging there for a while. She did what she always did: told herself to think about something else.

At ten-thirty Sophie returned from a truffle run to find the Js and several others again gathered around something in the reception area.

"What the hell?" she said, eyeing the humongous hammock. "Where did that come from?"

"Another mystery delivery," Jill informed her. "For you."

"Me?" Frowning, she walked over and read the tag that was attached to the steel frame. "'A summer classic, this beautiful hammock was handwoven of unbleached cotton by Mayan artists of the Yucatán to bring you many years of sumptuous pleasure.'"

"The Yucatán?" echoed Jill. "Is that anywhere near Ecuador?"

"What difference does that make?" Sophie countered.

"Isn't that where Shelby was going for the Peace Corps? Maybe she sent it to you . . . as a thank-you gift."

Sophie shook her head. "They aren't going to Ecuador for a few weeks. They're still in Hawaii on their honeymoon."

"How about her mother?"

"She's on a cruise. And I really don't see either of them sending me a hammock as a thank-you gift."

"Who do you see sending it?"

She closed her eyes. She saw Owen, of course, but that had nothing to do with the hammock. She saw him every time she closed her eyes.

"Well?"

"I can't think of anyone," she said, heading toward her office to eat a truffle in private.

"Wait," Jenna called after her. "What about the hammock?"

"It won't fit in my office," Sophie said. She sighed. "Help me push it against the wall for now and I'll think about it later."

When she got back from lunch, there was a red leather desk chair waiting for her. Or as Rae, who was sitting in it put it, a red leather desk chair extraordinaire.

"I didn't even know they made massaging desk chairs," Rae said, cozying up to the "scientifically calibrated massaging fingers." "Or chairs with coolers," she added, gleeful as she showed Sophie the underseat storage large enough to hold a specially designed ice pack and several beverage cans.

"This has got to be someone's idea of a joke," Sophie muttered.

"You mean like when people sign you up for magazine subscriptions or have pizza delivered to your house as a joke? My aunt once had to pay for a half-dozen pizzas she didn't order. With anchovies on them, which she hates. Does that mean you could get stuck paying for all of this stuff?"

"I hope not. But I may get stuck figuring out how to return all of it."

"Oh. Well, until you figure out how to return the chair, is it all right if I put it at my desk and sit in it?"

"Be my guest," Sophie told her.

By the end of the day, the hammock and chair had been joined by a fruit basket with what they all agreed was a genuine—and expensive—sapphire flower pendant tucked in between the pears and oranges. Also a birch sapling and an antique, glass-front display cabinet filled with an assortment of penny candy.

Sophie took off early. Partly because she felt a headache coming on and partly because she was afraid that whatever showed up next might have to be fed and taken home with her for the night. It turned out that there was no escape. She wasn't home an hour when the doorbell rang and she found a box containing a watch on the front step. It was a great watch. Very unusual, with a thin band of copper around the face and a copper band.

A tiger-lily plant in a bronze planter arrived next. Followed by a picnic basket with handmade ceramic plates and cups inside, then an intriguing small puzzle box made of hammered metal, and a while later a pair of designer sunglasses with stainless-steel frames.

The puzzle box frustrated her, but she really liked the sunglasses. And they looked good on her. She decided that if she had a choice, she would pay for them rather than send them back. Unless she ended up in prison for grand theft, in which case she wouldn't need sunglasses. It was possible all this stuff had been stolen. Which meant she was in possession of stolen property. She didn't think she could be held liable for it, and she wasn't about to call the FBI, but it couldn't hurt to call the local police in the morning and make a report of some kind.

She put the sunglasses on the nightstand when she went to bed and crossed her fingers that the doorbell didn't ring again that night. Or if it did, that the next package from her mystery gifter contained something useful . . . like earplugs.

Or a gift certificate for a Memory Wipe, if there was such a thing.

She thought about it some more and decided that even if there was a way to wipe her memory clean, she wouldn't do it. As much as it hurt now, she wouldn't give up one minute of the time she'd spent with Owen, or any of her Princess House memories.

For what seemed like the millionth time, she replayed that last afternoon in her head, and for what seemed like the millionth time, she wondered if she had made the right decision. She lay there torturing herself with all manner of possibilities and shades of meaning, and worried that maybe she'd been too critical of him for saying that he was proposing because he had no choice and that he didn't trust his feelings for her and didn't even want to feel whatever it was he felt, and in the end she came to the same conclusion she'd come to the first 999,999 times. She'd done the right thing. The words didn't matter. It mattered that what he was offering wasn't enough, and she wasn't going to settle for what wasn't enough.

The first days had been the worst. She'd stayed home from work and swum in a sea of self-pity. She bounced back and forth between anger and heartache. Which was dumb. It wasn't fair to be angry with someone for not loving you the way or as much as you wanted them to love you. She was angry just the same. Nobody ever said life was fair.

And she cried, even though she told herself she shouldn't because crying would only make her blotchy and not change a damn thing. She cried her heart out. Several times.

The crying was over.

She hoped.

Now she was taking it one day at a time. Eventually it would get better.

She hoped.

She punched her pillow and rolled over.

Think about something else, she told herself.

She wondered if there might be a truffle in her bag that she'd overlooked.

Something besides that, she told herself. Preferably something without calories.

She remembered the sunglasses and pictured herself walking into Seasons tomorrow wearing them. She wouldn't have thought she'd look good in steel frames, but she did. At least her mystery gifter had good taste. She liked the sapphire pendant a lot too, but she didn't think she could afford to keep it. She still couldn't figure out why whoever sent it had thought to stick it in a fruit basket, of all things. What did fruit have to do with sapphires? Or with jewelry in general? She turned it over in her mind. Fruit and sapphires. Fruit and sapphires. The pendant was shaped like a flower. Fruit and flowers?

Fruit and flowers.

She sat up and switched on the light. Fruit and flowers. Of course.

She glanced at the sunglasses on the nightstand. Steel frames. Steel, that was eleven. Fruit and flowers, that was four. Leather . . . the leather desk chair . . . three.

Leaping from the bed, she grabbed a notepad and pen and made a list just to make sure she was right, starting with the print . . . which was done on paper. Paper, the traditional gift for a first wedding anniversary. The second anniversary was cotton . . . as in a cotton hammock. The third was leather; the fourth fruit and flowers. The birch tree was wood. Year five. Candy and iron were traditional for year six . . . and the display case with the penny candy had iron fittings.

When she finished there were eleven items on her list, each one a perfect match for a traditional wedding anniversary gift. And she knew without a doubt who had sent them. Owen. She'd asked him not to call or e-mail or text her or try to see her. And she had been unhappy with his proposal. He'd tried to explain. She remembered how earnest he'd looked, and how devastated as he tried to explain that if he'd had more time he would have done better.

It seemed he was right.

By Friday, both her office and her condo had the look of a high-end bazaar sale. Lace, crystal, silver, pearls . . . Owen had covered all the bases. And as the years were ticked off, Sophie's impatience grew. The gifts were beautiful, but all she really wanted was to see Owen and hear what he had to say.

Late in the afternoon Rae called. They had it down to a routine now. But when she got to the front, there was no package waiting, only Owen, clean-shaven and dressed in a dark suit and carrying long-stemmed red roses. The urge to throw herself in his arms was almost overpowering.

"Hello, Sophie," he said, and it felt as if his slow smile was attached directly to her heart. He held the flowers out to her.

"A present? For me?" She shot him a teasing smile as she bent her head to inhale their fragrance. "They're beautiful. Thank you. . . . I feel like I should say that fifty times."

"I'd rather you didn't. Not yet. I actually have something else for you, but this is something I needed to deliver in person." He glanced around. "Is there someplace we could talk?"

"My office," she said, beckoning him to follow. She handed the roses to Rae as she passed. "Rae, do you think you could . . ."

"Put them in water for you? Sure." Her smile turned mischievous. "I know I saw a Waterford crystal vase around here somewhere."

The *J*s were still there and she could feel them watching. She was happier than ever for her cramped little office. At least it didn't have glass walls and had a solid wood door she could close for privacy.

As soon as she closed that door, Owen started to speak, ignoring her invitation to sit.

"I'm sorry for just showing up unannounced, but you made me promise not to call. Or text."

"It's all right. Actually, I was going to get in touch with you . . . eventually."

He looked incredulous. "You were? I figured after . . . you know . . . you'd never . . ."

"Not about . . . you know. It's about Ivy."

"Ivy? What about her?"

"Actually it's about Joseph. The librarian friend I asked to look into it finally got back to me, and I thought you'd want to know what she found out." She reached for a manila envelope on her desk. "This copy is for you; it makes for pretty interesting reading. I'll just quickly fill you in on the highlights. Most of the information comes from someone who Maggie—that's my friend—connected with while she was researching online. He's a doctoral student at Brown and he did a lot of his own research on the Hallidays for his thesis."

"He's writing his thesis on the Hallidays?"

"No, on Prohibition in Rhode Island. He came at it from that angle and more or less backed into the Ivy–Joseph mystery in the process. This is just his theory, of course, but he does have a lot of circumstantial evidence, letters and diaries, that kind of thing, to back it up. Plus he got his hands on the files of one of the private detectives Ivy's father hired to find Joseph."

"So what's his theory?"

"According to him, Ivy's older brother and a friend were involved in bootlegging, or rum-running, as I've learned is the preferred term when the booze is being smuggled over water. Prohibition was in full swing and the family's boatbuilding business provided the perfect cover."

"Was this with the old man's consent?"

"No. He wouldn't have stood for it. And evidently that was the rub . . . or at least the brother and his friend thought it would be. Joseph was a straight arrow and on course to become Mr. Halliday's fair-haired boy. The last thing they wanted was Joseph in a position to find out what they were up to and pull the plug. They met with him the night before the wedding. According to the theory, it was to offer him money to walk out of Ivy's life and stay out. Rumrunning was highly lucrative, so they would have had plenty to offer. Plus it was well known that the friend had always had a thing for Ivy, so he had even more reason to want Joseph out of the picture."

"So that's what happened? Joseph was paid to take a powder." He shook his head in disgust.

"Not so fast. Joseph refused. Emphatically, it seems. According to this guy's research, things got heated and turned physical between Joseph and the friend and Joseph ended up dead. The private detective tracked down a couple of witnesses who said it was accidental. Accident or not, it appears that when Mr. Halliday finally learned the truth, he paid to have the whole thing hushed up and the file sealed."

Owen reacted with a sound of disgust. "He was protecting his son."

"Yes. And who knows? Maybe he thought not knowing what her brother did would make things easier for Ivy too."

"Yeah, well, I'd like to have a talk with the old man about that. Poor Ivy. That's a long time to be left wondering." He swiveled his gaze toward Sophie. "I don't know how she did it. 'Cause honestly, this past week has almost been more than I could stand."

He took a deep breath.

"There's a lot I want to say to you, Sophie. A lot I need to say, and to explain. But there's something I want to do first. I've been thinking about it for days . . . practically from the moment I watched you drive away, and I can't wait any longer. I swear it's a goddamn miracle I managed to wait this long. You don't know how many times this week I wanted to say the hell with being patient and just walk in here and do it. I held back because the last time I just went with my gut, it didn't go so well. You may remember." His mouth slanted in a sheepish smile and everything inside Sophie went soft and warm.

"That does seem to ring a bell," she said.

"Never let it be said I don't learn from my own stupidity. This time I had a plan and I stuck to it. But I can't wait another damn minute to do this . . . if you'll let me."

She nodded, a shiver of anticipation dancing along her spine. She expected him to grab her and kiss her the way she wanted to grab and kiss him, and was stunned when instead he dropped to one knee and reached into his jacket pocket for a small black velvet box.

He flipped it open with his thumb as easily as if he'd done it many times before, but Sophie knew him too well to be fooled; she saw the slight trembling of his hand. Then she saw the diamond ring inside the box, the absolutely perfect diamond ring, the ring she had drooled over so many times in a magazine photo that the magazine she'd seen it in fell open to that page every time she opened it, and she gasped.

Owen smiled at her. "Miss Sophia Bennett, will you marry me?"

She was breathless, which made it hard to speak.

"You can give me your answer on a contingency basis if you want," he told her. "Believe me, I'm prepared to do as much groveling and explaining as necessary to make up for my first attempt at this. And I know it will take more than words to convince you that

I am crazy, out-of-my-head, heart-over-head-over-heels in love with you. It will take years. And I'm looking forward to every one of them. That's what gave me the idea of sending you anniversary gifts ahead of time. That's how many years I'm asking for this time . . . at least fifty, with a promise to renegotiate for whatever comes next. I want fifty years and I want to spend every minute of every one of them making you happy that you said yes and took a chance on a dolt who still doesn't have it all figured out but who wants to learn and needs someone with a doctorate in romance to teach him."

Laughing and crying at the same time, Sophie sank to her knees facing him.

He blotted a tear from beneath her eye.

"Say yes, Sophie."

"Fifty years? That's the deal?"

"There may need to be a subclause about children, but we can work that out later." He took the ring from the box and held her hand in his. "Say yes, Sophie."

She took a deep breath. "You're sure? You're sure this is what you want?"

"You're what I want. I want to wake up with you and go to bed with you and have babies with you. I love you, Sophie. I want to stand at the front of the biggest church we can find and watch you walk down the aisle in a white dress and promise you forever in front of however many people you want to invite. I get it now. Let me prove it to you. Say yes, Sophie."

"Yes." She swiped a tear. "Yes, yes, yes," she said, laughing and crying as she let him slip the ring on her finger and then he was kissing her.

And kissing her. She had no idea how much time passed before she became aware that someone was knocking on her office door.

They pulled back a little, but she kept her arms looped around his neck so she could stare at her left hand.

"Sophie?"

She recognized Rae's voice and was thankful it wasn't the *J*s she had to tell to get lost.

"Later, Rae."

"Uh . . . okay. It's just that you said to let you know whenever you got another delivery, and you just did. Get one, that is."

Pulling back another few inches, Sophie glanced quizzically at Owen, who immediately shook his head.

"This one's not from me," he told her at the same time Rae was saying that this package had a return address . . . or at least a name."

"It's from somebody named Ivy. Ivy Halliday. Do you want me to—"

Sophie yanked open the door and grabbed the package from Rae. The *J*s were standing right behind her.

"Sophie, what the hell is going on?" demanded Jenna.

Jill was trying to see around the door. "What's Winters doing here? Oh my God, is that a diam—"

The door shut.

Owen took hold of Sophie and spun her around and then rested his back against it to make sure it stayed shut.

"What do you suppose is in the box?" he asked.

"Don't you think a better question is how did it get here? Or when the heck did she send it?"

He shook his head, his expression happy and resigned. "Why bother? This is Ivy we're talking about, remember? She'd find a way."

"True." Placing the package on the desk, she hurriedly tore off the wrapping and opened the box inside and gasped with surprise.

"I don't believe it," she said, but of course she did. It was Ivy after all. Owen was right: she would find a way.

She carefully lifted the frame from the box.

"Look. It's the lace from my mother's wedding dress," she told him.

Owen rested his hand on her back as he looked it over. "Is that the same frame?"

She nodded. "Yes. It's exactly the same as I remember it . . . right down to the little wrinkle where I didn't get the lace quite flat. She said it would turn up when I needed it most," she murmured, already imagining how the lace would look adorning a bouquet of white roses and lilies of the valley. "How could she possibly—"

"There's a note," Owen pointed out.

Sophie reached for it. It was brief. She glanced at it and smiled. "It just says 'Leap . . . with love.' And there's a P.S. for you."

She handed it to him.

The P.S. read: *Well played, Mr. Winters. Well played indeed.*

"How about that?" he said, looking very proud of himself.

"Yeah, I guess when you get a seal of approval from on high, you know you're doing something right."

"And I plan to keep on doing it for a long, long time."

He reached for her. They kissed and laughed and kissed some more.

Outside the door there were noises and whispers. The *J*s didn't give up easily. Sophie looked forward to seeing their faces when she told them the news. But she was in no hurry for the kiss to end. And she could tell that Owen wasn't either.

There was no need to rush.

After all, they had forever.